RESURRECTION

Drummond watched the fist clenching the knife as it came bearing down on him, and saw his hand come up and catch it just behind the wrist. He turned slightly and, bracing his body, felt a slight bump as his hip connected with his assailant's body. Bowing slightly, he could hear the rustle of the punk's clothes as he slowly sailed past his head. Turning his neck slightly, Drummond watched as his would-be killer drifted past and vanished over the edge of the balcony.

In the moonlight, his attacker lay limply across the top of the railing, two ugly spikes projecting through the back of his black leather jacket. As Drummond watched, he stopped twitching and for a moment lay very still.

Then slowly, and with great determination, the attacker grabbed the top bar of the railing and simply pushed himself up off the spikes. . . .

KNIGHTS
OF THE
BLOOD

by
Scott MacMillan

**Created by
Katherine Kurtz**

A ROC BOOK

ROC
Published by New American Library, a division of
Penguin Group (USA) Inc., 375 Hudson Street,
New York, New York 10014, USA
Penguin Group (Canada), 90 Eglinton Avenue East, Suite 700, Toronto,
Ontario M4P 2Y3, Canada (a division of Pearson Penguin Canada Inc.)
Penguin Books Ltd., 80 Strand, London WC2R 0RL, England
Penguin Ireland, 25 St. Stephen's Green, Dublin 2,
Ireland (a division of Penguin Books Ltd.)
Penguin Group (Australia), 250 Camberwell Road, Camberwell, Victoria 3124,
Australia (a division of Pearson Australia Group Pty. Ltd.)
Penguin Books India Pvt. Ltd., 11 Community Centre, Panchsheel Park,
New Delhi - 110 017, India
Penguin Group (NZ), 67 Apollo Drive, Rosedale, North Shore,
Auckland 1311, New Zealand (a division of Pearson New Zealand Ltd.)
Penguin Books (South Africa) (Pty.) Ltd., 24 Sturdee Avenue,
Rosebank, Johannesburg 2196, South Africa

Penguin Books Ltd., Registered Offices:
80 Strand, London WC2R 0RL, England

First published by Roc, an imprint of New American Library,
a division of Penguin Group (USA) Inc.

First Printing, July 1993
10 9 8 7

Copyright © Bill Fawcett & Associates and Katherine Kurtz, 1993
All rights reserved

RoC REGISTERED TRADEMARK—MARCA REGISTRADA

Printed in the United States of America

PUBLISHER'S NOTE
This is a work of fiction. Names, characters, places, and incidents either are
the product of the author's imagination or are used fictitiously, and any resemblance to actual persons, living or dead, business establishments, events, or
locales is entirely coincidental.

The publisher does not have any control over and does not assume any
responsibility for author or third-party Web sites or their content.

This one's for my mom and dad.

Prologue

Los Angeles, 1972

Jack Sprague surveyed the crime scene before returning to the body. The alley showed signs of a struggle, and judging from all the blood between the trash cans and the dumpster, that was probably where the murder took place. It was Sprague's guess that after killing their victim, the assailants had placed the body in the dumpster, where it had been found by the driver of the refuse collection truck at approximately four-thirty that morning.

It was now five forty-five, and Sprague was developing a headache from too much coffee, too little sleep, and a lot of pressure from Parker Center to "keep it out of the papers." He walked back to the dumpster, where his partner stood talking to the driver of the garbage truck.

"Jack"—Demitter sounded as tired as Sprague— "I don't think we'll get much more out of Mr. Fuentes here." He gestured toward the fat man in greasy overalls and Angels baseball cap. "Think we oughta cut him loose?"

"Sure." Sprague was looking at the body again. "Let him go." The victim was a white male, early twenties, blond, and well-built.

"Looks like half the surfers at Zuma," Demitter commented.

"Yeah," said Sprague, "except that none of them have wooden stakes pounded through their hearts."

"I dunno, Kingfish. The last three we've met were all dressed that way." Demitter shook his head. "Stark naked, except for the stake."

Sprague ran a coffee-colored hand across the pepper-and-salt frizz on the top of his head. Demitter was the only person in the LAPD to call him "Kingfish" to his face, which was probably why Sprague refused to work with any other partner.

"Come on, Brother Andy, let's head back to the station."

Demitter grinned at his partner from under a thinning thatch of carrot red hair. "Yassum, boss."

Back at the station, the two police detectives reviewed their files for the umpteenth time.

"Okay," Demitter began. "Let's go over all of this again."

"Right," said Sprague, walking over to the chalkboard set up against one wall of their cramped office. "Here's what we've got."

He reached across to his desk and picked up an envelope marked "Los Angeles County Coroner," pulling out photos of the three victims, which he taped across the top of the chalkboard. Demitter fumbled in one of his coat pockets and produced a Polaroid photo of the most recent victim, taken earlier that morning at the crime scene. He tossed the Polaroid to Sprague.

"Here, might as well make the collection complete."

Sprague looked at the photo for a minute or so, then taped it up next to the glossy morgue shots.

"All right. Now we have *four* victims, all killed in the same manner, and all found in the same neighborhood." Sprague fiddled with a piece of chalk. He and Demitter had gone through this procedure with each of the previous killings, and would continue to do it until the murderer was caught. Somewhere there had to be a clue, a lead that would point them in the direction of the killers. "What else have we got?"

"Age. All in their late teens or early twenties." Demitter leaned back at his desk and looked at the ceiling. "All about the same size, between five foot ten and six feet tall. Same weight, 160 to 175 pounds."

While Demitter recited the vital statistics of the group, Sprague's precise printing made neat columns of facts under the four photos.

"And," Demitter continued, "no one has come forward to claim the bodies, and Missing Persons doesn't have anything on any of them."

Sprague turned to his partner. "That's almost as weird as the killings. These aren't street kids. They're in too good shape for that. But no one's looking for them. We hear back from the Army yet?"

Demitter rummaged through some papers on his desk. "Yeah. And the Navy, Air Force, and Coast Guard, too. I don't know about Number Four there, but the first three aren't AWOL."

Sprague was staring at the photo of Number Four. It had been taken by the crime scene boys, and showed the head and upper torso of the body as found in the dumpster. The face was contorted in a horrible grimace of pain, and the left arm was bent back, with the hand behind the head. As Sprague looked at the Polaroid for the hundredth time that morning, he saw something that he hadn't noticed before. Inside the left arm, up high near the arm pit, was a small tattoo.

"Hey, Amos. There anything in those coroner's

reports about any of the bodies having tattoos?" Sprague asked, pulling down the photo for a closer look.

Demitter picked up another batch of files and quickly sifted through them. "Naw. Although Number Two had scars that were similar to those inflicted by shrapnel. Why?"

Sprague flipped him the photo of Number Four. "Inside of his left arm. What's it look like to you?"

Demitter squinted, and then went back to the morgue photos in the coroner's reports. "Here, look at Number Three."

Sprague took the photo from Demitter's outstretched hand. Staring up at him from the eight-by-ten glossy morgue shot, Number Three was stretched out naked on the dissecting table, with an ugly black hole the size of a fist in his chest. Like the others, he was well-muscled, although he didn't look much over sixteen or seventeen.

Sprague slipped on his glasses and brought the photo close to his dark face. Peering intently at the inside of Number Three's exposed left arm, he could just make out what might have been part of a crude tattoo.

"Call Yamaguchi's boys and have them check these dudes for tattoos." He set the photo down and turned to Demitter. "I think we've found our link."

That afternoon, the county coroner's office confirmed that all four corpses were similarly tattooed under their left arms. Photos of the tattoos were sent to the Los Angeles County Sheriff's Department's forensic services lab, who identified the tattoos and forwarded their report back to Sprague at LAPD's Hollenbeck Division. When Sprague walked into his office the next morning, Demitter was already there.

"*Heil Hitler!*" Demitter snapped to attention, his arm upraised in a Nazi salute, a comb held under his nose in imitation of the Führer's moustache.

"I don't get it, Demitter. What's the joke?" Sprague removed his holster and gun and tossed them onto the back of his desk before plopping into his chair.

"Ze rrreports have just in-gecomming from der coroner's office, meine Kingfish!" Demitter clicked his heels. "Und guess vass?"

Sprague just shook his head.

"All of our dead surfers have Nazi army tattoos." Demitter dropped his phoney German accent. "To be precise, the guys in the Sheriff's Department have identified the marks as SS tattoos."

Sprague took the report from Demitter's desk and quickly scanned through it.

"I don't get it. What would a bunch of surfers be doing with Nazi tattoos?"

"How the hell should I know?" Demitter got up and poured himself a cup of coffee. "These surfers wear Iron Crosses and German army helmets. . . . You see 'em at the beach all the time. Maybe these guys are involved with the neo-Nazis out in El Monte. Who knows?"

Sprague was intently studying the chalkboard. "Let's go visit the Master Race."

A light rain was falling as they drove out to El Monte, turning the Pasadena Freeway into a slippery ribbon of concrete that snaked its way from downtown Los Angeles out toward the San Gabriel Valley. The dark blue unmarked police car turned east past El Monte Legion Stadium and headed out toward the bean fields and ramshackle houses that marked the boundary between the Anglo and Chicano neighborhoods in less than affluent East L.A.

The faded yellow house stood back from the street, about halfway down the block. Parked in front was an ex-Highway Patrol car, one of the black and white "freeway flyers," its doors crudely spray-canned black. In the drive was an old army command car, anchored to the driveway by spiderwebs and four flat tires.

Demitter drove past, made a U-turn, and parked across the street. "This is it."

Sprague grinned in anticipation of the coming confrontation. "The paperwork says the house number is 16421. This is 22006."

"These guys aren't exactly rocket scientists. We're parked across the street in front of 16422, and the only other houses on that side of the street are 16417 and 16429." Demitter shook his head. "Dumb shits. Real dumb shits."

The bell didn't work, so Sprague used his fist. Muffled voices answered the knock at the door, and Demitter eased his gun out of his holster. Sprague knocked again, and the door was opened by one of the Master Race.

The kid was skinny, about six feet tall with pimples and dirty, greasy-blond hair. His brown shirt was sweat-stained and grubby, and above the red-and-black arm band could be seen the stitch marks where an army corporal's stripes had been removed. The shirt was loosely tucked into a pair of filthy Levis buttoned only at the waist, the legs wadded into a pair of scuffed-up motorcycle boots. The voice was adenoidal, revealing broken yellow teeth when he spoke.

"Yeah. What do you want?"

Sprague nearly recoiled from the breath. "Police.

We'd like to speak with Commandant Steele." He held his badge up for the superman to see.

"Yeah? Wait here." The door closed. "Fuckin' nigger."

Demitter and Sprague looked at each other, and Demitter holstered his gun. A march started playing inside, and the young Nazi returned to the door, this time with his fly buttoned.

"This way. The commandant will see you."

Shabby doesn't begin to describe this place, Sprague thought. *It's more like pathetic.*

Even in the dim light screened by the tattered curtains, Sprague and Demitter could tell the place was filthy. On the wall was a large Nazi flag, and next to it was a photograph of Hitler. There were also framed photos of other Nazi big-wigs, along with snapshots of neo-Nazis armed with a variety of surplus army junk. Busted up furniture lined the walls, and a stained and torn carpet covered the linoleum-clad floor.

They followed along down a short hall, and Demitter held back just enough to get a quick look into two more rooms before they entered the "commandant's" office.

Steele was sitting behind a large desk, and stood up as the two policemen were ushered in by the pimply-faced storm trooper. Against one wall, a rack held two dozen cheap surplus rifles—Carcanos, like the one Lee Harvey Oswald used to kill Kennedy. There was a large bronze bust of Hitler behind Steele's chair, flanked on either side by an American and Nazi flag. A collection of Nazi daggers hung on one of the dark green walls next to a diploma from UCLA, and two wooden captain's chairs were drawn up in front of the desk. Unlike the squalor of the rest of the house, Steele's office was the very model of military spit and polish, as was Steele himself.

The commandant's uniform was as crisp as a new dollar bill. His black tie was neatly tucked into the front of his military creased shirt between the second and third buttons, and the brass buckles on his Sam Browne belt shone like gold against the deep russet of the leather. He was wearing a pair of old-fashioned cavalry-twill riding britches that slid smoothly into the tops of his glossy brown field boots. An SA leader's dagger hung at his left hip, and a red-and-black arm band encircled his left arm precisely two inches above the elbow. Three rows of military ribbons were centered above the left pocket of his heavily-starched khaki shirt, and below these, in the middle of the pocket, was a Nazi Party Leader's badge: a gold wreath surrounding the red-and-white roundel with the black swastika set spiderlike in its center.

Stopping just inside the door of Steele's office, the young Nazi stood at attention, giving Steele the stiff-armed Nazi salute.

"Two policemen to see you, *Herr Kommandant*." He remained at the salute until it had been returned.

"Thank you, Trooper. Show them in."

Awkwardly he pointed Demitter and Sprague to the chairs in front of the desk, then saluted once again.

"*Heil Hitler!*"

Steele perfunctorily returned the Nazi salute. "*Heil.*"

Sprague had seen combat in 'Nam with his army reserve unit, and quickly ran a soldier's eye over the ribbons on Steele's chest: Purple Heart, Silver and Bronze Stars, Soldier's Medal, and the Distinguished Service Cross for gallantry in action. Steele had won these the hard way in Korea, fighting at Inchun, Pusang, and the Yalu River. He might be a looney, but there was no questioning his personal bravery.

Before they were seated, Steele leaned slightly across the desk and extended his hand to the two officers.

"How do you do? I'm Commandant Steele."

"Detective Sergeant Demitter, and this is Detective Sergeant Sprague," Demitter said, shaking the offered hand. Sprague also reached out, expecting Steele to withdraw his hand rather than touch a black man, but to his surprise, Steele grasped his hand in a firm grip and shook hands with him like he meant it.

The formalities over, Steele settled back into his chair and surveyed the two officers before speaking.

"Well, gentlemen, what can I do for you?" His voice had the same casual formality of a loan officer at a bank.

"Mr. Steele—" Despite the uniform, Sprague refused to call him Commandant. "We're investigating the death of four young men whom we believe may have had some connection with your organization."

Sprague slid an envelope containing the morgue photos of the four dead men across Steele's desk. "We were wondering if you might be able to identify them for us."

Steele glanced at the envelope on his desk but made no move to touch it.

"Am I, or some member of my staff, under suspicion of having killed anyone?" he asked.

Demitter cleared his throat. "Look, Commandant, what we have here are four dead surfers. The only thing they have in common are some German army tattoos on their arms. We just want to know if you can help us identify them, that's all."

"Very well, then." Steele gave them a very impersonal smile. "I'll look at your photos."

Reaching across, Steele scooped up the envelope and dumped its contents out on the desk in front of him.

Sprague grunted. "Not very pretty is it?"

"Neither is the six o'clock news, Detective Sergeant Sprague," Steele replied without looking up from the photos on his desk.

Carefully Steele arranged the photos on his desk—but not, both Sprague and Demitter noted, in the order in which the victims had been killed. Steele reached into his desk and brought out a magnifying glass and stared intently at each photo for several minutes. Finally, he set down the glass and looked at the two policemen.

"Well, gentlemen, there are only three things I can tell you about these photos." Steele waited, until finally Sprague spoke.

"Okay. What?"

"First," Steele held up the index finger of his right hand, "I've never laid eyes on any of these guys before. They don't belong to my organization. Second—" the two fingers of his right hand made a vee "—I don't think they're surfers. These guys are butt-white all over—no tan lines. In fact, they don't look like they've been out in the sun for a long time. Finally, I doubt they're even Americans."

Sprague interrupted him. "How do you figure that?"

"Simple," Steele continued. "None of your victims are circumcised. Here in America, the medical profession is totally dominated by Jews, so virtually all boys are routinely circumcised at birth. In Europe, very few Jews are doctors, so their violation of newborn Aryans does not often occur."

Sprague and Demitter exchanged sidelong glances, and then Demitter spoke up. "Ah, aside from a shortage of Jewish doctors in Europe, is there anything else you'd care to expound on?"

"No, not really." Steele smiled his cold smile again, then added, "Except this. These tattoos are the sort that the SS used during the war to identify the blood-type and regiment of their soldiers, in case they were wounded or killed." He picked up the photo of Number Two and passed it over to the detectives, along with his magnifying glass.

"Now, see that mark that looks like a diamond balanced on the center point of a W? That's the mark of the *Prinz Eugen* SS Regiment. They were really tough front-line soldiers." He handed Sprague and Demitter another photo.

"This guy has the tattoo of the Death's Head Regiment. They were camp guards and special field police. I'd be willing to bet that the other two are probably from different regiments as well."

Sprague passed the photos and magnifying glass back to Demitter, who had been busily taking notes.

"So you think these men were in the SS?" Sprague asked.

"Of course not. They aren't old enough to have served in the armed forces of the Reich. I'd guess that their fathers may have been in the SS, and that they probably belong to some sort of SS family association." Steele was staring at the daggers hanging on the wall.

Setting down the magnifying glass, Demitter broke in. "So who killed them?"

Steele let out a long breath and adopted the tone of

voice used to explain things to a young child. "The Jews, of course. That pack of Bolshevik-Zionists down on Fairfax probably found out that they were in town, kidnapped them, and killed them, just as Abraham was going to sacrifice Isaac."

Sprague had a low tolerance for bullshit and had heard just about all he was willing to take from Steele.

"Are you absolutely certain that these men aren't part of your organization?" His voice was hard-edged and cold.

"If they had been my men, Detective Sprague—" Steele's voice was detached, but his expression was as hard as Sprague's "—they'd be alive now, and you'd be carrying around pictures of four dead Kikes."

It took all of Sprague's self-control to walk out of the Nazi headquarters without leaving two maimed and dying "supermen" lying on the beer-stained carpet. At the car, his anger was such that he tossed Demitter the keys.

"You drive, dammit. I'm too pissed off to get behind the wheel."

They were halfway to the Hollenbeck Precinct station when Demitter broke the silence. "Nazi Surfers From Hell. Sounds more like a movie than a lead."

Sprague just grunted and stared out at Los Angeles.

Chapter 1

The Holy Land, 1291

A plume of dust followed the riders across the desert floor, slowly settling as they thundered into the small oasis village of Wadi-al-Hifra and quickly dispersed among its buildings. From a vantage point on a hillock nearly a mile away, Henri de Beq and his armored men watched the operation with predatory interest. They had been hunting this quarry for weeks.

"Water for the horses, then for yourselves," de Beq ordered. "We'll give them time to get involved before we attack."

He was lean and grizzled, with a short-clipped salt-and-pepper beard and pale eyes permanently crinkled at the corners by more than two decades squinting under harsh desert suns. He swung down off his small Arabian mare without a wasted motion and loosened her girth, then unbuckled the chin-strap of his helmet and removed it, slinging it over the pommel of his saddle. From a goatskin bag he poured warm water into the helmet, holding it under the mare's nose so she could drink. Around him the other men were doing the same. The desert sun beat down on his mail coif, with its arming cap of padded cotton beneath, and he pulled up the hood of his white linen mantle for shade.

De Beq's horse shoved against him with her

head, demanding more, but when he grabbed a handful of skin on the mare's neck and let it go, the skin oozed smoothly back into place. The horse wasn't dehydrated, so de Beq felt no qualms about denying her another drink.

He must drink, though. Reaching back to the water-skin looped over the cantle of his saddle, he splashed more water into his helmet and forced himself to down several large swallows. It was brackish and rancid-smelling, and despite a quarter century in the desert, de Beq was unable to make himself gag down any more of it.

His horse had no such compunctions, and head-butted him in an attempt to get at the water. Reflexively, de Beq hit the horse as hard as he could on the neck with his fist. Then, having shown the mare who was master, he let her finish the water in his helmet.

The men around him were finishing. Leaving the mare with a serjeant, de Beq walked over to a small outcropping of rock that provided an unbroken panorama of the desert below. William of Etton, his second in command, was already standing there, gazing grimly at the oasis shimmering through the heat waves. As a shrill keening drifted upward on the breeze and the first puffs of white smoke began rising from the roofs of the houses in the village, de Beq tried to put out of mind what he knew was happening down there—and what he must *let* happen, to ensure that his quarry was sufficiently distracted not to notice the knights' threat until it was too late.

The oasis was known as Wadi-al-Hifra, home to nearly a hundred Christian Saracens and site of the chapel of Chalice Well. Legend had it that here the cup of Christ had been brought after the Crucifixion, and here a small shrine had been built long before the Frankish host had come to free the Holy Land. De Beq didn't know whether the part about the cup was true or not.

True it was that King Baldwin of Jerusalem had made a pilgrimage to the shrine at Chalice Well, accompanied by representatives of the Holy Father in Rome. The king had spent less than ten minutes in the small mud-and-wattle chapel, and the emissaries from Rome hadn't even bothered to enter. Bishop Tancred had pronounced the shrine "worse than a sty"; and when the hermit who functioned as keeper of the relic produced the so-called "chalice," the bishop dismissed it as nothing more than a common cup, made of horn and set round with brass—surely not the golden grail from which the Lord drank at the Last Supper. Dismissively, the bishop had remounted his mule and ridden out of the village, along with the king. A week later he was dead of dysentery, though that had caused little enough mourning among the Frankish host.

William touched de Beq's elbow—the plume of smoke was thickening—and de Beq recalled himself to the prospect at hand. Below, in the village, the Turkish devil known as Ibn-al-Hassad was proceeding with the methodical slaughter of the hapless inhabitants. For months he had been making lightning raids into the edges of the Principality of Galilee, killing entire villages and then vanishing into the desert before the Christian forces could muster to attack. When Hassad and his men had first struck in the northern bailiwick of the Order of the Sword, their Grand Master dutifully ordered his knights out to bring the Turk to justice.

Sire Henri de Beq, commanding the preceptory of Noire Garde, had been among those who tried.

Dashing out with a column from the castle entrusted to him by the Order, he had spent two weeks of fruitless searching before returning, with his men exhausted and two of his precious horses down with colic. At no time had they gotten closer than three days behind Hassad's trail.

De Beq screwed his eyes shut against the glare of the desert sun and pulled his hood farther forward. The rising pillar of smoke from the village below brought back memories of that first encounter with Ibn-al-Hassad. Neither his men nor their mounts had recovered from their first foray when word had come from a Saracen ally that a village a mere two day's ride to the east had been destroyed by Hassad.

Exhausted, and mounted on foot-sore horses, de Beq had led his men to an oasis village much like the one now before him. The ride to that village had taken its toll on the horses, with two of de Beq's mounted men-at-arms returning to the castle on foot before the end of the first day's march. By the time they had reached the collapsing walls of that oasis, all of the men were leading their mounts, and a few, like de Beq, were carrying their saddles as well.

Half a dozen men had squatted in the shade of their fleet desert ponies, clad in the black desert robes and *keffiyeh* favored by their tribe. At the approach of de Beq and his men they stood up, and their leader stepped forward. A light breeze gusted from across the hard-baked pan of the desert floor, lifting the green-and-red silk banner in salute to the approaching Christians. De Beq recognized the banner, as well as the figure of the slender, bearded man who walked out to greet him, black desert robes billowing in the breeze.

"Sharif!" de Beq called as he approached, handing off his helmet to one of his men.

Sharif Salim ibn-Faisal bowed gracefully, his right hand touching his chest, lips, and forehead in traditional Moslem greeting. In like manner, de Beq returned the salute.

"May Allah hold you dear," de Beq said formally, in Arabic only slightly tinged with a European accent.

"And may the Great Prophet always guide you," replied the Sharif, in tones that conveyed conviction in his statement.

The two men shook hands, then turned to move out of ear-shot of their troops.

"It is very bad, *el Beq*. This is a Moslem village, and all within have been killed." The sharif shaded his eyes from the sun. "I have seen inside the walls. The men who did this were not believers. They follow not the way of the Prophet *or* the way of the Christ. I have seen inside the walls, *el Beq,* and it is very bad."

"You called me here to see it," de Beq said, "so you'd better show me."

Declining further comment, Sharif Salim led the way around to the wooden gates of the oasis village. The breeze had come up again, but this time from another direction, bringing with it the stench of slaughter. De Beq had to grit his teeth to hold back the sudden flood of bile rising in the back of his throat, but he put a mail-clad shoulder to the gate and shoved, moving it back just far enough to let a man pass through. But as he made to enter the village, the sharif grabbed him by the arm.

"I warn you, my friend. I do not think you have seen anything like this before."

De Beq looked at the Saracen in surprise. "Does my friend not accompany me, then?" he asked.

"No, I will come with you," Salim said. "But this is something of which you may not have experience."

De Beq tried to imagine what horror of war he had not experienced—he had seen men killed in more ways than he cared to count—but it was clear that the sharif did not desire to go into greater detail. Setting his teeth in grim anticipation, de Beq turned and shoved through the narrow opening in the gates, Salim following with obvious uneasiness.

The village was small—not much more than eight or ten mud huts, a pen for a few goats, a fair-sized shed for storing dates, and the all-important well. There were no streets, just spaces between the huts wide enough for a few goats or a person to pass. The entire village was surrounded by a low wall no more than three or four feet high. Its purpose seemed more to keep the goats in rather than to keep anyone out, and in one or two places the stones had toppled over, dropping the wall height to not much more than a foot or so.

De Beq paused just inside the gates to get his bearings, studying the layout of the enclosure. His view of the well in the center of the oasis was blocked by one corner of the date shed. He looked cautiously to either side, his hand instinctively tightening on the grip of his sword, already aware in some deep-seated part of him that something was very wrong here. From far off he could hear one of the horses nicker softly, but other than that one sound, the entire village was blanketed in silence.

With his back to the village wall and Salim to his right, de Beq slowly began to circle to his left, hoping for a better view down the goat tracks that separated the huts. As he moved, he realized that he was becoming light-headed from the sun.

With his left hand, he reached over his shoulder and grabbed the brim of the straw hat hanging on his back, pulling it onto his head and tugging it down to shield his eyes from the midday glare. A deep breath of the air at midday scorched the back of his throat and reminded him to keep moving. He did so, always keeping his back to the wall, until his foot unexpectedly struck something soft on the ground.

At first he didn't recognize what it was. It was vaguely round, about the size and color of a coconut, but fleshy and bloated like a rotten date. He nudged it again with his boot, and it rolled over. De Beq took one look at the bashed-in face of the infant's head and all but retched.

"It gets worse, my friend," the sharif warned. "Much worse."

Closing his eyes briefly to regain his detachment, de Beq took another deep breath and continued on. As they came abreast of a wider passage leading toward the center of the village and its well, the sharif extended his arm in a gesture of invitation.

There were ten of them, men and women, dumped in a heap by the side of the well. They were bound hand and foot, with their heads cocked back at grotesque angles, and all of them bore the same jagged, dark purple wounds at their throats. Instinctively, De Beq eased his sword from its sheath as he stepped into the small clearing around the well, using the point of the sword to prod cautiously at the nearest body. It was ripe from days under the desert sun, and kites had been at the eyes, but it didn't look that different from thousands of others de Beq had seen during a score of years in the Holy Land. Neither infidels nor Christians held any sort of monopoly on savage cruelty, and it was all too common practice to slaughter entire villages during times of war. Men, women, children—all suffered the same fate if their village was in the way of a hostile army.

The binding of hands and feet *was* a little odd, though; and the identical throat wounds . . .

Inexplicably uneasy, de Beq glanced at Sharif Salim. The Saracen prince was watching him patiently, as if waiting for him to say something. When de Beq did not, Salim gestured toward the date shed. They had just started in that direction when a scraping sound came from within. De Beq might have ascribed it to an animal, or even the wind, but Salim instantly dropped into a crouch and drew his scimitar, dark eyes searching the front of the shed suspiciously.

Following his example, de Beq also crouched down, instinctively bringing his sword up in front of him, his right hand tight on the grip while his left moved instinctively to the pommel, enabling him to use the sword two-handed if needed.

"What is it?" he whispered.

Softly, the sharif shook his head. "I don't know," he said. "There's something in there that you need to see, but nothing should be moving."

Cocking his head toward the shed, de Beq strained to hear any further sound that might come from it. Nothing. Not even the buzzing of flies.

The realization sent a chill shiver through de Beq's body. Where were the flies? The desert was thick with flies; everywhere there were flies. Everywhere but here.

The sound scraped again. It sounded like a broom on a stone floor. De Beq forgot about the flies and concentrated all of his attention on the date shed. Sweat poured down his forehead, stinging his eyes and dripping from the end of his patrician nose, and he pushed the straw hat back off his head with an impatient gesture.

Scraape. Softly, seductively, the sound beckoned them toward the date shed. He could see the sharif's dark hands shifting on the hilt of his scimitar, and he really began to worry. If Salim ibn-Faisal was anxious—

Forcing himself forward, de Beq slowly began to advance toward the door of the mud-walled date shed. It was closed but did not appear to be latched. As the sharif glided to the right, setting his back against the wall, de Beq moved left and put the point of his sword against the top of the door and slowly pushed it open.

Standing outside in the bright sun, the contrast was too stark to see into the dark interior of the shed. De Beq swallowed hard and considered their options. Whoever was inside—if there *was* someone inside—would certainly have the advantage over a man entering. Temporarily blinded while his eyes adjusted from the bright sun outside, an enemy could easily kill him with a knife, sword, or spear. If the enemy had a bow, he could just as easily put an arrow in his throat before he had taken two steps into the room.

They had to go in, though. Drawing a deep breath, still listening for any movement, de Beq flattened himself against the wall in imitation of the sharif and mouthed in Arabic, "On the count of ten." He shut his eyes tightly then, drawing his sword up against his chest in a guard position, feeling the latent heat of the wall sinking into his back

through his armor as he silently counted: *huit . . .
neuf . . . dix . . .*

As he hit ten, de Beq pivoted around the door-
jamb and into the shed, Salim following suit, their
swords slashing to clear the darkness as they came,
eyes only opening when they were out of the glare
of the open doorway, backs to the walls on either
side. Slivers of light pierced the thatched roof of
the shed, and golden dust motes swirled through
them, reflecting the sunlight like a million tiny mirrors. A harsh rectangle of brightness fell on the floor
in front of the doorway, but the darkness of the rest
of the shed was no longer impenetrable. De Beq's
nose told him much about the contents of the shed,
even as his eyes began to pick out details.

Several dozen more bodies filled the date shed,
piled three-deep along either side wall, all of them
stripped naked and bound and slain like the ones
by the well. And hanging by their heels from the
center rafter were two more, gently swaying back
and forth like the pendulums used by infidel wiz-
ards to locate wells in the desert. Large brass bowls
were set under the two corpses, like those used by
the Jews in Jerusalem to catch the blood from the
animals their rabbis butchered in the marketplace.
The bowls were wiped clean, as were the faces of
all the dead. . . .

"I told you this was outside your experience,"
Salim whispered. "This slaughter was for more purpose than just to kill. The dead have been bled,
their blood caught in these bowls for—"

Scraatch. The sound again, right above their
heads.

As both of them looked up, a small black shape
plummeted out of the thatch and onto de Beq's
back, locking its fingers onto the edge of the mail

at his neck with a grip of iron. The chain mail inhibited de Beq's frenzied attempt to beat the thing off with either his fist or sword hilt, and despite slamming himself into a wall, it held on, its fingers now digging into his flesh.

De Beq bellowed as the thing on his back started biting at his neck and shoulders, and now Salim, too, was trying to beat it off. It screamed in pain as it broke teeth trying to bite through his mail, and then it found soft flesh again, this time on the side of de Beq's face.

De Beq batted at it with a mailed hand, then grabbed the thing's head and squeezed as hard as he could. Infuriated, the thing seized one of de Beq's fingers and nearly dislocated it as he wrenched away.

"Get outside! Get outside!" Salim commanded, battering at the thing with the hilt of his scimitar and urging de Beq toward the door. "They hate the sunlight! Get out!"

With blood streaming down the side of his face, de Beq staggered out the door and into the bright Syrian sun, Salim right behind him. The thing screamed and twisted, clawing for his eyes, but it did not let go, and the sharif's sword was useless at such close range.

Approaching exhaustion, de Beq flung himself to the ground, hoping to crush the thing with his own body weight. As the two of them hit the hard-packed earth, the thing shrieked and abandoned its grip on de Beq, scuttling back into the date shed on all fours before de Beq could get a clear look at it.

As de Beq rolled onto his back and shaded his eyes with one hand, gasping for breath, the sharif's shadow fell across his face.

"In the name of Allah! I had not expected *that*!"

He dropped to de Beq's side and helped the knight to a sitting position.

"And what *was* that?" de Beq demanded, grabbing Salim's sword-wrist with his free hand and pulling him closer.

The sharif's dark face went still and set, and he looked pointedly at de Beq's hand on his royal person. Exhaling softly, de Beq gave a nod and released him, gesturing toward the shed with his sword as he caught his breath.

"What was it, Salim? You said this was outside my experience, and you're absolutely right. Now, what are we dealing with?"

"I shall tell you after we've dealt with it," the sharif said. He rose and headed back toward the shed before de Beq could object, stationing himself to the right of the door as before, then turning to see if de Beq was coming. He was. The door was still open, and at the sharif's hand signal they eased inside to either side, searching the darkness overhead and keeping their backs to the doorjambs until their eyes adjusted to the dimness again, swords at the ready.

Silence. As de Beq tried to hear beyond his pounding heart, he strained to pick up any sound that would give away the position of the thing that had attacked him. After counting nearly a hundred heartbeats, he started to hear a faint sound from the far end of the shed: a soft sucking sound like a baby nursing.

Hardly daring to breathe, both de Beq and the sharif turned their gaze in that direction. In the heavy dimness of the storage shed, they could just make out a shape that had not been there earlier: almost child-sized, its thin arms locked around the head of one of the hanging corpses, face buried in the deep slash that had opened the dead man's throat.

"As I feared," the sharif murmured.

Even that faint sound was enough to alert the creature. Twisting around, it sprang at the two men in a series of bounding leaps. Instinctively, de Beq brought his sword point up in a stop-thrust, impaling the thing on the tip of his blade. It was the size of a child perhaps three years old, and it howled and writhed as the steel blade pierced it through the vitals. Afraid that it might thrash free, de Beq kept the sword pointed toward the ceiling, backing frantically out of the date shed and into the sunlight, Salim anxiously following.

Outside, the thing redoubled its screams and shrieks, convulsing on the blade and wrenching at de Beq's arm, which already ached with the effort of holding it aloft. With dreadful fascination, he watched as it howled and thrashed, until finally, with an agonized wail and one final spasm, the thing was still.

Slowly allowing himself to breathe again, de Beq cautiously began to lower his sword, intending to rid its blade of the abomination. But as he did so, the creature suddenly arched back into motion and grabbed the blade in both hands, making little grunting sounds as it tried to push itself free.

De Beq swung the sword skyward with a thrusting motion, driving the blade deeper into the creature's belly. Gasping, the thing doubled over and reached down the blade, reaching for de Beq, pulling itself closer by impaling itself still farther.

Half mesmerized by the thing's determination, de Beq glanced at Salim in disbelief, then turned toward the sharif, slowly lowering his sword until it was horizontal with the ground. As the thing

stretched toward de Beq again, making a mewling
sound in its throat and clenching at the air before
de Beq with a small, bloody fist, the sharif sprang
forward and, with a mighty swipe of his scimitar,
cut off the creature's head.

The head lay blinking in the sand at de Beq's
feet, its mouth moving once or twice as though silently mouthing a final curse of defiance. On the
blade of his sword, the body convulsed once more,
then went limp. Only at the sharif's cautious nod
did de Beq let his sword arm lower, letting its
weight pull the sword down and allowing the impaled body to slide at last from the weapon and
onto the sun-parched ground. For a moment de
Beq stood frozen to the spot, simply staring at it.
Then, almost mechanically, his right arm rose and
fell. It took him three cuts to hack the body of the
child in two.

"Holy Mother of God." De Beq's heart was
pounding beneath his mail as he straightened and
crossed himself in awe, with his sword still in his
fist. "What kind of child was that?"

"That was no child as you or I know them."
Salim was wiping the damascened blade of his scimitar with a green silk scarf. "It was a demon. Hassad created it and left it here to starve."

Stooping to rub sand on his sword blade, de Beq
glanced up at the sharif in bewilderment.

"I don't understand. What do you mean, he created it? It doesn't look like a demon to me. It looks
like a child." He rolled the bottom half of the torso
over with his boot. "A girl, not more than three
years old."

"Yes, a girl child, but one Hassad decided to
dedicate to the evil of blood." The sharif slowly
returned his delicately curved sword to its scabbard.

"Hassad and his men live on the blood of the living, be it the blood of their horses or the blood of men. They are *afreat,* accursed of the Prophet. Their very existence is a blasphemy, and Allah wills that they should wander the earth forever driven by a desire for blood—the blood they need to purify themselves."

De Beq crouched quietly looking at the sharif. It was true that there were demons and devils. He had discussed this many times with Father Andre, the confessor. They had agreed that demons and imps were almost human, but somehow he had expected scales, and fins, and horns . . . not a grime-encrusted three-year-old girl.

"I accept that what you say is probably true—" de Beq cocked his head to one side "—but my books teach me that demons are the work of the Devil."

"Ah! Yes, it is so. *Shaitan* controls Hassad, but it is Hassad who poisons his followers with a desire for blood." The sharif squatted in a meager pool of shade. "That is what he did to this unfortunate child."

De Beq was staring at the little girl's severed head. "But why? Why do this?"

"For sport, perhaps. Perhaps because he is evil and delights in torture and pain. For his amusement, he made the child like himself and his men. He set the hunger, but then he left her with no blood to drink. In a few more days, she would have left this place seeking blood and would have been slowly roasted alive under the desert sun."

De Beq stood up and slowly sheathed his sword. "Salim, my friend, we must find this Hassad. We must find him and kill him."

"Alas, that is not for me to do, *el Beq,*" the sharif had replied. "*You* must find him. My men will have no stomach for fighting Hassad and his men after today. There is magic here, evil magic, and my men fear that far more than death in battle. I will send word, if I learn of his whereabouts, but *you* must kill Ibn-al-Hassad. . . ."

Nearly a month had passed after the slaughter at the oasis, and during that time de Beq and his men had bided their time at Noire Garde, waiting for word to come concerning the movements of Ibn-al-Hassad. During that time, only one visitor had come to the fortress of the Order of the Sword—a Greek priest called Father Georgilas. He had stayed for three nights, breaking his journey to the Patriarch of Antioch, and during that time he and de Beq held several long talks on the subject of *afreat* and Ibn-al-Hassad.

"Of course I know of such things." The Greek wiped his greasy hands on a disreputable-looking beard before pouring himself another mug of wine. "As a boy in Greece, I was reared on the island of Santorini, where we had many troubles with the *vrykolakas* and the *vrykolatios*. They are like these *afreat* you speak of."

He drained half the mug in a single quaff and wiped his sleeve across his drooping moustache before continuing.

"From what you have described of what happened at the oasis, there can be no doubt about it. This Turk you are after—he must be a *vrykolatios* of the most evil kind."

"A *broucolaques*?" De Beq's command of Greek was limited, and his phonetic pronunciation of the language twisted many of the words into the Franco-Norman patois common to the knightly class in the Holy Land. "What exactly are these *broucolaques*?"

"*Vrykolatios,*" Father Georgilas corrected, looking at his empty mug and reaching for the wine jug.

"Put most simply, they are the un-dead. They drink human blood and shun the sunlight, and often they leave their graves at night and come out to torment their relatives."

"Excuse me, holy Father," de Beq interrupted, "but Ibn-al-Hassad doesn't live in a grave. He does drink blood, but he moves across the desert and kills Christian and infidel alike, and is not afraid of the sunlight."

"Ah ha!" roared the priest. "Exactly why I said he was a *vrykolatios* and not a *vrykolakas*! He does not fear the sunlight. He moves about with others of his kind, and from what you tell me of the little child who attacked you, he creates other *vrykolatios* when it pleases him. The vrykolatios feeds on the blood of his enemies, and his enemies are the devout, be they Christian—" the bearded cleric crossed himself twice "—or heathen Saracen." In his outburst, Father Georgilas had spilled some of his wine, which he mopped up with the sleeve of his habit and squeezed out over his mug.

"But tell me, Father." De Beq leaned forward and topped up both their mugs with the sweet Cypriot wine. "How did Hassad become a *vryko—vryko—*"

"*Vrykolatios,*" the priest supplied. "Holy Church teaches that there are eight ways in which a man may become *vrykolatios*. Those who are buried without the rites of the Church as well as those who commit suicide or die unavenged will surely be so condemned. So, too, will children who were conceived on one of the great Church festivals, as well as those who die unbaptised or apostate."

Father Georgilas took another long, thirsty pull from his mug, surrendering a clarion belch before continuing.

"Let me see, what else? Yes. Those who led an immoral or evil life, as well as those over whose dead body a cat or other animal has passed, will also become *vrykolatios,* as will those who have eaten the flesh of a sheep that was killed by a wolf."

Father Georgilas leaned back in his chair, his eyes suddenly looking startlingly glazed as his head lolled slowly from side to side. De Beq had been trying to keep count of the eight ways as the priest rehearsed them, ticking them off on his fingers, but he was afraid he had lost track at seven—and that Georgilas had, too.

"Father Georgilas," said de Beq, "you said there were eight ways in which a man could become—" here de Beq tried his hardest to pronounce the Greek word "—*vrykolatios,* but I think you've mentioned only seven. What is the eighth way?"

The priest drew himself upright in his chair and with great effort forced his eyes to focus on the knight.

"Those who practice . . . the Black Arts . . . also . . . become . . . *vryko* . . . *vryko* . . . *vry* . . ."

The priest's head slammed forward onto the table, and de Beq gave a heavy sigh. He should have curtailed the priest's consumption before he passed out. Now it would be morning before they could speak on the subject again. Resigned, he had three of the serving brothers carry their unconscious guest to a pallet in a corner of the hall to sleep it off.

The next day around noon, de Beq was in the stables checking on the condition of the horses when one of the men-at-arms brought him word that the Greek priest finally had recovered from the previous night's drinking. Giving a few instructions to the native groom who looked after his men's horses, de Beq went back across the courtyard and up the stairs to the great hall. The priest was sitting at the long trestle table opposite de Beq's chair, holding his head in his hands and nursing an untouched cup of thin local beer. No one else was in the hall besides a few servants at the kitchen end, cutting bread trenchers for the main meal later on. As de Beq sat down, the priest looked up through bloodshot eyes and moaned.

"Sire de Beq," the priest croaked, "I feel all of God's punishment for my sins in my head. Not for all the money in the world would I wish to be archbishop of Cyprus. The wine would kill me."

De Beq didn't care if the Cypriot wine killed the priest or not, but he did want to know one thing further from their conversation of the night before.

"Tell me, blessed Father, how do you kill a *broucolaques* in the Greek lands?"

"*Vrykolatios,*" the priest corrected automatically. He drew a deep breath and held it for several seconds before expelling it, looking very pale behind his beard. For a moment, de Beq thought the sodden cleric was about to be sick and instinctively moved back, just in case.

"To kill a *vrykolatios,* you must drive a spear or sword through its heart," the priest informed him gravely. "Cutting off its head is even better." The priest closed his eyes as a mighty belch rumbled up from his guts. "Finally, they may be killed by burning them to ashes—oh, Mother of God!"

The priest belched again. The red veins on his nose stood out from the purpled flesh, and his eyes began to water. Expecting this, de Beq jumped back, just as the priest turned his head and was violently sick on the stone floor of the great hall.

De Beq surveyed the scene with disgust and got to his feet. The Greek priest turned back to de Beq with a weak smile and a look of apology, but appeared as if he was about to be sick again.

"Thank you, Father," was all de Beq said, and then he left the hall.

For the next three weeks, de Beq had concentrated all of his efforts in preparing his men for the inevitable confrontation with Hassad and his men, going on the assumption that all of them might well be *vrykolatios,* as the priest had suggested. Contrary to the rule of his Order, de Beq fed his men three full meals a day, with meat served both morning and evening. Regular devotions in the chapel were increased as well, with daily attendance at Mass and reception of communion—for if the *vrykolatios* were also *afreat* or demons, as Sharif Salim maintained, and accursed by Allah, de Beq had to suppose that any fortification from the Christian God could only assist Christian knights in carrying out His will.

Meanwhile, de Beq did not neglect the practical side of his preparations. Prayers were well and good, but prowess with cold steel held its own grim reassurance. De Beq worked his garrison hard, requiring the men to spend extra hours swinging at the pells with their heavy swords and throwing heavy spears at stuffed "Turks" hanging from the quintain in the training yard. Nor were tactics overlooked. Shoulder to shoulder, the men grunted under the morning and afternoon sun as they formed *schiltrons* bristling with spears and trudged back and forth between the tower and stable, practicing a maneuver used to clear the streets of lightly armed combatants.

Some of the men grumbled about the training,

especially the older knights and serjeants, who were annoyed at having to mount their regular patrols on mules, their horses having been relieved of all duty in order to keep them in good condition for the confrontation. In the stable yard, de Beq saw to it that the horses were carefully brought up into condition. Extra rations of grain were fed from the carefully harbored supply in the tower, and the native exercise boys were required to walk the horses for two hours before sun up, and again for two hours after sun down.

De Beq kept careful note of the progress of all of the men and horses under his command, and at the end of the first two weeks' training had already decided which of the one hundred and ten men would go and which would stay, when they galloped off in pursuit of Ibn-al-Hassad.

The serving brothers would be left behind, of course, as would the chaplain and three of the knights. Fifteen serjeants and forty-two men-at-arms would also remain at the castle, along with the mules, lame horses, dogs and native servants. This would leave de Beq with forty men to lead across the desert—surely a more than adequate force to seek out and destroy the *vrykolatios*. . . .

Now, standing on the outcropping of rock above the small village of Chalice Well and preparing to do just that, de Beq again surveyed his troops. The reliable and competent William of Etton was at his side, awaiting his orders. They had two dozen men-at-arms and a complement of four archers. The six serjeants were well-armed and mounted. Like the men-at-arms, they carried heavy, eight-foot-long boar spears in addition to the broadswords slung at their waists and the iron maces that hung from each

pommel. Crouched apart from the serjeants and
men-at-arms in the shade of their mounts were the
rest of the knights that de Beq had selected to ride
with him—five of them.

The knights were the elite, of course. They were
taller than the other men—the benefit of having
been born into noble families, where greater abun-
dance of food and a more balanced diet combined
to give the knightly class a physical stature denied
to the lesser orders.

The physical superiority of a knight was reflected
in everything he did. In a secular setting, his defer-
ence to his superiors was pragmatic; a knight held
his estates only so long as he provided military service to his overlord. His concern for the well-being
of the men under his command centered not on
altruism but on their ability to follow his orders on
the field of battle. A knight was a law unto himself,
beyond the civil jurisdiction of the courts, and an-
swerable only to his feudal lord.

Knights professed to a religious order, like the
Order of the Sword, surrendered some of that au-
tonomy, but their noble status still set them apart
from those of lesser birth. If they survived for long
in the desert, they soon learned that cooperation
was essential. When the invading European host
had first arrived in the Holy Land, many of the
knights had objected to serjeants and men-at-arms
riding horses, feeling that being mounted was solely
the prerogative of their class. This was especially
true in the early years of the kingdom of Jerusalem,
when many of the European war-horses had perished from the change in climate and diet. Knights,
keen to defend their social position, had mutinied
on several occasions when horses were assigned to
lesser fighting men.

Twenty-five years of desert warfare, however, had had a leveling effect on the society of warriors. Neither knights nor men could survive for long without the cooperation and assistance of the other. As a result, it no longer seemed to bother the knights to see a short Burgundian peasant armed and mounted as a serjeant or even a man-at-arms. De Beq's men had long since cast aside any such prejudices, though each man knew his place within the structure.

It was time. Feeling the rising tension that always preceded going into battle, de Beq turned and went with William of Etton down to where the rest waited, mentally checking each man's equipment as he moved among them and assessing the condition of their mounts. The horses looked fit enough for the gallop down to the village, after their long march to get here; the men looked no worse than their horses.

He had done almost all he could do to prepare them. Drawing his sword, he sank to one knee to do the rest, grasping the blade of the sword with both mail-mitted hands and holding the cross-hilt before him, as the others did the same all around him. The archers lowered the top ends of their bows to the ground in salute, heads bowed, and the knight who held the standard, Sir Myles Brabazon, dipped the colors to trail in the dust.

"Not to us, Lord, not unto us, but unto Thee be the glory!" de Beq prayed, as generations of crusader knights had prayed, bowing his head at the men's answering, "Amen," as it whispered around him.

Then he was kissing the relic in the pommel of his sword, rising to slip the weapon into its sheath, setting his boot in the stirrup of the horse that one of the serjeants brought up, while his men mounted all around him. Beside him, the brilliant banner of the Order unfurled above Myles Brabazon's fists— a blue cross *patonce* outlined in gold, floating on a crimson field. Between the arms of the cross were four golden cramponned crosses, turned forty-five degrees, so that a distance, they looked like X's within a golden circle.

Beneath their flowing mantles of white linen, the knights bore this device on their red surcoats, with their personal arms displayed on short, open sleeves at either shoulder. The serjeants bore the same device, but without the demi-sleeves. The men-at-arms displayed the device as well, but in a roundel on the left breast. It was a noble and inspiring device, and had never been dishonored.

Picking up his horse's reins, de Beq turned in the saddle and surveyed his command, waiting until everyone was mounted and settled, awaiting his orders.

"Quietly, now, *mes confrères,*" he said with a wolfish grin inside his helmet, holding up a mitted hand for silence. "We have an appointment with Ibn-al-Hassad, and we would not want to alarm him prematurely."

Chapter 2

The wind coming up off the Syrian plain brought with it a fine grit that worked its way between skin and padded gambeson as the Knights of the Order of the Sword rode across the desert floor towards Chalice Well. The gates to the settlement were open, and de Beq led his men quietly through, drawing them up to dismount inside the village.

Leaving four of his men-at-arms to guard the horses, de Beq quickly formed his serjeants and remaining men-at-arms into skirmishing parties of three to four, each led by a knight. Should they need to beat a hasty retreat, he sent his four archers up onto the walls to provide covering fire. Spread out at ten-yard intervals, the archers could prevent even the most determined enemy from making any headway between the tightly packed houses and the perimeter wall. Each man had thirty arrows, and at the distance they had to cover, there was no doubt that each shaft would find its mark. With his protective cover in place, de Beq raised his sword and gave the signal for his men to advance down the narrow paths between the houses.

The skirmish parties started to move out, boar spears at the ready, each followed by the knight who had command. In the event that anyone was foolish enough to offer resistance, the men-at-arms and serjeants would stab and slash with their broad-bladed spears. If attacked from the rear, the knight would turn and hold the enemy while the men behind him raised their spears, turned around, and pressed forward to assist the knight. It was a technique that had been developed over the years to deal with the occasional uprising, and given the discipline of the Europeans, one that usually worked well.

As each skirmishing party passed a building, it halted while one of its number checked to see if it was empty. The party remained at the halt until it caught sight of the skirmishers on either side of it before moving forward again. At each stop, de Beq would jog from one group of men to another, providing them all with unified command and the assurance that he was leading them. Finally, after passing by a dozen empty huts and sheds, de Beq and his men came to the clearing in the center of the village.

The wind continued to blow grit, turning the sky a copper-bronze and muffling any sound. Through the slit in his helmet, de Beq could see shadowy lumps lying on the ground around the well. At first he thought they were goats, but then the wind abated and the dust died down, and he realized what they really were: the bodies of children. In the sudden stillness, he could also hear the agonized cries of villagers coming from behind the buildings opposite the well and the sadistic laughter of the Turks.

Swinging his sword-arm in a slow arc high over his head, de Beq grimly led his men across the clearing toward the sound of the screams. They had nearly reached the first few buildings when two

Turks suddenly came around a corner, dragging a body behind them.

Sir Myles Brabazon was less than twenty feet from them and reacted without hesitation. Despite the more than seventy pounds of chain mail weighing him down, Brabazon sprinted directly at the two momentarily bewildered Turks, smashing his shoulder into the chest of the smaller of the two men and sending him sprawling while, at the same moment, he swung full hard with his sword and caught the other Turk just above the right ear. He managed to cleave right through the head and neck, but his sword stuck in the Turk's body as it dug into his breast bone.

The Turk sagged to the ground, blood spraying up from the severed arteries, and Brabazon placed a foot against his chest and pushed the dying Turk off his blade. The other Turk, recovered from the shock of Brabazon's impact, scrambled to his feet and took a vicious swipe at the knight's leg with his scimitar.

The thin, curved blade of the Turkish sword bit cleanly through the knight's sheepskin legging and sank into the muscles of his calf. Brabazon's leg buckled under the blow and he crashed to the ground, instinctively rolling away from his adversary and bringing his sword up in a defensive parry, deflecting a cut that had been intended to slide beneath his helmet and connect with his throat. Before he could recover, the Turk was at him again, this time with a bruising blow to his forearm, mercifully deflected by Brabazon's mail sleeves. As the knight tried to stand, the Turk swung his scimitar with both hands, axelike.

Brabazon ducked down and caught the blow full on his helmet, the force of the impact once again sending him crashing to the hard-packed earth. Fortunately, before the Turk could close in for the kill, one of the serjeants dashed forward, driving his boar spear into the enemy's gut.

The Turk staggered back, screaming as he pulled himself free from the broad-bladed spearhead. Blood gushed from his abdomen in such a torrent that the serjeant drew back in disbelief, spear still at the ready—for the Turk still had a sword locked in his fist. But though the Turk should have collapsed, he suddenly straightened and, with speed uncanny even for an unwounded man, lunged forward and knocked the spear aside, thrusting his sword into the serjeant's eye and driving it through the socket, deep into the brain.

Reflexively, the dying man dropped his spear and grabbed the sword with both hands. Screaming, he spun around in a circle before staggering into the side of a building and collapsing onto his knees, his body going into death spasms. Two men-at-arms raced forward with spears ready to avenge him, but at their approach the Turk turned and ran between the buildings, headed back from where he had come just a few minutes before.

Without waiting for the command to follow, the skirmish party took off at a dead run after the wounded Turk, one of the serjeants stopping to help Brabazon to his feet, propping him up with the aid of a spear before hurrying on. As the serjeant came even with the Turk that Brabazon had dispatched with one blow of his sword, the mutilated corpse pushed itself up into a sitting position, its nearly severed head flopping grotesquely to one side.

The serjeant froze momentarily in his tracks as the corpse struggled to regain its feet; then, with the utmost deliberation, he swung his sword in a downward plunging arc, completing what Brabazon had started. The severed head bounced several times and then rolled to a stop near the horrified Brabazon, and the body collapsed to move no more. Without further regard for the *vrykolakas,* the serjeant threw the knight a grin and a triumphant salute, and took off after his companion and the wounded Turk.

The wounded Turk was almost twenty yards ahead of the crusaders when his body, now drained of blood, toppled forward, pitching his conical spiked helmet into the open space in front of the Chapel of the Chalice. The helmet rolled across the barren earth and came to a halt against the naked and battered body of an old woman, savagely raped before her throat was slashed. Other corpses littered the courtyard, some horribly mutilated, others hardly touched. All, however, had had their throats cut.

The crusaders passed into the courtyard with only a passing glance at the bodies. They were looking for the Turks, not the sign of their passing. Death was their stock in trade, and the death of the villagers elicited only casual professional interest.

The chapel of the shrine of Chalice Well lay across the square, and de Beq and two of the men from his skirmishing party trotted out in front of the rest of the crusaders and made their way across to it. The door was closed and barred from within, but inside they could hear the wailing moans of someone pleading for mercy, punctuated by screams, and the laughter and coarse chatter of the Turks.

Quietly, de Beq beckoned for one of the burlier serjeants to come and boost him up so he could look through a tiny window above the door. With a leg up from a man-at-arms, he climbed shakily onto the serjeant's shoulders and stood up, hooking his fingertips over the windowsill. By stretching, he was just able to peer through the lower part of the little window.

Inside, to blasphemies and hoots of derision, seven or eight Turks had singled out the guardian of the shrine for their special attention. The old priest had been stripped naked and nailed to the top of his altar, a spike driven through each of his outstretched hands and another pounded through his feet in sacrilegious parody of the crucifix looking down from the wall above him—no work of any Christian or even of Moslems, who at least honored Jesus of Nazareth as God's prophet, even if they did not accept him as God's son.

Not satisfied with this profanation, the Turks were flaying the priest alive, one of them peeling long, bloody strips from his tightly-stretched chest with a wicked, curved dagger while his fellows crowded round and took delight in each new contortion. Blood streamed from the priest's wounds, befouling the altar with gore and the sweat of his terror and anguish, but the raw agony of his screams was weakening with every breath he managed to draw.

The man with the dagger—somehow de Beq knew it could only be Ibn-al-Hassad himself—gave a maniacal laugh and flayed another strip of flesh, then bent langorously to lick the raw wound with an obscene, blood-stained tongue. The old man's scream shifted into a long, despairing wail of anguish at this new outrage, caught just at the edge of madness, but the sound, coupled with his writhing, only served to goad his torturers on.

De Beq had seen enough. He knew their number, their unredeemable depravity, and he also knew that there was no other way out of the place besides the door below him. Letting himself down from the sill, still balanced on the sergeant's shoulders, he turned and took the up-stretched hands of two of his knights and vaulted lightly to the ground, beckoning them silently aside.

"He's in there with about half a dozen of his men," de Beq said. "They're torturing the priest. There's nothing we can do for him, but I don't intend that Hassad should leave this place alive. If they don't simply tire of their sport and kill him, the priest should last long enough for us to make our preparations. Michel," he called to one of the serjeants, "take two of the men, go back to the horses, and bring up the archers."

Without waiting, the serjeant tapped two men on the chest, and the three of them trotted off in the direction of the horses. Satisfied, de Beq turned back to his knights.

"Now, we're going to need something to use as a battering ram. Armand, take three men and see what you can find, and be quick about it. You others, keep looking for more of the Turks. They *all* may be *broucolaques*. Father Georgilas said they fall into a kind of stupor when they're sated with blood, and they're hard to rouse. But don't waste time stabbing and cutting—just cut off their heads—or burn them in the huts where you find them, if you have to. This whole place goes, when we're done.

"And William—as soon as the archers get here, I want you to position them opposite the chapel door. Put a double row of men with spears at either side of the door. If any of those bastards come out,

I want them facing a gauntlet of steel and a shower of arrows. The minute they're down, behead them."

He kept two knights and half a dozen men-at-arms with him, in case he had overestimated the priest's endurance, and set them in readiness outside the chapel door. Because the fighting would be close when they eventually went in, he took off his helmet and spurs and directed his men to do the same. Some of them put aside their swords in favor of maces or axes. De Beq decided to keep his sword, but did take off his scabbard.

The rest of his men finished their sweep of the village in the quarter hour it took the archers to return, and came back blood-stained and satisfied looking. François Mansard reported that they had accounted for a good score of the Turks, all drowsing in a blood-induced stupor in one of the sheds, surrounded by the bodies of slain villagers.

Listening grimly, de Beq watched William deploy the returning archers, integrating them with the returned serjeants and men-at-arms exactly as he had ordered. On either side of the chapel door, eleven men were drawn up in a double line of six men backed up by five more. They were crouching on the ground, facing diagonally towards the door with their spears at the ready. Beyond them by some fifty feet were the archers, protected by a German knight named Hano von Linka and the limping Myles Brabazon, easing his wounded leg with a boar spear for a crutch. If the Turks broke out of the chapel, they immediately would face a hail of arrows that either would drive them onto the broad points of the boar spears or force them back inside. The death trap was well set.

All that was lacking now was the battering ram.

The hoarse screaming from inside the chapel had diminished but little while they made their preparations, and de Beq found himself wondering how the old priest could take so much pain. As the screaming shifted abruptly to anguished pleading again, de Beq handed off his sword and vaulted up on his serjeant-observation post again to see what the sudden quiet betokened. Before he could look, the men sent for a battering ram finally returned with a hacked-off trunk of a date palm, and de Beq signaled them into position as he stretched up to peer inside one more time.

Hassad was standing nearer the old priest's head now, one hand stroking the gasping throat while the other slowly turned the blood-stained dagger before the doomed man's suffering gaze. One of his men had already seized the cup—a simple thing of horn, bound with brass—from its little shrine behind the altar and in it Hassad caught the first spurting gush of blood as he suddenly plunged the dagger into the side of the old man's neck.

The double act of sacrilege and desecration immobilized de Beq for just a stunned instant, as the cup brimmed to overflowing almost in an eye-blink and Hassad lifted it in mocking salute to the figure on the crucifix before draining it off at a single draught. As the Turk filled it from the source again and offered it to one of his followers, himself bending to the wound itself, de Beq ducked back sharply and half-fell to the ground, at the same time motioning to the men with the date palm trunk. Seconds later, backed by the weight of a dozen grim-faced men, the battering ram made short work of the chapel door on the first blow.

"The Sword of Christ!" Someone screamed, as

the first of de Beq's crusaders burst into the chapel, maces and axes clearing everything in their path.

Like men possessed, the Turks turned on the Europeans and began fighting their way to the door of the chapel. Hassad stayed back, a scimitar now in his hand, watching the progress and occasionally urging his men on. One of de Beq's men lost his footing, went down in the rush, and was immediately seized by a Turk who stood on his chest and ripped his head off with his bare hands. Unable to withstand the pressure of the Turks in such close quarters, de Beq's men tumbled back through the door and into the courtyard again.

De Beq rallied them. An iron mace pulped the skull of the first Turk to charge after them, while the next two were hacked to bits by knights rushing to de Beq's side. One of the serjeants had run to the door of the chapel with his boar spear, ready to impale the next Turk through the opening. He reached the doorway just as a small Turk emerged brandishing a scimitar. The serjeant thrust at the Turk, who deftly parried the spear on his small round shield and then dashed back inside, the serjeant hot on his heels.

De Beq and his men raced after, but not in time to save the hot-headed serjeant, whose dying eyes reflected eternal surprise and disbelief as he sagged to his knees just inside the door, trying to gather up his entrails in his arms. De Beq nearly tripped over him, but recovered in time to avoid a similar fate as a fat Turk lunged at him with a dagger and missed.

The Turks had been momentarily stunned by the Europeans' attack, but now they reacted with discipline as de Beq's men renewed their offensive. The Turk who had cost the serjeant his life leaped forward, slashing at de Beq with his scimitar, but William of Etton parried the cut with his mace and swung hard at his attacker. The Turk brought up his shield defensively and managed to deflect the knight's blow. William kicked out with all of his might and caught the Turk on the side of his knee.

The small man's leg buckled under the impact and the Turk went down. Screaming imprecations, he turned his attention to William now, going for the knight's leg, but the larger man was raining blows on him so hard that his attack had little effect. Eventually, William's mace connected with the Turk's elbow, turning the joint into shattered pulp. The Turk screamed in pain as his arm fell useless to his side, and the knight was able to sink his mace into his adversary's conical helmet.

Martello held one of the Turks at bay with his spear as two more grappled with serjeants Joffre and Brandstadter. Joffre's hand-and-a-half sword was too long to be used effectively in the confines of the chapel, and Brandstadter had to grasp his axe by the middle of the haft in order to wield it.

Joffre had his sword wrenched away in the struggle and was easily overpowered by his foe, who forced the stocky Breton to his knees as though he were a child, bashing his face to pulp with his bare fist. Joffre fought with all his strength to break free, but despite punching and kicking in every direction he could think of, he was unable to escape the beating he was receiving. As Joffre slipped in blood on the floor, he instinctively threw out his arm to catch himself. His hand found a conical spiked helmet, and picking it up, he rammed it into the Turk's chest.

Joffre felt the Turk's grip on his throat weaken as the spike drove into flesh, and the Turk staggered back. Winded, Joffre wrenched himself free, dropping to all fours, gasping for breath. As he looked up at the Turk in the dim light, one eye blinded by blood, he froze in astonished horror as the Turk reached up to his chest, grabbed the helmet with both hands, and slowly withdrew the bloody spike from his chest. Before Joffre could even throw himself to one side, the Turk rammed the spike of the helmet down on Joffre's back, killing him instantly.

But with Joffre out of the way, de Beq was able to swing his sword in a round-house blow at the Turk's neck. Sensing the motion, the Turk tried to duck, and instead of beheading the Turk, de Beq's sword took off the top of the Turk's head. The Turk screamed but kept coming, even with his brain exposed, dashing forward and tripping over Joffre's body. De Beq slipped in the growing slick of blood on the floor of the chapel, but still managed to launch himself after the Turk and aim another slash at him, this time burying his blade deep in the shoulder of his opponent.

The Turk turned with such sudden ferocity that de Beq's sword was torn from his hands. With the sword still deeply embedded in his shoulder, the Turk sprang at de Beq, his hands grabbing the edge of his chain mail coif, tightening it around the knight's neck as he tried to choke him to death. The blood roared in de Beq's ears, and a blackness seemed to be overtaking him, coming from far behind his eyes, as he twisted and struggled to break free of the Turk's viselike grip. Repeatedly de Beq drove his knee into the Turk's groin, but failed to loosen the Turk's choking hold on his throat.

De Beq felt his legs begin to buckle as he started to lose consciousness. In desperation, he began to flail wildly against the Turk, his weakening blows pummeling the man's back and sides without effect. The Turk pulled de Beq closer to his mouth, going for the jugular with sharpened yellow teeth. The intended bite became but a nip as de Beq flinched away, his iron-mitted fingers trying desperately to gouge the Turk's eyes. The Turk reflexively turned his head aside, escaping the mailed mitt that tried to blind him, and de Beq's fingers connected with his brain.

De Beq dug in harder as the pressure on his throat relented and he realized the Turk was going into spasms. He gritted his teeth and dug harder still, and the Turk let go with a deflated gurgle and collapsed completely, leaving the horrified de Beq holding a fistful of brain.

De Beq fell into a seated position, gasping for air as the roaring in his ears and the great blackness that had engulfed him both receded into the pain of his badly bruised throat. All around him, the battle still was raging. Flinging away what was in his hand, de Beq looked around to see who needed help next and saw Brandstadter's axe methodically rising and falling—and for the first time was conscious of the German serjeant's screamed curses as he hacked one of the Turks to bits. Struggling to his feet, de Beq staggered over to where Brandstadter was kneeling in a growing pool of his own blood, bringing his axe down on a nearly limbless form. The object of his attentions screamed in rage and pain as the serjeant hacked off his remaining arm and left him to squirm in the gore like an obscene worm.

But the dark pool around Brandstadter had grown larger with his exertions. The German serjeant's face was a pale bluish white, and as he raised his axe for what was clearly the last time, de Beq could see the golden hilt of a Turkish dagger protruding from under his left arm, and the wetly glistening torrent of blood staining his surcoat a darker crimson.

For an instant, Brandstadter reared up in his final glory, the two-handed axe poised above his head at the apex of the swing, his coif pushed back and his thin blond hair matted with sweat and blood, a look of elation blazing in the pain-taut face. Then, with the supreme satisfaction of those who know they die in a just cause, if die they must, the axe flashed down, severing the head of the armless and legless Turk and embedding deeply in the floor. The light was already fading from Brandstadter's eyes as he toppled forward across the torso of the Turk.

The fighting was almost over, though. Fresh men-at-arms had pressed into the chapel, beheading several more Turks with their two-handed battle axes and clearing a way for Martello and two more serjeants with boar spears, who now drove the Turkish chief to ground in an angle between the altar and the chapel's back wall, using the spears to spar with his blade. Myles Brabazon had brought three of the archers into the back of the chapel, too, and roared for the men in the center of the chapel to stand aside as three heavy war bows were brought to full draw, barbed arrows aimed unrelentingly at Ibn-al-Hassad.

Suddenly, de Beq realized that all of the Turks were dead except Hassad. A hush descended as the men realized it, too, and weapons were guardedly lowered as all eyes turned fearfully to regard the trapped Turkish leader. There was still a danger so long as Hassad lived, and at de Beq's signal, the knights Armand du Gaz and Hano von Linka pushed forward to join the three serjeants with more boar spears, unintimidated by Hassad's glare. The other knights and serjeants pressed into the chapel as well, as many as would fit, all of them with weapons still at the ready, should Hassad try to escape.

Aided by one of the men-at-arms, de Beq dragged himself to his feet and made his way toward the profaned altar and Hassad, picking up a spear from off the floor and hefting it as he eyed the Turkish chief. Hassad still held a bloody scimitar in his hand, but now he flung it away and glared at them with haughty contempt.

"You cannot harm me," he declared in French. "I am eternal."

De Beq was as much shocked by Hassad's use of French as he was by what the Turk said. Some of the men shifted uneasily, as though instinct warned that if they stood too close, he could in some way destroy them. Some of the others crossed themselves. De Beq, however, stood his ground.

"Only our Lord is eternal, Turk," he said evenly.

"I think not," Hassad retorted, spitting on the altar beside him. "I have drunk the blood of your Lord, and he is nothing! *Nothing!*"

There was something in Hassad's voice, an evil that went beyond mere blasphemy. De Beq could sense the threat that it might affect his men, causing them to falter—possibly even causing them to weaken, giving Hassad an opportunity to escape.

"Pin him to the wall,' de Beq said, not even raising his voice.

Without the slightest hesitation, Hano von Linka and Armand du Gaz rammed their spears hard into Hassad's shoulders, the blades sinking to the bars on the ricasso and the points digging deep into the wall as Hassad gasped. At the same time, the archers let fly arrows into Hassad's thighs, three of the shafts slamming through the flesh and pinning him there as well.

"I shall kill you all!" the vampire roared, sweeping a forearm across the arrows and snapping them off like so many matchsticks, nearly pulling his thighs free as he arched his body away from the wall and wrenched at von Linka's spear. "I shall kill you all and drink your blood before you die!"

Still pinned by the spears, apparently oblivious to pain, Hassad kicked out at the crusaders and continued trying to tear himself free. Other men rushed forward and drove more spears into arms and legs, putting their weight behind the hafts, two to a spear, as his superhuman strength threatened to overwhelm even these efforts.

De Beq had seen enough. Moving swiftly to the altar, with the dead priest's body still staked out upon it, he bent down and retrieved the cup that the old man had died to protect—the cup that Hassad had used to drink the old man's blood. Hefting his spear, he held the cup aloft for Hassad to see, righteous rage propelling him into vengeance.

"I will hear no more of your blasphemy, Turk! This holy relic is the cup of our Lord. You profaned it by drinking the blood of its keeper. Now we will purify this cup. The last thing you shall see before I send your soul to hell will be this cup resanctified!"

Without further preamble, de Beq moved a single step closer and plunged his spear into the Turk's side. Hassad gasped, his head snapping back as he felt *this* wound, but he could do nothing to stop the blood gushing out of his side and down the shaft of the spear, to be caught in the cup which de Beq impulsively thrust beneath it.

"I curse you, Christian!" Hassad ranted. "You and yours shall live to regret what you do here! I call upon the nine demons of Hell to torment you, to smite you for your presumption! You cannot kill that part of me which is immortal! I curse you! I curse youuuu. . . ."

At that point, de Beq had ceased caring about any part of Hassad, whether or not it lived forever. He was thinking of the horror Hassad had wrought upon countless hundreds, perhaps thousands—and in particular, of the blameless old priest still staked to the altar beside Hassad in the anguish of his death, whose tortured pleas for mercy had fallen upon deaf ears. De Beq's ears were likewise deaf as he lifted up the blood-filled cup and, to astonished gasps from his own men, pressed it to his lips and drank, never taking his eyes from Hassad's as he swallowed once, twice, again.

But eager hands were waiting to take the cup when he had drunk, passing the cup from man to man and back to de Beq each time it was emptied. Hassad's cursing had given way to maniacal laughter. The gush of blood from the Turk's side slowed—surely the wound was not closing of its own accord!—and de Beq had to twist the spear to make the blood continue flowing, until all who desired had shared the gory communion, even those in the yard pressing inside to partake—all save the archers, who had melted back to the courtyard murmuring among themselves when de Beq's intention became clear; for their service to the Order was by contract, not as true members, and they did not share the other men's thirst for blood-vengeance.

Hassad was still laughing weakly as de Beq set the little cup carefully on the altar, but reason no longer lit the dark eyes. De Beq almost pitied him as he took the sword that William handed him and, after kissing the holy relic in its hilt, struck off Hassad's head.

His men's shouts of approval reverberated in the little chapel as Hassad's body arched once more, blood spraying them all in bloody baptism, then subsided on the spears that pierced it. The head came to rest on the floor at de Beq's feet, and he shuddered, suddenly sobered, as he thought he saw a fleeting smile pass briefly across the dead Turk's lips.

But then the moment was past. Justice having been done, and having been *seen* to be done, the men immediately withdrew from the desecrated chapel to see to their dead and wounded and set about the more pleasant business of looting what valuables they could from the village. De Beq remained for a little while, staring in numbed reflection at Hassad's body, then set himself the grisly penance of removing the priest's remains from the altar. He could not budge the spikes pinning the old man's hands and feet, so he had to force the limbs free, wincing as he tore the lacerated flesh even further—not that the priest could feel it.

When he was done, he closed the staring eyes and folded the pierced hands on the flayed breast, intending to take the body elsewhere; but on reflection he realized that the altar could never be exorcised of the sacrilege that had been committed upon it. Better to cleanse the whole place by fire.

Before leaving to give the order, he picked up the cup from which they had all drunk, turning it reverently in his trembling hands, wondering whether what they had done had only compounded the sacrilege begun by Hassad; wondering whether God would punish them for trying to cancel blood with blood. He wiped the cup as clean as he could with a piece torn from one of his slain men's mantles, then tucked it into the front of his surcoat and went outside, transferring it to his saddlebag as soon as someone brought his horse up.

Chapter 3

De Beq felt less uneasy when he had gotten outside. There he heard the toll in lives that the day's work had cost them—a worry he knew how to deal with. Three of his serjeants, five of his men-at-arms, and an archer were dead, another man-at-arms would be dead before nightfall, and fully a dozen of various ranks bore wounds that would be long in healing, though Gaspar, the serjeant-hospitaler, thought that they could ride.

And ride they must, to get away from this godforsaken place. After ordering one of the serjeants to have the fit ones fall in by the well and start refilling their water-skins for the long journey home, de Beq looked around for William of Etton. William was over by the rather sparse pile of loot that had been accumulating over the last hour, rummaging through it with Armand du Gaz who, as one of the few knights who could both read and write, was trying to inventory the meager haul.

"Brass cups. Nothing but brass cups. By the Blessed Virgin, none of these are fit for drinking wine. They make anything taste foul." As he tossed a cup on the pile, Armand gave him a withering look.

"William, *mon cher ami,* if you don't quit tossing

'brass cups' on the wrong pile, I may have to break your skull."

With a shrug of apology, William put the cup back on the right pile and crouched down next to Armand, as the Frenchman dipped his Persian pen into an ink horn and made another notation on a piece of papyrus.

"Armand, why do you always make a list of the pillage?"

The French knight finished what he was writing, then handed the papyrus to William with an eyebrow raised in droll patience.

"Just give it to Henri," he said, stashing his pen in its wooden case, and closing the ink horn. "Without this list, it is just possible that some of the plunder might not make it back to the castle."

Before William could protest the suggestion that a member of their order might be less than honest, a horn sounded by the well where de Beq was now waiting, and both knights moved off to obey its summons, leaving the plundered treasure in the dust.

Drawn up in front of their leader, the crusaders stood around in more or less even ranks waiting for final orders. Several had been set to drawing water from the well, where an impromptu bucket brigade filled the water-skins that others brought. All of the knights were present, two of the serjeants, the three remaining archers, and sixteen of the men-at-arms, most of them nursing some kind of wound. Gaspar, the serjeant-hospitaler, was crouched in the shade of one of the buildings fronting the square, where two of the men-at-arms were cradling a third in their arms. The man's moans carried weakly to where de Beq stood, and de Beq glanced only briefly at the inventory William handed to him, before beckoning to Hano von Linka, whose wounds were slight.

"Take the men you need to bring our dead into the chapel, Hano. I want all the Turks out. Pile the rest of the bodies all in one building and then set fire to it." The knight nodded and started to leave, but de Beq raised a hand to stay him.

"One last thing. Bury the priest under the altar of his shrine. When that's done, then burn the entire village."

"The chapel, too?" Hano asked.

"Especially the chapel. The presence of our dead will re-hallow what has been defiled."

As the men dispersed to their duties, some of them starting to pack up the booty, de Beq turned and walked over to the shade where the dying man lay. The man was an Italian named Fortunato—a good fighter, but not a lucky one today. The dark eyes mirrored agony and delirium, its source a gaping abdominal wound, which his twitching hands could only partially cover. The serjeant Gaspar looked up as de Beq approached, as did the two men trying to comfort their comrade-in-arms.

"How long?" de Beq asked.

Gaspar shook his head, lips pressed together grimly. "It could be hours, Sire."

"We can't wait. You know that," de Beq said.

At the serjeant's silent nod, de Beq drew his sword and, grasping it under the quillons, knelt down beside the dying man, presenting the cross-hilt before the man's pain-glazed eyes.

"You have fought the good fight, Brother Fortunato," de Beq murmured, slipping his free hand underneath the man's head so he could lift him up to touch the cross. "If you can hear me, kiss the cross, in token that you go into God's great Heaven as his soldier, faithful even unto death."

The man stirred a little in de Beq's arm, and de Beq pressed the cross-hilt of the sword to the trembling lips, at the same time glancing at the two men-at-arms and nodding. The usual method for administering the *coup de grace* was by severing the great veins and arteries in the neck, but all of them had seen too much of *that* form of death in the days and weeks just past; so his comrades drew their daggers across the veins in his wrists instead. It was slower, but the dying man slipped into death with a gentleness denied all the others who had died today at Chalice Well.

De Beq held his sword to the silent lips long after he knew the man was gone, head bowed in wordless prayer, finally sealing the departed soul's passage with the words that had taken them into battle.

"Not to us, Lord, not unto us, but unto Thee be the glory."

As the others whispered "Amen" and crossed themselves, de Beq stood and slipped his sword back in its sheath, not watching as the men picked up the body and carried it into the chapel with the rest of the Order's dead.

Smoke was already spiraling up from the first of the fires as de Beq mounted up and led the crippled remnants of his command out of the ruins of Chalice Well. Half an hour later, the spirals had become a black, greasy pall hanging over the oasis, as von Linka and the six men charged with the task of burning the village set spurs to their mounts at last and galloped off to catch up with the rest of the Order of the Sword.

A fever seemed to accompany the crusaders as they covered the long, simmering miles back to their castle of Noire Garde, and not only among the wounded. Men became drowsy, literally falling asleep in the saddle and sometimes tumbling to the ground as they rode along. Appetites waned, though their thirst remained undiminished and even increased, and was little eased by the tepid water they carried.

De Beq told himself that it was the water itself, brackish and rancid from the goatskins that were the only means of carrying the water they needed to sustain horses and men for the long ride home; but he could not remember a thirst like this before. His head throbbed, too, behind his eyes, and his joints seemed stiff. He said nothing to his men, but this mission seemed to have taken more than the usual toll on them as well—except for the wounded, who felt the heat and fatigue no less than anyone else, but whose injuries seemed not give them as much distress as de Beq would have expected.

They reached Noire Garde on the fourth day of march, exhausted, thirsty, and with a gnawing hunger in their bellies. De Beq had a serjeant sound a horn as he and his men approached the castle, and from inside the massive gates were unbarred and swung open. The cobbled courtyard rang under the hooves of the horses, many of which had pulled up lame on the hard march back and had to be led. Grooms came out of the stable block to take charge of the horses as those still mounted swung down, and two serjeants emerged from the donjon to begin gathering up the armor and weapons the men-at-arms discarded, noting which swords needed sharpening, what armor needed mending. The archers, always a little apart from the knights and men-at-arms, moved off to their quarters with their own priorities, where bows must be wrapped in damp rags to safeguard them from the desert heat and arrows carefully stored in special boxes in the armory.

Gradually, the men staggered off in the direction of the lavatorium, with its well, there to strip off gambesons and undergarments and wash the desert grime and the killing from their weary bodies before donning the long white robes and mantles that were their habit within the castle. With red-rimmed eyes and ashen faces, the men gathered briefly in the chapel to offer numb thanksgiving for their safe return, before staggering upstairs to the great hall, where serving brothers of the Order waited to begin bringing in the evening meal.

The arrival home had not much relieved Henri de Beq. Like his men, de Beq was suffering from the same strange fever and growing lethargy that had followed them from Chalice Well. His headache had not diminished, and every joint and muscle in his body seemed to ache. He had eaten but little during the four-day march, despite a driving, gnawing hunger, and although he knew that a meal soon would be set in the hall for him and his men, the thought of that meal filled him with revulsion. Nor had the fresh, clean water of the castle well really slaked his thirst, though it had helped a little.

Wearily climbing the turnpike stair that led up from the courtyard, de Beq paused to look into the tiny intramural chamber that was his sleeping place— the rest of the men slept in large dormitory rooms above the great hall and stable, according to their rank—checking to see that a serjeant had brought up his saddlebags from the yard below. Then he continued up another straight flight of stairs in the thickness of the wall and entered the great hall.

Of the six knights he had taken with him to Chalice Well, all had returned. He wished he could say the same of his serjeants and men-at-arms. William of Etton, looking near death, was already sitting next to de Beq's place at the refectory table drawn up in front of the large fireplace that was set into one wall along the side of the hall. In front of him was a silver goblet filled with heavy Lebanese wine and a wooden plate with a fresh loaf of bread. Armand du Gaz and the injured Myles Brabazon had claimed a bench along the opposite side, where Brabazon could prop up his wounded leg, both of them staring numbly at the hall's whitewashed walls. Two of the three remaining knights from the venture, Hano von Linka and François Mansard, were helping a limping Etienne Lefroi to a seat.

The three knights he had left behind were huddled at one end of the serjeants' table, quietly conversing with the serjeants who had come back. De Beq supposed that they were pumping the men for information about what had happened at Chalice Well, which was certainly inevitable. Lower down the hall, the men-at-arms who had gone and who had stayed were mixed indiscriminately, though those newly returned would be too weary to give their curious comrades many details.

The men all rose as de Beq entered the hall, but he waved them back to their seats with a weary gesture. As was his privilege, he sat down at the head of the long, carved table in a cross-braced chair with a tooled leather seat and back. His goblet was already filled, and he picked it up and tried to drink, but the mere effort of lifting the cup to his lips seemed to require more strength than he could muster. Exhausted, he set the goblet down, splashing some of the wine on the table. Lethargy crashed over him like a wave, and for a moment he thought he was going to faint. The other knights at table seemed in no better shape.

Several serving brothers entered the hall carrying platters of freshly cooked meat, setting them on the table in front of the knights and then retiring to the far end of the room where they could keep an eye on the meat and wine, ready to bring more if needed. The chaplain said the blessing, and all were free to eat.

Absently, de Beq tore a piece of bread from the loaf in front of him and sopped it in the juice swilling around the meat on one of the platters. He had no appetite for it, but he knew he had to eat something. With some effort, he managed to bring the soggy crust to his lips and push it into his mouth. A wave of something near to nausea flashed through his body as he tasted it, but despite his queasiness, he swallowed.

Within seconds, his hunger turned to a craving—a craving for more of the juice from the just-cooked meat. Tossing aside the chunk of poorly cooked pork, de Beq picked up the platter and brought it to his lips, tipping it up to drink as much of the bloody juice as he could.

He staggered off to his bed then, and slept the sleep of the dead for the better part of two days, until William of Etton roused him with the news that Acre had fallen—Acre, the capital of the Kingdom of Jerusalem.

While de Beq dressed to come down and receive the messenger who had brought the news, William filled him in on what was known thus far. It had taken the Chevalier Humphrey d'Urbot six days to reach de Beq's garrison by camel, pressing the beast hard and traveling mostly by night to avoid any Saracen patrols that might be searching for refu-

gees. On the fifteenth of May, 1291, as de Beq and
his men had been celebrating their defeat of Ibn-
al-Hassad, the Mamaluk army under Sultan al-Ashraf
had breached Acre's walls. Within hours, news of
the disaster reached the city of Tyre, directly north
of Acre on the Mediterranean coast, causing wide-
spread panic among the populace. The next day,
Tyre was abandoned to the Moslems without a
fight, its Frankish population scattering in all
directions.

"The king, along with most of his nobles, has
fallen back to Cyprus," d'Urbot reported to de Beq
in the castle's chapter room, as his council of
knights also listened. "Our master, the Prince of
Galilee, is determined that the castle of Noire
Garde should not be allowed to fall into the hands
of the Saracens. To prevent this, he commands you
to slight the castle and then accompany me to Armenia, where we will join with the King of Armenia
in raising an army to retake Jerusalem."

Having relayed the orders of the prince, Chevalier Humphrey d'Urbot sat down and poured himself a cup of wine.

Slowly standing, de Beq surveyed the faces of the
knights present at the table.

"It is not possible that all of us accompany you,
Chevalier. Of the thirty men who returned from a
mission we undertook last week, at least half are
not yet recovered. I would propose that you take
the main part of the garrison tomorrow, leaving behind those who are still not recovered from their
fever. I will retain an additional complement suffi-
cient to slight the castle, when we are ready to
leave, and follow you with the rest, in as many days
as it takes to regain our strength."

Chevalier d'Urbot looked down the table to

where de Beq stood, his thick fists resting on the tabletop. "How many would I take with me?"

"About sixty, perhaps a few more. They will be useful to the prince. Most of them are soldiers, only a few are serving brothers."

D'Urbot looked around the room and decided that his chances of reaching Armenia would be improved if he didn't have to slow down to nursemaid fifteen fever-ridden men.

"An excellent plan. I shall start out tomorrow with the main garrison, then, and you can follow when you're fit." D'Urbot raised his cup. "The Sword of Christ."

De Beq had no wine before him, but he bowed slightly in answer to the salute.

"The Sword of Christ, Chevalier."

Next evening, de Beq watched alone from the tower battlement as the garrison rode out, d'Urbot at their head on his swaying camel. De Beq had kept behind all of the men who returned with him from Chalice Well save the archers. When the departing column was only a plume of dust on the darkening horizon, he went back down to the great hall. He wondered if he looked as pasty-faced as the knights who were waiting for him. Even d'Urbot had remarked upon it, before climbing up on his camel.

He stayed the men from rising as he came into the room, suddenly struck by the realization that one of them, Hano von Linka, appeared to be dramatically improved over his fellows. Unlike the other five, Hano had a hint of color in his cheeks, and the brightness in his eyes was different from the look that came from fever.

"Hano, you're looking almost fit tonight," de

Beq said as he walked around the table to take his seat at its head.

"*Ja*. I think the medicine may be working," Hano replied.

"Medicine?" de Beq asked.

"Well, not medicine, really," said the lanky blond knight. "When I was a boy in Styria, my father's surgeon would make us drink pig's blood if we were ill. So last night and today, I drank a cup of blood from the animals they butcher for the kitchen." The Chevalier von Linka leaned back against the wall. "It sounds disgusting, I know, but I feel much better."

An hour later, under Hano's direction, another pig was brought squealing into the hall and stunned with a blow from a mace before being strung up by the hind feet and having its throat cut. They caught the blood in a pan held beneath—imagery all too reminiscent of the brass bowls in the date shed, to de Beq's way of thinking—and from there, the dark, frothy fluid was ladled out to the knights and other men remaining at the castle. De Beq misliked the similarity to the other blood they had drunk together, remembering the blood-stained cup he had brought back in his saddlebag, but he ordered them all to drink, and no one disobeyed.

Hano's homegrown remedy seemed to work. In the morning, the men seemed to have taken on some color, and again that evening a pig was butchered. Fortified by blood, the men's normal appetites began to return as well, so that after a week, all of them seemed nearly returned to normal health. Even the wounded continued their remarkable recovery, enabling de Beq to set a definite schedule for slighting the castle and readying for their departure.

The methodical dismantling of the castle began. Since the fever appeared to have run its course, there seemed no further need to slaughter animals for their blood, so de Beq ordered that the treatment be halted. Within days, however, symptoms of the fever began to return, and the slaughter of animals for their blood had to be resumed. Not much blood was required—less than a cupful per man, and only every three or four days. But without it the fever came back, and the hunger began to rise, to the exclusion of all other hungers.

Trying not to think about it, de Beq set a rigorous schedule for slaughter, hoping the animals would last, and kept his energies concentrated on finishing the destruction of the castle. By the end of the third week, it was nearly complete. The battlements had been hurled to the ground, and the defensive bawn wall had been pulled down close to the tower. All that remained to do was destroy the gates and set fire to the roof of the tower.

On their last night at Noire Garde, de Beq called a council meeting of all his knights and serjeants. For several days he had been thinking about the situation in the Holy Land, and wondering about the advisability of trying to reach Armenia. Finally he had reached a decision, but one which he felt should be ratified by all of the knights and serjeants.

"Mes confrères," de Beq began, calling them to attention once he was sure everyone was there. When it was built, the great hall of the castle had been designed to accommodate nearly a hundred men, but with fewer than a dozen, the very size of the hall became intimidating, and the men clustered together for reassurance around the cold ashes of the fireplace.

"Mes confrères," de Beq said again, "as you

know, the Prince of Galilee has taken flight, along with the king, to Cyprus. Most of our brothers-in-arms have fled with him, or gone to Armenia where they hope to raise an army to free the Holy Land of the Saracen."

There was a general muttering of agreement among the men, who were all aware of the situation.

"We have been told to go to Armenia," de Beq went on, "yet we are only twenty miles from the sea. It's obvious that the only purpose in sending us north to Armenia was to draw off any Saracens that might have been tempted to follow our king and prince across the water to Cyprus. We were," here de Beq looked around the room to make sure that everyone understood what he was saying, "to be decoys, sent out to die so that the king and our prince might escape."

William of Etton was quick on the uptake. "Since the king and the prince have escaped to Cyprus, is it not our duty now to join them, rather than go haring off to Armenia?"

"It *would* be, if there was any chance that the king would be returning to the Holy Land," de Beq replied. "Jerusalem fell forty years ago, and now Acre and Tyre are in Saracen hands as well." The full import of de Beq's words was beginning to sink in.

One of the serjeants spoke. "Sire, do you think the kingdom is lost?"

"Only if the king stays in Cyprus." De Beq's eyes swept around the waiting faces seated around the table before him. "It will take another crusade to free Jerusalem. Until that crusade is organized, we will return to my castle in Luxembourg and wait."

He did not tell him that there was another reason for his decision, one which had nothing to do with the possible betrayal by their overlord or even the failing military position in the Holy Land. Not for many a month would he reveal how he had reached his decision—how he had knelt by his bed one night in his private quarters pondering a once-holy cup, now befouled by the blood of an infidel Saracen demon—and how it slowly had come to him how the Turk's curse was coming to pass, damning him and his men for all eternity unless they devoted the rest of their very long lives to prayer and penance. . . .

Chapter 4

The Ardennes, 1944

The pale ivory face of the Madonna in the triptych above the altar gazed serenely down on the flickering points of light that danced on votive candles. On the walls of the chapel, a fresco of angels poured their blessings upon armored men preparing to do battle with the forces of Satan. The strident colors of the murals were muted by the soft golden glow of the candles, the outward symbol of the burning devotion of the twenty men kneeling before the tortured carving of Christ crucified.

Heads bowed, their heavy white robes offering some protection against the midwinter cold of the small stone chapel, the men were deep in meditative prayer when the door to the chapel was kicked open and one of their number staggered in carrying the naked body of a dead man.

"Master!" he cried as he struggled to carry the body to the front of the chapel. "They're in the woods. They've come again!"

Standing as he crossed himself, the man addressed as master came quickly to where the body had been laid at the foot of the altar steps. Even by candlelight, the body had a waxy bluish tinge to it, the outward sign that it had been drained of all blood. But beyond that, the body had been horribly mutilated, one arm hanging in shreds and a huge wound gaping in its back. Looking closely at the face of the corpse, the master decided that the dead man had been perhaps eighteen years old, certainly not more than twenty. He turned to the man who had carried in the corpse.

"Where did it happen, Pageau?"

"I found him near the edge of the wood, along with many others."

"Others?" Concern flashed across the master's face.

"Yes. About twenty. They had been dumped in a pile, by the men with the steel helmets."

The master turned to the other men in the chapel who had been standing silently listening, his hand dropping casually onto the hilt of the sword belted over his heavy white robe.

"William, take ten men and go with Pageau. The rest of you, secure the castle." Then, turning to the two men nearest the body, he added. "Take this one to the great hall."

"Shall we prepare him for burial?" One of them asked.

"No, not until William returns with the leader of the Steel Helmets."

Outside, a full moon reflected off the snow, making it easy for the white-mantled men to make their way from the castle to the edge of the wood several hundred yards away. Following the footprints made by the man returning with the corpse, the lightly armored men continued on into the wood and had no difficulty finding the pile of fresh corpses Pageau had reported. As they cautiously approached the small clearing, two black-clad men with a stretcher added another victim to the pile and turned back in the direction from which they had come.

Crouching low, the knights followed along behind, drifting invisibly in and out of the shadows, their white cloaks enabling them to blend in with the crusty snow on the ground.

Another twenty yards beyond the small clearing was a larger one, the scene of much activity. A field generator chugged away at the near side, providing electricity for two outside work lights as well as a small field hospital set up in a tent not far away. From the far side of the clearing came a slow but steady stream of stretcher bearers bringing wounded men under the work lights, where a medical triage team inspected the wounded, directed some to the hospital tent, and treated those they could. Those men too badly wounded—or who were already dead—were sent to a sideless shelter at the edge of the clearing nearest the generator.

Here the bearers stripped the uniforms off the dead and dying and placed them naked on a crude table. A bored-looking medical orderly then inserted a large needle into an artery in the arm—or, if the arms were too badly mangled, in the leg— and attached it by rubber tubing to a small vacuum pump. Another tube ran from the pump to a rack of glass bottles, and the medical orderly would attach this tube to a new bottle before starting to turn the hand crank on the pump. The blood thus drained from the dying or dead soldiers could be used for immediate transfusion in the field hospital just a few yards away.

To avoid any possible error in typing, each soldier had his blood-group tattooed under his left arm, as well as stamped into the metal disc worn around his neck on a string, and it was the job of one of the stretcher bearers who brought each man in to copy this information onto an appropriate number of adhesive strips used to label the bottles, before returning with his partner to pick up more wounded men.

In shock, or delirious from the pain of their wounds, most of the dying only moaned softly as they were slowly bled to death by the medical orderly who methodically turned the handle on the pump, pausing only to change bottles when they filled. A few, however, realized what was happening to them, and had to be held by the stretcher bearers for the first few minutes, while they screamed and wept and pleaded for their lives to be spared. That was why the table was located near the generator; its unmuffled chugging drowned out the cries of those men still clinging to the hope of life.

The figures in the white robes stood transfixed, unable to comprehend the technological efficiency of the slaughter they were watching. Nor did they grasp the difference between the khaki-green uniform of one of the stretcher bearers, staring in horror at the spectacle under the work lights, and the black uniform with twin lightning bolts as worn by the medical orderly.

On a given signal, the knights silently fanned out along the edge of the clearing, their swords at the ready. The orderly removed his needles and tubes from the dead man before him and labeled the last bottle of morbid blood. Two more stretcher bearers brought up another dying soldier, lifting the body of the dead man clear of the table before hoisting up the next to give his all for the fatherland. The young man in the khaki-green uniform fell to his knees beside the dying man on the table, pulling a strip of purple ribbon from the pocket of his battle-dress jacket, and was about to make the sign of the cross on the man's forehead when the knights attacked.

With a shout of *"Deus Veult!"* the knights crashed into the clearing behind the hospital tent, hacking and slashing at the German soldiers. Father Francis Freise, Chaplain, 3rd US Army, still on his knees beside the dying soldier, watched in frozen horror as the knights cut down those medics who tried to defend themselves with their blunt-pointed medical daggers, throwing up empty hands and offering no resistance when one of the knights roughly jerked him to his feet and marched him off at sword point. Within the space of less than a minute, the knights had captured Father Freise and three of the Germans as well, pummeling two of them into silence with sword hilts before hurrying all of them into the woods.

Torches blazed in their sockets in the great hall, casting more than enough light on the body lying partially under a blanket on the long table in the center of the room. De Beq and another knight stood over the body, deep in conversation.

"What do you think, Henri? Is it the *broucolaque*?"

"I'm not sure, Hano. The blood is gone, look." De Beq took a dagger from his belt and made a deep incision on the arm of the corpse. "No blood. None. I've never known a *broucolaque* to take so much."

The other knight leaned closer. "Perhaps it was drained out by the wounds?"

"I think not. Have you ever known any wound that would take all of the blood from a body?"

Just then the doors of the great hall opened and the returning party of knights entered with their captives, shoving them to their knees in front of their commander.

"So," said de Beq, "these are the *broucolaques*."

"Some of them," said William of Etton. "We killed several back in the woods."

"Please tell me everything," said de Beq, as he examined the Red Cross dagger of one of the Nazis.

SS *Sturmbannführer* Wilhelm Kluge ignored the moans of the wounded as he and his men quickly surveyed the clearing behind the field hospital.

Partisans! he thought. *Butchering bastards who can only be heroes by attacking hospitals!* Well, they wouldn't get far, and by God, they'd pay. He looked around and saw the reassuring bulk of *Scharführer* Baumann glowering at him from behind his eyepatch.

"Well, *Scharführer*, where are they?"

"Headed northwest, sir. I think there are eight of them, maybe ten. With possibly two or three prisoners." Baumann glanced around the clearing at the bodies. "Shall I organize a patrol, *Herr Sturmbannführer*?"

"No. Take three men and come with me. We won't need a patrol to deal with this lot."

Baumann saluted and trotted off to where several SS privates stood shivering in the cold. He singled out three of them, and then returned to Kluge. Without another word, they unslung their weapons and began to follow the tracks left by the knights in the fresh snow.

De Beq set down the Nazi dagger and walked over to one of the captives. On the man's left sleeve was an eagle similar to the one cast into the cross guard of the dagger, and clutched in its talons was a wreath surrounding a cross similar to the gammadion that was set between each of the arms of the cross of the Order of the Sword. But where the gammadion of the Order was of polished gold, with its arms curved to embrace the true faith of the Lord, the cross worn by the captives was black, with flat, angular arms.

In the symbolism of his time, this subtle difference spoke volumes to de Beq. Gold, the color of Light, had been replaced with black, the color of Evil. And where the gammadion of the knights curved like loving arms embracing the most noble of all ideals, the harsh angular arms of the black cross turned it into a hammer, meant only to destroy. De Beq decided that it wasn't an eagle clutching the wreath and swastika on his captive's sleeve, but a vulture, poised to devour.

"Tell me, William, what language do these men speak?"

"I'm not sure. The ones in the black uniforms speak something like German. The other one was mumbling in bad Latin when we took him prisoner."

De Beq turned and faced the man in khaki-green. "Who are you?" he asked in flawless medieval Latin.

Father Francis Freise sensed, rather than understood, the question, but he did his best to answer in the same language. "I am an American soldier, and a prisoner of those men," he said, indicating the Germans next to him.

"You're right," de Beq said to William. "His Latin is horrible. Did you make out what he said?"

"Something about being a soldier. I think he's probably their prisoner," he inclined his head toward the SS men.

De Beq grunted and walked over to the table where the dead soldier was covered with a blanket. "What do you know of this?" he asked, ripping the blanket from the body.

Father Freise crossed himself, and the three SS field medics stepped uneasily closer to one another.

Kluge and his men had reached the edge of the forest that surrounded the castle and, following Baumann's signal, spread out to five-meter intervals. Baumann pointed to the man on the extreme left of the group, who immediately trotted along the edge of the shadows until he was opposite the gates of the castle. After a few moments' wait, the moon was swallowed by clouds and the SS man sprinted to the gates.

Waiting in the dim glow of the half-hidden moon, Kluge studied the castle through a pair of Zeiss field glasses. Even in the half-light of the night, he could tell that the castle was in excellent repair, the stone well-pointed and the massive gates set well on their hinges. Scanning the silhouette of the keep, Kluge thought he could make out a thin spiral of smoke climbing skyward from one of the chimneys.

A light snow started to fall, and Kluge put his binoculars back in their case and pulled out a map. Using his pocket torch, he scanned the sector, looking for some reference to the castle, but found none. German maps were precise in their detail, yet here was a major castle not marked on the map. It could only have been left off on purpose. But why?

Somewhere in the back of Kluge's mind there stirred half an answer, trying to gnaw its way into his consciousness, but for the moment it would have to wait. The soldier at the gate flashed his signal to the men in the woods, and Kluge and the others sprinted forward to the gates of the castle.

Kluge was in excellent condition and crossed the one hundred or so meters to the castle ahead of his men, throwing himself into the shadows of the gate house, his P-38 pistol ready for action. Rolling into a seated position against the wall, Kluge dug his heels into the hard ground and, pushing with his legs, slid up the wall to a standing position.

Baumann and the other two SS privates were halfway across the clearing when the moon burst out from behind the clouds, flooding the open space between the castle and the woods with a flat incandescence. Instantly, the three men threw themselves down on the ground and lay perfectly still, waiting for the moon to vanish once again and hide them under a cloak of darkness, before crossing the remaining fifty meters to the castle. As Kluge also waited, he took the opportunity to have a closer look at the heavy gates before him.

The gates were made of thick oak planks, banded together with iron straps and heavy iron rivets—not so very different from those at the Castle of Wewelsberg, the mystical fortress that SS leader Heinrich Himmler had reconstructed as the spiritual shrine of the SS. Kluge had been assigned to the research staff of Wewelsberg for a time, searching out the artifacts that legend said were imbued with mystical power. It had been Kluge's job to locate these talismans and bring them back to Wewelsberg Castle, where they would be laid upon special altars and used in the magical rituals of the SS.

Struck by the similarity of this castle to that at Wewelsberg, Kluge stepped back a little to look up above the gates, still keeping to the shadow at one side. At that same moment, the moon brightened slightly, just before vanishing once again behind the clouds, and he was able to catch a clear look at the heraldic device carved into the stones above the gates.

The keystone set into the gate-arch was chiseled

into the shape of a shield, and carefully carved on the stone was a cross potent, with four of the curved-armed swastikas called sun-wheels set within the angles of the arms of the cross. In only one other place had Kluge seen anything like such sun-wheels, and those were painted on the walls of the inner temple of the SS shrine at Wewelsberg.

The moon vanished behind the clouds then, and Kluge's men sprinted the last fifty meters to the castle.

Standing behind the body of the dead German soldier, de Beq stared at Father Freise and then asked him—slowly, in Latin—why he had crossed himself. Freise struggled with the awkward vulgate tongue, hoping that he had correctly understood the question before replying.

"I'm a priest," he said reaching into his field jacket and tugging out his pectoral cross—for he had lost his stole in the confusion of his capture. *"Sacerdos."*

"I see," de Beq said, nodding with some unknown satisfaction. "And who are these others?"

"The enemy."

Kluge and his men pushed cautiously against the small postern door set into the gates of the castle, and were rewarded for their efforts as the door swung silently open. Easing through the small opening, alert for any movement within, they found themselves in a large, silent courtyard opposite the main tower of the castle. Built out from the walls of the castle were a number of buildings that lined the courtyard and provided stabling, a smithy, kitchen, and chapel for the knights. Kluge and Baumann took it all in in a glance, and without a word being spoken, led their men along the eastern-most wall of the castle, staying well hidden in the deep shadows as they approached the tower.

Inside the castle, de Beq turned his attention to the three SS medics identified by the priest as the enemy. He had tried to speak with them in German, but it was obvious that they couldn't understand him. He was trying to decide on a different tack when one of them stepped forward, snapped to attention, and with a click of his heels gave de Beq a smart, stiff-armed salute.

Somewhat taken aback by the soldier's actions, de Beq was even further surprised when the man stepped forward and raised the left arm of the corpse and pointed to the tattoo on the inside of the bicep. Then, pulling off his own tunic and shirt, he showed his own tattoo to de Beq.

It was obvious that both men wore the twin lightning flashes on the inside of their left arm. Just what that was supposed to mean, however, was lost on de Beq. He turned to William of Etton, who had been quietly sizing up their captives, and asked for his opinion.

"Well," said William, "I suppose that the men in the black uniforms all belong to the same order. They must all swear an oath to be branded, so they can tell their dead if they are stripped by the enemy. This other one—well, he's certainly not one of them"—he inched his head toward the SS men—"and since he wasn't armed when we caught him, I suppose he *might* be a priest."

"Well, there's one way to find out," said de Beq.

"How?" asked William.

"Priest," de Beq spoke slowly in Latin, "I want you to offer Mass for us."

"Henri, do you know what you are saying?" William whispered, eyes wide, as several of the other knights also exchanged apprehensive glances. "If we are damned for our transgression—"

"If we are damned, then it is long past time we perished," de Beq said softly. "But I tell you, William, that to endure more than six hundred years without the sacrament of our Lord is long enough. Whether it heals or condemns, I am prepared to place the matter in His hands. Do you agree, *mes confrères*?" he finished, glancing also at the others.

At their low-voiced murmurs of agreement, de Beq turned back to Freise.

"Well, Father, do you agree?"

Freise had not been able to follow the urgent murmurings among his captors—he thought they might be speaking French, but he knew only a few words of that language—but the request for a Mass seemed relatively clear, if a trifle oddly timed, under the circumstances.

"You wish me to say Mass?" he said in halting Latin.

"Yes, the Mass," the head knight replied. "*Corpus et Sanguis, Hostiam et Calix*—both, together."

Freise nodded. They wanted it under both species, then, host and cup. The request was unusual, other than in a religious community—but maybe they *were* a religious community. The white robes suggested it—though Freise had never heard of an order like *this* before. . . .

"We will go to the chapel, then," de Beq said. "Pageau, bring some bread and wine."

Kluge and his men were deep in the shadows of the stable when the knights and their prisoners started down the wooden stairs outside the tower.

Holding back to watch, the Germans saw their comrades and the American priest marched at sword point across the courtyard and into the chapel.

As Kluge and his men were about to dash across the courtyard to the chapel, more than a dozen more white-robed figures began to emerge from the castle and also went into the chapel. Kluge and Baumann waited until the last of them had entered the building—and then another five minutes, to be sure of stragglers—then dashed across the courtyard with their men. The door to the chapel was closed but not latched, and yielded soundlessly to Kluge's slow pressure.

Inside, the long chapel was illuminated only by a few votive candles at the sides and a blaze of altar candles on the reredos behind the altar. The five SS men crept silently into the vestibule beyond and eased the door closed once more, then Kluge signaled his men to work their way closer on their bellies, guns at the ready. He could see the American priest up at the altar, reading from a G.I. issue missal held by one of the white-robed men, but the rest were kneeling with their backs to the door, in a ragged semi-circle in front of the altar, their attention obviously focused on the priest.

The three SS captives sat tensely in seats carved out of the wall at the right of the altar, guarded by three knights who leaned on their naked swords, watching their captives as closely as they watched the priest. Kluge counted about two dozen of the men in all, but they were occupied for now. It gave Kluge time to consider all his options—for a single glance around the chapel had given him the answer to the question that had been gnawing at his subconscious since he first saw the cross and swastikas carved above the gates. He was in the castle of the Order of the Sword.

As he crouched in the darkness, Kluge tried to piece together what little he knew of the Order of the Sword. He recalled them having been a crusading order of knights, bodyguards to the Prince of Galilee . . . but there was something else, something sinister, that he tried desperately to recall.

At the altar, the Mass was approaching its climax. Reverently, Father Freise held up a small loaf of bread, carefully pronouncing the words of consecration.

"Hoc est enim Corpus meum."

Kluge found himself watching avidly as the priest put the loaf down, genuflected, then held the loaf aloft for the men to see. There was something, just at the edge of memory. . . .

The priest continued in Latin, setting down the loaf, genuflecting again, and picking up the chalice. This he gazed upon with equal reverence, again speaking the words of consecration.

"Hic est enim Calix Sanguinis mei. . . ."

Calix sanguinis mei, the cup of my blood—*blood.*

Suddenly Kluge knew why the castle wasn't on his map. The Order of the Sword had been declared anathema by the Pope at about the same time that the Templars had been suppressed in France. Unlike the Templars, there was no accusation of heresy. No, the charge against the Order of the Sword was far greater. They had been accused of being vampires.

As the priest elevated the chalice—*now containing the Blood of Christ,* if the Christian faith were true—Kluge stared at the gray-haired knight kneeling closest to the altar, perhaps the leader of this strange, white-clad band. Carefully, he took in every detail of the man—the chain mail showing under robe and mantle, the hand-and-a-half sword belted around his waist.

The full realization of what he was witnessing flooded over Kluge, crashing on him like a crimson wave. In an instant, he realized that the knights waiting to receive communion were centuries old. The pale luminance of their skins, the rapturous expressions on their faces as the priest lifted the loaf in one hand and the chalice in the other—all confirmed the darkest of the legends surrounding the Order of the Sword.

Himmler had modeled the blood rituals of the SS on those alleged to have been practiced by the Order of the Sword, and Kluge realized with a chill of elation that having been initiated into the bloody rites of the SS, he was in communion with the knights now kneeling in the chapel—knights with the blood of vampires in their veins, knights who would live forever!

Kluge took another look around the chapel, its walls painted in the style of most medieval churches. But unlike other churches, the murals on the walls of the chapel were not decorated with religious scenes, but instead covered with a continuous painting depicting the history of the Order of the Sword. Quickly Kluge scanned the stylized figures of the knights and horses, following their exploits around the room until, in the north, he came to a large triptych depicting the battle at Chalice Well.

The first panel showed the knights fighting with the Turks in the chapel, as a radiant Christ crucified looked on. In the next panel, the knights had pinned one of the Turks to the wall with heavy spears. Blood was gushing from another spear wound in his side, almost in parody of the crucified Christ, and the knights were drinking the Turk's blood from cups offered to them by their leader. The figure of Christ on the cross now had an anguished look on its face, as though He were suffering far greater agonies than the Turk whose blood was being consumed.

The last panel showed the knights moving through the darkness, leaving the chapel. The crucifix was still there, only now Christ had turned His head away from the knights, and His face was not visible.

So. The Knights of the Sword had committed sacrilege, and been cursed by their God, and had retreated here to their castle in Luxembourg to make amends. But meanwhile, they were vampires!

Vampires! The thought of their total power electrified Kluge. It did not take a genius to see that Germany was losing the war, and yet here was a way in which some men could survive, and no matter what the outcome of the battle now raging in the forests around them, could rise out of the ashes of defeat and rebuild the Aryan race.

And now the vampires who could give Kluge this power were waiting to receive Christian communion. Kluge's theology, based on childhood catechisms mostly forgotten, was hazy; but if the words of consecration truly did transform ordinary wine into the Blood of Christ, he had to wonder what such blood would do to a vampire. Would it provide the same kind of nourishment as human blood? Or would it destroy them utterly for daring to profane so sacred a thing? If vampires *were* cursed of God, the Blood of Christ would surely destroy them the instant it touched their lips.

Kluge decided he did not want to wait to find out. The potential gift was too precious to risk losing it by the pious self-sacrifice of six-hundred-year-old knights who had decided it was time to pay the

price for a sacrilege committed long ago in the Holy
Land. Even now, the young priest was dipping a
fragment of the consecrated bread into the cup,
touching it to the edge to stop its dripping, holding
it a little above the cup as he looked into the ancient eyes of the leader of the knights.

*"Corpus et Sanguis Domini nostri Jesu Christi
custodiat animam tuam in vitam aeternam. Amen,"*
he said.

And as the vampire knight also murmured,
"Amen," and extended his tongue to receive,
Kluge and his men opened fire.

The first shots slammed into de Beq and several
other of the knights kneeling nearest the priest.
Freise sprang back, instinctively throwing himself
to the floor and rolling to his right, scrambling behind the cover of a thick pillar that supported the
roof of the chapel. He was still holding the chalice
as he drew himself into a huddled ball behind the
pillar, but the wine had spilled across the floor of
the sanctuary. Freise grimaced at the sight, but he
decided that it was more important not to spill any
of his own blood just now, than to worry about
Blood already spilled. Surely the Lord would not
fault him for this.

Meanwhile, 9mm slugs were slamming into the
mailed bodies of the knights, shredding their white
mantles and punching ragged holes through centuries-
old chain mail. The knights reeled under the impact
of the bullets, but struggled to their feet nonethe-
less, already drawing their swords and staggering
forward to charge Kluge and his men.

Baumann and the SS troopers with him poured a
deadly fire into the three men nearest them, finally
managing to knock them off their feet—but they
got back up! Another of the mailed men charged

at Kluge, his heavy sword raised high above his head. The pistol in Kluge's fist barked twice, but the slugs thudded into the chest of his attacker with no apparent effect. Coolly taking aim, Kluge fired a third round into the man's forehead—and *that* dropped him, twitching, at his feet.

A crossbow bolt slammed into the door behind Kluge, missing him by inches and sending him diving for cover as another warrior bore down on him with an axe. Firing wildly at the man's head, Kluge managed to slow him down only when one of his bullets struck and shattered his assailant's jaw. His pistol empty, Kluge grabbed the sword from the dead man at his feet and, swinging it with all his might, nearly severed the head of his latest attacker. Dropping the sword and crouching low, he reloaded his P-38 on the run as he made his way towards Baumann and his other men.

"Down!" boomed Baumann's heavy voice, and instinctively Kluge dropped flat on the ground and tried to cover his ears. He heard the metallic clatter of the grenade hitting the stone floor, followed seconds later by the deafening blast as it went off.

All of them were momentarily stunned by the concussion of the exploding grenade. The sharp smell of cordite stung Kluge's nostrils as he gasped for air, while the chapel filled with a combination of smoke from the grenade and plaster dust from the damaged walls. The ringing in his ears made it impossible to hear anything, but instinctively he knew that he had to act before the knights recovered their senses.

Pushing himself up onto his hands and knees, Kluge shook his head and tried to clear his vision. The concussion grenade had done its job: Kluge's nose was bleeding, his own men only faintly stirring, and the knights were collapsed in disoriented heaps around the chapel. The triptych on the north wall had fallen down, almost on top of Kluge; and as his eyes finally focused, he found himself staring at the center panel, at the scene of the knights sharing their sanguine communion.

Even in his stunned condition, Kluge knew immediately what he had to do. Half crawling, half walking, he tottered his way to the nearest downed knight, fumbling inside his battle-dress jacket as he fell to his knees beside the man. The knife he withdrew had a gravity-operated blade—the sort usually issued to paratroopers—and with a flick of his wrist, he opened it. He had to struggle to roll the stunned knight over, but his blade slit the man's throat with hardly any effort.

Blood gushed from the wound, and Kluge looked around belatedly for something to catch it in; but seeing nothing in reach, he bent down and pressed his mouth over the wound. Now was not the time to be fastidious. He drank greedily of immortality, swallowing as much of the knight's blood as he could stomach.

The others were stirring by the time Kluge raised his head. From behind the pillar, a groggy Father Freise watched in stunned disbelief as Kluge, gorged on the fallen knight's blood, lurched unsteadily to his feet and staggered over to two of his men, shaking their shoulders and rousing them to consciousness.

One of the captive SS orderlies had been hit by stray bullets and would not be going anywhere, but the other two were dragging themselves upright, starting to stumble towards Kluge, too. Another gained his legs a few feet away and helped Kluge get the others standing.

All around them, the knights were stirring, too, and with a signal to Baumann and the other SS men, Kluge dashed for the door of the chapel and out into the courtyard. Most of Kluge's men were through the door to the courtyard when William of Etton and a few others managed to find their feet, but they had not reckoned on the speed of the vampire knights.

The SS medical orderly stared in disbelief at the knight whose sword had just sliced through his torso, before the top half of his body toppled to the cobblestones just outside the chapel. Bursting into the courtyard, the knights fell about the nearest Germans with incredible ferocity, literally hacking the men to pieces as they ran for the gates and the safety of the war beyond.

Kluge had just dived through the postern door when he heard something smack into the man right behind him. Turning, he saw one of his men catching himself on the sides of the door jamb, wide-eyed, the point of a crossbow bolt jutting out through his forehead. Baumann had been hit as well, the iron bolt passing nearly through his shoulder. Grabbing the *Scharführer* by the front of his battle jacket, Kluge yanked him through the opening and, half carrying, half dragging the wounded soldier, made for the wood at the edge of the clearing.

Back in the chapel, as the sounds of fighting subsided in the courtyard beyond, the trembling Father Freise finally dared to venture out from behind his sheltering pillar. Averting his gaze from the dead and dying all around him, he crept stealthily back to the rear of the chapel and peered out cautiously. Outside, he could still see a few of the strange white-robed inhabitants of the castle, but they seemed to be preoccupied with caring for their wounded and searching for any remaining Nazis. If Freise was to have any hope of escape, he must try it now.

Closing his eyes briefly in wordless prayer, Freise crossed himself nervously, drew a deep breath, then began making his way stealthily along the shadows of the walls of the castle, heading for the open castle gates and the moonlit meadow beyond. When he had managed to reach the shadowed arch of the gatehouse unobserved, he crossed himself once again, then dashed across the hundred yards to the woods and began to make his way south, toward the advancing American troops.

Chapter 5

Los Angeles, 1991

The silhouette target danced its way back to the firing line, the twelve small holes neatly grouped in a tight cluster crossing the ten-ring.

"Good shooting, Captain," was the range master's only comment as he initialed Drummond's score card.

"Thanks," said Drummond. He was more intent on wiping down his Beretta and reloading its magazine than he was in verifying his qualifying score.

Drummond holstered his pistol, picked up his shooting card, glanced at it—292 out of 300 possible—and headed down the stairs, pausing to turn in his card before heading on down the hill. The parking lot of the Los Angeles Police Academy was a sweltering asphalt square, and his red BMW 635 was parked at the far side. Before opening the driver's door, Drummond pressed a small button on the key fob to deactivate the car's alarm system. He let the hot air escape from inside while he moved around to the back of the car, opened the trunk, and locked his pistol in his briefcase. When he had closed the trunk lid, he circled back to the front of the car and slid in, grateful that the sheepskin seat covers didn't soak up the heat the way leather seats did.

He started the car and let it run for a few seconds

before turning the air-conditioning on, then opened
the sun-roof to let the hot air out, fastened his seat
belt, and closed the door. Slipping the shift lever
into first gear, he eased the BMW out of the parking lot and turned right past Dodger Stadium, heading out of Elysian Park into downtown Los Angeles.

In the 1930s, City Hall had towered over Los
Angeles, then a medium-sized town basking in the
last days of Southern California's golden era. Now,
as Drummond moved along the Harbor Freeway,
heading toward the off-ramp that would take him
to the municipal archives, City Hall was overshadowed by more than a dozen buildings that shot skyward, reaching for skies that were once again
turning blue. Drummond's father had been one of
the top camera men in Hollywood before he retired, and his critical eye had taught John Drummond how to look at his city, to see beyond the
chrome and glass of the Bonaventure Hotel and to
admire the town that had once been there.

Drummond turned the BMW into the security
parking lot of the archive building and hunted for
a parking place well away from the acre-and-a-half
of Japanese jalopies that brought in most of the
three thousand city employees every day. Finally
parked, he retrieved his briefcase from the trunk of
the BMW, turned on the alarm, and headed for the
cool basement of City Hall.

The stairway leading down to the archives was
lined with marble, and despite the glossy sheen on
the banister, smelled of corroded brass. At the bottom of the stair, a large bronze door opened into
a windowless basement room filled with hundreds
of oak filing cabinets. In front of the cabinets was
a counter presided over by a formidable black

woman of more than ample proportions: the city archivist.

"You again, huh?" she said with mock hostility.

"Yup. Still working on the same old case."

"Sugar, you ain't never gonna crack this one." She smiled at Drummond before waddling off to retrieve his files.

Drummond moved over to a small table in the corner of the room, opened his briefcase, and tossed his jacket over the back of the chair. He had no more than sat down when the city archivist returned to the counter with the thick file.

"Honey-chile, I don't mind dragging this outta the dust for you, but I ain't gonna lug it over to your desk."

Drummond got up and walked over to the counter. "Thanks, M'Azee."

The archivist gave Drummond a huge smile. "You're welcome, Captain Drummond. Need anything else?"

"No, this should do me for a while."

"Okay, then. I'm going on my break. You want anything from upstairs?"

"Yeah," said Drummond, "a big iced tea. I'll buy if you'll fly." He handed her a five-dollar bill.

M'Azee grinned and stuffed the fiver in the pocket of the baggy sweater she was wearing.

"Back in half an hour, Mr. Man."

Strictly speaking, Drummond shouldn't have been opening the folder that M'Azee had handed him. Department regulations were clear on accessing the "unsolved crimes" section of the archives. Anyone who wanted to see anything had to have departmental clearance, and because of the eager-beaver work of a cop trying to break into the movies as a

writer, some years back, the department no longer
gave permission to access unsolved murder cases.

Fortunately, Drummond did a lot of routine research for Homicide Division, so no one had questioned his asking for the file on a series of unsolved
murders in 1972. Not that Drummond was interested in turning the gruesome events of two decades
ago into a movie for television. On the contrary, as
a part-time student at USC, Drummond was using
this case as the matrix for his master's thesis in
criminology.

From the academic point of view, it was nearly
perfect. A series of six unsolved murders, sensa-
tionalized by the press and with no suspects. The
victims were never identified, and almost as quickly
as the crimes had been uncovered, the entire case
was overshadowed by the events of the Watergate
scandal. As the press hounded the President of the
United States out of office, the East L.A. "vampire" killings were quickly forgotten.

Drummond undid the string that held the folder
closed and spread out the contents on the desk in
front of him. It took about five minutes to sort the
jumble of papers into neat piles, and then he was
ready to begin.

The photos were first, both the crime scene shots
and those taken before the autopsy had begun. The
carefully typed reports of the investigating officers
were next, and as Drummond placed these in
chronological order, he made a mental note to
check with personnel to find out what had become
of Detective Sergeants Sprague and Demitter.

There should have been more in the file, but
there wasn't. There was no suspect sheet, no list of
interrogations, and no summary of events—the gut
feelings of the officers involved—in the folder. It

was as if the crimes had occurred, been reported, logged in, and then filed away. Even the referral to the DA's office was missing from the file.

M'Azee came in with Drummond's iced tea. As she set down the large paper cup, she picked up one of the photos.

"Mmm-mmm! This sure was a fine-looking boy before he got himself killed. Must have made his mamma real unhappy when he died." She dropped the picture back on the desk. "Here's your change. You catch that killer, and the next iced tea is on me."

That evening at home, Drummond reread the photocopied reports of the killings for the umpteenth time. The reports, all six of them, were virtually the same. The location of the discovery of the body varied in each report, but other than that, it was as if each report had been photocopied and added to the file.

Drummond placed one report on top of the other and held the two of them up to the light. While the reports didn't exactly line up, the signatures of Sprague and Demitter did. Exactly.

Drummond grabbed another report and held it up behind one of the two he had already checked. The signatures were identical. He checked the rest of the signatures in the same way, and all were identical copies of the first one. That could mean only one thing. Someone had doctored the original reports and had copied them above the genuine signatures of Sprague and Demitter. But why?

The next morning, Drummond stopped off at Personnel to find out the whereabouts of Sprague and Demitter. The blonde twenty-year-old behind the counter spent nearly ten minutes trying to access the records of Detectives Sprague and Demit-

ter on the city's computer before she had to throw
in the towel.

"I'm sorry, Captain Drummond, but unless they
retired within the last five years, they won't be in
the system." She smiled at Drummond.

"Do you think that you could call down to pay-
roll and see if they're still drawing their pension
benefits?" Drummond asked.

"Sure, no problem." She turned on her Valley
girl smile again. "Try back after lunch."

After lunch, Drummond's luck hadn't improved.

"I'm *real* sorry, Captain, but I'm afraid I've hit
a blank." Her pout was unbelievable. "Both those
officers are dead, and no survivor bennies have
been paid for—oh, let's see." She picked up the
hard copy of her computer printout. "Yes, here it
is. Mrs. Sprague last received a check three years
ago." She handed Drummond the hard copy. "I'm
sorry." Her Valley girl smile was on at full volume.

Drummond took the paper, thanked the girl, and
headed back down the hall to his office. Later that
afternoon, he stopped by the Los Angeles City Library and pulled the microfilms of the *L.A. Times*
from three years back, scrolling through the obitu-
aries until he found the entry for Mrs. Sprague.
After noting the name of the cemetery where she
had been buried and the names of her surviving
children, he rewound the microfilm, turned off the
projector, and dropped the film off at the librarian's
desk as he headed out to his car.

Before starting home, he stopped at an LAPD
sub-station and ran the names of Mrs. Sprague's
children through the Department of Motor Vehicles
computers, but drew a blank. Even more curious
now, he climbed back into his car and drove over
to Forest Lawn in Glendale.

Some wit had once described Forest Lawn as a Disneyland for shut-ins. As Drummond pulled up in front of its mock-Tudor offices, he mused that whoever had first coined the term hadn't been far off the mark. The sprawling cemetery had been built in the 1920s and endowed with a significant degree of wealth. The founder and early promoter of Forest Lawn had been a gentleman of exquisite taste, with a fine sense of proportion. So, in true California style, he had set about acquiring great works of art—or perfect replicas—for his cemetery. Only Disneyland had knocked it from the number one slot in the tourist parade.

The interior of the offices wouldn't have been out of place in an English country house, or on the set of an old Basil Rathbone film. Smooth leather, thick carpets, and burnished paneling all added to the dignity of the somber office. A woman in a severe dark suit greeted Drummond as he entered the offices, and once he had identified himself as a police officer, ushered him into the office of the manager.

"Mr. Kelso? I'm Detective Captain Drummond, LAPD." Drummond stuck out his hand, and the other man took it.

"Yes, Captain Drummond. What may I do for you?" Kelso's voice was well-modulated and positively oozed sincerity. Drummond wondered briefly what the man would sound like if he laughed.

"I'm here to inquire about the graves of Sergeant and Mrs. Jackson Sprague. We've lost track of the family and were wondering if you might have an address for next of kin."

Drummond could tell from the way that Kelso knitted his brow that it was unlikely he would get any assistance.

"Well, our files are strictly confidential, but . . . let's see what we can do." Kelso got up and went to a filing cabinet behind his desk. He returned after a few moments with a three-by-five card and pressed the button on his intercom.

"Miss Lambert, could you bring me Plot Book 126, please?" He eased back into his chair and smiled at Drummond as though he were sizing him up for a pine box.

Not that Kelso would ever stoop to selling pine boxes, Drummond decided. No, Mr. Kelso was more the bronze-with-gilt-handles type.

Just then Miss Lambert came into the room carrying a thick black book and handed it to Kelso. Kelso opened it, thumbed through a number of pages, and finally found the one he wanted. Using the edge of the three-by-five card as a guide, he quickly skimmed down the page until he found the entry he was looking for.

"Ah, here it is. Mrs. Mary Sprague, plot 1114, right next to her husband. He was buried by the Los Angeles Police Department—but then, I'm sure you know that. Her grave was paid for by the Prudential Insurance Company. And the headstone was paid for by," Kelso squinted at the page, "a Mr. Lincoln Sprague."

"Do you have an address for Mr. Sprague?" Drummond asked.

"Yes, indeed. We *always* keep a record of the name and address of the next of kin, just in case there are any problems at a later date."

"Problems?" Drummond arched an eyebrow.

"Heavens, yes," said Kelso. "Quite often families want to re-bury someone, and it's vitally important that we make sure we're giving them the right remains."

"I see."

"Anyhow—" Kelso took a crisp white piece of paper from his desk and quickly wrote on it, then handed it to Drummond. "Here's the address of Lincoln Sprague. If I can be of any more help, just call."

"Thank you, Mr. Kelso. Good-bye."

As Drummond walked out to his car, he had a sinking feeling that the trail was growing colder by the minute.

The address that Kelso had given him was in San Marino, the last bastion of white, Episcopalian wealth and power in the San Gabriel valley. Drummond checked the address in his Thomas Brothers Guide and then headed up Glendale Boulevard to the Foothill Freeway. In twenty minutes he was in San Marino, driving up Huntington Boulevard to the address given as the home of Lincoln Sprague.

The house was a large Spanish colonial hacienda, the type popular with millionaires just after the First World War. It was set well back from the street, and three ancient eucalyptus trees provided nearly an acre of shade on the front lawn. Drummond turned into the sweeping drive and parked in front of the door.

Up close, the door to the house looked as if you could bounce cannon balls off it, and as Drummond pressed the polished brass bell, he could hear the distant sound of muffled chimes. After a few minutes, the door was opened by a thick-set Mexican woman wearing a maid's uniform.

"May I help you?" she asked.

Drummond produced his badge. "I'm looking for a Mr. Lincoln Sprague," he said.

The woman eyed him impassively. "Please wait

here, señor," she said, and closed the heavy oak door.

A few moments later the door was reopened, and Drummond was ushered in. The walls in the entryway were covered with blue and white tiles, and the floor was done in large terracotta slabs. A fountain dominated the center of the entry, its gentle splashing sound almost as cooling as the air-conditioning itself. The maid led Drummond past the fountain and into a small white-washed room with a high beamed ceiling. As he entered, a petite, well-dressed woman somewhere in her sixties stood up and extended her hand.

"How do you do? I'm Cecelia McBain."

Drummond took her hand and introduced himself.

"Captain John Drummond, ma'am. I'm looking for Mr. Lincoln Sprague," he began.

Mrs. McBain interrupted him. "Is Linc in any trouble, Mr. Drummond?"

"No, ma'am. I'd just like to talk to him, if I could." Drummond found the woman's concern somehow touching.

"If you give me your word that you won't arrest him. . . ." Her voice trailed off, and she stared intently at Drummond.

"Scout's honor, ma'am." Drummond grinned and held up the first three fingers of his right hand.

"That's fine, then. I'll call him over now." She picked up a telephone and turned to the maid who had reentered the room. "Two iced teas, Maria." Then she dialed Lincoln Sprague's extension.

Lincoln Sprague was tall, and well-built for a man in his seventies. He was dressed in a black three-piece suit with a crisp white shirt and black silk tie. When he entered the room, he looked past Drummond as if he wasn't present and addressed himself only to Mrs. McBain.

"You called for me, Miss Cecelia?"

"Yes, Lincoln. This gentleman," she gestured toward Drummond, "would like a few words with you. If you've no objection."

Lincoln looked at Drummond for a long second before he replied. "No, Miss Cecelia, I've got no objections at all."

"Very well, then. You may speak here, if you wish. Or if you'd prefer, you may take Mr. Drummond to the coach house." Mrs. McBain stood and extended her hand to Drummond.

"It has been a pleasure meeting you. Now, if you'll excuse me." So saying, she turned and walked toward the door that Lincoln Sprague now held open for her. As she was leaving, Drummond heard her tell Maria to serve the iced tea in the coach house.

Drummond followed Lincoln back to the garage, and was impressed the moment he walked through the door. The garage contained three Rolls-Royce motor cars and a Bentley. All were in immaculate condition, and all were at least thirty years old.

"This is quite a collection, Mr. Sprague. Do you drive all of them?" Drummond was admiring a red Silver Wraith fitted with the most extravagant two-passenger convertible body he had ever seen.

"No, sir, I don't." Lincoln took a soft cloth from out of his pocket and wiped an errant smudge from the door handle of the dark blue limousine next to him. "Miss Cecelia drives the Bentley, and when he was alive, Mister Mac drove the two-seater. I drive the blue car, and in the evenings when the weather is fine, I take Miss Cecelia out in the tourer."

Drummond looked at the tourer, a dark claret-colored Rolls-Royce convertible fitted with a small windshield between the front and rear seats. Lying on the pale gray leather of the rear seat was a mink wrap, casually tossed to the side in case the weather should turn chilly.

"Yup. We used to have some great times taking these cars up to the big house in Montecello." Lincoln took a sip from his iced tea. "But you didn't come here to look at the cars, sir. What can I do for you?"

Drummond set down his empty glass on a small desk in the corner of the garage. "Mr. Sprague, I'm hoping you can tell me something about a case your brother was working on in 1972."

Over the next half hour, John Drummond explained the details of the case he was studying, in the hopes that he might gain some further information from Jackson Sprague's brother. Despite Lincoln's willingness to discuss his late brother's career, he was unable to offer any insights into the murder case his brother had been working on nearly twenty years before.

Finally, it was time to go. As Drummond made to leave, he turned to Lincoln with a final question.

"Lincoln, does Mrs. McBain ever drive the Rolls-Royces herself?"

"No, sir." Lincoln Sprague smiled. "Miss Cecelia says that a lady or a gentlemen *drives* a Bentley, but is *driven* in a Rolls-Royce." He laughed softly. "She's right, too. You see all these people driving up and down in Beverly Hills in their Rolls-Royces—well, they might be rich, but not one of them's a lady or a gentleman. Like Mister Mac used to say, 'Any fool can make money, but only God can make a gentleman.' He surely was a gentleman."

"So are you, Linc." Drummond pulled out his wallet. "Here's my card. Call me if you remember anything."

Walking past the red Rolls-Royce convertible, Drummond tried to imagine what it must have been like, cruising up Pacific Coast Highway toward Santa Barbara in the late 1940s with the top down, and Lincoln following behind with the luggage. "Wonderful" was the only adjective that came to mind.

Several days later, John Drummond was taking care of the routine paperwork that occupied most of his time in Homicide Division when a cadet officer escorted the tall black man with the visitor's badge clipped to his immaculate black suit into his office.

"Visitor, Captain," the cadet said.

Looking up, Drummond recognized the visitor at once.

"Mr. Sprague, what a pleasant surprise. Come on in and sit yourself down."

"Thank you," said Sprague, easing himself into the chair opposite Drummond's desk.

"Coffee?" Drummond offered as he moved a stack of papers from in front of him.

"No, thanks, I can only stay a minute. I have something for you that might be useful. After you left the other afternoon, I went out to my son's home. He's a manager with Safeway Stores, lives out in North Hollywood. Anyhow, I keep a bunch of boxes of stuff in his garage, including some things of my brother's."

Lincoln shifted in the uncomfortable chair. "Well, I went scratching through his stuff, and I found his notebooks—what he used to call his 'Cop-cyclopedia'—and some official-looking papers in an old manila envelope. I brought them along, just in case you could use 'em."

"Well, that's great, Mr. Sprague. Thank you very much. I really appreciate it. If there's any way I can return the favor . . ."

"There is, Captain." Lincoln Sprague grinned. "You can haul all that stuff out of the trunk of my car."

Sprague was parked in the underground lot behind Parker Center, and was waiting patiently next to a dark blue Mercedes when Drummond drove up in his BMW.

As Drummond got out of his car, Sprague opened the Mercedes' trunk.

"I'm surprised, Mr. Sprague. I thought you'd be in one of the Rolls'," said Drummond.

"No, sir. I prefer German engineering to Old World craftsmanship. Besides, my kids gave me this car for my sixty-fifth birthday. Now, how's that for a present?" Lincoln Sprague smiled in pure delight.

"Unbeatable," said Drummond as he shifted the two boxes from one car to another. "You sure must have a great family."

"I do, indeed." Lincoln carefully closed the trunk lid of his Mercedes, then turned back to Drummond.

"You know, it would mean a lot to me and my family if this could close the file on Kingfish's case." Lincoln put out his hand. "Good luck, Captain Drummond."

The two men shook hands, then climbed into their cars and went their separate ways. Lincoln Sprague went back to the gentle elegance of old San Marino, and John Drummond returned to the tedium of the paperwork sitting on his desk. By end of the watch, at four o'clock, Drummond was able to put most of the forms in the "out" basket on his desk, switch off his computer, and knock off for the day.

He followed surface streets home, avoiding the mess that the Hollywood and Harbor Freeways were at that time of day, and was soon headed out Sunset Boulevard toward the beach, well ahead of the heavy rush hour traffic.

Half an hour later, he was stepping out of the shower in his beachfront condominium and climbing into a well-worn pair of Levi's. He pulled a navy blue Lacoste shirt over his head and slipped on a pair of canvas deck shoes before heading into the kitchen to pour himself an iced tea. Then he turned on the stereo and sat down in front of Lincoln Sprague's boxes.

It was nearly eleven when Drummond stopped to build a sandwich and pull a cold bottle of *Dos Equis* from the refrigerator. Returning to the paperwork covering his table, he carefully made room for the sandwich and beer before picking up the small spiral-bound steno pad he had saved until last.

It was what he'd hoped he'd find. Not only had Jack Sprague carefully cataloged all of the murders, he had also listed his leads and, best of all, had written down his hunches—those invisible sixth-sense feelings that all policemen get when working on a case—no matter how trivial.

Drummond read with wonder and amazement. Sprague had not only been a good cop, he had been a damn good cop. From his notes, it was possible not only to reconstruct the case but to see who the prime suspect in the murders had been. Sprague had been able to interview this suspect twice, and had felt so strongly about the person's guilt that he had gone to the DA's office to swear out an arrest warrant.

Two days later, the shit had hit the fan. Sprague's notebook gave the complete picture:

21 July: Went with file and partner to DA to collect warrant for arrest of suspect. Arrived office 1015 hrs and was asked to wait in DA's lounge. 1242 hrs: Deputy DA asks Demitter and self to accompany him to office of District Attorney. 1255 hrs: DA tells us that case is closed, and hands us court order to deliver all files to his office by 1400 hrs or face arrest for contempt of court. Deputy DA accompanies us back to Parker Center, and all files are transferred to his custody in presence of Watch Commander at 1325 hrs. Code 7 at 1330 hrs. 1445 hrs: Called into Captain's office and told to forget entire episode or could cost my badge. As I leave, Demitter called in, presumably for same warning. This is bullshit.

The rest of the notebook was blank, but it told Drummond all he needed to know. The reason for the dummy file was clear. For some reason, the City of Los Angeles had decided to cover up the murders of six young men, all between the ages of 16 to 24.

Drummond stared at the papers piled on the table in front of him. He had more than a class project to work on now. He had a twenty-year-old series of homicides to clear up.

Finishing the last of his beer, he decided that first thing in the morning he'd pay a call on the man named in the warrant: a Father Francis Freise.

Chapter 6

Drummond pulled off the Harbor Freeway at Soto Street and drove the six blocks to Saint Agatha's Catholic Church. The barrio—East L.A.—hadn't come to life yet, but Drummond still was wary about leaving the BMW on the street, even in front of a church. Still, it couldn't be helped. Parking the dark red sports car directly in front of the doors, he set the alarm and climbed the steps, only to find the doors locked. A small sign in Spanish gave the Mass times and indicated that anyone needing the priest should call at the rectory around the corner.

Drummond climbed back into his car and drove to the rectory, pulling the car onto the parched lawn, rather than risk leaving it on the street. His knock was answered by a young man in a tank top, basketball shorts, and sandals.

"Good morning. I'm looking for Father Francis Freise, and wonder if you might be able to help me," Drummond said.

"Father Freise, huh?" the young man answered. "I don't know, that's well before my time here. Come on in and I'll see what I can do for you. Oh, uh, I'm Father Tom Berringer," he said sticking out his hand.

"John Drummond," was the reply, as the two men briefly shook hands.

"Have a seat, Mr. Drummond, and I'll see if the parish register has any information on Father Freise."

The priest left the room and returned a few minutes later carrying a worn-out address book.

"Let's see," he said, thumbing through the pages. "Yeah, here it is." He wrinkled his brow. "That's funny. It says to forward all his mail to the archbishop. Huh. He left here about twenty years ago, and there's no forwarding address." He looked up at Drummond. " 'Fraid that's about it. Why are you looking for Father Freise, anyhow?—if you don't mind my asking."

"He and my dad went to school together, and he wanted me to try and track him down for a class reunion," Drummond lied.

"Well, sorry I can't help you. You might try the chancery office, though." Father Tom started to stand up, then changed his mind. "Maybe Mrs. Gonzales would know. She used to take care of the priests here at Saint Agatha's, back in the sixties and seventies." He flipped through the address book again. "Yeah, here she is." He picked up a note pad and pencil and scribbled out the address. "Lupe Gonzales. She lives out in Montebello." He handed Drummond the piece of paper. "Maybe she can help you. Hope so."

Both men stood and walked out onto the porch, where the BMW had already attracted a swarm of fascinated young Chicano boys, who scattered as Drummond and the priest emerged.

"Wow, is that your Beemer?" Father Tom asked.

"Mine and the bank's," was Drummond's reply.

"You know," said Father Tom, "sometimes I almost wish I hadn't decided to be a priest. I really love cars."

Back on the freeway, Drummond drove as though on auto-pilot, his thoughts focused on the thus far elusive Father Francis Freise. He put his foot to the floor as he swung the BMW through the interchange and onto the Pasadena Freeway, and the red car shot forward, settling onto its springs as it hugged the gentle curve of the transition on-ramp. Ahead of him, Drummond saw a Porsche 928 sitting in the number three lane, moving along in the sparse Saturday morning traffic at a steady sixty. Holding the throttle to the floor, Drummond shot past him at nearly twice his speed and, with a deliberate push on the wheel, changed lanes to merge onto the Glendale Freeway. He lifted off slightly as the speedo needle touched 130, settling back to a solid one hundred miles per hour as the car sped up the Glendale Freeway and merged into the Foothill Freeway.

Traffic thickened, and Drummond slowed to a safer 55-60 miles per hour as he continued east, eventually making the transition to the 605 Freeway. Half an hour later, he was pulling into the last remaining A&W Root Beer stand in the San Gabriel Valley for a quick lunch. While he waited for his food to be brought to his car, Drummond stared at a faded Norman Rockwell print plastered against the wall of the drive-in.

A fresh-faced blonde in a car-hop's uniform was offering a tray of chili-dogs and root beers to an all-American family in a maroon sedan. Judging by the kids' crew-cuts, the father's hat, and the mother's gloves, Drummond figured that the poster had to date from the forties or early fifties. America, locked in a time capsule, and hidden behind a drive-in.

The chili-dog wasn't the greatest, but the frosty

mug of creamy root beer more than made up for it. Drummond turned on his headlights, signaling to the car-hop that he was through. A heavyset teenager sitting in the shade of the building by the kitchen came over and sullenly took the tray from the side of the car. As she waddled back to the shade, Drummond reflected how different the reality had become in just two generations.

Drummond had a quick look in his Thomas Brothers Street Guide and verified the location of Lupe Gonzales' street before pulling out of the A&W parking lot and heading back onto the freeway. Twenty-five minutes later, he was knocking on Mrs. Gonzales' door.

The house was one of half a dozen Spanish-style houses on the street, with glaring white walls and reddish pink tiles on the roof. Unlike the others, it had a deep green lawn, with neatly trimmed shrubs flanking the large French-paned window. His knock was answered by Mrs. Gonzales, who allowed him in only after thoroughly scrutinizing his police ID.

"Do please sit down," she said, her English only slightly softened by her Californio accent. "Now, *Capitán,* what can I do for you?"

"Well," he began, "I was hoping you could put me in touch with Father Francis Freise."

"What makes you think I could do that?" she asked.

"Father Tom, over at Saint Agatha's, thought you might know where Father Freise is."

She stared at Drummond for a few moments before she next spoke. "Why do you want to contact Father Freise?"

Drummond thought about lying, telling her that he was helping out his father with a class reunion, but looking around the room he decided against it.

On every wall there hung a crucifix, with small votive candles set below them, and over the door at every window, garlands of garlic were strung, as though Mrs. Gonzales were trying to prevent some sort of evil spirit from entering her house.

"I need him to help me with a problem," he said truthfully.

"You're not going to arrest him?" she said.

"No, not at all. I just need to speak with him, to talk with him about something that happened a long time ago."

Mrs. Gonzales pulled a crucifix out from under a pillow on the couch next to her. "Kiss this," she said, "and swear to God that you are telling me the truth."

Drummond reached over and took the cross from her trembling hands. Gently he brought it to his lips and kissed it. "I swear to God," he said. "That's all I want to do."

Mrs. Gonzales looked relieved, but obviously was still unsure whether she should trust Drummond.

"Okay," she said at last. "Give me your address and I'll pass it on to Father Freise."

Drummond wrote his home phone number on the back of one of his cards and passed it over to Mrs. Gonzales, then rose to go.

"Thank you very much, ma'am," he said before heading out the door and climbing into his car.

In the two weeks following his visit to Mrs. Gonzales, Drummond's section of LAPD's Homicide Division had processed nearly thirty cases—murders in which either the suspect had been apprehended or, if still at large, was at least known to the authorities. The LAPD prided itself on solving cases, and solving them quickly. Fewer than two percent of all homicides ever went unsolved.

Drummond finished reading the file in front of him—the straight-forward murder of a known prostitute. The suspect, currently in custody, was her pimp. From the arresting officers' report, it would seem that the pimp had simply walked up to the girl on a street corner, pulled out a gun, and shot her three times in the stomach. Unfortunately for the pimp, one Arfons De La Rouix, two of the other "prostitutes" on the same corner were undercover cops, and they effected an immediate and lawful arrest. The suspect, attempting to avoid capture, had tried to draw his pistol from the front waistband of his trousers, but in his haste the gun had discharged, causing what the two officers called a "grievous wound" to the pimp.

Drummond smiled ever so slightly to himself as he initialed the paperwork necessary to send the case on to the district attorney for prosecution. "Grievous wound" was a euphemistic understatement. According to the report from the hospital, Mr. Arfons De La Rouix was no longer equipped to partake of the service he had supplied to so many of his former customers. Drummond could only reflect that the universe sometimes did dispense its own kind of justice, regardless of what fate the courts might have handed out in this particular case.

Tossing the folder onto the growing pile in his out-tray, Drummond stretched and then got up from his desk and headed toward the coffee machine, raising a hand in greeting to Special Agent Sandy Morwood, a recent addition to the LAPD Homicide Division. Morwood worked for the United States Department of Justice, and was

agent-in-charge of the program known in law enforcement circles as FLASH—Federal Legal Assis-
tant in Solving Homicides. He had escaped from
his federally-funded computer center and was pouring his own mid-morning cup of coffee when Drummond walked up.

"Hey, good morning, Cap'n."

"How's it going, Sandy?" Drummond replied.

"Not so bad. Anything exciting in the current
crop of killings?" Sandy Morwood added creamer
to his coffee and gave it a sloppy stir with a pencil.

"Nah. Same old stuff. Pimps killing hookers,
drug deals gone bad, gang disputes. Nothing really
exciting." Drummond mopped up Morwood's mess
before setting his own cup down on the coffee
table. "Anything exciting on FLASH?"

"Hmm, not really." Morwood took a sip of his
coffee. "One sort of interesting item from Canada,
though. Seems some doctor was operating a private
blood bank up in Vancouver. You know—special
blood, AIDS-free, that sort of thing." Morwood
took another sip of coffee.

"Well, it seems that he got a little greedy and
started taking a bit more blood from his patients
than he should have done. Anyhow, one of them
checked into a local hospital after collapsing in the
street. Guess what?"

Drummond arched his eyebrows. "What?"

"The guy was nearly three pints low. This led to
an investigation by the medical authorities, who got
nowhere with the doctor, so they called in the police. The cops went out to this doctor's blood bank,
and found several hundred *gallons* of blood, but no
doctor.

"Now, two days later, the police get a call about
a dead body in a dumpster behind the blood bank."

Morwood took another sip of coffee and wrinkled up his face. "Jeez, this is bad! Anyhow, the body in the dumpster *looks* like a suicide. Male caucasian, mid-thirties, well-dressed, wearing a lab coat and with both wrists slashed. ID on the body identifies the stiff as the doctor who ran the blood bank. Open and shut, right?"

"Sounds like it," Drummond said.

"Sure. Everybody figures that the doctor climbed into the dumpster and cut his wrists rather than face the embarrassment of an official inquiry into his blood bank. Except it turns out that the guy in the dumpster isn't the doctor, and get this—he didn't die from slashing his wrists. It looks like he was drained dry by the doctor, and *then* dumped in the alley, and a few pints of blood were poured in the dumpster to make it look as if he'd bled to death." Morwood dumped the remaining contents of his cup.

"Vancouver PD have put out an APB on FLASH, along with a composite drawing of the doctor. I'll drop it by your office, if you're interested."

"Thanks," said Drummond, setting down his own cup of now-tepid coffee. "I'd very much like to see that."

"Okay, Cap'n. I'll trade you for the report on the pimp who blew his dick off."

Drummond nodded amiably at Morwood's grin, but as the special agent returned to his office, Drummond was left with the chilling feeling that somehow the blood bank in Vancouver was inexplicably linked to a small Catholic church in East Los Angeles.

*   *   *

That evening when Drummond got home, a message was waiting for him on his answering machine.

"Hello, Mr. King? This is Father Freise calling from Angel of Mercy Sanitarium in Auburn, New Hampshire. It's about your uncle. He's taken a turn, and I think you'd better come out here right away." The machine beeped off.

Drummond played the message again, then went out onto the balcony and sat gazing out to sea for nearly an hour. Freise had called, told him where he was, and asked for a meeting. But why? Drummond tried to think of a dozen possibilities, but none of them made sense. And there had to be a reason that Freise had called him Mr. King and asked him to come to New Hampshire right away. After playing the tape for the final time, Drummond made a tuna salad sandwich, washed it down with a glass of milk, and turned in for the night.

The next morning, Drummond called Personnel and requested four days' personal leave. He then called his travel agent and booked the next flight to New Hampshire.

The "next flight" to New Hampshire flew as far as Boston's Logan Airport, where Drummond picked up a Corvette from the Avis rental desk and headed north up Interstate 93. The sign said "Live Free or Die," as he crossed from Massachusetts into New Hampshire, and within half an hour he was in Auburn. The local Gulf station filled the tank in the Corvette, and the pimply-faced cashier provided vague directions to the Angel of Mercy Sanitarium. Twenty minutes and two wrong turns later, Drummond eased through the gates of the sanitarium and headed up its long, winding drive.

It was like driving through a well-manicured park, Drummond thought—then decided that the grounds looked more like a golf course than a park: gently rolling lawns with only a few scattered trees. The drive swung around to the right, and Drummond's rented yellow Corvette pulled up in front of the Gothic, cut-granite mansion house.

Drummond had long ago decided that one of the truly great crimes against society was the rape of architecture—fine buildings wantonly destroyed to make way for shopping centers and parking lots, others vandalized by their owners as they were converted into apartments, offices, factories, and hospitals. In its heyday, this mock Elizabethan mansion had probably been extremely elegant, although it was hard to imagine what it must have looked like originally. Grafted onto the building were a variety of additions, mostly constructed from unadorned concrete blocks—although a few were stuccoed and painted a pale, lavatory green.

A light rain began to fall as Drummond got out of his car, causing him to make a dash up to the front door. The door was locked, and as Drummond rang the bell and stood waiting for someone to come and let him in, the skies opened up and he was drenched. When the door did open, he found his way barred by a petite, hard-faced woman with shocking red hair.

"Yes, what do you want?" the woman asked.

"My name is King. I've come to see about my uncle. He's a patient here," Drummond said, "and I'm getting soaked. Can I come in?"

Reluctantly, the woman admitted him into the foyer. "Wait here," she said, then vanished behind a thick door set into one of the walls.

At one time the room had been attractive, but that was before the institutional minds that controlled the sanitarium had set about converting the building from a mansion into a hospital. The same sort of people who would be the first to complain about some kid with a spray can putting graffiti on a wall had painted the carved oak paneling of the foyer a light, industrial gray. They had covered the hardwood floors with the sort of linoleum usually encountered on the floors of enormous supermarkets, and had replaced what undoubtedly had been stained glass windows in the stairwell with modern double-glazed units that were framed in extruded aluminum. A single light bulb, modestly hiding its nakedness behind a fly-specked cardboard shade, dangled down on a length of greasy-looking black flex from where a chandelier had graced this once noble room.

A man's voice interrupted Drummond's personal anger at the faceless criminals who had robbed the room of its dignity.

"Mr. King?"

Turning around, Drummond came face-to-face with an elderly priest. He was nearly six feet tall, and although heavyset, Drummond guessed that the priest had been stocky but well-muscled when he was younger.

"Yes," Drummond said.

"I'm Father Freise. I'm the one who phoned about your uncle." Freise averted his eyes from Drummond for just a moment; then, looking back at him, said, "Perhaps you'd better come with me to the chapel."

The two men walked silently down the maddeningly gray hallway that led from the foyer to the chapel. Father Freise paused just inside the door to cross himself with holy water, and Drummond did, too. Inside, they sat down next to each other on one of the simple pews. Drummond waited, determined that Freise should be the first to speak.

"I'm sorry to have to tell you this, Mr. King," the priest finally said, "but your uncle passed away during the night." Freise looked intently at Drummond.

"Oh, I see. Well, I guess some arrangements will have to be made." Drummond kept his voice low.

"Yes. Well, I've seen to most of the details, but perhaps you could tell me whether you would like your uncle buried here or at the army cemetery." Freise nodded almost imperceptibly toward the door.

"I'm not sure. Maybe you could show me your cemetery, and then I'll decide." Drummond hoped he'd made the right choice.

"Certainly," said Father Freise. "Wait here and I'll be right back with some umbrellas."

Outside it had stopped raining by the time Freise returned, and the old priest leaned on one of the furled umbrellas like a walking stick as he and Drummond crunched along the gravel path that led toward the small cemetery, several hundred yards from the house. Only when they had nearly crossed the distance did Freise break the taut silence.

"You were trying to reach me, Captain Drummond. What can I do for you?"

Drummond stopped walking and turned to look the priest in the face. "For starters, you can tell me who killed six young men in Los Angeles in 1972."

For a few seconds, the only sounds were some birds off in the bushes. Then Father Freise spoke very softly.

"I did," he said, then turned and continued trudging along the path to the graveyard, with Drummond following speechlessly behind.

Chapter 7

A Victorian wrought iron fence surrounded the small private cemetery, and it took Father Freise a few seconds to unlock the gate and push it open so that the two of them could enter the grounds. Continuing on a little way, Father Freise sat down on a stone bench underneath a little summer house, resting both of his large hands on the handle of his black umbrella.

"Did the police know?" Drummond asked, settling down gingerly beside him.

"Of course they knew," snapped the priest. "I told them."

"But—then, why weren't you arrested?"

"Ha!" Father Freise snorted. "I'll tell you why. Because it wouldn't look good to arrest a priest for murder, and then have him get up on the witness stand, put his hand on the Bible, and swear that the men he killed were vampires. That's why. So the archbishop had a meeting with the DA's office, and they agreed to drop the investigation, so long as the Church kept me out of the way. That's how I ended up here."

"Vam—" Drummond instinctively had started to question the vampire allegation, but suddenly he decided that was a subject he really didn't want to get into, just yet. "You mean that you've been here, all these years—"

"As a prisoner? Yes," Father Freise interrupted. "Go ahead and say it, because its true."

"As a prisoner," Drummond continued, "for nearly twenty years?"

"Yup. A life sentence without parole, Captain Drummond."

"But—did the Church actually think that they could hide you out here, and that no one would ever ask any questions?"

"Sure they did. And they were almost right, weren't they?" Father Freise heaved a great sigh. "By the time the police knew I was responsible for eliminating those vampires, Watergate had already crowded the story off the front page and buried it back in the want-ads. Nobody cared, so long as no more killings took place. And with no families demanding that someone be brought to justice— well, it solved a lot of problems, if I just quietly vanished.

"As far as my 'hiding out' goes, do you know what sort of place this is?"

Drummond shook his head.

"Well, it's a very exclusive hospital. It was founded right after the First World War as a place where soldiers, mostly officers, could be brought, who were so horribly mutilated that there was no place left for them in society. Men without faces, arms, or legs, blobs of burned and charred scar tissue that continued to live, despite the gross violation of their bodies.

"The family that donated this estate to the Church did so because their son was so horribly deformed by the war that no hospital in America would admit him. Just the sight of that boy would cause men to faint. I won't go into all of the details, because there's no point. Just let me say that their son looked like a badly charred ham with one pale blue eye. I know, because I met him when I first came here. He lived—if that's the word for it—until about fifteen years ago. He was seventy-eight when he died."

"If it's been that terrible, why did you stay?" Drummond asked.

Freise gave him a wan smile. "Despite the fact that you may think me a murderer, Captain, I'm a priest, and this is my parish. I can't go, even though there are no chains holding me back. These men need me, and I could never desert them." Freise looked away from Drummond, anguish on his face and a moist glint in his eyes.

Drummond stood up and walked a few paces away from Father Freise, then turned and came back. Either the priest was nuttier than a Hollywood party, or Drummond was about to be caught up in a black abyss of terror. There was only one way to find out.

"Tell me, Father, how did you know those men you killed were vampires?"

Freise shot him a sharp look. "Are you humoring me?"

"No. I'm genuinely interested."

Freise sighed and looked off into the distance. "I recognized one of them from the war, when I was taken prisoner by the Germans."

"Tell me about it," Drummond urged.

"All right. Do you know what triage is?" the priest asked.

"It's a medical term. Has to do with sorting casualties, separating the critically injured from the less seriously injured ones," Drummond replied. "Why?"

"Well, when I was captured by the Germans, I was sent to one of their field triage hospitals to help out as a stretcher bearer. Some German doctor would look at the wounded and decide if they were savable or not. The ones beyond help were taken to a little hut behind the generator, where an SS medic would hook them up to a pump and drain out all of their blood." Father Freise looked out across the neat rows of graves in front of them.

"That's where I was working—carrying the wounded *into* the hospital, at first—but then hauling mortally wounded young men *away* from the hospital, back to a table where they could give their last drop of blood for the Third Reich. Actually, they say it isn't that bad a way to die, especially by battlefield standards. The victim simply loses consciousness, fades away. . . ."

He shook his head, swallowing noisily, making himself return from the horror of the past to a yet uncertain horror, at last called to account for his deeds.

"Once I realized what was happening, I didn't carry any more stretchers," he went on. "I put on my stole and began to give the last rites to the boys they brought out of the hospital. I guess the medical orderly must have been a Catholic, because he didn't try to stop me.

"Anyway, I was on my knees praying when we were attacked by what I thought was a band of partisans armed with axes and swords. They dragged me and a couple of German medics back into the woods and took us to a castle about a mile away. Inside the castle we were interrogated, and when they found out I was a priest, they asked me to offer Mass."

Drummond shook his head. He had been listening to Father Freise's story for only a short while, but he had formed a definite opinion about the priest. He might be mad—and probably was—but he was also sincere. The events he recounted were real, even if they had only happened to him in his imagination.

"Let's go back to the men who captured you the second time, when you were taken prisoner at the German field hospital," Drummond said. "You said you thought they were partisans?"

Freise shrugged. "I did at first. But when we got to their castle, I noticed they were all wearing chain mail. Then, when they took us into the great hall, there were these shields on the walls—a couple dozen of them." He pulled a pen and notepad out of his breast pocket and began to sketch.

"The shields were all painted bright red," he went on, "with a light blue cross in the center, like this, and gold swastikas in between each of the arms of the cross. They were unusual swastikas, though. The arms were curved, so they'd fit into a circle. . . ."

His voice trailed off as he finished drawing one of the swastikas and stared at it, and Drummond glanced at the sketch with some skepticism.

"These symbols were on the walls?" he said, to get the old man talking again.

Freise nodded, still staring at the sketch. "On the shields. I still don't understand it all. These guys had attacked us like partisans, but when we got back to their headquarters, they had Nazi symbols all over the place. At least I thought they were Nazi symbols, at the time.

"But the leaders, there in the castle, wore long white robes and mantles, almost like a religious community. And the big surprise was yet to come.

When they started to question me, they spoke medieval Latin."

"Latin?" Drummond murmured.

Father Freise managed a wry, strained smile, as if he still couldn't fully comprehend what had happened to him all those years ago. "As you can imagine, I was pretty well confused at that point."

"Yes, I imagine you were." Drummond tried to sound nonjudgmental, and hoped that Father Freise wouldn't take offense at his comment.

Father Freise shot Drummond a sidelong glance. "Anyhow, they asked me who I was, so I told them I was a priest. That seemed to get their leader's attention, and the next thing I knew, we were all being hustled to the chapel."

"Excuse me, Father, but you said 'we.' Who was there with you?"

"The three Krauts taken prisoner with me, and about a dozen or so of the men in armor." Father Freise rolled his head from side to side, as if trying to relieve a stiff neck.

"Once we were inside the chapel, I was told to offer Mass, so I did. The Nazis were led off to one side, and our captors started coming forward to receive communion. But before any of them could receive, some SS men crashed into the chapel, and all hell broke loose."

He grimaced as he relieved the memory.

"The Germans started shooting everything in sight, so I dived for cover behind a pillar. But it wasn't the massacre you might have expected. The men in armor fought back with swords and axes, and the bullets just didn't seem to have much effect on them. I don't know, maybe they couldn't penetrate the chain mail—and the Germans were being hacked to bits by swords and axes."

Drummond tried to imagine just what sort of thin-gauge wire loops could stop a 9mm slug traveling at over 1000 feet per second. He couldn't. A 9mm bullet could punch holes in a car door or shatter a concrete block. This part of Freise's story didn't make any more sense than the rest of it had.

"So then what happened?" Drummond asked.

"One of the Germans threw a concussion grenade, and for a moment or two everyone was stunned, including me. I couldn't move, but I could see their officer, just as plain as I can see you. He was lying on the ground next to a stunned knight, and before he got up and ran for the door with the rest of his men, he pulled a knife and cut the other man's throat—and then he started drinking his blood!" He closed his eyes briefly against the memory. "It—seemed like ages before he got up and dashed for the door." Father Freise reached into his pocket and pulled out a handkerchief and blew his nose. "Damn hay fever."

"So, how did you escape?" asked Drummond, when the old priest had had a few seconds to recover.

"Well, I waited until all the knights had gone charging out into the courtyard after the Nazis. Then, while they were preoccupied with their wounded, I just walked out. When I got to the edge of the woods that surrounded the castle, I started heading back toward our lines. A patrol found me the next morning, and three days later I was back with my unit."

Drummond rubbed his eyes with his left hand. He understood now why the LAPD had been willing to let this case slide out the door. The priest was obviously unbalanced, probably from his experiences during the war. Still, he had to find out why

Father Freise had chosen those six random victims to die.

"Father, this is all very interesting, but I don't see how it relates to what happened in Los Angeles. What made you think that the young men you killed were vampires?"

"Like I told you, I recognized one of them from that night at the castle. He was one of the SS orderlies captured with me." A hint of exasperation tinged Father Freise's voice. "I was helping out at the local fire station. They were having a blood drive . . ."

Drummond felt as if he were looking over the edge of a pit so deep that its bottom was swallowed up in darkness.

". . . and I had organized the cookies and juice. Anyhow, I went up to give blood, just like anybody else, and the technician drawing blood looked kind of familiar. Well, I'm a priest and I meet a lot of young people, so at first I didn't give it much thought. But then, when he put the needle in my arm—boy, did it all came back in a flash . . ."

FLASH . . . Drummond suddenly remembered the blood bank in Vancouver, the missing doctor, and the dead man drained of blood. . . .

". . . the last time I'd seen that young man was in 1944 in the Ardennes."

"Excuse me, Father, but was that a Red Cross blood drive?" Drummond asked.

"No, it was some private firm out on Whittier Boulevard. Why?" Father Freise looked almost owllike in the late afternoon sun.

"Just curious. Tell me, how did you kill the vampire?" Drummond asked.

"It wasn't easy. I followed him back to the blood bank, thinking I'd burst in and confront him. Once

I got there, though, I realized that alone I didn't have a chance. I needed help, and I knew that the cops wouldn't give my story the time of day. I also knew that the Church frowns on executing vampires, to put it mildly, so that my help had to come from somewhere else. So I turned to the only other help I could think of."

"And who was that?"

Father Freise glanced at the ground, then shook his head.

"It doesn't matter if I tell you now, because he's dead. Miguel Gonzales helped me. He was Lupe's husband. I won't go into details, because that doesn't matter, either, but we did fine, until Number Six. That one was on to us, and he—infected Miguel before we realized what was happening. We—finally got Number Six, in the end, but then I—had to deal with Miguel."

As a cop, Drummond had not thought he could be easily shocked, but he found himself listening aghast to Father Freise's account.

"Jesus, do you mean you killed Miguel, too?"

Freise swallowed hard and nodded, not looking up. "He begged me to do it, Captain. He knew what was in store for him, if he waited for the curse to take him over. I—couldn't let that happen to that decent, God-fearing man.

"So I agreed to go up into the mountains with him. I helped him dig his grave. We said Mass together, and I gave him the Last Rites. He took some sleeping pills then, and laid down on the ground beside his grave with his arms outstretched in the form of a cross. It wasn't a fatal dose, though, because that would have been suicide, and I wouldn't let him do that. It was bad enough that

I must be the instrument of his death—this man that I had come to love like a brother.

"And then, when he had fallen asleep, I—did what had to be done, and buried him, and came back down the mountain to comfort Lupe. The story we'd agreed on was that he'd gone back to Mexico. No one would ever question that in the Hispanic community. And when my—troubles began with the police and archdiocese, no one thought to connect his disappearance with what I'd done."

Drummond found he had nearly stopped breathing as Freise's story unfolded, and he was shivering inside as he drew a shaky breath. Not six murders, but seven. The priest was clearly mad—or was he? The latter possibility was infinitely more frightening than the first.

"You don't believe me, do you, Captain?" Freise asked gently, all passion spent, now that he had bared his soul to the man who could still bring him to conventional justice. "You think I've made up all this part about the vampires to justify the acts of a madman. I can't say I blame you."

Cold inside, Drummond drew a tentative breath. "Does anyone else know about Miguel?" he asked.

Father Freise shook his head. "Only Lupe, of course. I've never even told a confessor. What possible penance could he assign, much less grant absolution?" The priest smiled and glanced at his hands, still holding the pen and notepad. "Are you going to arrest me, Captain?"

Answering Freise was one of the most difficult things Drummond ever had to do in his professional career. "I'll simply ask you not to leave this place for now," he said evenly. "And if you don't mind, I'd like to have that sketch you made."

The old priest's eyes lit with something a little like hope. "Then, you *don't* think I'm mad?"

"I didn't say that," Drummond replied. "May I have the sketch?"

With trembling hands, the old priest tore the page from his notepad and handed it to Drummond.

"God bless you, Captain," he murmured, as Drummond rose to go. "God bless you—and be careful!"

And before Drummond could leave, the priest pressed a much-used rosary into his hands, lifting a hand in benediction as Drummond beat a hasty retreat toward his waiting car.

Chapter 8

In the two weeks following his return from meeting with Father Freise, Drummond's investigation had run up against a stone wall. In trying to verify at least some of the priest's story—though without mentioning that he had seen Freise—he contacted the archivist of the Archdiocese of Los Angeles. The bespectacled priest who granted him an interview at the chancery was polite but evasive. He was too young to have been involved in an incident of twenty years before, but he obviously had been ordered not to give any information on Freise. Unless Drummond wanted to disclose his sources—which he most certainly did not—the Church was not going to be very helpful in this case.

He had rather better luck regarding the sketch Freise had given him—at least in finding out how to learn more about it. One of his neighbors had an interest in chivalry and heraldry, and referred him to a private research library in San Pedro.

Drummond parked his car in front of the small, sun-faded building on Catalina Street, tucked in between the local post office and a used-book store. A discreet brass plaque on the door announced that this was the library of the International Institute of Noble and Heraldic Studies. Thumb-tacked below the plaque was a small card instructing those desiring entrance to press the button to the left of the door.

Drummond pressed the button, and after a few seconds a metallic voice responded.

"May I help you?"

"I hope so," Drummond replied. "A friend of mine suggested that you might be able to help me with a research project I'm involved with."

"Okay," said the metallic voice. "If you can wait just a second, I'll let you in."

Drummond was waiting for the click of a remote control lock when the door was opened by a conservatively dressed gentleman wearing a dark blue blazer and regimental tie.

"Please come in," the man said.

There was a small counter just inside the doorway, and after locking the door behind him, the man stepped around Drummond and gracefully moved behind the counter.

"I'll have to ask you to sign in, please," he said, as he opened a guest book on the counter. "It's one of our rules here at the library. The other one is 'No Smoking.' "

Drummond picked up a pen from next to the book and signed just his name.

"Now, Mr.—er," the man turned the book around to read the signature, "Mr. Drummond, what can I do for you?"

"Well, I'm trying to find out about a coat of arms," Drummond said. "I think it's from around the Ardennes, perhaps the Luxembourg area, and I'm told it might belong to some kind of religious order." Then, extending his hand toward the other man he added, "I'm sorry, but I didn't catch your name."

"My name's Keating, and I'm the director of the

institute." He glanced awkwardly at Drummond's outstretched hand. "I hope you'll forgive my not shaking hands, but I have arthritis. . . ." His voice trailed off.

Drummond smiled slightly. "Of course," he said.

Beyond the counter where Drummond had signed in, the library stretched to the very back of the building, shelves lining the four walls as well as forming neat little islands on the floors. The smell of books, especially old books, was an aroma that Drummond found as intoxicating as any perfume.

Hundreds of small shields, each brightly painted with a coat of arms, looked down on Drummond as he followed Keating back to the rear of the library, passing stacks of books that dealt with every aspect of heraldry, chivalry, and the nobility. Pausing briefly, Drummond noted that the books were in every imaginable western European language, and many of them, to judge by their elegant bindings, were privately printed.

Keating halted outside a door marked HERALDIC RESEARCH and fumbled in his pocket for a key.

"I'm afraid I'll have to apologize for the condition of these files," Keating said. "I had a retired colonel who used to come in from time to time to sort things out, but he died a few months ago, and I haven't had a chance to get back here and tidy things up."

Turning the key, Keating opened the door to the small room. A leather-topped table with a brass lamp filled the center of the room, and around the four walls, reaching from floor to ceiling, were filing cabinets. Not the large sort of cabinets found in offices, but the smaller ones usually used to index books in libraries. Keating pulled out one of the drawers filled with index cards.

"Here's how it works. The files with white ID cards are filed by the name of the organization." He pulled out one of the cards. "This one is for the Order of Malta. On the front of the card is the coat of arms, and on the back its blazon, which is the technical description of the arms, as well as the date granted." Keating smiled. "I don't suppose you know the name of the religious order you're looking for, do you?"

Drummond shook his head.

"I was afraid not." Keating sounded almost dejected. "In that case, you need to search the files that have the blue ID labels. This is going to take a while longer, because on this side of things, Colonel McEwan died before he got it cross-referenced." Pulling out one of the drawers, he held up one of the file cards and continued.

"Each coat of arms is recorded by three things: the color of the shield, the design on the shield, and the color of the design." Keating slowly shook his head. "Unfortunately, the colonel wasn't computer friendly, so he did all of his work by hand. What you're looking for is probably in here," Keating waved his hand around the room, "but finding it may take quite some time."

"I can see that," Drummond said. "Any suggestions on where I should begin?"

"That depends on what you've got, so far. Have you got a sketch of the arms?"

Drummond produced the page torn out of Freise's notebook and showed Keating the cross with its four swastikas.

"The cross is blue," he said. "And the swastikas are gold."

Keating nodded, studying the drawing. "I'm

afraid it doesn't ring any bells for *me*. I don't suppose you know the background color?"

"Red," Drummond said, with the most conviction he'd been able to muster about anything in this case so far. "The shield is red."

Keating grinned. "I can see you're not a herald, Mr. Drummond. But red it is. That narrows your search to *these* drawers." The sweep of Keating's hand took in an entire corner of the room. "Good hunting."

Three hours later, Keating stuck his head in through the door. "Can I offer you a cup of tea or coffee?" he asked.

"No, thanks, unless you can do an iced tea," Drummond replied, aware that he was coming down with a massive headache.

"Afraid not. How's the research coming along?" Keating asked.

"Not so hot. I haven't even made a dent in the red shields, and already I'm coming down with eyestrain." Drummond stretched. "It isn't easy."

"Research never is. Look, do you mind if I make a suggestion?" asked Keating.

"Go ahead," replied Drummond.

"There's an organization in Switzerland, the Priory of Sion, that keeps tabs on this sort of thing. From time to time, we contact them regarding information we need here at the library. If you'll give me as much information as you can, I'll write to them and we'll see if they can help."

Drummond looked around the room at the hundreds of small files neatly stacked one on top of the other. It had taken him three hours to go through the contents of only a few of those drawers.

"Mr. Keating," Drummond asked, "how much do I owe you for the postage to Switzerland?"

*   *   *

Another two weeks passed, filled with the routine paperwork that occupies most of a career police officer's time. Despite the midsummer heat of Los Angeles, Drummond had fewer than twenty homicides to contend with, none of them sensational. Most were gang-related—Asian gang members killing Chicanos, and the Chicanos retaliating—pretty much open and shut stuff, most with the killer apprehended within three or four days.

Turning from the completed crime files in front of him, Drummond was going over the expense vouchers turned in by the men under his command when Special Agent Sandy Morwood came in through the open door to his office and dropped into a chair opposite his desk.

"John," Morwood said, "I've got another one for you."

"Another what?" Drummond asked.

Morwood held up the faxed copy of a report from FLASH. "More bodies without blood."

"Like in Vancouver?" Drummond had set aside the expense vouchers and was giving Morwood his undivided attention.

"Not quite. This one's in from Germany—Hamburg, to be precise." Morwood put on his glasses and scanned through the report. "Seems a lot of street people have been disappearing in the docklands of the city. Local police didn't think too much of it until last week, when some big developer started tearing down buildings in the area and discovered what they thought was a mass grave—you know, the sort that would have been leftover from the war."

Drummond nodded.

"Anyhow, the developer called in the police—

and you guessed it—these were fresh bodies. And—" Morwood tossed the report onto Drummond's desk "—all of them were about six quarts low."

Drummond stared at the folder. "Empty, huh?"

"That's what the report says. Anyway, they flashed it over to us to see if we had anything similar. We haven't, of course—at least not in L.A.—but I thought you might be interested." Morwood pushed himself out of his chair and grinned as he jammed his hands into his pockets. "Uh, do you have anything you'd like me to send out on FLASH? Uncle Sam would like to justify my salary this month."

"Nothing today, Sandy, but if anything weird comes up, I'll let you know."

When Morwood had left the office, Drummond picked up the report that had been tossed on his desk. Thumbing quickly through, he noticed that all of the victims seemed to have been clinically drained of their blood, as none of them bore any wounds that could result in so much blood loss.

The phrase "clinically drained" leaped off the page at Drummond. Rummaging in his desk, he turned up the report from the Vancouver Police concerning the blood bank murder. Scanning down the report, he stopped when he came to the coroner's report on the victim found in the alley behind the blood bank.

". . . *despite deep lacerations to the wrists of the victim, it was obvious from the nature of puncture wounds in the arms that the blood had been clinically removed from the body sometime prior to its being placed in the dumpster.*"

Picking up the phone on his desk, Drummond buzzed his secretary.

"Alicia, do we have any old phone books here in the office?"

On the other side of the glass division, the petite young Chicana looked at the shelves behind her desk. "How old, *Capitán*?" she asked.

"The late sixties, early seventies."

"The oldest I've got is about two years old. I think you'd have to try archives if you want anything older."

"Okay, Alicia, thanks."

Drummond hung up the phone. Reaching across his desk, he picked up the pile of expense reports in front of him and, without bothering to check the figures, initialed all of them in the appropriate box. Scooping them up, he headed out the door, dropping them on Alicia's desk as he left the office.

The reference section of the central library in downtown Los Angeles was on the third floor, although it turned out that the old copies of the *Yellow Pages* were kept in the basement. It took nearly half an hour for the slightly built young man with the thick moustache to bring up the three volumes covering 1971, 1972, and 1973.

"Now, here you are, sir," the young man said as he dumped the three dusty phone books on Drummond's table.

"Thanks," Drummond said to the retreating librarian.

Starting with the 1971 edition, Drummond checked the listings of all the blood banks in the East L.A. area. Shifting to the 1972 edition, he cross-checked the listings and found that while two companies no longer were listed, three had been added. Turning to the 1973 *Yellow Pages,* only one company Euro Plasma Services, had dropped its ad. Its address, he noted, was on Whittier Boulevard—which at least

supported part of Freise's story. Scratching the information in his notebook, Drummond headed
back to Parker Center.

Back in his office, Drummond gathered up all of
the files on the vampire killings, put them in his
briefcase, and headed down the corridor to Sandy
Morwood's office.

"Hey, Sandy, you got a minute?" Drummond
asked as he walked into the special agent's office.

"Sure. What can I do for you?" Morwood moved
a stack of files from the center of his desk as Drummond sat down.

"I need a favor." Drummond leaned across the
desk. "I'm working on a dead case, one that's been
officially closed for twenty years. I think it may be
tied in with the blood bank murder in Vancouver
and the mass graves in Hamburg."

"Jesus, John. What kind of case is this?" Morwood pulled out a legal pad and started to take
notes.

Drummond reached out and put his hand on
Morwood's wrist. "Sandy, this has got to be totally
off the record."

"I don't know, John. I mean, FLASH isn't for
personal use."

"Look. All I need is one piece of information.
No names, nothing important. Just one small bit
of info that may tie all of this together." Drummond released the other man's hand. "And if it
does, I'll waltz it all in here and you can put it
on FLASH."

Morwood tossed his pencil on the desk. "Okay,
what do you want?"

"The name and address of the blood bank in
Vancouver."

"Is that it? I mean, that's all?" Morwood sounded slightly suspicious.

"That's it. Swear to God." Drummond gave Morwood what he hoped was a sincere look.

"Okay. I'll have it for you tomorrow." Morwood sounded relieved, if not totally convinced.

Drummond stood up. "Thanks, Sandy. I mean it." Picking up his briefcase, he headed out the door and down to the parking lot below Parker Center.

When he got home, Drummond climbed into an old pair of jeans and a faded T-shirt before opening a *Dos Equis* and heading down to collect his mail. The pale ivory envelope stood aloof from the bills and junk mail that had piled up in Drummond's mailbox over the last few days. Unlike the computer-generated labels that nowadays were stuck on all of the mail, this letter had been addressed by hand, in an elegant, cursive script that neatly floated between a pale green Austrian stamp and the golden coronet that occupied the upper-left corner of the envelope.

Back in his condo, Drummond slit open the envelope with a steak knife, careful not to damage the stamp. The letter paper inside was as elegant as the envelope. The pale ivory paper was embossed with the sender's crest and edged with gold. The aristocratic penmanship was as interesting as the message itself.

> *My dear Mr. Drummond,*
> *I have been informed by a colleague in Switzerland of your interest in a certain august society, and am writing to you in that regard. If you would care to meet with me in Vienna to discuss this matter, I would be only too happy*

to assist you in obtaining the interview that you seek.

Sincerely,
Baron Anton von Liebenfalz,
Chevalier de Saint Germain

Also inside the envelope was a small, neatly engraved business card with an address and phone number in Vienna for a place called *Ritterbuchs.*

The next morning, Drummond was tied up in staff meetings, so it was nearly lunch time before he made it back to his office. The first thing he noticed as he sat down at his desk was the pale yellow Post-it note stuck to the center of his computer screen.

Euro Plasma Services Ltd.
112379 Queen Adelaide Street
Vancouver, British Columbia

Drummond picked up the phone on his desk.

"Alicia, would you get me the German Consulate on the phone? I need to speak to the trade secretary. Thanks."

Replacing the phone, he opened his briefcase and took out the slim file that contained his notes on the vampire killings. Opening it up, he stared at the photo on top, the German Army tattoo just visible under the victim's left arm.

The phone buzzed softly, and Drummond picked it up.

"Yes? Okay, thanks. Put him on.

"Mr. Spangenberger? I'm Captain John Drummond, with the Los Angeles Police Department, and I was hoping that you might be able to help us with one of our investigations."

"Certainly, Captain. What can I do for you?"

Drummond looked at the note stuck to his computer screen. "We're trying to locate a German firm that is in the blood or blood products industry."

"Do you know the name of this firm?" Spangenberger's voice was soft, with only a hint of accent.

"We think it's called 'Euro Plasma Services,' although that may be a translation of its German name." Drummond glanced at the address he had copied from the *Yellow Pages*. "They had an office here in L.A. about twenty years ago."

"Very well, Captain Drummond. Leave it with me, and if they are still in business in Germany, I'll send you what information I have."

Drummond thanked the German diplomat and hung up the phone. He thought for a minute, staring at the Post-it note on his computer screen, then pulled it off and stuck it to the inside of the file folder. He picked up the receiver again as he ran his finger down a list of personal phone numbers, then punched up an outside line and dialed.

"Good morning, Cochrane, Smith, and Hamilton," came the cheery voice on the other end.

" 'Morning, Yoko, this is John Drummond. Is the boss in?"

"She sure is, Captain Drummond. I'll put you right through."

Drummond was on hold for less than ten seconds before a brisk but cordial voice said, "John, hello. Have you been watching the market this morning?"

"Nope, haven't had time," he said, looking again at the Post-it note. "That's what *you* get paid for. Listen, Nance, I need a favor. There's a company I'd like you to check on for me. It may be out of business, and I don't know if it's ever been on the board, but it's called Euro Plasma Services. They do blood and blood products."

"Euro Plasma Services, eh?" the woman replied. "Are you thinking of getting into pharmaceuticals? Your portfolio is already pretty diversified."

Drummond smiled. "No, this is something else. If I stop by after lunch, do you think you might have something on it?"

"I'll do my best."

"Thanks, Nance."

When he had hung up, Drummond tossed the file folder into his desk, stretched, and headed out to lunch.

The "Nightwatch" was halfway up the hill to the court house, and as usual was packed with cops. Drummond grabbed the door handle, an old police billy club, and pulled the door open. Inside it was cool, and Drummond found a seat at the counter next to a young Chinese officer. After a few minutes Paula, one of the waitresses, came over to take his order.

"What'll it be today, Captain?" Paula asked.

"Same as always. Reuben and an iced tea, please."

"You want potato salad with that?" Paula shook her head from side to side as she asked the question.

"No, thanks," replied Drummond. "Think I'll give it a miss."

"Probably a wise decision," Paula said, before sliding off to take care of the other customers at the counter.

While he waited for his food, Drummond reread the letter he had received from von Liebenfalz the day before. Like Father Freise's telephone call a few weeks earlier, it was clear that von Liebenfalz wanted a meeting—but in Vienna, not New Hampshire. As he munched his way through the Reuben sandwich, Drummond decided that he'd try to phone his mysterious contact in Vienna, and failing that, he would have to take some vacation time to meet with him in Austria.

There was a small travel agency next to the "Nightwatch" that specialized in package tours, and on his way back to Parker Center, Drummond stopped in to check on flights to Vienna. The prim young man behind the counter produced an armload of brochures and suggested that the "Sound of Music" package really was the best tour to take.

"Really?" asked Drummond.

"Oh, yes. Actually, it starts in Munich, then goes on to Salzburg and *then* Vienna, but it's very good value for your money—and it leaves every Thursday from LAX. You get to see the film on your flight over, and then when you arrive in Munich, a deluxe coach takes you to all of the lovely locations used in the movie. It's breathtaking." The young man seemed on the edge of fainting with excitement.

"I'm not really much of a Julie Andrews fan myself," Drummond began. "I don't suppose there's some sort of cheap charter available, is there?"

"Hmmm, let me see." The young man's slender fingers tapped the keys of his computer. "Well, there might be space on the Austrian Opera Tour in November—that's a little cheaper—but I'm afraid that's about it."

"You're sure that's it?" Drummond asked. "The Mary Poppins tour is the only one available?"

"It's the Sound of Music Tour, *sir,* and if you don't like Julie Andrews, I'd suggest you try for tickets to a Bette Midler concert." He threw his head back and gave Drummond an icy stare. "It's probably more your style."

Drummond scooped up the brochures and headed out the door. "Thanks. I'll be in touch."

His next stop was Cochrane, Smith, and Hamilton. Drummond winked as he walked past the pretty oriental receptionist, going straight through to Nance Hamilton's office. The elegant Nance was finishing a carton of yogurt and watching the market quotations on an amber computer monitor, looking like a million dollars—which, in fact, was only a fraction of her net worth. She beamed and put the carton aside as Drummond came into the office. Her russet silk suit precisely matched her mane of red hair.

"John Drummond, long time no see," she said, wiping her hands on a pale yellow kleenex. "Have a seat. Not only do you make me a fair amount of money, but you are definitely one of my more interesting clients. Where did you hear about this Euro Plasma Services?"

"Oh, around."

She chuckled and shook her head. "Okay, be cagey. You won't make any money on this one, though. It's gone, defunct, kaput."

"Out of business, eh?" Not that Drummond was surprised.

"If you were interested in the one in L.A., it is," she replied. "However, there *was* a prospectus for shares in general stock in a San Francisco company called Euro Plasma plc."

"I *see*," said Drummond.

"Unfortunately, that was in 1986."

"Damn," Drummond muttered under his breath.

Nance chuckled. "I thought that might be your reaction, so I called our San Francisco office. Guess what? They had a copy of the company's annual report for that year in their files."

"San Francisco, eh?" Drummond said. "What are the chances of getting a copy of that report in the next few days?"

Nance smiled and reached into her desk drawer, withdrawing a stack of FAX flimsies.

"Somehow I had a feeling you were going to say that," she said, handing them over. "You sounded really interested, so I had them FAX me the whole thing. The company showed promise in the early eighties. They were on the cutting edge of the early AIDS research." She craned her neck to look over the top of the document as he leafed through the pages.

"Unfortunately, for some reason the company went belly up and never did go public. I couldn't get a feel for what actually happened, but the offering was withdrawn and the company just disappeared."

Drummond raised an eyebrow and looked up at her. "Disappeared?"

"Poof! Right off the board, just like it never existed," Nance replied. "If you're still interested, there are a few other things I can cross-check, but I'm afraid it's a dead issue."

"That's okay, Nance. You've told me what I need to know. Thanks. I owe you one."

He spent the next half-hour after he got back from lunch going over the 1986 annual report for Euro Plasma plc. He wasn't sure what he'd thought he might discover by reading it, but it didn't seem to be very helpful. Just the usual collection of sales figures and market strategies, with several photos of clean-cut looking blood donors being bled, a mobile blood bank with the Euro Plasma logo on the side, and earnest technicians looking at test tubes full of blood and doing things with unknown medical equipment in which Drummond had no particular interest. The name had to be more than coincidence, though.

Drummond had just checked his watch and calculated the time difference between Los Angeles and Vienna when the phone on his desk buzzed.

"Hi, boss." Alicia's Valley girl voice never failed to amaze Drummond. "It's someone from the German Consulate. I didn't get her name."

"Thanks, Alicia. Put her through, would you?"

The voice on the other end of the line was harsh, and the accent was heavy. Drummond guessed that, whoever she was, she probably looked like an East German Trabant.

"Captain Drummond? I am Uda Kreise, Dr. Spangenberger's secretary. He asked me that I should phone you about a company in Germany."

"Ah, yes. I need the name of a company—" But before Drummond could finish, Miss Trabant-voice cut him off.

"Yes. That is so. The name of the company you want is only one in our directories for blood." She paused, and Drummond realized that listening to her was giving him a headache. "It is called Europa Plasma Technik."

"Could you repeat that, please?" Drummond asked, hardly believing his ears.

"Ja. Europa Plasma Technik. They are on Bindler Strasse in Hamburg."

Drummond furiously scribbled the information on his note pad. "Thank you very much. You've been most helpful. Please thank Dr. Spangenberger for me."

Reaching across his desk, he punched one of the outside extensions on his phone, glancing at one of the brochures from the travel agent before quickly dialing their number.

"Hello, Melody Travel? Yes, I'd like to book your Sound of Music Tour. Yeah. The one that leaves next Thursday."

At the German Consulate on Flower Street, Uda Kreise sat at her typewriter carefully filling out a Trade and Commercial Development form. All requests for information concerning German businesses were processed in the same way. The person who had requested contact with a German firm was sent the appropriate information. As a backup, the firm itself received a copy of the report so that they could contact the client themselves. A model of Teutonic efficiency, and the sort of double-tracking system that had contributed to the "miracle" of the post-war German economy.

It was odd, she thought, that the Los Angles Police Department would want to do business with a German blood bank. Maybe the police were afraid of AIDS and were looking for a supply of clean blood.

Carefully she typed in the name of the business contact: Captain John Drummond, Los Angles Police Department. Then, removing the form from the typewriter, she inserted an envelope and carefully typed the company name and address:

EURO PLASMA TECHNIK
Bindler Strasse
Hamburg, DEUTSCHLAND.

Chapter 9

Vienna

The old Jew shuffled along the uneven sidewalk, the collar of his shabby coat turned up against the light rain. From a vantage point in the shadows of the building across the street, only his crisp white shirt-collar dimly visible, Wilhelm Kluge watched intently as the old man stopped under the flickering street lamp to catch his breath before climbing the stone steps to the front door of his apartment block. Kluge smiled to himself in the darkness as he noted that the door to the apartment house was unlocked. This would be easier than he possibly could have hoped for.

As the door closed behind his prey, Kluge tried hard to imagine where he might have seen the old Jew before. Probably at one of the camps, but he hadn't a clue which one. Not that it mattered. He would have had no reason to remember any of the concentration camp inmates with whom he came in contact, although those who had survived the war would undoubtedly remember him.

Kluge licked his lips and waited, watching for a light to come on in the correct window. His hunger gnawed at his consciousness, demanding to be fed.

Within a week after the attack on the crusader castle, Kluge had known what his hunger demanded. And he knew how to feed it.

It was simple. Shoot a prisoner in the neck—or better still, cut his throat—and as he lay dying, just suck a mouthful or two from the wound. Kluge had to be careful that he wasn't observed, but fortunately very few Germans wanted to know what an SS officer was doing with prisoners that were marched out of the camps, and his victims never survived to complain.

He had come to terms with his hunger fairly easily. At first it had demanded blood on a constant daily basis, but then it seemed to become a part of him, rather than trying to consume him, and Kluge had found that he needed to feed less often. Before the arrival of spring, Kluge had found that he needed less than half a liter a week to satisfy his craving. It need not even be human blood, though that was the most satisfying.

Kluge stared at the building across the street. Although it was dark, and only one street lamp was working, Kluge was able to see everything in sharp detail, even deep into the shadows of the decaying brick building. The vision wasn't bright, but it was clear, like a television with its contrast levels set too low, the brightness gone from the picture. It had come upon him gradually, as his initial hunger evened out. He remembered the first time he became aware of his keen powers of night vision. . . .

His patrol moved quietly through the snow, trying to stay ahead of the advancing Allied Army. Darkness had come early, and with it a light snowfall that obscured vision and deadened sound. Kluge halted his men and pulled out his map, carefully tracing his finger along the line of their march. As he studied the map in near darkness, *Scharführer* Baumann stepped over to him and shined a flashlight onto the map. The pool of pale yellow light hurt Kluge's eyes, causing him to squint as if he were trying to read the map under the glare of a noonday sun.

"Turn off that light," he ordered. "Do you want to draw enemy fire?"

The *Scharführer* snapped off the torch, and in the enclosing darkness Kluge realized for the first time that he could see as well at night as most of his men could see on a rainy afternoon. Taking his bearings carefully, Kluge directed his men north-west, heading them away from the approaching American troops.

But despite their hard push to elude the Americans, General Patton's Third Army raced ahead and outflanked them, and in less than a week Kluge and his men found themselves cut off from the main German retreat. Moving only at night, Kluge and his men managed to make it as far as the Czech-German border before coming into contact with the enemy.

What fools! thought Kluge, as he watched a detachment of British Tommies brewing tea beside a small stream. There were ten of them, and the way they were clustered together, Kluge knew he could kill most of them with a single hand grenade, and then rush in with his men and finish the rest. In 1941, he probably would have done just that, but by early 1945, Kluge had become cautious. He knew that, militarily, Germany was on the edge of total collapse, and if the Reich was to salvage anything out of its defeat, it would be necessary that he, and others like him, survived to carry on the struggle.

Kluge's men circled around the British soldiers while he and another sharpshooter armed with sniper rifles fitted with telescopic sights moved into position. The stock of the Austrian-made Mannlicher hunting rifle was cold against his cheek as he sighted carefully through the 2.5-power scope, picking as his target a young-looking British soldier who had stepped up to a tree to relieve himself.

Kluge's index finger pulled the rearmost of the twin triggers fitted to his rifle, setting the front trigger to go off at four ounces of pressure. Through the scope, he could see a dark stain appear on the trunk of the tree and steam rise up in the cold morning air.

Centering the cross-hairs of the sight on the soldier's back, he touched the front trigger. The crack of his 6.5mm hunting rifle was the signal for the rest of his men to open fire. Within seconds, four Tommies lay dead or wounded on the snowy ground.

Kluge watched dispassionately as the man he had shot staggered backwards, away from the tree, and fell writhing on the ground. Bringing his right hand back, Kluge slid his fingers up under the butterknife bolt handle of his rifle and pulled it back, ejecting the spent cartridge and chambering another one as he slid the bolt forward in a single, fluid movement. Staring through the scope, he panned across the open ground and caught just a glimpse of another British soldier peering up from the stream bank, his head almost hidden behind his tin helmet.

Kluge waited as the soldier slowly raised his head another inch to get a better view of his surroundings, placing the cross-hairs over the soldier's left eye—and fired again.

The 130-grain bullet raced across the open ground between Kluge and his target at three times the speed of sound. The impact of the bullet equated to more than three quarters of a ton, causing the soft, pointed projectile to mushroom on impact. The force of the bullet passing through the soldier's skull ripped his helmet from his head and tore it open like the lid on a can of tomatoes. He collapsed like a bundle of wet laundry.

Five of the Tommies were down now, and two more were trying to ford the icy stream in a desperate attempt to make for the woods on the other side. Two shots rang out from the underbrush, and the soldiers in the stream jerked and sank beneath the black water, disappearing soundlessly. The three remaining British soldiers threw down their rifles and raised their hands above lowered heads, with cries of *"Nicht schutzen, nicht schutzen . . . Kameradin!"*

No more shots rang out. Through the eyepiece of his telescopic sight, Kluge watched as the men got slowly to their feet, glancing around warily, hands above their heads. Glancing aside at the man on his left with a slight nod, Kluge took careful aim on the soldier in the middle and set the trigger. As he fired, his partner did the same. Two of the Tommies fell, and the third one balanced and remained standing, eyes screwed shut, trembling hands stretching even higher above his head.

"Don't shoot," he pleaded. "Please don't shoot."

Slinging his rifle, Kluge climbed up from the frozen ground and walked into the clearing where the lone British survivor stood trembling, his hands still above his head. The stripes on his sleeves declared him a corporal, and he was very young.

Unbuckling the flap of his holster as he approached, Kluge drew his pistol and set its muzzle against the soldier's forehead. The touch of the cold barrel elicited a gasp, and startlingly blue eyes popped open to stare at Kluge in dreadful fascination.

"Which way to your lines?" Kluge asked in heavily accented English.

The boy looked very young and scared, and sweat was running off his face, even with the snow all around.

"West, sir." He moved his head slightly in the direction the two dead men in the stream had been running.

"How far?" Kluge asked.

Tears welled up in the corporal's eyes, choking his voice as he answered, "About a mile—maybe a bit less, sir."

Kluge stared at him for a moment—a scared kid in a corporal's uniform, trying to hold back his tears. Kluge's voice softened.

"Thank you."

The young soldier blinked and looked at Kluge. Kluge smiled slightly—and pulled the trigger. . . .

Nearly half a century later, Kluge reflected that he might have made something of that young man, had things been different. The boy had been weak, but that was the fault of the system that had bred him. The British were fellow Aryans, after all. With the right leadership, they might have shared in the dream of the Third Reich. But they had chosen to deny their common blood and set themselves to thwart the Führer's plan for the Master Race. . . .

A battered gray Volkswagen van pulled up in front of the apartment house, and two youths in leather jackets, studded wrist-bands, and skin-tight black jeans got out and crossed the dimly lighted street, heading toward the shadows where Kluge stood waiting. The burlier of the two had shaved his head bare and wore a dangling silver earring of a skull in one earlobe; the more slender one sported a technicolor Mohawk and a rose tattoo on one cheek. As they approached him, Kluge could feel the contempt begin to boil up inside—contempt for the nihilistic punks that he must gather around him to carry out the work of rebuilding the Reich. History, it seemed, had come full cycle. Just as the Party had needed the Storm Troopers in the early days of Hitler's rise to power, so they were needed again to bash into line anyone who would oppose Kluge's will.

Modern day SA men, thought Kluge. *Necessary, but totally expendable.*

For some of his followers, the night of the long knives would come very soon. These two were already on a short tether, though for sheer expediency, Kluge thought he might salvage one of them, if he sacrificed the other. He looked at them disdainfully as they approached in the pale light of the single street lamp, weighing which should be which.

Half a century ago, the Gestapo would have sent this scum to a labor camp, he thought, as he gave the two a half-smile of recognition.

The one with the tattoo on his cheek spoke first, and with respect.

"Good evening, sir. What are your instructions?" His speech was slightly slurred, and when he spoke, gaps were plainly visible where his front teeth should have been.

"Up there." Kluge pointed across the road at the shabby apartment house. "On the second floor, in the front. An old Jew by the name of Stucke." He looked at the two punks in front of him. "The door to the building is not locked. His own door may be. Take him, quietly, and bring him to the warehouse."

"What if he resists?" It was the skinhead who spoke this time, and Kluge could tell from his tone of voice that he was looking for an excuse to beat someone tonight.

Kluge stepped slightly out of the shadows so the two of them could see his face.

"If you so much as leave a mark on the Jew," he said, though his voice never rose above a whisper, "I'll rip your balls off." He punctuated the whispered threat by violently grabbing the skinhead by the throat and crotch and slamming him against the wall. "Do you understand?"

The skinhead's eyes were bugged wide in terror and pain, but despite the viselike grip on his throat and testicles, he managed to croak, "Yes!"

Releasing him, Kluge stepped back into the shadows.

"Excellent. Now, go."

A light drizzle started to fall as the two punks trotted across the road and went up the stone steps of the apartment building, neither daring to speak until they got inside. But once they were out of Kluge's sight, the skinhead stopped and doubled up, groaning, one hand pressed to his bruised throat while the other dropped to massage his crotch.

"You okay?" asked the tattoo.

"The pig-fucker! I'm gonna mess him up good!" the skinhead muttered under his breath, though he managed to straighten and continue up the stairs with his partner.

"Hey, man, don't even think shit like that!" The tattoo looked nervously at his mate. "If he even *thought* you were a threat, he'd kill us both."

"Asshole. I'll show him," the skinhead said, still rubbing his aching crotch.

"Shut up. This is it." The tattoo raised his hand and tapped quietly on the door to Stucke's apartment. There was no immediate answer, so he tried again, only this time a little harder. Still there was no reply. He was just trying the doorknob when they both heard the sound of a toilet flushing somewhere behind them.

They turned around just as Hans Stucke stepped out of the small toilet, there on the landing opposite his apartment door. The old man looked at them with mingled curiosity and wariness, clearly uncertain what to do. When neither of them spoke or made a move toward or away from him, Stucke spoke.

"Excuse me, please, but you are in my way," he said.

As he tried to push past the two punkers, the skinhead started to step aside, then lashed out with a vicious kick, his Doc Martin catching Stucke on the side of the knee and sending him crashing down onto all fours. Before the old man could even draw breath to cry out, the tattoo was on him, pinning his head back in a full-Nelson and jerking him roughly to his feet, where the skinhead slugged him in the groin before drawing a strip from a roll of duct tape and slapping it across the old man's mouth. Stucke sobbed and struggled feebly, his rheumy eyes watering from the pain, but he subsided to a whimper as his assailants seized him roughly by both arms and hustled him down the stairs to the waiting van.

Watching from across the street, Kluge allowed himself a thin smile as his henchmen emerged from the building and bundled the weakly struggling Stucke into the Volkswagen. When they had driven off, turning the corner to vanish down a darkened alley, Kluge turned up the collar of his expensive suit and headed back up the street toward his parked Mercedes, satisfied—for now.

Kluge let himself anticipate the rest of the night's work as he drove north along the Donaukanal. When he had crossed the river, he followed along the east bank for about twenty minutes, until he at last approached a cluster of industrial buildings on the very outskirts of Vienna.

Turning into the complex of warehouses and small factories, Kluge eased the Mercedes past the deserted buildings and pulled up in front of a moderate-sized warehouse set next to an abandoned garage. He opened the glove-box and pressed a button on a remote control box, and a steel door on the building rolled up. Kluge drove in, and the door rattled down behind him.

Inside the building, Kluge climbed out of his car and headed across a small loading bay toward a steel door marked "Private." The door had a push-button combination lock instead of a conventional doorknob, and when Kluge punched in his personal code, the door swung open. An electric eye turned on lights and closed the door behind Kluge as he made his way purposefully toward a darkened video monitor with a control console below it. He flicked a master switch as he sat down, and the screen came to life, revealing a grainy black-and-white picture of the front of the building.

Running his fingers down a row of softly illuminated buttons, Kluge quickly pressed each one in turn to check the security devices that guarded the building. The system would not have been obvious to anyone casually surveying the building—which appeared to have been abandoned for some years—but it suited Kluge's purposes quite well. No one

was likely to come prowling here without invitation.
The immediate area had become known as a haven
for thieves, drug addicts, and worse. Some who
were worse were gathering under the eye of one
of Kluge's cameras even now, quite aware of his
occasional scrutiny and not caring, for they came at
his behest.

Smiling, and satisfied that the area was deserted,
save for those he expected, Kluge punched up camera four on the monitor. The picture on the screen
showed him the narrow alleyway between his building and the deserted garage next door, which was
also encompassed by his security system. By manip-
ulating a small joystick next to the control panel,
Kluge panned the camera to the left, gaining a
clearer view of the alley. Then, his eyes fixed on
the small screen, he settled back to wait for the
arrival of the Volkswagen van.

Inside the van, Hans Stucke was now blindfolded
as well as gagged, with his hands bound behind him
with more of the duct tape that sealed his mouth.
They had dumped him on the floor of the van and
covered him with a heavy canvas tarpaulin that
reeked of oil and mildew. The van lurched and
swerved as his captors deliberately took a winding
route around Vienna, gradually heading for their
rendezvous with Kluge at the garage.

As they neared a wooded area to the west of the
city, the skinhead, who was driving, pulled the van
off the road and headed down a small lane, to the
silent consternation of his companion. A few hundred yards on, he stopped in a lay-by underneath
some trees at the side of the road and switched off
the lights, though he left the engine running.

"Jesus, Jurg, what are you doing?" the tattoo asked anxiously.

"I've gotta piss. Jeez, Egon, fuckin' lighten up."

The skinhead swung open the door of the van and dropped out onto the soft mulch under the trees. Unbuttoning his jeans, he pointed himself in the general direction of the woods and sprayed the surrounding ground. His scrotum still ached from where Kluge had grabbed him, and as he finished urinating, he gently touched himself to feel if any serious damage had been done.

"Fuckin' asshole!" he muttered again under his breath—though he knew he would never dare to do anything to Kluge, despite his anger. The man displayed almost superhuman strength at times. He scared Jurg—and Jurg was not afraid of much in this world.

But if fear made him bottle up his rage at Kluge, it also helped turn it into a desire to hurt and humiliate someone else as much as Kluge had hurt and humiliated him. As Jurg stood there in the darkness, remembering the pain and the shame, he knew who was to blame, and who had to pay. Without bothering to button his jeans, the skinhead climbed back into the van.

"You drive," he said to the tattoo, as he squeezed between the two front seats and into the back of the van. "I've got some business to settle with this old fucker back here."

"Holy shit, Jurg! Didn't you hear the Man, back in the alley?" Panic edged the tattoo's voice. "He said he didn't want any marks on the guy. Shit, you beat him up, and we're dead meat!"

The skinhead gave a snort and a sneering chuckle and pulled the tarpaulin off Stucke.

"Just drive, Egon. And don't worry. I'm not going to leave any marks on the sonofabitch."

As the tattoo reluctantly scrambled across into the driver's seat, Jurg bent down and grabbed the old man by the belt, pulling him across the floor of the van and rolling him onto his back. With both hands, he grabbed the waistband of the old man's trousers and tore them open, bursting the zipper as he yanked them down to his knees. Though still bound, blindfolded, and gagged, the old man struggled bravely against the assault, his muted groans punctuated by metallic bangs as his feet kicked the sides of the van—and occasionally Jurg.

"You sonofabitch!" Jurg roared, as one hard-soled kick connected with his shin and he cuffed the man on the side of the head.

"Goddammit, Jurg! Stop it!" the tattoo screamed. "Stop right now! You're going to get us both killed!"

"Shut the fuck up and drive!" the skinhead ordered, slamming his fist as hard as he could between the old man's legs.

The old man groaned and fell heavily onto his side, reflexively drawing his knees up to his chest, and Jurg reached for him, jerking him onto his knees and shoving his head into a back corner of the van. As the skinhead dropped to his knees, shoving his jeans down onto his thighs, the tattoo slammed the van into gear with a head shake of dismay and pulled the Volkswagen back onto the road.

"Hey, old man," the skinhead said hoarsely, punctuated by a grunt, "how's this feel?"

The old man's moan of anguish was stifled behind his duct-tape gag, but it struck a chord of raw terror in the tattoo. Looking fearfully into the rearview mirror at the convulsive thrusting of the skinhead, the tattoo broke out in a cold sweat.

"Jesus Christ, Jurg," he whispered into his death-grip on the steering wheel. "If *he* finds out, we're both dead meat. . . ."

Chapter 10

He, meanwhile, had been staring at the picture on the television monitor for more than half an hour, occasionally switching to other cameras to continue his scrutiny of the building's security, but becoming increasingly impatient.

His mood had not been improved by the letter in his pocket bearing a Los Angeles postmark. It was a routine communication from the German Consulate there, addressed to Kluge under one of his several aliases, informing him of an inquiry by a Los Angeles police captain concerning one of Kluge's companies. The letter itself occasioned no cause for alarm, but if whatever was happening in Los Angeles somehow connected with events of nearly twenty years ago, the implications could be startling indeed.

Kluge's last and only undertaking in L.A. had cost him six good men, in a manner that suggested that someone knew precisely what they were dealing with. There had been very little publicity, and no suspect had ever been named—as fortunate for Kluge as for the perpetrator.

Still, Kluge found it mildly disconcerting that any such inquiry should arise just now, just when he was having to deal with the annoyance of Stucke's snooping. He made a mental note of the policeman's name—a Captain John Drummond—then shifted his attention back to more immediate matters as the gray Volkswagen van finally appeared on his screen.

Kluge leaned forward and moved the little joystick. The surveillance camera panned slightly to the left, and he watched as Egon and Jurg climbed out of the van and opened a small side-door of the abandoned garage. As Egon held the door open, Jurg returned to the van and dragged Stucke out into the night. The van partially blocked Kluge's view, but he could tell by the way the old Jew moved that something wasn't right.

Rage boiled up in Kluge like an underwater explosion, sending fury flooding through every fiber of his being. They had defied him! Despite an explicit order to the contrary, they—or more likely, Jurg—had done something to the Jew, and it could ruin Kluge's carefully conceived plan.

Taking a deep breath, Kluge turned off the monitor and strode purposefully from the control room. Walking briskly across the loading bay past his car, he climbed a cast iron stairway set into the far wall and used a large skeleton key to open a heavy padlock securing a door at the top of the stair. Behind the door was a small locker room.

Without bothering to turn on the lights, Kluge quickly undressed and stored his expensive suit in one of the lockers that lined the walls. A new black cotton overall lay neatly folded on the top shelf in the locker, and Kluge pulled it on and zipped it up to his throat. After tugging on a pair of black canvas shoes and slipping something into his right-hand pocket, he glanced at a ladder in the corner of the room, then quickly climbed up into the attic above. He had to crouch low as he made his way expertly along rafters and catwalks to the far end of the building, where he opened a window and peered into the street below.

A light rain had started to fall, and from this vantage point, he could see that the streets around the garage were still deserted. Stepping out onto the windowsill, Kluge looked across to the roof of the deserted garage next door, some twelve feet away and slightly lower. Taking a deep breath, he crouched low and then leaped.

With less sound than a cat jumping off a bed onto the floor, he landed lightly on the opposite roof, dropping to crouch for an instant on all fours as he listened for a reaction. Then he moved quickly into the shadows and, still crouching low, made his way to a door on the opposite side of the roof. The door was unlocked, and he opened it silently and went down the stairs beyond, down to the level of the garage.

Jurg and Egon were standing with their backs to Kluge, over by a workbench beside the garage's wash racks, trying to adjust the light coming from a small, gas-powered camping lantern. For a split second, Kluge considered sending both of them to Hell right now, but instead he quietly coughed. The sound caused both punkers to nearly leap out of their skins.

"I'm sorry. I didn't mean to startle you." Kluge's voice was soft, almost effeminate in its tone.

Jurg was the first to recover his wits, and tried hard to be nonchalant.

"Hey, that's okay, man. Been waiting long?"

Kluge noticed that the skinhead's jeans were only partly buttoned.

"No," he said. "Only a few minutes."

"We put the Jew in the box," Egon said, nodding

toward a bright red shipping container in the middle
of the big garage. "Was that right?" He was sweat-
ing, his eyes darting nervously, anywhere except to
connect with Kluge's steady gaze.

"Yes. That was right." Kluge looked at the two
punkers for a long moment, then asked, "Did he
give you any trouble?"

Jurg and Egon answered simultaneously. "Yes."
"No."

"Come now, Egon. Did he give you any trouble?" Kluge's voice was seductive in its demand for
an answer.

Egon's ears burned red, and he stared at his feet,
gulping for air before answering. "Well, he sorta
thrashed around in the van. . . ."

"He kicked me in the head," Jurg interrupted,
"and I had to hold him down so Egon could drive."

"I see," said Kluge. "I suppose it couldn't be
helped, could it?"

"That's right," said Jurg, his voice expressionless.
"It couldn't be helped. Isn't that right, Egon?"

Egon continued to stare at his boots. "Yeah."

Kluge had already made up his mind, but decided
to let them sweat a while longer.

"All right," he said. "Come with me."

The two punkers looked at each other before
moving off with Kluge towards the box. When they
reached the container, which was chocked up on
blocks about two feet off the ground, Kluge turned
casually to look at them. The double doors were
closed, but he could see a thin edge of light along
the bottom edge.

"Is he secure?" he asked.

"Yes, sir," said Egon. "I tied him to the wall."

"Excellent," Kluge said. "I want you to go in
there and strip him, and then bring his clothes out

here, and put them on that bench." He pointed back to the workbench with the lantern on it.

Egon nodded nervously and swung open one of the bright red doors, stepping up to disappear into the container. Smiling slightly, Kluge motioned for Jurg to move a little away from it, out of line of sight or hearing of what Egon was doing inside.

"I'm afraid that Egon lied to me about the Jew," he said softly to the skinhead. "I'm going to have to teach him a lesson."

"Whatever you say, boss." Jurg's tone was flat and noncommittal, totally abandoning his partner to his fate. Kluge looked at him and was about to say more, when Egon jumped down from the container, Stucke's clothes balled under one arm. The tattoo took one look at Kluge and Jurg, then ducked his head and hurried over to the workbench.

"Jurg, wait for me in the box," Kluge said, then followed Egon over to the workbench, where the tattoo was neatly but nervously folding Stucke's clothing.

"I'll be back in a few minutes. Don't leave. Understand?" His soft voice stabbed into Egon's guts like a bayonet, but Egon merely nodded mutely as Kluge turned and headed back across the warehouse to the container.

The inside of the box was the same bright red as the outside, lit by a single naked bulb hanging from a length of flex strung along a row of tie-down rings welded along the top of the right-hand wall. Stucke was tied spread-eagled to more of the rings on the other wall, his head sagging down on his chest. The tape was off his mouth. Naked, his skin had the pallor of a plucked chicken, and the contact of the cold metal sides of the container had made his flesh erupt with goose flesh. His right leg showed new bruising in several places, and a thin trickle of blood had run down the back of his thighs and dried.

Kluge took it all in at a glance. Very well. Jurg had not been *quite* as stupid as Kluge had feared— Kluge had already figured out how to divert attention from the damage—but the blatant disobedience required more urgent attention.

Silently Kluge stepped up into the box, laying a finger over his lips to signal silence as Jurg looked up in brief alarm. At his beckoning gesture, Jurg came quietly nearer, if a trifle warily. In an almost comradely fashion, Kluge laid one hand on the skinhead's leather-clad shoulder, masking his disgust.

"Watch closely now," Kluge whispered, "and I'll show you *real* power."

Without further preamble, Kluge walked slowly over to where Stucke was tied to the wall, slipping his right hand into his coverall pocket while his left reached out to take the old man by the chin and lift his head up off his chest. Slowly Stucke's eyes focused on Kluge's face, and the weight of his chin lifted from Kluge's hand.

Disoriented, his body aching from the beating and assault, it took nearly a minute for him to recognize the man coldly gazing at him. The last person Hans Stucke had ever hoped or expected to see in this lifetime stood smiling before him.

"You!" he tried to croak. But his voice failed him, only a pitiful mewing sound escaping his lips.

Something flashed in the harsh light of the box as Kluge brought his hand out of his coverall, and the old man's eyes darted to it, widening in horror and disbelief. Kluge raised it closer, turning the shiny object to catch the light so Stucke could see it better. Still standing against the wall behind, Jurg was barely able to breathe as he watched Kluge slowly pass the open straight razor back and forth in front of the old Jew's eyes, like a hypnotist swinging his watch in front of his subject or a snake fascinating its prey. The old man could not seem to look away.

Smiling, Kluge gently tilted Stucke's head back and then rolled it slightly to one side, still holding the man with his gaze. Terror filled the old man's eyes as his captor's intent became unmistakable, but all he could do was tremble in his bonds, the rheumy eyes pleading, knowing there was no escape.

Kluge looked over his shoulder at Jurg, now totally motionless and staring, wide eyes riveted on the razor, Kluge and his terrified victim.

So, he thought to himself, *you questioned my power? Watch and learn, you stinking pile of excrement—for all the good it will do you!*

Turning back, he brought his face close to Stucke, his long fingers caressing the handle of the razor.

"It's time now, Jew," he whispered. "I don't tolerate men who betray me. I especially don't tolerate meddlesome Jews. You should have looked away, when you saw me on the street that day. . . ."

"No, please—" Tears rolled down the old man's cheeks as he tried to shake his head. "Please," he gasped. "I won't say anyth—"

Kluge's razor flashed in the glaring light, and the old man's desperate plea became a choking sound, and then a gurgle. Pumped by Stucke's pounding heart, his blood spurted from his wound in a hot, foaming geyser, mostly missing Kluge, but showering Jurg and the inside of the box as he convulsed against his bonds.

Jurg felt the bile exploding in the back of his

throat and flooding into his mouth. Gagging, he half-turned away and clutched at the metal wall for support. To his disbelieving dismay, Kluge seemed hardly discomfited at all, and calmly bent to press his mouth over the old man's spurting wound like a man drinking from a water fountain—drinking his blood!

Horrified anew, and choking on another rising flood of vomit, Jurg fell retching to the floor, pressing both hands to his ears to shut out the obscene slurping sound and the weakening struggles of their victim.

After a little while, Kluge stepped back from Stucke and turned coldly to where Jurg lay heaving on the floor. Grabbing him roughly by a handful of leather collar, he jerked the skinhead to his feet and gave him a shake, shifting his other hand to clamp the back of Jurg's neck. Jurg whimpered and tried to cringe away, his hands half-lifting in a gesture of refusal and fear, but Kluge only pulled him closer.

"Now, Jurg," he whispered, as he looked pitilessly into the terrified eyes. "Now I will share my hunger with you." Relentlessly he turned Jurg's head toward Stucke's still twitching body.

"Drink," he said through blood-stained lips. "Drink deep—" and shoved Jurg's face hard against the bright gash at the side of Stucke's neck.

The hot, thick blood filled Jurg's mouth and made him gag and then retch again, but Kluge's grip was unyielding. Kluge held him by the scruff of his neck, his vicelike grip preventing Jurg from dropping to the floor of the box.

"Come on, Jurg, drink. You can do it," he said, his breath purred in Jurg's ear. "You wanted to share my power? This is how it's done."

Jurg froze for just an instant, then twisted around slightly to stare at Kluge, terror suddenly giving way to understanding. He had seen men kill before, but never had they fed on their victims. Now, looking at the black-clad man in front of him, he realized at last where his power came from.

"Please." The tremble in his voice had an almost erotic quality to it. "I understand now. Make me like you."

One corner of Kluge's mouth turned up ever so slightly as he released his grip on Jurg's neck and allowed the punk to sink to his knees.

"Drink his blood."

Slowly Jurg hauled himself to his feet, swaying unsteadily in front of Stucke's still-bleeding form. The old man was unconscious now, but blood still pulsed from the terrible wound in his neck. Bracing his arms against the wall of the container to either side of the old man's lolling head, Jurg lowered his mouth over the wound and began to suck. The blood was hot and slightly salty, filling his mouth, but despite a renewed reflex to gag, Jurg forced himself to swallow. His stomach churned as the blood went down, but he closed his eyes and kept on blindly swallowing.

Behind him Kluge watched with arrogant contempt as Jurg continued to go through the motions that—for him—would never gain him eternal life. Finally, Kluge reached out and grabbed him by the shoulder, pulling him away from what was now a corpse.

"Enough," he said. "Cut him down, and then let's get him out of here."

Numbly Jurg unsnapped the pouch on his belt and pulled out a Puma folding knife. With leaden fingers, he opened the knife and crouched down, cutting Stucke's feet free as Kluge threw back both doors of the container and jumped down to the concrete floor. Jurg stood up to saw through the ropes holding Stucke to the wall, then took the full weight of the dead man in his arms and dragged him to the end of the container. At Kluge's command, Egon had brought up a wheelbarrow and was retreating again in the direction of the wash rack. With Kluge's help, Jurg lowered the lifeless body into the wheelbarrow, then jumped down beside him. Kluge had hardly any blood on his black coverall, but Jurg and the body were bloody almost from head to foot.

"Take him over to the wash rack and hose him off," Kluge said. "I don't want any blood left on him, understand? While you're at it, clean yourself up and get rid of those things you're wearing. You can put on the Jew's clothes, for now. He won't be needing them."

Glassy-eyed, Jurg did as he was ordered, picking up the handles of the wheelbarrow and pushing it over to the corner of the garage, next to the wash rack, wondering how long it would take to feel different. Turning on the hose, he waited for it to build up pressure, then began spraying it over Stucke's corpse, flushing the congealing blood from the body. Twice he had to stop to tip the bloody water from the wheelbarrow, but after three or four minutes, Stucke's body glistened a bluish gray in the soft light cast by the primus lamp.

Kluge went back into the container to retrieve his razor while Jurg worked, making a cursory inspection of the blood-spattered interior. It didn't show much, against the red-painted inside—which was the whole point of the exercise—but he would have Jurg hose it out, too. When he returned to the door of the box, Jurg had finished washing down Stucke's body and was stripped to the waist, sitting on the ground with his blood-soaked jeans down around his knees as he struggled to peel them off. He started to get up as Kluge appeared in the doorway—white-faced and anxious in the light of the primus lamp—but Kluge only gave him a mild nod of acknowledgement.

"Rinse yourself off, and then hose out the inside of the box before you get dressed," he said, jumping lightly to the ground.

He appeared to put Jurg out of mind as he strolled idly along the edge of the shadows, apparently just marking time while he waited for Jurg to finish. The skinhead pulled his jeans off the rest of the way and tossed them on the bloody heap with his jacket and shirt and boots, then scrambled to his feet. Naked, and shivering as much from after-reaction as from cold, he turned modestly toward the wall as he held the hose over his head, using his free hand to scrub away at the clotted blood sticking to his face and scalp. In the dim light cast by the softly hissing primus lamp, his body glowed a pale ivory, surrounded as it was by darkness. As he headed toward the box, dragging the hose with him, Kluge nodded slightly to himself.

It was time. Stepping back into the shadows, Kluge walked softly back to where Egon was waiting in a darkened doorway. Jurg was climbing into the box, bracing himself against the side to pull himself some slack in the hose.

"Are the others all here?" Kluge asked Egon.

Egon nodded, his eyes as big as saucers. "Yes, sir."

"Good. Then let them in—and unless you want to die right now, don't even *think* about running away."

Ducking his head in alarmed agreement, Egon reached back to the door behind him and opened it wide. A dozen more leather rats walked quietly into the room, men and women mixed, the studs on their jackets and wrist bands bouncing tiny points of yellow light across the room.

Silently they spread out, forming a half-circle around the end of the box, Kluge trailing behind their double line. Inside, the sound of the spray hitting metal walls rumbled like mock-thunder, hollow and tinny. At a signal from Kluge, the leather-clad punks began rhythmically clapping their hands.

The sound produced the desired effect. In a hollow scramble of bare feet on wet metal, Jurg appeared in the doorway with the hose, wide-eyed and startled. Instantly, the clapping was punctuated by whistles and catcalls, and cries of, "Faggot!" and "Queer!"

Instinctively, Jurg cupped one hand over his crotch, the other hand still stupidly holding the hose.

"Hey, little boy," one of the girls shouted, "can't cover up what you don't have!" Her voice was oily and edged with nastiness.

"Or what you're not going to have much longer!" another voice chimed in, followed by a chorus of obscene laughter.

Jurg backed away from the slowly advancing punkers until his buttocks smacked up against one side of the box, only then remembering he still had the hose in his free hand. In a panic, he let out a throaty cry and started to spray his tormentors, only to have one of them whip out a Buck knife and cut the hose outside the box, smugly holding up the cut end that was the mate to Jurg's. As several of the nastier-looking of the men started to climb up the back of the box, Kluge moved a step nearer.

"*Halt.*" The voice was quiet, yet totally commanding. The punkers froze in their tracks, those partway into the box sinking down to a crouching position to glance respectfully back toward their leader. Kluge stepped to the very edge of the light coming out of the box.

"I gave this *swine* an order tonight," Kluge said softly, "and he disobeyed it. As a result," Kluge surveyed the punkers standing around him, "the one I was going to give you died."

A groan of angered despair rose in a dozen throats, quickly silenced by Kluge's upraised hand.

"I've made other arrangements, however. Come out, Jurg," he said, crooking a finger in invitation.

Jurg's shaved head moved back and forth in distraught negation.

"No—please—"

"I'm sorry, Jurg, but you've been a naughty boy. Now, if you don't come out on your own, they'll have to come in and get you—"

"No, please—you can't!"

All out of patience, Kluge gestured with his chin to the two punkers crouched nearest Jurg. Leering obscenely, the two uncoiled and sauntered back to where Jurg stood cowering against the metal side, his hands clasped over his crotch. He sagged as they pinned back his arms, moaning softly, offering no resistance as they half-dragged

him back to the doorway and held him there,
right on the edge.

Kluge walked quietly over to the pile of Jurg's
clothes, reaching down to unsnap the pouch that
hung from the belt attached to his jeans. Taking
out Jurg's knife, he flicked it open. The soft light of
the primus lamp glinted blue-white off the brightly
polished blade. Dropping the jeans back on the pile
of clothes, Kluge returned to the box, where Jurg's
trembling body was still supported by two of the
punkers. At his gesture, they forced him to his
knees, one of them bending back his head to expose
the throat.

"You wanted to share in the power, tough boy?"
Kluge held the knife high enough for Jurg to see.
"No way. No *way*! I told you to be careful with my
Jew," Kluge went on. "You disobeyed. You could
have ruined everything."

Jurg's breath was coming in short, sharp gasps,
and his eyes were wide and terrified as he watched
Kluge pass the knife to the punk with the free hand.

"So, it's feeding time, tough boy."

As Kluge stepped back and nodded, the knife
flashed, and Jurg's last scream was drowned out
by the triumphant shouts of the punkers as they
closed in on their flailing feast. Without looking
back at his victim, Kluge walked over to where
Egon stood shaking next to the wheelbarrow containing Stucke's body. The tattoo suddenly looked
very tame and respectful. Somehow Kluge knew he
would not have to repeat tonight's lesson for Egon.

"Take him back to his apartment," Kluge said,
nodding toward the wheelbarrow. "I'll meet you
there in an hour."

Egon glanced past Kluge in dread fascination, to

where the twelve punkers were feeding on a now supine and motionless Jurg.

"Yes, sir," he said softly.

As he picked up the handles of the wheelbarrow to follow his instructions, Kluge had already vanished back into the shadows.

Chapter 11

Munich

The Trapp Family Singers, fresh from their triumph at the Salzburg Festival, had just eluded their Nazi pursuers and were busily hiking over the Alps as the captain of the Lufthansa jetliner turned on the "Fasten Seat Belt" signs and began his descent to Munich's Riem Airport. The fat woman next to Drummond was still humming, "The Hills Are Alive," as the wheels screeched into contact with the runway and the pilot threw the jets into reverse-thrust to slow the big Boeing 747, preparatory to taxiing up to the terminal building.

Once the plane had come to a complete stop, Drummond unhooked his seat belt and tried stretching his legs in the confines of his mini-seat. The flight—all eleven hours of it—would have tried the patience of even Maria Von Trapp. Wedged into a seat designed to accommodate a bicouperal amputee, Drummond had been unable to escape the babbling of the woman next to him.

Across two continents and an ocean, he had been subjected to an oral biography of Julie Andrews that would have embarrassed even the most puerile fan magazine. Between snippets about Julie's pets and her dietary foibles, the immense Mrs. Mac-Dowell had regaled him with a scene-by-scene re-telling of the film, commenting along the way that it was far better than the real life adventures of the Trapp Family Singers.

About the time that Drummond was seriously beginning to think about applying his thumb to her carotid artery, the cabin lights dimmed and the in-flight movie flickered into life on a wavy screen pulled down six feet in front of him, and Julie sprang into view larger and more distorted than life. Far from quieting down Mrs. MacDowell, the flickering image of her celluloid goddess at once gave her the gift of second sight, enabling her to accurately predict what would happen next in each and every scene.

Drummond decided that he was somehow fundamentally flawed—the result, no doubt, of being that rarest of all earthlings, a native Californian. That same laid-back temperament that allowed him, and hundreds of thousands like him, to live perched on the edge of potentially the most cataclysmic seismic disturbance in the history of the planet, without the least concern that at any moment their entire glittering civilization could be dashed into the sea, also made him constitutionally unable to be rude to the fat lady in the seat next to him.

Perhaps, he thought, *if I'd been born in New York, I could lean over and tell her to take it outside, or I'd serve her up a knuckle sandwich.*

But even the thought of behaving like some misfit from the Big Apple drove Drummond deeper into a cocoon of courtesy. Instead of shoving his thumb against her neck and putting her to sleep for a couple of hours, he found himself making polite noises.

Finally, Julie warbled her last song, the plane landed, and 357 people all leaped to their feet, anxious to crowd the narrow aisles of the aircraft as they pushed and shoved their way toward the door, so that they could be first to the baggage claim area—where their eleven-hour flight could be extended by at least another hour waiting for their luggage. Drummond decided to wait until the flood of tourists had ebbed somewhat before diving into the crowd that streamed past his seat.

He had not reckoned on the edelweiss-fueled desire of Julie Andrews' roving genealogist to join in the lemming-like race to the land of lost luggage.

"Excuse me, would you please get up so I can get out?"

"I'll be getting up in just a moment," Drummond said, almost apologetically.

"No, I mean could you get up now? We might be missing something." Mrs. MacDowell sounded like a kid at Disneyland pleading to go on a ride.

"Well," Drummond began, "I can't really get up; there's no room in the aisle just now."

Mrs. MacDowell stood up, stooping to avoid banging her head on the reading lights and air vents above her seat.

"Well, then, if you'll just let me squeeze past," she said, as she started to half-climb over Drummond's lap, visions of chrome-plated luggage carousels, complete with the Trapp Family Singers perched on long-lost suitcases, undoubtedly dancing in her head.

It was the last straw. After eleven hours of Julie Andrews trivia, even an LAPD cop snaps.

"Look, lady. It's been a long flight. I'm tired, my eyeballs feel like they've been rolled in sand, and my brain is numb from your nonstop recitation of thrilling facts about Julie Andrews." Drummond took a deep breath. "So why don't you sit down and wait for the crowd to clear out, before I give you an in-flight knuckle sandwich?"

The pudgy features beneath the over-inflated hair wrinkled into a scowl. "New Yorkers," she said contemptuously, "are *the* rudest people in the world."

Drummond narrowed his eyes. "We're also homicidal maniacs," he said in flat tone. "Now, sit down!"

Defeated, the fat lady huffed back down in her seat. After a strained minute or two, there was a momentary break in the shuffling flow of tourists squeezing past Drummond's seat, so he took the opportunity to get up and step into the aisle. Standing firmly in place, he held up those passengers from farther back in the aircraft while the lady seated next to him crawled out clutching a large canvas bag and, without so much as a thank-you, headed determinedly down the aisle toward the open hatch.

Inside the terminal building, Drummond shifted his carry-on to the other shoulder and handed his passport and landing card to one of the green-uniformed *Grenzpolizei,* who quickly scanned them, stamped his passport, and then handed it back to him.

"Herr Drummond," the Grepo said, "I see on your landing card that you are a police officer, yes?"

"That's right. I'm a captain with the Los Angeles Police Department. Why?"

"Oh, professional courtesy. You are here on police business?" the Grepo asked, pressing a small button on the counter next to his stamps.

"No, just a vacation. I'm headed to Vienna."

"Ah, Vienna. A beautiful city. Enjoy your stay, *Kapitän. Auf Wiedersehen.*" He gave Drummond a nod and a slight smile, and turned to the next passenger in line.

In the baggage arrival hall, nearly six hundred people milled around waiting for their luggage to magically appear on one of the conveyor belts that led from only-God-knew-where to the stainless steel carousels that were surrounded six-deep by people anxious to recover their luggage so that they could stand in line for half an hour while the customs police conducted a series of random spot checks for smuggled goods.

Drummond saw his canvas-and-leather Gurka bag snake down the conveyor and tumble onto one of the carousels. Fighting his way past a family of Iraqis, he managed to retrieve his bag on its first go-round. Moving back out through the crowd was more difficult with his bag than it had been going in to get it, but somehow he managed to get clear of the mob. He was heading for a row of glistening baggage trolleys when another of the green-uniformed frontier police came up to him and saluted.

"*Kapitän* Drummond?"

Surprised by the sudden appearance of the policeman, it took Drummond a beat to reply.

"Yes," he said. "I'm Drummond."

"Come with me, please, *Kapitän*," the Grepo said, relieving Drummond of his larger bag.

Not sure what to think, Drummond accompanied the policeman over to the Red and Green customs channels, packed with several hundred people all being carefully interviewed by the customs police. To the left of the Red Channel entrance was a small door marked "Security Personnel Only." The man with Drummond's bag tapped in his code on the keyboard next to the door, and within seconds a metallic click announced that the door was unlocked. The Grepo held open the door for Drummond, then followed him through.

A customs official inside glanced up from his desk at the two men, said something to Drummond's escort in German, and went back to reading a dog-eared copy of *STERN*. Several small, glass-fronted rooms opened off the office, but the German police officer led Drummond past them to another door at the opposite end, there turning to face Drummond and hand him back his bag.

"This is as far as I can take you, *Kapitän,* but the airport lobby is just on the other side of the door." Smiling, he reached into his pocket and brought out a small card. "If you require any assistance while you are in Germany, please call this number, and one of our fellow officers will do whatever he can to help you." He held out his hand. "Enjoy your holiday in Germany."

"Thanks," Drummond said shaking the man's hand. Fumbling in his back pocket, he pulled out his wallet and removed one of his own cards. "Here," he said handing it to the German policeman. "If any of you are ever in Los Angeles, give me a call."

The Grepo smiled, and then with a salute opened the door that led out into the airport concourse.

Munich's international airport was a lot like any airport in the United States, Drummond decided, if you could overlook the policemen carrying submachine guns. On the far side of the concourse, he could see the familiar red-and-white Avis sign, and deftly skirting the crowd of people waiting for arriving passengers, he made his way to the car rental desk.

A smiling blond girl in a pert Avis uniform spoke

to Drummond in German as he handed her his pre-paid car rental voucher.

"Guten Tag, mein Herr. Danke schön."

"I'm sorry," he said. "I don't speak German."

"No problem," said the young woman, with an east Texas drawl you could cut with a Bowie knife. "I speak Yankee just fine." She flashed Drummond a Pepsodent smile as she spread out the voucher. "My husband is over here with the Army, and I'm what Uncle Sam calls a dependent."

Her fingers flew across the keyboard next to her desk. "Now, Mr. Drummond, if I could have a look at your driver's license, please?"

Drummond pulled out his badge case, opened it, and removed his driver's license from behind his police ID card.

"Here you go," he said as he handed it over to the girl.

"That's fine," she said as she checked the expiration date and matched the photo on the license to Drummond's face. "If you don't mind my asking, are you a police officer?"

"Yeah, I'm with LAPD. Why?"

She handed back Drummond's license. "My husband's an MP, and his enlistment is up in six months. We were thinking of moving to L.A. when he gets out. You know, maybe getting a job with the LAPD or something."

"Well," Drummond said, pulling another of his cards from his wallet, "if you do come to L.A., give me a call. I can't promise anything, but at least I can tell you where its safe to park your car."

"Oh, gosh, thanks. A captain in homicide—Jim'll be thrilled!" She tucked his card under the edge of a book on the desk and looked back at the computer screen in front of her. "Now, let's see.

Hmmm. Your voucher entitles you to a group C car. . . ."

"What's a group C car?" Drummond asked, as he stuffed his badge back in his pocket.

"Well, it's a Ford Fiesta." She screwed up her lips and made a face.

"Any good?"

"Well, not according to my husband. We've got one, a real old clunker, and Jim is always complaining that his foot keeps slipping off the gas pedal." She tapped the keyboard again, and a new list of cars appeared on the screen.

"Were you serious about us calling you, if we came to L.A.?" she asked wistfully, looking up from her computer.

"Yeah. Why?" Drummond looked puzzled.

Her face brightened. " 'Cause in that case, I'm gonna upgrade you to a Mercedes!" She tapped in the code number of Drummond's voucher, and a moment later the printer next to her buzzed out a copy of his contract. Taking off the top copy, she put it in a folder envelope that she handed to Drummond.

"You're in parking slot 74. Our courtesy bus is just outside the door." She smiled radiantly. "Have a nice day, sir."

The courtesy bus that took Drummond to the Avis parking lot passed a huge coach parked near the front of the airport. As they drove by, Drummond looked at the painting of Julie Andrews dancing across an Alpine meadow that decorated its flanks and shuddered.

Thank God for pretty girls from Texas! he thought, as he watched the first of the Americans climb on board for the Sound of Music Tour.

In the Avis lot, the cars were parked with Teu-

tonic efficiency, neatly lined up at attention, all of
their bumpers in perfect alignment. Drummond had
the feeling that if he shouted, *"Sieg Heil,"* all of
the hoods would snap open in salute as he walked
by. As he approached the end of the line of cars,
Drummond could just catch a glimpse of a
snowflake-white car standing to the right of an otherwise sober row of metallic gray and silver Fords.
When he got to slot 74, he had to check the license
plate against the number printed on the key tags to
make certain he had the right car.

Several of his friends at the department had Mercedes 190's, and Drummond had always thought of
them as boring, bland, and gutless. The car in slot
74 was none of those things. The snowflake-white
Mercedes was the AMG high-performance version
of the already incredibly quick 190E. The sculp-
tured body kit improved the car's drag coefficient
significantly, while the lowered and stiffened sus-
pension, allied to a set of Metzler ultra-high perfor-
mance tires, gave the car superior handling and
cornering capabilities. Drummond whistled softly as
he tossed his bags into the trunk, locked it, and
climbed into the red leather interior of the car.

After fastening his seat belt, he started the engine, allowing it to warm up while he adjusted the
power-operated mirrors on both doors. As the en-
gines revs fell back to a comfortable 800 rpm, he
put in the clutch, slipped the shift lever into first
gear, and pulled out of the parking lot. Following
the signs out of the airport, he was soon on the
autobahn and headed east toward Linz and Vienna.

German autobahns, unlike the car-clogged freeways of southern California, have no speed limits.
Drivers push their cars along as fast as they can,
realizing that to drive faster than is safe is to risk

arrest on the spot for dangerous or reckless driving. Surprisingly, the Germans seem to have fewer accidents than the Americans, who are mesmerized by the steady roll of 55-65 miles per hour on an eight-lane super highway.

The transition from the Munich ring-road onto the autobahn heading east toward the Austrian border loomed up, and Drummond shifted down into third gear. Turning the steering wheel to the right, he put his foot down and felt the twin turbochargers cut in, the car squatting down on the pavement as the tachometer raced up toward the 7000 rpm redline. Lifting off slightly, Drummond shifted up into fourth gear at a hundred and ten miles per hour and, as the speedometer nudged 225 kilometers per hour—a hundred and forty miles per hour—he shifted into fifth gear and let the speed fall off to an easy hundred and ten cruising speed.

According to the guide books, Munich was 381 miles from Vienna, and despite the effortless manner in which the Mercedes devoured the miles, Drummond soon could begin to feel jet lag overtaking him faster than he could overtake the other cars on the road. Pulling into a lay-by, he checked his map and decided to call it a day when he reached Braunau, just across the border into Austria.

The frontier post spanned the autobahn, and Drummond slowed as he approached it, getting in line with the other traffic that was crossing into Austria. As he pulled up to the booth, the guard gave him a casual glance and waved him through. Braunau was clogged with trucks stopping for customs checks, so consulting his map again, Drummond decided to press on to Ried, some twenty miles farther east.

Following the signs marked *zentrum,* Drummond

drove into the center of Ried and parked the white Mercedes in a small parking lot across the square from the local tourist information office. The young man behind the desk spoke flawless English, and in a matter of minutes Drummond was back in his car and headed out of town, looking for a small turning to the left, sign-posted *"Hotel Schloss von Dielstein."*

Chapter 12

The hotel was an old castle perched on the edge of the river, one of the tributaries that fed into the Saltzach River that formed part of the frontier between Austria and Germany. As Drummond pulled up on the graveled forecourt in front of the castle, a servant came out to take his luggage—a thin, bald-headed little man in dark green trousers and a vest with green and gold horizontal stripes. He was waiting for the trunk key before Drummond switched off the engine, and had it open before Drummond could unfold himself from the driver's seat, moving stiffly from sitting so long. Indicating with a wave of his hand that Drummond should proceed him, the little man followed along intently with Drummond's two expensive bags.

The interior of the castle gave Drummond the immediate impression that he was in someone's home, rather than a hotel. The furnishings, for the most part nineteenth-century copies of medieval furniture, glowed with the patina of expensive antiques lovingly cared for. On the walls, hundreds of small chamois antlers crowded around portraits of aristocratic-looking cavalry officers neatly inset into the darkly carved paneling. At one end of the room, an otherwise cold and forbidding fireplace was filled with a huge arrangement of wild flowers.

Above the carved stone mantelpiece, a magnificent portrait of Emperor Franz-Josef gazed down serenely at Drummond and his leather-edged canvas bags.

At an immense carved desk in one corner of the room, an attractive dark-haired woman in her mid-thirties was speaking on an old-fashioned telephone. As Drummond approached, she smiled at him but made no attempt to get rid of the caller. After a few minutes, she said good-bye and put down the receiver, giving Drummond her full attention.

"I'm sorry to have kept you waiting," she said, standing up as she spoke. "That was my grandmother, and you know what they are like, I'm sure." She smiled again. "You must be Herr Drummond."

"Yes, I am," Drummond said.

"Well, I have your room all ready for you." Her accent was as soft as her chestnut-colored hair, done up in two braids on the side of her head. Looking past Drummond for a moment, she spoke to the servant in German.

"Joachim, nehmen Sie an der Generalszimmer das Gepäck des Herr Drummond, bitte."

"Jawohl, Baronin." The little man clicked his heels as he spoke, then lifted the bags off the thick carpet and turned and left the room.

"Now," she said, returning once again to Drummond, "if you will please fill out a registration card?" She handed him a thick black fountain pen and a largish card. "Just your name, occupation, and nationality is all that is necessary."

Drummond filled in the blanks, and then handed the card back to the baroness. She quickly scanned the card, one elegant eyebrow raising slightly.

"Thank you, Herr Drummond. Dinner will be at eight o'clock. If you would care for a drink, just ask."

"Oh, not right now, thank you. I'd like to clean up first, change—that sort of thing." Drummond smiled. "So if someone could show me to my room?"

"Certainly. Please come with me."

Following the baroness down the elegant hallway, it suddenly occurred to Drummond that dinner *might* be a formal affair.

"Excuse me, but will a jacket and tie be appropriate for dinner?"

"Of course, Herr Drummond. Actually, you are the only guest here at the castle tonight, so you needn't worry too much about dressing for dinner." She stopped outside a heavy oak door. "If you don't mind, I usually have a few friends for drinks before going in to table. Perhaps you'd care to join us, if you're not too tired after your trip."

"Thank you, I'd be delighted to meet your friends," he said, as she handed him the key to his room.

"Good. Then I'll see you downstairs for drinks at seven-thirty." Far away, at the other end of the castle the sound of a ringing phone could just be heard.

"Oops, the phone. Excuse me, please." And with that, the baroness turned and walked briskly down the corridor.

Drummond collapsed into his room, the built-up jet lag hitting him like a flower pot dropped from a fourth-floor window. Sinking onto his bed, he realized that if he put his head down for as much as a minute, it would be sometime tomorrow before he lifted it up again. Struggling against the urge to lie down, he took off his jacket and tossed it over the back of the nearest chair, then kicked off his loafers.

Barefoot, he headed into the white-tiled bathroom, pulling off his shirt on the way. Joachim had unpacked his bags and placed his shaving kit next to the basin; Drummond unzipped it and, after rummaging through it for a few seconds, pulled out a bottle of vitamins. He shook two of the pills into his hand and popped them into his mouth, then filled a glass with water and took a long drink.

Soon he was stripped and under the hot shower, enjoying the tingle of the high-pressure nozzle after his long flight from Los Angeles. Ten minutes under the shower convinced him that he might be good for several more hours before he collapsed from lack of sleep, so long as he went easy on the booze. He toweled off, then wiped the steam from the mirror and set about shaving. A few minutes later, he was padding back into the bedroom to pull his navy blazer and gray slacks from the wardrobe. What was it his mother had always called it? The man's basic uniform, appropriate to wear anywhere except a nudist colony or a black tie dinner.

By the time he finished dressing, it was nearly seven-thirty and time to meet the baroness and her friends before dinner. Heading out the door and down the hall toward the lobby, Drummond found himself idly speculating on what she'd be wearing. She had looked very attractive in the traditional loden of earlier this afternoon, when he arrived, and he wondered what a baroness wore for drinks.

Joachim was seated by the door in a leather-covered porter's chair, his small frame nearly hidden in the deep semi-domed recess of the chair's back, and as Drummond approached, he slid out of the chair and stood stiffly to attention. Bowing deeply, he led Drummond across the lobby and through a carved oak door into the library.

The baroness and her friends were standing in a bay window overlooking the terrace as Drummond entered the room, the men dressed much as Drummond was. Immediately, the baroness left them and walked across the deep burgundy carpets to where Joachim had halted just inside the doorway.

"Herr Drummond, how good of you to join us." She took him by the elbow and led him over to her friends.

"Everyone," she said as the two of them walked over, "this is Herr Drummond, from Los Angeles."

Drummond smiled politely. "How do you do."

One by one, the baroness introduced him to her other guests. "This is Dr. Polinsky, and his wife," she indicated a short balding gentleman to Drummond's right, who immediately shook hands with him. "Professor Detweiller," she continued, "whose wife will be joining us later, and Police Commandant Reidl." The two policemen shook hands.

"If you two will excuse me a moment," the baroness smiled at both of them, "I'll get Herr Drummond a drink." She turned to Drummond. "What would you like?"

"Scotch, please, with just a little water," Drummond replied.

"Coming right up," she said, and then with a smile she turned and walked across the room toward a heavily carved table laden with crystal decanters filled with a variety of spirits. Drummond watched as she fixed his drink. She was elegantly dressed in a pale ivory-colored silk gown that came just below the knee, close-sleeved and closed at the waist with an ostrich hide belt that matched her delicate high-heeled shoes. The chestnut hair now was coiled low at the nape of her neck, apparently held in place only by one strategically-placed tortoise-shell pin. A pale topaz evening ring glittered on the index finger of her right hand, and at her throat a double strand of pearls fell casually across her firm breasts. All in all, she was the perfect expression of casual elegance.

"She is lovely, isn't she?" Commandant Reidl's voice was barely louder than a whisper.

Drummond flushed slightly. "I'd say she was something more than that." He hunted for the right words. "My father was a cinematographer. He would have said she had presence, a natural grace that goes beyond merely being physically attractive."

"And you? What would you say?" asked Reidl.

"I'd say Dad was right." Drummond smiled as the baroness returned with his drink. "Thank you."

"You're welcome," she said handing him a crystal tumbler filled with an aromatic scotch. "Has the commandant been telling you all about the crime of the century?"

"No, he hasn't." Drummond was beginning to feel the combined effects of jet lag along with the first sip of his scotch, and was beginning to wonder if bed might not have been a better idea than dinner.

"Well, I'm surprised. I thought two policemen would be eager to talk shop." She grinned at Reidl. "He's with the Los Angeles police, Franz. Why don't you tell him about your body in the woods?"

Reidl looked a little incredulous as he sipped his drink. "Nothing much, really. Just some skinhead punker with his throat cut. Probably a drug deal gone bad. I suppose he was killed elsewhere, and then his body dumped here in the woods."

"Not much crime in this part of Austria, then?" asked Drummond.

"Oh no, we get a lot. Poaching, smuggling, an occasional burglary. But drug dealing? No, that's for the boys in Vienna."

"Then, what makes you think the body was dumped?" Drummond asked.

"Well, for one thing, the boy—somewhere between seventeen and twenty, maybe twenty-two, according to the pathologist—the boy was naked. And for another, there was virtually no blood at the scene. You cut someone's throat, there's lots of blood—but not here. So the killing must have taken place somewhere else, the body stripped, and then driven out here and dumped." Reidl drained his glass. "So much for the 'crime of the century,' as Maria calls it."

"Well, I'd say you've probably got it figured pretty close." Drummond made a mental note of the baroness's first name, just in case.

"So tell me, Herr Drummond," Reidl's voice took on a slightly patronizing tone, "what do you do in the police in Los Angeles?"

Usually laid back, Drummond picked up on the quiet challenge Reidl had laid down. "I'm a captain, in charge of the homicide division at police headquarters in downtown Los Angeles." He stared levelly back at Reidl, who was looking at him in the same way cops all over the world stare at suspects. Then suddenly Reidl relaxed, a broad smile spreading across his face.

"Please, *Kapitän* Drummond, call me Franz." He turned and made a pouting face at the baroness. "Maria, darling, why didn't you tell me your guest was an officer?"

The baroness laughed. "How was I to know? His

registration card just said 'policeman.' And, since you're the only policeman I know, I thought I'd invite you up for a drink."

"Forgive me, *Kapitän*," Reidl began.

"Please, if you don't mind, call me John, okay?"

"John. Yes. John, please forgive me, but there is something you should know about Austrians. We are title crazy. If you have a title, use it. Otherwise, you will receive very little respect here."

The baroness joined in. "It's true. I'm afraid we are all terrible snobs, unlike you Americans. Even Joachim, my butler, has a title that he uses socially. In the village, he is known as *Jagdmeister*—hunting master—because he is in charge of the shooting here on the estate. To live in Austria and to not have a title, places one on the very bottom of the social totem pole." She smiled. "I hope you can forgive us, John."

Drummond chuckled softly. "Sure. In Los Angeles, we have the same sort of snobbery, only it's based on the sort of car you drive. If you drive a Ford, then no one wants to know you."

"But *I* drive a Ford," said Reidl—then he burst out laughing, as did the baroness.

"Come along," she said, taking each of the men by an arm. "Dinner is waiting in the private dining room."

Led by the baroness and her two "escorts," the seven of them trooped out of the library and into a small dining room.

"This used to be my grandfather's smoking room, but after he died, and I had to open the castle to the public, I had it turned into a small dining room for my own use."

The room was painted a deep, rich red, with the windows and mouldings picked out in white. The floor was rosewood—dark, almost black wood with a reddish brown grain that complemented the polished mahogany dining table set in the center of the room under a tented damask ceiling. A Bohemian crystal chandelier hung down above it, with real candles illuminating it, rather than electric ones.

The paintings in this room, unlike the military subjects in the library and great hall, were eighteenth-century landscapes, and to judge by their color and composition were of English rather than continental origin. Heavy white tapers set in solid silver wall sconces cast a pale yellow light into the shadowy corners of the room, while the crested china and silver dinner service glowed with the reflected light of the chandelier overhead.

The baroness and Reidl sat at opposite ends of the table, with Drummond to the right of his hostess, sandwiched between her and Madame Polinsky. Opposite Drummond was Professor Detweiller, who—much to his relief—spoke excellent English. During the course of the evening, it transpired that Madame Polinsky spoke far better Spanish than English, with the result that Drummond was able to carry on conversations with all of his immediate dinner companions. One couldn't be a cop in Los Angeles, these days, without being reasonably fluent in Spanish.

It wasn't until the last course was removed from the table that Drummond realized he could remember nothing of the meal just consumed—only the conversation that had sparkled as much as the excellent champagne that had been unstintingly poured into the tall crystal flutes.

The women excused themselves from the table, leaving the men to enjoy their cigars before joining them in the library for coffee. In the lull that inevitably follows the departure of the ladies from any well-bred dinner party, Reidl leaned forward onto his elbows to speak to Drummond.

"So, John, you are going to Vienna tomorrow?" he said.

"Yes, I am. I had hoped to get an early start, but I doubt I'll hit the road much before ten." He stifled a yawn, exhaustion racing up on him, now that the table had quieted down.

Reidl and the others chuckled. "Ten is still pretty early, here in Austria. You'll be in Vienna in time for lunch. Where do you stay?"

"I'm booked into the Hilton," Drummond said.

"The Hilton? That's a tourist trap." Reidl reached into his coat pocket and brought out a small leather notebook and a gold pen. "Before you leave tomorrow, call this number and ask for Inspector Eberle. Tell him you are a friend of mine, and that I said he was to put you in a decent hotel. Okay, John?"

"Okay, Franz. Thanks." Drummond took the note, folded it in half, and placed it in his pocket.

"So," said Dr. Polinsky, "now we join the ladies, drink some coffee, and maybe go home to bed."

Laughing, the men got up from the table and headed back into the library.

The baroness was sitting in front of the fireplace pouring delicious-smelling Turkish coffee into delicate little cups, each emblazoned with a black two-headed eagle. Reidl sat down next to her and began handing out the steaming demitasses to the guests. Drummond sipped the thick, sweet coffee and chatted politely with the just-arrived Madame Detweiller, who, he was surprised to learn, was a well-known Austrian singer.

"And so where are you singing now?" he asked.

Laughing, Madame Detweiller said, "Ah. I am

engaged for the next ten days in Salzburg, where I will be singing for some visiting Americans."

"Oh, really?" Drummond said, supposing that it must be some sort of trade fair or diplomatic function. "What sort of group are you singing for?"

"It's the 'Sound of Music' tour. I sing all of Julie Andrews' songs from the film." She positively beamed. "Do you know it?"

Chapter 13

It was after ten by the time Drummond managed to prise himself out of bed and stumble into the shower the next morning. At first the stinging sensation of the water jets hitting his body seemed to be happening to someone else, but gradually his sense returned as he recovered from the combined effects of one drink too many allied to thirty-two hours without sleep. Lathering up, he had just about decided that he could spend all day in the shower when abruptly the hot water changed to cold. Madly spinning the taps by the edge of the tub did nothing to restore the hot water, and gritting his teeth, Drummond finished his shower under the ice-cold spray. Frozen to the bone, he briskly dried off and climbed quickly into his clothes. His teeth were still chattering as he made his way downstairs to breakfast.

Sitting at a small table in the bay window of the morning room, Drummond thought he could feel himself thawing out as the sun beat down across his shoulders. He allowed himself one last shiver as Joachim approached with a silver tray, set it down next to the table, and poured Drummond a steaming cup of coffee from an elaborate silver coffee pot.

"Danke schön," Drummond said—then, remem-

bering the previous night's discussion about titles, quickly added, *"Herr Jagdmeister."*

A smile struggled at the corners of Joachim's mouth, and only partly managed to overcome the butler's strict sense of decorum. Joachim bowed deeply.

"A pleasure, *Kapitän,"* he said, and then returned to the pantry.

Drummond finished a hearty breakfast of orange juice, eggs, bacon, smoked sausage, and toast, and poured himself a second cup of coffee. The baroness came into the room and smiled as she walked over to his table. She was wearing old-fashioned tan riding britches, a khaki shirt with a silk scarf at her throat, and a pair of well-polished russet leather riding boots. Drummond could tell from the dusty marks on her instep that she had only just taken off her spurs.

"Well, I trust you had a good night's sleep?" she asked.

"Terrific, except I could have easily slept for another twelve hours. I didn't realize how tired I was. May I pour you a coffee?"

"Thank you, no. It's the jet lag," she said.

"Well, that's a relief. For a moment I was afraid I might be allergic to champagne!"

They both laughed at Drummond's little joke, then the baroness smiled and glanced back at the door.

"Well, I'd love to stay and chat, but I must get changed and be about the day's business. I've left your bill in an envelope on the desk, next to the telephone. Joachim will settle up with you." She extended her hand to Drummond, *"Auf wiedersehen, Kapitän* Drummond. It's been delightful having you."

Drummond stood up and took her hand in his. "The pleasure has been mine, Baroness." Bowing slightly, he kissed her hand. *"Auf wiedersehen."*

The baroness gave him a dazzling smile, then turned and left the morning room. Drummond, standing next to the small table in the bay window, watched her disappear through the doorway that led out to the lobby.

Reidl, he thought to himself, *is one lucky sonofabitch.*

After packing, Drummond brought his bags down to the lobby and walked over to the heavily carved desk in the corner. There, propped up next to an antique telephone, was a small white envelope with *"Kapitän Drummond"* written across the front in gothic script. Inside was a gracious note thanking Drummond for having stayed at the castle, along with a bill for what seemed to Drummond to be a ridiculously small amount for his stay.

Joachim materialized from deep within his porter's chair and bowed deeply to Drummond.

"The *Kapitän* has found everything to be in order?" he asked.

"Yes, although this hardly seems enough," Drummond said, handing Joachim his bill and a credit card.

Joachim took them from Drummond's outstretched hand and vanished down the hallway, only to return a few minutes later with the credit card slip ready for Drummond to sign. Drummond signed it, took his copy and credit card, and slipped both in his pocket. He reached for his bags, but Joachim beat him to it.

"I will take these to the *Kapitän's* car," the servant said. "You may use that telephone to call Herr

Reidl's friend in Vienna." Picking up the bag, Joachim turned and marched out the door.

Fumbling in his coat pocket, Drummond found the slip of paper that Reidl had given him the night before. He picked up the telephone on the desk and dialed the number he'd been given. A woman's voice answered.

"*Inspektor Eberle, bitte,*" Drummond said, exhausting most of his meager knowledge of the German language.

"*Ein moment,*" the voice replied, followed by a hollow metallic click.

Nearly a minute passed before a man's voice crackled on the line.

"*Eberle hier, kann ich helfen Sie?*" There was authority in the voice, but more than that, definite kindness.

"Inspector Eberle, this is Captain John Drummond of the Los Angeles—"

"Ah, yes." Eberle cut Drummond off. "Franz Reidl phoned me this morning to say you'd be calling. Where are you now?" Eberle's English was flawless, without a trace of accent.

"I'm still at the castle." Something instinctively told Drummond he was going to like Eberle.

"Okay, here's what you want to do. You're about one hundred miles from Vienna. Get on the autobahn and head into the city. Just before you get into town, the freeway splits, and you want the A1. Take that to the end of the highway, and then follow the signs toward the Schönbrunn. I'll meet you out front and guide you to your hotel." Eberle paused, then added, "Franz tells me you've got a red-hot Mercedes, so you should have no trouble meeting me in—say, an hour and a half?"

"Sure," replied Drummond. "Just so long as I don't get nailed for speeding."

"Not to worry, my friend." Eberle chuckled. "Franz gave me your license number when he called. I've already tipped the Bahnpoz not to bother you. See you at the Schönbrunn, Captain." Then he hung up.

Drummond replaced the receiver on the polished brass cradle. One thing was certain: professional courtesy in Austria knew no bounds. He could just imagine the response he'd get calling up the CHP in Los Angeles and asking them to look the other way when some foreign cop came blistering by on the Harbor Freeway.

Heading out the door, Drummond glanced at his watch. It was just eleven thirty; according to Eberle, he could make Schönbrunn by one. Climbing into the freshly washed Mercedes, Drummond fastened his seat belt, switched on the engine, and pointed the white car towards the autobahn.

The turbo-charged Mercedes clung to the road like an abalone on a rock, and Drummond soon had it cruising at well over a hundred miles an hour. The gently curving blacktop between Linz and St. Pölten flashed by beneath the thick Metzler tires, Drummond only occasionally slowing as he approached the odd intersection, or a cluster of cars traveling at significantly slower speeds. The last twenty miles, from just before St. Pölten to where the Al branched off into Vienna, saw the needle of the speedometer sit at a rock-steady 250 kilometers per hour—slightly more than one hundred fifty miles per hour.

Stepping on the brakes as he approached the Al, Drummond hauled the car down to a safer seventy-five miles per hour and quietly took back everything he'd ever said about Mercedes-Benz being an old man's car. Changing down directly into third, he stood on the gas and felt the car leap forward as the twin turbochargers took over. In less than five minutes, he covered the last ten miles of Austrian autobahn and found himself slowing down to what seemed to be a crawl as he wound his way off the autobahn and on to the wide boulevard that led off to his right, following the signs that pointed the way to the Schönbrunn Palace.

Schönbrunn Palace would dwarf either Buckingham Palace or the White House, its elegant classical facade stretching along the main road leading into Vienna for four long blocks. The sheer splendor of the pale yellow palace was a lasting monument to the Hapsburgs, the old imperial Austrian dynasty that had created an empire which, by 1900, was greater than the common market for today's modern Europe.

As he approached the palace from the north, Drummond saw the sign directing traffic to a parking lot opposite the main gates of the palace. Signaling to turn left, he turned as if to cross the bridge that spanned the Wien Fluss—the Vienna River—but then he turned immediately right into the parking lot where Eberle had said he'd meet him.

Drummond checked his watch—12:58. The Mercedes had effortlessly done its job, and Drummond was smugly satisfied that he'd arrived on time.

A black BMW 530 pulled up next to the Mercedes and a dumpty man in his mid-forties got out, tugged up his trousers, and walked over to Drummond's side of the car.

"Hello, Captain Drummond." The man crouched down to the open window of the Mercedes. "I'm

Markus Eberle," he said, through a grin that displayed two stainless steel teeth set into an otherwise perfect smile.

"My pleasure, indeed," Drummond said, sticking his hand awkwardly out the window.

Eberle grabbed it with both of his fists and pumped it up and down.

"Had lunch yet?" he asked.

"Nope, just got here."

"Well, then, follow me to your hotel, we'll get you checked in, grab a bite, and then I'll show you some of the sights." Eberle's smile was infectious, and Drummond decided that he definitely liked the man.

"Lead on, Inspector, lead on."

Eberle pulled smoothly into traffic, and Drummond tucked in behind him. In tandem they moved along the Schönbrunner Strasse, then Eberle led him through a maze of small alleys and side streets, jigging left and right until they reached Prinz Eugen Strasse, where they turned to the left. At the bottom of the street, Drummond could see a tall pillar with a statue of a soldier on top of it, who seemed to be resting his hand incongruously on top of a very large toilet seat.

Just before they got to the pillar, Eberle turned to the right up a driveway, through an elaborate wrought iron gate. Drummond followed and found that they were in the forecourt of a baroque palace—smaller, but infinitely more elegant, than the Schönbrunn.

Eberle pulled up, and two servants in gold-striped vests and black trousers immediately stepped out from the large double door opposite the cars and stood to attention. Eberle climbed out

of the police car and walked back to Drummond's
Mercedes.

"Well, this is home. Hope you like it," he said.

"I'm impressed. I just hope I can afford it,"
Drummond replied.

"Sure you can." Eberle winked. "You get the
police discount."

Drummond got out of his car, and he and Eberle
headed toward the door now being held open by
one of the servants. Inside, a discreet counter to
the right of the door told Drummond that this was
probably one of the most expensive hotels he'd ever
been in. He wasn't far from wrong.

The man at the desk was wearing a cutaway coat
and striped trousers, and as Drummond approached,
greeted him by name.

"*Kapitän* Drummond," he said with a cultured
voice. "Welcome to Palais Schwartzenberg. Allow
me to show you to your room."

Taking a large key from a small pigeon-hole behind the counter, he led the two men up a short
flight of stairs and then down a curving corridor
hung with tapestries, finally stopping in front of a
pale ivory door set with a silver plaque engraved
with the number 45. Using the large key, he opened
the door and let Drummond and Eberle into a small
hallway.

"Over here is your kitchen," the man in the swal-
lowtail coat said, gesturing to a door on the right.
"And in here," he opened an elaborate door on
the left, "is your sitting room."

The three men entered the sitting room, which
was furnished with traditional rather than modern
furniture indicative of taste rather than opulence.

"Upstairs," the hotel manager gestured toward
the carved banister at the far end of the room, "are

your study, bedroom, and bathroom. I hope you find everything satisfactory?"

"This is just fine, thank you," Drummond said, as the manager placed the key in his hand.

"Very well, then, *Kapitän*. I will have your bags brought up." He bowed stiffly and, walking backwards, withdrew from the room.

"Quite impressive," Drummond said. "I hope the police discount is a big one."

"Oh, it is," said Eberle. "Now, go pee so we can head out to lunch."

Eberle's idea of lunch was a small Hungarian restaurant around the corner from Palais Schwartzenberg that specialized in fresh game. During a meal of venison in a Hungarian pepper sauce, complimented by a rich, ruby-red wine, Eberle enthused about his city, the most beautiful city in Europe. Drummond could find no reason to dispute Eberle's claims—certainly what he'd seen of the city so far confirmed that Vienna was without equal.

As the last of the dishes were cleared away, Eberle patted his ample stomach with both hands.

"Ah, that's what I call lunch," he said. "Now, can I show you some of the sights?"

"Sure," said Drummond, "but I've got to make a phone call first." He looked at his watch. "It's nearly three-thirty, and I have to meet a man tomorrow, if he can see me."

"Okay, how about this? You go back to the hotel and make your calls, and I'll come back for you at—say, seven-thirty. Then, we can either take in the nightlife or, if you'd prefer, we'll answer a couple of calls with the local homicide team." Eberle gave him a quizzical look. "I'm sure some of the boys would really like to meet you."

"See you at seven-thirty for some police work," Drummond said.

"Great," Eberle replied. "I'll walk you back to your hotel."

Back in his room, Drummond was surprised to discover that some of his clothes seemed to be missing from his closet. Picking up the phone, he rang the desk.

"This is Captain Drummond," he began. "I seem to be missing a suit and a couple of shirts from my closet."

"Yes, *Kapitän*. The porter has sent them out to be pressed. They should be back about four-thirty, if that's all right, sir."

Amazing, thought Drummond. "Yes that's fine," he said. "Thank you," and then he hung up. *I'll probably own American Express when I get home*, he mused.

Reaching into his pocket, he brought out a small notebook and flipped through it until he found the page he was looking for. Carefully he dialed the number for Ritterbuchs.

The phone purred softly in Drummond's ear repeatedly. Finally, just as he was about to hang up, an elderly voice answered on the other end.

"Bitte?" the voice asked.

"Baron von Liebenfalz, please," Drummond replied.

"Ah. Who is calling, please?"

"John Drummond. With whom am I speaking, please?"

"This is Liebenfalz. How may I help you?"

"Well, sir, you wrote me in Los Angeles and suggested that we meet here in Vienna to discuss—"

"Ah, yes. Now I remember. So you would like to meet. Is tomorrow convenient, at—say, eleven?"

Von Liebenfalz spoke quickly, although without much of an accent.

"Eleven o'clock tomorrow morning will be fine, sir," Drummond said.

"You have my address, Herr Drummond?" von Liebenfalz asked.

"Yes, on your card."

"Good. Then, I see you tomorrow. Good-bye." There was a click and the line went dead.

Drummond stared at the phone for a few seconds, then dropped it back onto its cradle. With nothing to do but wait for his suit to come back from being pressed, he decided to head upstairs and take a nap.

The shabby stucco-fronted building in another part of Vienna had been a modest middle-class home when it was built shortly before the First World War. The revolution that had followed the abdication of King Carl after the war had changed Vienna, and by the time the Second World War was over, there was no middle class left in Vienna who could afford to keep the house. Like other houses whose owners were either dead or simply vanished, the building was taken over by the municipal authorities and converted into numerous small apartments.

Frau Kettleman had lived in the small ground-floor flat since the winter of 1947, when her husband had secured the job of building janitor. She kept to herself and rarely spoke to any of the other tenants, especially the old Jew in the apartment above her own.

Hans Stucke kept to himself, which was exactly how Frau Kettleman wanted it. It was loathsome, she thought, that the old Jew should have returned to Vienna after the war. "Why couldn't he have gone to Israel with the rest of them," she used to ask her husband, "instead of coming back here to make the rest of us feel guilty, as though we had committed some sort of crime?"

Still, he paid his rent: on time, every week, for nearly thirty years. Except for this week. It had been due two days ago, but this time his rent payment envelope had not appeared in the box next to Frau Kettleman's front door. At first, she didn't think too much of it; most of the tenants were usually behind in their rent.

Today, however, when the dark stain appeared on her ceiling, and water began to drip down on her carpet, Frau Kettleman remembered the late rent and went upstairs to confront Hans Stucke, and to complain about the water coming from his apartment.

When Stucke didn't answer the pounding on the door, Frau Kettleman unlocked his door with her pass key and let herself in. It was dark inside, with the lights off and the blinds pulled down to the sill of the room's only window.

"Herr Stucke?" she called, trying to be heard over the sound of the running shower without actually shouting.

There was no reply; only the hissing of the shower running in the small bathroom next to the kitchen.

Frau Kettleman walked across the room to the bathroom door, the water-logged linoleum slick beneath her shoes. She rapped on the closed door.

"Herr Stucke?"

The sound of the shower was the only reply. Convinced that the room was empty, Frau Kettleman pushed open the bathroom door. In the half-darkness of the apartment, the bathroom looked empty. It wasn't until she reached across the tub to turn off the shower that Frau Kettleman realized that Hans Stucke, slumped in the corner of the tub, was staring at her.

The phone next to his bed had rung several times before Drummond was awake enough to realize where he was and answer it. When he did finally pick it up, Eberle was on the other end.

"Time to rise and shine, amigo. The Vienna PD is anxious to show you how we tackle crime on the Donau." Eberle was buoyant.

"Gimme five minutes. I'll be right down."

Drummond half-heartedly considered a quick shower, but settled instead for washing his face, a fast shave, and a fresh shirt. A quick glance at his Rolex told him that it was almost eight-fifteen. His suit had reappeared in the closet, along with the missing shirts, so he donned the suit instead of his blazer, also pulling a pair of Rockport shoes out of the closet. When he was dressed, he headed down to the lobby to meet Eberle.

Like Drummond, Eberle had changed clothes from that afternoon. In place of his light brown suit was a dark tweed jacket, a gray shirt with black tie, and charcoal trousers. Also like Drummond, he was wearing a pair of thick-soled black shoes, of the kind designed for standing in for hours.

Eberle grinned at Drummond. "Okay, sleepy-head, let's go."

On their way to the car, Drummond asked where they were heading.

"A dead body, over in the sixth district." Eberle shook his head with disappointment. "Not much excitement tonight, I'm afraid. It was the best I could do."

Drummond laughed. "Markus, don't worry. It'll be exciting enough."

The sixth district was a shabby working-class neighborhood full of cheap apartment houses and empty shops. Eberle's BMW pulled up to the curb opposite the front door of one of the apartments, and the two policemen got out.

"The body's upstairs," Eberle said as they crossed the street. "Call came in about ten minutes before I left to pick you up."

The men climbed the two flights of stairs that led to the dead man's apartment, pushing past a knot of curious neighbors on the landing outside the door. A uniformed police officer stopped them just outside the apartment, but Eberle produced his ID, said something in German, and with a smart salute from the policeman on duty, they entered the small flat.

The cramped apartment had, at one time, been one room of not over-generous size. After the war, when housing in Vienna had been at a premium, a couple of flimsy partitions had been put up, and a small kitchen and bath installed. The rest of the apartment had been turned into a bed-sitting room that measured not much more than nine by twelve and was dominated by an ornate brass bed.

A chest of drawers and a small bookcase stood to either side of the bed, and a pair of ancient leather armchairs were huddled next to an enameled stove, the only source of heat for the apartment. A wardrobe was tucked into one corner of the room, and next to that a small fold-top table and two small cane-back chairs stood pressed to the wall under the only window in the room.

Drummond would have described the room as tidy, if it hadn't been littered with cops. Pressing his way into the room with Eberle, Drummond squeezed past a half-dozen of Vienna's finest, most of whom were engaged in cop-talk, the universal chatter of policemen comparing crimes, the latest court rulings, and changing departmental policy. Drummond didn't have to speak German to know what the men were saying; he was part of that universal brotherhood, the freemasonry of law enforcement. Like policemen the world over, he saw society as divided into two classes, the good and the bad, separated only by a thin blue line. As part of that thin blue line, policemen tend to withdraw into a society of their own—a society with its own rules and mores, and a universal language all its own, understood by all cops, regardless of their mother tongue.

"Well," Eberle asked, "what do you think?"

"I think this is a little over-crowded, for one thing," Drummond replied.

"Yeah. Real crime of the century stuff, for most of these guys." Eberle said. "Actually, most of 'em are rookies, still doing their probationary years. They've been called out so that they can see a real live stiff—sorry about that." He gave Drummond a sour grin and continued. "I've had a word with Sacher, the chief investigating officer, and he thinks this was probably a suicide. Subject's name was Hans Stucke."

"What makes him think it was suicide?" Drummond asked.

"Well, take a look for yourself—although before you go into the bathroom, I'd better warn you that the body has been under the shower for at least a week."

Drummond moved past the two young police officers standing at the door to the bathroom and elbowed his way into the cramped little room. A policeman wearing a gray boiler suit and elbow-length plumber's gloves was furiously working away with a snake as he tried to clear a blockage in the drain of the tub. Finally, with a tremendous tug, the snake pulled free and the water began to slowly subside in the porcelain hip bath. The body was leaning back in the corner of the deep tub, its head lolled back against the white-tiled walls, a deep, clean-washed gash opened in the right side of the neck.

As the water began to recede from the edge of the tub, Drummond could see why Eberle had warned him about the condition of the corpse. The spray of the shower had been directed against Stucke's left leg, slowly softening the tissue until it began to fall away from the bone, like some piece of meat left to simmer too long in a stew pot. Finally, the flesh of Stucke's calf had separated from the bone and sunk to the bottom of the tub, momentarily clogging the drain and causing the tub to start filling with water.

But each time the tub filled, Stucke's parboiled flesh had floated to the surface, only to plug the drain again as the tub slowly emptied. During the next few days this cycle was repeated over and over, until several chunks of flesh became impacted in the drain pipe and the tub finally overflowed, attracting the attention of the now sedated Frau Kettleman. Drummond had seen the parboiling effect before, in Los Angeles, when people had died in their hot tubs and their bodies hadn't been discovered for days, or even weeks.

The level of the water in the tub had dropped

enough by now for Drummond to see the pinkish bones in Stucke's lower leg, shreds of skin still clinging to his ankle and foot. The policeman in the rubber gloves was carefully feeling around the bottom of the tub, at once trying to prevent the drain becoming blocked and at the same time searching for something.

"Ah-ha!" he said, holding up an old-fashioned straight razor.

In response, the drain made a thick sucking sound as the last of the water sluiced down the pipe and headed toward the Donau. Another officer was shaking out a black plastic bag, watching a little queasily as his gloved partner began fishing out the soggy chunks of flesh now lying on the bottom of the tub. Trying not to breathe too deeply, Drummond moved back into the sitting room, where he found Eberle talking to another detective.

"John," Eberle said, "I'd like you to meet Alois Sacher, the officer in charge of the investigation."

The two men shook hands.

"So tell me, *Kapitän* Drummond, what do you think of our suicide?" Sacher's accent was heavy, and hard to understand.

"Well," began Drummond, "it was messy enough. What makes you suspect it was suicide?"

"Ha." Sacher's laugh was humorless. "The body of the man is in his bathtub, his razor is lying on the bottom of the tub, and his throat has a cut just so." Sacher brought his index finger up to the side of his neck, indicating Stucke's wound.

"Did he leave a note?" Drummond asked.

"No. But then, his kind rarely do." Sacher made a face.

"His kind? I'm afraid I don't follow." Drummond stared blankly at Sacher.

Sacher looked at Eberle and said something in German, causing Eberle to nod his head in agreement.

"What Alois means, John, is that Herr Stucke over there in the sitzbath was mentally unstable." He gave Drummond a knowing smile, as if to say, *I agree with you, Sacher is jumping to conclusions, but it's his case.*

Drummond smiled at Sacher, and tapped his head with his index finger. "Crazy, huh?"

Sacher smiled. "Yes. That is so. He was in the local precinct offices all the time, claiming that he had seen a Nazi."

"Had he?" Drummond asked.

"Nein, nein," Sacher said impatiently. "When he filed his first complaint, it was sent to Special Investigations. They checked out his 'war criminal,' but the man was at least thirty years too young to have been in the war, let alone the SS."

Drummond could feel a cold knot in the pit of his stomach. "Did Herr Stucke identify the man from photos?"

"Ja—and the resemblance *was* amazing. I suppose almost like a twin." Sacher shook his head. "But from the Special Investigations office we were told that the accused was in his early thirties, and a well-respected businessman. When Herr Stucke came back later, I told him this, but he did not want to believe it. It's often the same with former concentration camp inmates. They think they have seen one of the old guards, and nothing will shake that from their mind." Sacher pulled out a small cigar case from his pocket. "Smoke?"

"No, thanks," said Drummond.

Sacher lit his cigar and blew out a long stream of blue-gray smoke. "Anyhow, Stucke insisted that the man he'd seen was an SS officer by the name of

Kluge, and every week he would come into my office and rant and rave that Kluge should be arrested."

"Kluge? Was that his name?" Drummond asked.

"What? No. Kluge was the SS man. The man Stucke saw was named Hartmann. Why?"

Sacher's discourse was interrupted by the arrival of two ambulance attendants with a stretcher, which they barely managed to maneuver around the bed and set down. A black plastic body bag lay on the stretcher, and one of the men deftly unzipped it and folded it open before glancing expectantly at Sacher, who spoke to them in German and gestured toward the bathroom door.

Drummond had no idea what the one attendant said in response, as they headed toward the door, but it elicited a guffaw from his partner. The partner's laugh died in his throat as they pushed past the policemen and entered the bathroom. Out in the sitting room, Drummond and the others could hear the explosive sound of retching, followed immediately by the curses of several policemen.

A few minutes later, ashen-faced and silent, the two ambulance attendants emerged carrying Stucke's body, which they carefully laid in the open body bag. The older of the two returned to the bathroom, to reemerge a moment later with a smaller black plastic bag that he set squeamishly between the corpse's legs. Zipping the body bag closed over Stucke's remains, they hoisted the stretcher up and carried him down to the waiting ambulance on the street below.

"No stomach for the work," Sacher said, drawing heavily on his cigar. His face brightened. "Let's go have a beer. The boys here can clean things up. Okay?"

Chapter 14

The taxi that collected Drummond from Palais Schwartzenberg the next morning moved through the heavy traffic of Vienna and turned to join the slowly moving parade of cars inching along the inner ring road. As they passed the office building of OPEC, the driver turned slightly toward Drummond and said, "There it is. In the most beautiful city in the world—the ugliest building in Europe!"

Looking out the taxi window, Drummond had to agree. The chrome-and-glass box, surrounded by the baroque splendors of the city, was as ugly as the inside of a barrel of crude oil.

The taxi slowly cruised past OPEC and headed toward the university, finally turning off on Schindler Allee and then threading through a maze of small streets and alleyways until it finally pulled up in front of a dusty yellow building with a faded blue "17" painted above its door.

Drummond paid the driver, got out of the cab, and thoughtfully watched it pull away and vanish down a side street before turning his attention to the building directory. A discreetly polished brass plaque, neatly engraved with a Maltese cross, quietly announced that "Ritterbuchs" was located on the second floor.

Drummond pressed the small button to the side of the plaque.

"Bitte?" The voice was thin and metallic.

"I'm sorry, I don't speak German. I'm John Drummond. I have an appointment with Baron von Liebenfalz."

"Ah, yes. Please come on up, Mr. Drummond."

The metallic voice was replaced by the thick buzz of the security lock. Drummond pushed against the door and entered the lobby of number seventeen. It was like stepping through the doorway of a time machine, instantly taking him back to the gilded age that was Europe before the First World War.

The lobby of the building was a temple to the Vienna school of art nouveau, with glittering mosaics by Muscha adorning the walls and a double staircase sweeping gracefully along two sides of the room, its intricate bronze railings a delicate shade of blue, replete with gold-leafed foliage. Rising out of the cream-and-green tiled floor between the wings of the staircase was the elaborately gilded dome of a baroque elevator, appropriately framed by a veritable forest of potted palms.

Drummond made his way under the crystal chandelier to the elevator and slid back the golden grill to step in. A large brass panel set at eye level housed a row of mother-of-pearl buttons, each engraved with a small portrait of Venus. Drummond paused for a moment before pressing the one next to a card marked "von Liebenfalz."

From behind the panel he heard a muffled click, but nothing happened. He pressed the button again. Another click, but still the elevator remained earthbound. He was about to press the button a third time when a voice drifted down to him from somewhere up above.

"Herr Drummond. You will have to use the stairs; the lift is out of order."

Stepping out of the elevator, Drummond headed up the stairs two at a time.

The only door on the second floor was painted a deep green, and before Drummond could even raise his hand to knock, it was opened by a tall, elderly gentleman with the same air of genteel breeding as the men he had met when he dined with the baroness.

"Please come in, Mr. Drummond. I'm Baron von Liebenfalz."

The baron's apartment was as aristocratic as his accent. The first thing Drummond saw as he followed his host inside was a silver-framed photograph of Dr. Otto Habsburg, occupying a place of honor on a small giltwood table opposite the door. Next to it was a silver box bearing the arms of Imperial Austria and the cypher of King Carl, last of the Austro-Hungarian emperors. A large parchment document hung above the table, in a severe gold frame, boasting several coats of arms and with the signature of the Emperor Franz-Josef at the bottom.

Von Liebenfalz led Drummond past all of this and through a tiny formal sitting room, ushering him into a larger study-cum-library, where the aroma of Viennese coffee mingled with the dusty smell of old leather-bound books, tinged with the subtle bouquet of fine pipes and heady tobacco. Above the pale marble fireplace, a beautiful woman in an equally pale blue silk ballgown of an earlier century gazed down serenely on two worn leather club chairs and a small fruitwood table groaning under the weight of a silver coffee service.

"Please, sit down," von Liebenfalz said, indicating one of the chairs with a graceful gesture. "I hope you like coffee."

"Certainly." Drummond took the delicate cup and saucer the baron offered him. "Thank you."

"Austrian society—that is to say, Viennese society, which *is* Austrian society—runs on coffee," von Liebenfalz explained, "just as Rolls-Royce cars run on petrol." The baron took a sip from his own cup. "Ah, excellent." He smiled, obviously pleased not only with his coffee, but with himself as well.

"Now, Mr. Drummond. In his letter of introduction, Mr. Keating indicated that you had expressed interest in the Order of the Sword." He set down his cup and saucer on the table. "Do you mind if I ask why you would wish to enter this ancient order of knighthood?"

An order of knighthood? It took Drummond several seconds to reorient his thoughts.

"I wasn't sure that the Order of the Sword was an order of the knighthood, sir. I thought that it was a religious order of some sort, something like the Trappists."

Von Liebenfalz refilled the two cups from the silver coffee pot.

"Oh, it *is* a religious order—but a religious order of chivalry, not monks." He handed Drummond his cup. "I am afraid that I must have misinterpreted Mr. Keating's letter. I thought you wanted to be admitted to its ranks."

Drummond balanced the ridiculously small cup and saucer between his hands. "No, I'm not interested in becoming a knight, or whatever you'd call it. I'm interested in finding out about the Order of the Sword for a research paper I'm working on, back home in California."

"Ah." Von Liebenfalz set down his coffee and

stared at the ceiling. "Normally, Mr. Drummond, I receive a small honorarium for providing—how shall I put it?—an introduction to the various orders of chivalry, once a person has been admitted. . . ."

Drummond was quick on the uptake. "Naturally, sir, I would expect to pay a research fee to reimburse you for your efforts on my behalf."

Von Liebenfalz smiled at Drummond. "That's very thoughtful. As it happens, I have already prepared a brief history of the Order of the Sword." He stood and walked across the room to a well-polished oak desk, where he picked up a file folder and removed several neatly typed pages. He brought these to Drummond and handed them to him, but he did not sit down.

"This should answer most of your questions, I think. If not, then please telephone me and we'll discuss the matter in greater detail." Von Liebenfalz' manner indicated that their meeting was over, and Drummond got to his feet, folding the pages and slipping them into an inside pocket.

"Thank you," Drummond said. "What about your fee?"

"I have your address in America. I'll send you a fee note—or, if you'd prefer, I shall send it to your hotel."

"The hotel will be just fine. I'm staying at Palais Schwartzenberg."

Von Liebenfalz arched one eyebrow slightly. "I know it well. Unless I hear from you in the next day or so, then, I shall send the bill to the Palais." The baron shook Drummond's hand. "Now, if there are no more questions?"

"Only one, sir."

Von Liebenfalz looked puzzled. "What is that?"

"The woman in the painting—" Drummond gestured toward the pale vision still gazing down at them. "Do you mind if I ask who she is?"

Cocking his head to one side, von Liebenfalz gazed up fondly at the portrait.

"That," he said, "is Carlotta, Empress of Mexico. She was a distant cousin of mine." He smiled slightly at the lovely face of the woman in the painting. "She is beautiful, isn't she?"

"Yes, sir, she is."

Von Liebenfalz walked Drummond to the door then, shaking hands again before bidding him a final good-bye. When the American had disappeared down the stairwell, von Liebenfalz closed the door softly and returned to his study, where he went quickly to the telephone and dialed a number. He waited nervously for what seemed like an interminable number of rings, until a hollow series of clicks indicated that the line had been picked up.

"Your Eminence, this is Liebenfalz," the baron said. "I have just spoken with the man inquiring about the Order of the Sword—"

A voice on the other end of the line said something, interrupting von Liebenfalz before he could finish his sentence.

"Certainly, Your Eminence. I will attend to it immediately."

The line went dead, and von Liebenfalz carefully replaced the handset on the cradle. Then, opening the center drawer of his desk, he removed a small screwdriver and, without bothering to close the drawer, left his apartment and trotted down the stairs to the lobby below.

There was no sign of the American. Entering the elevator, von Liebenfalz undid the four screws that held the elevator control panel in place and pulled it away from the wall. A small Leica camera was mounted behind, and he removed it and rewound the film before opening the back. When he had removed the exposed film, he dropped it in his pocket, replacing it with a fresh roll from a niche behind the panel before carefully setting the camera back in place. He replaced the control panel and snugged down the four screws quickly. Then, fingering the roll of film in his pocket, he returned to his apartment, and the small darkroom set up adjoining his kitchen.

Drummond, meanwhile, had found himself obliged to walk several blocks before he could find a taxi stand after leaving von Liebenfalz' apartment. When he climbed into the dark blue Mercedes, however, he handed the driver a slip of paper with an address written on it. He tried to look at von Liebenfalz' report as he settled back for the ride across town, but he had hardly gotten past the first page, when the cab pulled up to the curb in front of a nondescript office building on the edge of the business district.

He paid the driver and got out of the car, glancing around him with the automatic assessment of a cop as he walked toward the entrance. Sunlight reflected off the small brass plate that identified the offices of the Simon Weisenthal Center, and he opened the door and went in. Inside, a pert, dark-haired receptionist at a large circular desk looked up as Drummond approached. He was surprised to be greeted in English.

"Can I help you, sir?" The receptionist looked and sounded like a typical Valley girl.

"Well, I hope so. I'm looking for some information on a former SS officer by the name of Kluge."

"You'd need to see one of our researchers." She pouted slightly. "Did you have an appointment?"

"No," said Drummond, "I don't. Do I need one?"

"Well, yeah, sort of. I mean, we're really busy and kinda short-handed, so it's always best if you write to us and ask for an appointment." She gave Drummond a room-temperature smile.

Drummond reached into his jacket pocket and brought out his ID case.

"I'm a police officer," he said showing her his badge, "and I need this information for a case I'm investigating." He gave the girl his most ingratiating smile. "Do you think you could find a researcher for me?"

"Wow, an American cop! For sure." She picked up the telephone next to her and pressed some buttons. Someone on the other end of the line answered, and in halting German the receptionist made an inquiry. Replacing the receiver, she turned her full attention to Drummond.

"So, where're you from in the States?" she asked.

"L.A. How about yourself?" Drummond could have guessed.

"Encino. I'm Button Horowitz." She held out her hand. "What's your name?"

"John Drummond, ma'am. LAPD." Drummond did his best to sound like Jack Webb.

"Oh, that's neat! You sounded just like Dan Akroyd in the movie, *Dragnet*."

Drummond decided that her room-temperature smile probably masked a room-temperature IQ.

"So tell me, Button—" he couldn't believe the name; her parents ought to be shot "—what are you doing here?"

"My parents wanted me to get in touch with my heritage—you know, work on a kibbutz or something. Anyhow, that sounded like a real bummer, so I wrote to the center here, and they offered me a job for the summer. I mean, if you had a choice between some yucky farm or Vienna, which would you choose?"

Before Drummond could agree with her, he was saved—if that was the word for it—by the arrival of a woman he assumed was the researcher. Whereas Button was tall and full of life, this woman was short, dumpy, and looked at him over her glasses with the zeal of the totally committed.

Drummond wondered what she would do in another fifteen years, when the youngest of the men she was dedicated to tracking down would be over ninety. He felt sorry for her, because time was now her enemy. With each passing day, another decrepit war criminal slipped silently into his grave, having eluded the dogged pursuit of the researchers there at the center. Eventually the last of them would die off, and the center would have no real purpose. It might remain as a memorial to its founder, or perhaps be converted into a museum, but its real purpose would be gone forever. And its employees, like the mousy woman from research, would be nothing more than hollow ghosts whose lives had been spent in the pursuit of old, old men whom most of the world no longer really cared about.

"How may I help you?" The researcher's voice was as plain as the rest of her.

"I'm looking for information on an SS officer named Kluge," Drummond replied.

"And why do you want this information?"

"It's part of an investigation." He showed her his badge. "I'm with the police in America."

She looked at his ID card. "You are *Kapitän* Drummond?"

Drummond nodded. "Yes, that's me. And you are?"

"Magda Krebs. I work in the research department here at the Weisenthal Center." Her voice sounded drained in life. "Do you have any other information on this Kluge?" she asked.

"Nope. Just a name." Drummond tried to read some reaction on Magda's face, but all he saw was a blank.

"Well, come with me, and we'll check the main files."

The files at the Weisenthal Center were housed in hundreds of filing cabinets crammed into every room on every floor of the building. Trudging up a flight of dimly lit stairs, Magda led Drummond into a narrow corridor lined with files.

"These are service records of SS officers. They aren't complete, because we simply don't have the files on everyone who served in the SS between 1923 and 1945. This section covers J and K, and they are more or less in alphabetical order."

She gave Drummond an exhausted look. "You start here," she indicated one of the dark green filing cabinets, "and I'll start over there."

Drummond didn't relish the prospect of several hours digging through the gray folders stuffed in the file cabinets.

"Excuse me, Ms. Krebs, but it's just possible that the file may have been recently copied for the Vienna Police, Office of Special Investigations. If that's the case, would it have been returned to these files, or put somewhere else?"

Drummond knew that if this was anything like the Los Angeles Hall of Records, it could take months for a file to be returned to its rightful place.

"Ah. If the OSI had a copy of the file made,

then it would be downstairs in the activity center."
A glimmer of interest sparked behind the woman's
eyes. "Come with me, *Kapitän*."

Trudging down the stairs, they walked past Button Horowitz, talking animatedly on the phone behind the reception desk, and went into a small but
well-lit office that overlooked the street. Stepping
behind a high counter, Magda pulled out two large
ledgers from the shelf below and dropped them
down in front of Drummond.

"In this one are the police requests," she shoved
the book across to Drummond, "and in this one
the civil requests. You check out the police."

It took Drummond only a few minutes to find
the entry he was looking for.

"Here it is," he said, turning the book and sliding
it back to the other side of the counter.

Magda Krebs made a note of the file number,
then turned to a large Rolodex next to her. Slowly
turning the wheel on the side, she stopped when
she came to the index number that matched the
number in the ledger Drummond had been searching.

"Well," she said, "your Wilhelm Kluge is a popular man. The Vienna police want to know about
him, and an old man named Stucke wants to know
about him. I'll get the file for you."

She turned away from the counter and vanished
through a door on the other side of the room, and
Drummond took the opportunity to check the dates
in the Rolodex and also to take down the address
of Hans Stucke, which he had neglected to note last
night. Stucke's request for the file had been made
almost two months ago, and it had been nearly six
weeks since the Vienna police requested the file.

Drummond glanced out the window as he did
some quick calculations. Stucke's body had been in

the shower for at least a week, and it had probably taken the office of Special Investigations a couple of weeks to hunt down the Kluge look-alike. That left not more than three weeks of Stucke's life open to speculation, as far as Drummond was concerned.

Suicide, eh? He'd bet all the strudel in Austria that Alois Sacher wouldn't bother to check into the last three weeks of the old man's life.

The researcher returned, carrying a slim gray file. "Here it is, such as we have. I can make a copy for you, if you care to come back tomorrow. Our Xerox machine is down right now." She handed Drummond the file.

Drummond flipped through it quickly before handing it back, but it was mostly in German. He would need a translator if it was to be of much use, but he'd worry about that later.

"Yes, I think I *would* like a copy, please. What time tomorrow can I pick it up?"

"Any time after lunch. Here." She handed Drummond a form to fill out. "I need your name and address here in Vienna, just on those two lines— so." She pointed to the spaces Drummond had to fill in. "When you come back tomorrow, ask at reception and they'll have your copy of the file ready." She took the form from Drummond's hand and glanced at it. "The Palais Schwartzenberg. That's fine, Herr Drummond. *Auf wiedersehen.*"

"*Auf wiedersehen, Fräulein,*" Drummond replied, watching her perk up at the form of address. "And thank you."

Outside the Weisenthal Center, Drummond hailed a taxi and handed the driver the piece of paper with Stucke's address written on it. He recognized the outside of the building from the night before, as his driver pulled up across the street, and he handed him a one hundred schilling note as he climbed out of the car.

"Wait here, *bitte,*" Drummond said, pointing at the ground next to the cab. "Here. Stay here. Okay?"

"Ja," said the driver. *"Hier."*

"Good," said Drummond as he turned and started to cross the street to Stucke's apartment. He hadn't made it to the opposite curb before the taxi pulled away and drove off down the street.

"Shit!" was all Drummond could say, as the cab vanished around the corner.

Drummond had worried about making himself understood, but he was able to overcome his lack of German by handing the concierge a thousand schilling note in exchange for the key to Stucke's apartment. Unlocking the door, he stepped quietly inside and closed it behind him, trying to get a better feel for the place, now that all the police were gone.

Little details suggested that someone had been through the place pretty thoroughly. Not the police, he guessed, if official procedure here was anything like at home. In cases of suicide, any official search was apt to be extremely casual, confined to a cursory look-around for suicide notes and the like. In circumstances like this, though, it was quite likely that another search had been made after the police left—possibly the building's concierge, looking for anything of value before the state assessor came to impound everything, ultimately to be sold at auction if Stucke had no heirs.

Drummond quickly glanced around the room and decided to start his own search in the chest of drawers beside the bed. What he was looking for would not have appealed to the police or to avaricious landlords.

A quick search through the drawers revealed a few pair of socks and some underwear, a few shirts, nothing else. The wardrobe in the corner held a shabby overcoat, a worn-out pair of trousers, and a pair of galoshes that had been mended with black electrician's tape, but was otherwise empty. Checking under the bed, Drummond struck pay-dirt.

The battered cardboard box at first appeared to contain only a thick stack of girlie magazines; but after lifting up only two, Drummond uncovered a fat scrapbook and a copy of SS *Sturmbannführer* Wilhelm Kluge's file from the Weisenthal Center.

Sitting on the edge of the bed, Drummond took a quick look at the copy of the file, then turned his attention to the scrapbook, which was filled with newspaper cuttings. He flipped through the book page by page, trying to make some sense from the German headlines that were neatly pasted on each page. Suddenly he came to a banner headline that even he could understand. One word in heavy black type covered the entire top of the page: "EICHMANN."

So, he thought, *this is it. A collection of newspaper clippings that relate to Nazi war criminals.*

He thumbed through a few more pages. Maybe Sacher was right, and Stucke *was* emotionally disturbed. The scrapbook certainly was the work of an obsessive personality: neat, with precise margins, every clipping carefully pasted into place.

Drummond looked around the room. Other than drawers left slightly ajar from the search, everything was in precisely the right spot. The coat and trousers in the wardrobe, the socks and underwear in the dresser, the shoes . . .

He hadn't seen any shoes. Setting the scrapbook aside, Drummond went back to the wardrobe and opened the door. Inside were the trousers and coat, and on the floor the worn-out galoshes, but no shoes. Dropping to his hands and knees, Drummond looked under the bed and dresser.

No shoes. None in the kitchen or bathroom, either. Nor, as he looked more closely at the bathroom walls, did this look like a place where a man had slashed his throat with a straight razor. He should have noticed it before, but there had been too many people crowding the tiny room. Blood should have been everywhere. It couldn't all have washed down the drain.

Having searched both rooms, he came back into the sitting room and had one final look around before closing the cardboard box on the girlie magazines and sliding it back under the bed. He tucked the scrapbook and Stucke's copy of the file on Kluge under his arm, heading out of the apartment and downstairs to the street below. On his way out, he paused to drop the key through the mail slot of the concierge's door.

Outside in the fresh air, in the late afternoon sun, Drummond started walking, clutching his bundle under his arm. He now was certain of one thing: Stucke had been murdered, and his body brought back to his apartment and stuck in the shower to make it look like suicide. Whoever killed Stucke had either carried off his blood-soaked clothes, or had left them behind at the scene of the crime. Including the missing shoes.

Drummond brought his hand up to his neck. Where was it Sacher had indicated the wound? He placed his fingers over his carotid artery on the right side of his throat. Deep within the muscles of his neck, he could feel the steady throb of arterial blood. No, an old man with a straight razor wouldn't cut his own throat. The pain would be too intense; he would have to cut too deep.

There was something else, too. Briefly screwing his eyes shut, Drummond tried to recall a mental picture of the body in the hip bath. Stucke's blue-white corpse was leaning back in the corner of the deep tub, his head lolled against the white-tiled walls. The shower might have washed away some of the blood, if he'd really done it in the tub, as Sacher maintained, but not all. No, the tile walls were spotless, as if they had been wiped clean. If Stucke had killed himself, the walls and ceilings would have been sprayed with blood pumping from the severed artery.

There was no longer any doubt in Drummond's mind. Stucke had been killed somewhere else, and his body brought back to his apartment to make it look like suicide. Leaving the shower running on the corpse had been a clever touch. The combined effect of the heat and the pressure of the water on the body would cause the flesh to fall away from the bones, enough to distract most cops from the absence of blood on the walls.

The absence of blood . . . Drummond let the thought trail off. A sudden gust of wind made him shiver as early evening closed in on Vienna. Across the street he saw a taxi, and dodging an electric streetcar, he hurried to where it was parked.

"Palais Schwartzenberg, *bitte*," he said as he climbed in.

The driver grunted and pulled out into the closing darkness.

Chapter 15

The concierge met Drummond in the lobby of Palais Schwartzenberg and handed him his room key and a small buff-colored envelope.

"Your telephone messages, *Kapitän*."

"Thank you," Drummond said as he pocketed the envelope.

"You are welcome, *Kapitän*," the concierge said, and bowing slightly, returned to his desk.

Drummond took the half-dozen steps to the corridor that led to his room two at a time. Sliding the key into the lock, he had just opened the door when the phone rang. Leaving the door open, he stepped into his sitting room and picked up the phone.

"Hello?"

"Hi, John. It's Markus." Eberle sounded his usual buoyant self.

"How are you doing?"

"I'm starving to death. How about dinner?"

Drummond looked at his watch. It was nearly seven-thirty, and he realized that he hadn't eaten since breakfast.

"That sounds like a great idea. Where and when?"

"The 'where' is a surprise. The 'when' is in about

twenty minutes. That give you enough time to shave, shower, and shampoo?" Eberle asked.

"Sure," said Drummond. "See you at eight." And then, almost as an afterthought, "Hey, Markus, how fancy is this place we're going to?"

"Not fancy at all. Don't bother with a tie. See you at eight." With a chuckle, Eberle hung up.

Drummond set down the phone and opened the envelope the concierge had given him to look at his phone messages. Eberle had phoned twice, obviously trying to touch base about dinner. There had been a call from the Weisenthal Center—Drummond wondered if it had been Button or Magda—and a call from von Liebenfalz.

Looking at his watch, Drummond decided that all of the calls could wait until morning. Draping his suit jacket over the back of a chair, he headed upstairs for a fast shower.

Clean but hungry, Drummond dressed in a hurry, pulling on a pair of blue corduroy trousers, a starched white shirt, and black Gucci loafers. He had just picked up a lightweight gray leather jacket and was going out the door when the phone rang. Imagining it must be Eberle in the lobby, Drummond closed the door and headed down the corridor.

The huge beer hall was crowded, and Egon felt mildly uncomfortable sitting across the table from the unattractive woman Kluge had sent him to meet. He felt awkward anyway, because Kluge had told him to get rid of the technicolor Mohawk. Egon still wasn't used to the skinhead look, though he had to admit that it was much less conspicuous.

Returning his attention to his dinner companion, Egon found himself wondering if she had ever slept with a man. Not that he thought she might be a lesbian, but rather that she looked like the sort of woman whose features and personality would keep most men away. He couldn't tell how old she was, but then Kluge didn't look his age, either.

Maybe, he thought, *she's one of us*.

Egon still couldn't really believe that Kluge had finally shared his power with him. For a moment, he thought back to the night that Jurg had been killed, when Egon had been sure that his own death was only a matter of time—a *short* time.

He had taken the Jew's body back to the apartment as ordered, not daring to disobey. When he got there, Kluge had been waiting outside in the shadows. Together they had wrapped the dead man in the tarp in the back of the van, and then Kluge, tossing the body over his shoulder like a sack of potatoes, had carried it up the stairs to the apartment.

Inside, Kluge had placed the old man's body in the hip bath and then turned on the shower, making sure the spray was focused on the dead man's leg. Then, reaching into his coverall pocket, he had produced an old-fashioned straight razor and flicked it open, staring at its blue and gilded blade in the half-light of the apartment.

"Come here, Egon."

The voice had been dispassionate but commanding. In his soul, Egon felt he was about to die, but he was unable to offer any resistance. Despite the total dread that encompassed his very being, he managed to walk over to where Kluge stood in the semi-darkness, just outside the bathroom.

Only the pale light of the single streetlamp down on the sidewalk below found its way into the apartment through the one tiny window in the sitting room. Staring at Kluge, Egon watched as he slowly unzipped his black coverall to the waist, exposing the smooth white flesh of his chest.

Lifting the razor in his right hand, Kluge pressed the blade against his chest until the steel corner suddenly punctured the skin. Pulling downward on the polished bone handle, Kluge made an inch-long incision in his chest above his heart.

Egon watched with horrible fascination as the blood welled up around the blade and trickled down Kluge's chest like a rivulet of blackness in the shadow light of the apartment. As Kluge's hand took the blade away, letting it fall to the floor, the distant hissing of the shower seemed to drown out any other sound save Kluge's soft voice.

"Come here, Egon."

Clutching Egon's head between his hands, Kluge forced Egon's mouth over the wound on his chest.

"Drink."

Egon sucked at the wound, his mouth filling with Kluge's hot blood. He swallowed, the hot, salty fluid clutching at his throat. He sucked harder, swallowing more of Kluge's blood, feeling himself growing weak at the knees. Kluge sensed his impending collapse and put one of his arms under Egon's arm pits, holding him up.

"Drink," he commanded again.

Egon obeyed, and it became an almost sexual euphoria. Finally, when Egon thought he could bear no more, Kluge pushed him away and let him collapse boneless to the floor, at the same time retrieving the straight razor.

Walking into the bathroom, Kluge carefully wiped the handle clean of any fingerprints, then dropped it into the tub by Stucke's feet. Still a little dazed, Egon watched as Kluge returned to the darkened sitting room, pulled shut the bathroom door, then turned and looked at him, smiling slightly as he placed his hand over the cut on his chest and pinched it closed, holding it between his thumb and forefinger for a few seconds while he stared at Egon. When he let go, it had stopped bleeding, although an angry red welt remained where the wound had been. Egon simply could not summon up the will to move.

Kluge zipped up his coverall, then leaned over and pulled Egon to his feet. Half dragging him by the wrist, he took him downstairs and out to the van. Shoving him behind the wheel, he stared hard into Egon's eyes.

"Go back to the warehouse and collect Jurg's body. Take it out to the country and dump it."

Egon nodded.

"Any mistakes, and you'll wish you had died with him. Understand?" Kluge's voice was as clear as ice water.

Egon nodded, wide-eyed, but Kluge leaned closer to grasp his bicep again.

"*Do you understand,* Egon? Say it."

"Yes, Master," Egon managed to whisper.

"Excellent." Kluge released him and smiled. "And Egon—"

"Sir?"

"Get rid of the hair?"

Egon nodded without speaking, any thought of disobedience gone forever, and started the van. . . .

Sitting opposite the woman Kluge had sent him to meet, in the noisy beer hall, Egon found himself reflecting that it all seemed like it had happened a hundred years ago. He wondered what it would be like in another hundred years, when he would still be twenty-two. How old would the woman be?

The waiter brought two plates of wurst and sauerkraut, along with two steins of beer, and set them down in front of the oddly matched couple. They consumed the meal in silence, and after paying the bill, the woman handed Egon a slip of paper with an address on it. Egon nodded; he and the woman both got up to leave.

Outside, a black BMW pulled up in front of the beer hall and parked under the "No Parking" symbol. Grinning, his two stainless steel teeth flashing in the light of the streetlamp, Eberle tossed a PO-LICE VEHICLE sign up on the dash.

"Come on, John," he said. "Now I'm going to treat you to some real Austrian food."

The two men got out of the car and headed inside. Past an entry vestibule, the huge, low-ceilinged room was filled with long tables crowded with students drinking to excess and all talking at the top of their voices. Scattered around the edge of the room were smaller tables, and in the very back, obscured by the blue haze of cigar and cigarette smoke, were half a dozen booths.

"This way," Eberle shouted, to make himself heard above the din. "I've reserved us a booth in the back."

Grabbing Drummond by the elbow, he steered him down a half-flight of stairs and past the noisy tables of students. As they approached the booths, a short, fat man with bald head and drooping walrus moustaches stepped in front of them, blocking their path.

"Name?" he demanded in German. "Gotta have your name. All these booths are reserved. No name, no booth."

Eberle grinned at the man. "Hitler. Name's Hitler. Haven't been here for about fifty years, but I'm sure you remember me."

Distracted by Eberle's baiting of the waiter, Drummond hardly noticed the punker with the tattoo on his cheek and his mousy female companion, just getting up from one of the small tables near the wall. The two were far less memorable than many of the patrons of the establishment. He had determined to enjoy himself as he followed Eberle and the waiter to their booth.

Eberle had been right about the food. It was delicious. The wurst was tangy and succulent, and the kraut, served with applesauce, had a zest of its own. Washed down with several steins of beer, it was one of the most satisfying meals Drummond could ever recall having eaten. The bohemian atmosphere created by the raucous students at the long tables provided the perfect backdrop to the meal as the two men settled back to their coffees, Eberle lighting up one of his ubiquitous cigars.

"So, John, what did you see today?"

"Not much in the way of tourist attractions, I'm afraid," Drummond replied. "I spent most of the day doing some research for my master's thesis."

"Oh, really?" Eberle blew a lazy smoke ring at the ceiling. "Where was that?"

"At a place called Ritterbuchs, over on the edge of the second district. It's run by—"

"Baron von Liebenfalz," Eberle supplied.

"Yeah. Do you know him?" Drummond asked.

Eberle cleared his throat. "Let's just say that he is not unknown in our professional circles."

"Really? Is he one of the regulars on the fraud squad lists?"

"Oh, no. Nothing so uncomplicated as fraud." Eberle reached for his coffee. "During the war, when Austria was occupied by Hitler's Reich, his home was the headquarters of the *Ahnenerbe*."

"What's the *Ahnenerbe*?" Drummond asked.

"Oh, it was a special branch of the SS. They spent all of their time investigating witchcraft, occult sciences, Freemasonry, and the like. Anyhow, in 1938, two days after the *Anschluss,* they rounded up a bunch of Freemasons, took them to 'Number 17,' as the *Ahnenerbe* headquarters was known, and executed them."

Drummond set down his empty coffee cup. "Why wasn't von Liebenfalz arrested as a war criminal then, when the war was over?"

"He was in Switzerland at the time—an iron-clad alibi. Besides, after the war, the Austrian government decided to prosecute the *German* officer in charge of the executions, instead." Eberle looked at his watch.

"Gads, it'd nearly midnight. We'd better head back. I've got to be in court in the morning." Tossing two hundred-schilling notes on the table, Eberle stood up and stretched. "Drop you back at your hotel?"

"No thanks, Markus." Drummond smiled at his friend. "I think I'll walk."

The night air was crisper than he thought, and Drummond could feel it reaching through his lightweight leather jacket like some gigantic cold hand slowly squeezing the breath out of his lungs. Ignoring the cold, he walked on towards the heart of the city, retreating to the comfort of a taxi only when a light rain started to fall.

Back at his hotel, the night porter greeted him at the door, and Drummond made his way back to his room. The room was stuffy and overheated. Obviously the staff had turned on the heat to compensate for the cold front that was moving through Vienna, but Drummond found the temperature uncomfortable. Walking over to the French doors that led to a small balcony outside his room, he opened them wide, then shed his jacket and tossed it over the back of a nearby chair.

Stucke's copy of the report from the Weisenthal Center was lying on top of a small writing desk in one corner of the sitting room. The report was in German, so Drummond was unable to do more than just look at the first few pages of closely typed material. Further on were German military forms, but even without a dictionary, Drummond had no trouble figuring them out.

Kluge must have been the embodiment of Hitler's "ideal" Nazi. Looking at the photocopy of his ID picture, Drummond saw a ruggedly handsome young man with neatly clipped blond hair in an immaculate black uniform, the silver SS runes and three pips of a second lieutenant on his collar tabs.

Next to the photo, Kluge's physical description tallied with Drummond's first impressions. After a bit of number crunching, Drummond decided that at 183 centimeters tall and 75 kilos in weight, Kluge had been just on six feet tall and weighed just under a hundred and seventy pounds. According to his birthdate, he had been just twenty when the picture was taken, which would have made him twenty-six in 1944. The rest of the page was unintelligible, although Drummond guessed that most of it must have related to Kluge's overall physical condition.

The next page seemed to be some sort of assessment sheet. Down one side of the page there were a number of questions, and opposite these were five boxes. Most of the tick marks were in the first two boxes, with only one showing a tick in the last box. Drummond immediately resolved to buy a German-

English dictionary, so he could find out what Kluge's one apparent failure was.

The next page was a list of place names, and Drummond speculated that it might be a list of Kluge's duty assignments. Running his finger down the list, he saw that the first entry was for Lichterfelde. The dates next to it indicated that Kluge was there for nearly two years before being transferred to Wewelsberg.

After less than a year he was posted to Wien—Vienna—arriving there in December of 1937. In April of 1938, he was again posted to Wewelsberg, this time until May of 1944. After that date was written *Sonderkommado der Ahnenerbe-SS*. Drummond wondered what it meant.

The last page in the file was a copy of a document in English, prepared by the U.S. forces occupying Vienna at the end of the war. After the usual military headings and codes there followed three very short paragraphs.

1. This department has conducted a thorough investigation into the execution of twelve civilians on 15 March 1938 in the alley adjacent to SS HQ at 17 Dietrich Eckart Strasse.

2. All evidence indicates that the victims were arrested and executed on the direct order of SS Haupsturmführer (Captain) Wilhelm Kluge.

3. This department therefore requests the Judge-Advocate General to prepare an indictment citing the above named German officer as having committed war crimes on the date first set out in this document.

Wm. Logsdon, Major AUS

Drummond stared at the document for several minutes, slowly gathering his thoughts. The scenario that confronted him seemed impossible, but just as Sherlock Holmes said to Dr. Watson, "Once you have eliminated the possible, what remains, no matter how impossible it may seem, is the truth."

Drummond had several impossibles to deal with. He had a priest who admitted killing half a dozen "Nazis," as well as a Mexican gardener, in Los Angeles back in the early seventies, because they were vampires. The priest had vaguely connected the vampire notion with an obscure order of knights supposedly living in a castle in Luxembourg.

His only lead for more information on the knights had brought him into contract with an eccentric Austrian aristocrat whose home was the former headquarters of some strange branch of the SS dedicated—or so it would seem—to the eradication of Freemasony.

Then there was Stucke—some pitiable survivor of Hitler's holocaust who turns up dead in a bathtub within a month of telling the police he's spotted Wilhelm Kluge, the man the U.S. Army said was responsible for the execution of the twelve Freemasons at von Liebenfalz' home.

The room was getting chilly, and Drummond decided to close the doors to the terrace. Neatly stacking the papers to one side of the desk, he stood up and turned toward the open doors.

The intruder froze where he was for just an instant, and then, as Drummond turned to face him, sprang forward with all his might.

In his surprise, Drummond was taken totally unawares, and crashed to the floor as his assailant slammed into him. Reflexively, Drummond tried to roll away from his attacker, but found himself tangled in the broken legs of the writing desk. Struggling to distance himself from man who had leaped on him, Drummond saw the glint of something bright in his adversary's right hand.

Lashing out with both feet, Drummond kicked himself free, and struggling to his knees threw a round-house punch that landed square on the side of his assailant's head. Reeling under the blow, the punk sagged slightly, and Drummond was able to scramble to his feet.

In an instant, the punk was after him, taking a vicious swipe with his knife that came within inches of laying open Drummond's belly. Drummond jumped back, and instantly dropped forward into a crouching position, well-balanced on the balls of his feet.

The punk lunged again, and Drummond caught his wrist in both hands, twisting and pressing down as he pulled his attacker closer. Shifting his weight, Drummond suddenly lifted straight up and heard a loud *pop* as the arm was dislocated from the shoulder.

The punk sagged slightly, then delivered a vicious kick aimed at Drummond's groin. Letting go of the punker's wrist, Drummond jumped back, the kick glancing painfully off the point of his hip.

Eyes blazing, the punk stepped away from Drummond and put his back against the wall. Crazily, Drummond noticed that he had a tattoo on his right cheek—the tattoo of a rose. Slowly lifting his dislocated arm, the knife still clutched in his hand, the punker suddenly gave an almighty jerk—and the arm snapped back into the shoulder socket.

Drummond watched in utter amazement, his only thought that the skinhead had to be on drugs in order to withstand that much pain. The punk slowly circled around towards Drummond, who now stood with his back to the wall. Drummond took advantage of his position and moved closer to the open

French doors, determined to make a dash for it if he had the chance. The chance came.

There was a heavy pounding on his door as the concierge shouted, "*Kapitän* Drummond, *Kapitän* Drummond, are you all right?"

For an instant the punk hesitated, and Drummond made his dash for the open doors. The punk leaped at Drummond but missed. Crashing to the floor, he grabbed Drummond's ankle, causing him to trip. Drummond recovered his balance and turned to face his attacker, just in time to see the knife coming arching down toward his chest.

Somehow Drummond was detached from what was happening, almost as if he were watching someone else fighting for his life. It was as if everything in the world was happening in slow motion, and he had a ringside seat. He watched the fist clenching the knife as it came bearing down on him, and saw his hand come up and catch it just behind the wrist. He turned slightly and, bracing his body, felt a slight bump as his hip connected with his assailant's body. Bowing slightly, he could hear the rustle of the punk's clothes as he slowly sailed past his head. Turning his neck slightly, Drummond watched as his would-be killer drifted past and vanished over the edge of the balcony.

Suddenly the world was moving at full speed again. Drummond heard a scream as the punk went over the edge and crashed down on the spikes of the ornate wrought iron railing that surrounded the Palais Schwartzenberg. Breathless, he ran to the balcony and looked down.

In the moonlight, his attacker lay limply across the top of the railing, two ugly spikes projecting through the back of his black leather jacket. As

Drummond watched, he stopped twitching and for a moment lay very still.

Then slowly, and with great determination, the attacker grabbed the top bar of the railing and simply pushed himself up off the spikes. For a moment, he balanced himself straight-armed on the top rail, then swung his legs to the side and over the top with the ease of a gymnast and dropped to the ground below. Impossibly, disappearing in the shadows and darkness, he trotted off in the direction of the Belvedere Palace.

The door to Drummond's room slammed into the wall as the concierge and night porter burst into Drummond's sitting room.

"My God, what has happened?" The concierge sounded on the verge of hysteria.

"Someone came in through the window and attacked me." Drummond surveyed the room for the first time. Aside from the shattered desk and a few pictures that had been knocked askew on the walls, the room had survived pretty much intact. The night porter came back from the balcony carrying a large, high-power flashlight just as two uniformed policeman came through the door.

A quick exchange in German ensued between the concierge and the police, then the concierge turned to Drummond.

"The police would like you to go with them to make a statement at the police station, *Kapitän*." The concierge made the police request sound like an apology.

Drummond walked over to his jacket, still draped on the back of the chair, and stuck his hand into his jacket pocket, pulling out his badge wallet and something else—the rosary Father Freise had given him several weeks before. Drummond looked at it for a second, then stuck it back in his pocket. Turning to the two policemen, he handed them his ID.

"Tell these gentlemen," he said to the concierge, "that I'll be happy to make a statement in the morning. I've pulled a few muscles, and I'd like to have a hot bath before I tighten up. If they have any questions, they can check with Inspector Markus Eberle."

The concierge translated for Drummond, and one of the policemen saluted as he handed back Drummond's ID. They spoke with the concierge for a few more minutes, then left.

"The police will send a car for you tomorrow at ten, if that is convenient." The concierge looked around the room. "Perhaps the *Kapitän* would prefer to be moved to another room?"

Drummond was exhausted. "No," he said, "that won't be necessary. You can clear up this mess in the morning while I'm downtown giving my statement."

The concierge bowed slightly and started to leave.

"Oh, there is *one* thing you could do for me this evening." Drummond went to the closet and pulled a small notebook from his suit coat pocket. "I need to call the United States."

"Of course, *Kapitän*." The concierge bowed. "I'll have our operator set up the line."

When the phone jangled beside his bed five minutes later, Drummond direct-dialed the Angel of Mercy Sanitarium in Auburn, New Hampshire. The phone rang half a dozen times before it was answered by a woman who sounded more like a warden than a receptionist.

"Angel of Mercy, can I help you?" The voice had a harsh edge to it.

"Father John Freise, please." Drummond was put on hold, and then a man's voice came on the line.

"This is Father Conklin, can I help you?"

"Yes, I hope so. This is John Drummond from the Veterans Administration, returning Father Freise's call." Recalling their first furtive telephone encounter, Drummond hoped that he wouldn't have to play twenty questions with Father Conklin in order to get through to Father Freise.

"Could you tell me what this call is in regard to?"

"I wish I could, Father, but I just have a message to call back Father Freise. I've no idea why he called." Drummond hoped that he sounded convincing.

"Where are you calling from?" Father Conklin asked.

"Ogden, Utah. That's where our phone center is located. Why?" *Christ*, thought Drummond, *what's with this guy?*

"I only asked because it sounds like you're a million miles away. Just a moment and I'll get Father Freise."

The phone went dead, and Drummond found himself wondering how much it cost per minute to be on hold. Just about the time he'd decided to hang up and call back, Father Freise came on the line.

"Mr. Drummond? Are you the gentlemen I'm supposed to speak to about survivor benefits?" Freise's voice sounded guarded.

"That's right, sir. It's in regard to the late Mr. King's military insurance." Drummond could hear Father Freise breathe a sigh of relief.

"Certainly. What can I do for you?" Freise's tone of voice was level.

"Are you free to talk?" Drummond asked.

"No, not at the moment."

"Okay then, just listen. Remember when you asked me if I thought you were crazy?"

"Yes."

"Well, you're not. I was just attacked by one of your Nazi vampires a few minutes ago." Drummond realized that his voice had a slight tremble in it.

"Well, that's very interesting, Mr. Drummond, but I don't see how I can really be of much help."

"Do you have a passport?" Drummond asked.

"Certainly," the priest replied.

"All right, which is your nearest big airport? One where you could catch a flight to Europe?" Drummond's mind was racing.

"Let me see." Father Freise paused for a moment. "Yes, I think I spoke to a Miss Logan in your Boston office."

"Okay. Tomorrow there'll be a ticket waiting for you at the TWA desk at Logan Airport. Can you make it?" Drummond felt his throat going dry.

"Just as soon as I get the paperwork, Mr. Drummond, I'll hop right on it." Father Freise was playing his part to perfection.

"Thank you very much, Father."

"I'm glad to help out. Good-bye."

Father Freise replaced the phone on its cradle. The man seated behind Father Conklin's desk leaned back in the leather chair, his fingertips brought together under his chin. Light flashed off the large oval-shaped sapphire on his index finger.

"So tell me, Father," he asked, "who is this Mr. Drummond?"

"The police officer from Los Angeles who was here last month, Your Eminence."

There was a rustle of crimson silk as the man behind the desk opened a folder and produced the photographs of Drummond that had been taken in the elevator at von Leibenfalz's apartment.

"Is that him?" he asked, handing the photographs to Father Freise.

"Yes, Your Eminence. He's asked me to meet him in Europe. He needs my help." Freise looked beseechingly at the cardinal seated behind Father Conklin's desk.

"You mean he needs the help of the Church," the cardinal corrected him.

"Yes, Your Eminence."

"Then in that case, you had better pack."

The cardinal extended his hand, and Father Freise bent down to kiss the ring.

"Go with God," the cardinal said. And almost as an afterthought, he added, "Oh, and tell Father Conklin I won't be needing his office any longer, will you?"

Chapter 16

It was raining when Drummond woke up the next morning. Despite the hot bath he had soaked in the night before, every bone in his body seemed to ache as he hauled himself out of bed and headed into the bathroom.

Small wonder, he thought, as he surveyed himself into the large bathroom mirror and gave up trying to count the welts and bruises scattered across his body.

After a long, hot shower he felt decidedly better, and by the time he had shaved and dressed, only the ugliest of the bruises gave him any real discomfort. Adjusting the knot on his silk foulard tie, he slipped on the jacket of his navy double-breasted suit and went downstairs for a light breakfast. In the middle of his coffee and croissant, one of the waiters approached his table carrying a cordless telephone.

"Excuse me, *Kapitän,* but there is a call for you."

Drummond took the phone, and the waiter withdrew from the table.

"Hello, Drummond here," he said.

"John, it's Markus." There was concern in Eberle's voice. "I'm still at home, but I've just heard about last night. Are you all right?"

"Couple of minor bruises, nothing serious." Drummond poured more coffee into his cup from the small silver pot on the corner of his table.

"Listen, I've pulled some strings, and this is going to be given top priority," Eberle said. "We're going to need you to make a statement, so if you don't mind, I'll have a car collect you at your hotel at eleven o'clock. I'm in court in—shit, I'm late!— half an hour, or I'd collect you myself. I hope that's all right?" Eberle sounded rushed, but at the same time willing to do anything Drummond might ask of him.

Drummond picked up his cup. "That's just fine, Markus. I think I can handle it."

"Okay, pal. I'll see you at the station as soon as I'm free." Eberle hung up, and Drummond signaled the waiter to come and retrieve the phone.

Looking out the window at the rain, Drummond cursed to himself that he hadn't brought a raincoat. There was time to buy one, though, thanks to the hour's reprieve before he was due at the police station. After signing for his breakfast, he walked over to the porter's desk and asked for a taxi to be called. While he waited for it, he borrowed an umbrella and went outside to look at the railings under his window.

The drop from Drummond's balcony to the top of the railing was a good four feet—more like seven, from the top of the stone balustrade around the balcony. The railing below was of wrought iron, with slender spear points jutting up every ten to twelve inches. It would have been impossible for anyone to fall on them and survive.

Drummond had just about convinced himself that in the poor light of the previous night he had been mistaken in what he thought he saw, when he noticed the dark puddle of congealed blood pooled at the base of the railing. Directly above it, one of the spear points was bent, as though the weight of the falling body had shoved it slightly forward.

Reaching down, Drummond dabbed one finger in the reddish puddle and sniffed it. It was blood all right. No mistaking the cloying smell, even in the rain. As he went back to the porter's desk to return the umbrella, he found himself almost wishing he had thought to put Father Freise's rosary in his pocket.

The rain had worsened by the time Drummond's taxi arrived at the hotel. Armed with the address of a travel agent and a men's clothing store, Drummond climbed into the waiting taxi and headed out into the city.

The first stop was Herter's, an exclusive men's shop in Vienna's fashionable third district. As the taxi pulled up to the curb, Drummond couldn't help but compare the street with Beverly Hills' famous Rodeo Drive. The shops tended to be as small as their merchandise was expensive. Rolex, Gucci, and Cartier were nestled side by side with Bally, Hermes, and Zolli, while out front the street was lined with Mercedes-Benz and Rolls-Royce motorcars.

Pushing open the door of the taxi, Drummond paused to glance up at the driver.

"Bleiben Sie hier, ja?" He had gotten the phrase from the porter, in hopes of not being abandoned again. *"Hier. Nicht gehen. Verstehen Sie?"*

"Ja, ja," the man replied, turning off the ignition as he nodded in the rearview mirror. *"Ich verstehe."* The fact that Drummond had not yet paid him probably also helped to get the point across.

Slamming the door, Drummond dashed across the rain-slicked pavement and into Herter's. An impeccably dressed salesman in his early sixties came immediately to his assistance, his English as crisp as his freshly starched shirt. Leading him to the back of the shop, he showed Drummond an impressive array of raincoats. Drummond selected a dark slate-blue leather one that, like his suit, was double-breasted. He also took a dark charcoal-gray hat, tried it on, and handed the man his credit card. Five minutes later, dry and warm at last, he was back in the cab, handing his driver the address of the travel agent.

The young lady behind the counter spoke flawless English with a slight British accent, and immediately set about booking Father Freise's flight from Boston to Vienna.

"Now, sir, the Boston flight arrives in Munich at nine-thirty tomorrow morning, and connects with our flight at seven-thirty the following morning, arriving in Vienna at eight thirty-five." She looked up from the amber computer screen. "Would you like me to book a hotel room from your friend for the night?"

Drummond was stunned. "That's a twenty-two hour layover. Can't you manage any better connection than that?"

The young lady shrugged and tapped the keys of her computer again. "I'm sorry, sir. I've tried routing him through several different ways, but everything is booked solid."

"What about other airlines?"

"They're all in the computer, sir. There's simply nothing available tomorrow between Munich and here."

Drummond thought for a moment. Twenty-four hours ago, he would have taken the delay all in stride. The twenty-year-old trail of a series of unsolved homicides in Los Angles had hardly seemed urgent in Vienna, the land of Strauss and cream-filled tortes.

But that was before one of Freise's Nazi vampires had tried to kill him. Drummond didn't want to believe that was what the punker was, but he didn't know of any human being who could impale himself on a wrought iron fence and walk away. He needed to talk to Freise, someplace that Freise didn't have to be afraid to level with him. And he was not about to wait another forty-eight hours.

"Just book the flight through to Munich. I'll *drive* to Munich and meet the plane when it lands."

The keys clicked rhythmically for several seconds before the young lady paused and asked Drummond for his credit card. Handing her his American Express card, Drummond tried not to think about how much all of this was costing.

"That's fine, sir," the ticket agent said, when he had signed off on the charge slip and was putting his copy and the credit card back into his wallet. "Your friend's ticket will be waiting for him in Boston. Have a pleasant drive to Munich."

His faithful taxi driver was still waiting when he came out, and he handed the man an extra hundred-schilling note when he got out again at the Palais Schwartzenberg. A police car was pulled up outside, to the obvious disapproval of the porter, and a young, fresh-scrubbed looking uniformed police officer was waiting for Drummond in the lobby of the hotel. As Drummond came through the door, he walked over to him and saluted.

"*Kapitän* Drummond?"

Drummond nodded slightly by way of returning the compliment.

"I'm Drummond."

The young policeman stood at rigid attention. "*Kapitän*. Inspector Eberle has asked me that I drive you to police headquarters."

"Let's go, then," Drummond said.

"Yes," replied the policeman. "We go now." He turned on his heel and opened the door for Drummond. Following him over to where the car was parked, he stepped ahead of Drummond and opened the back door of the BMW.

Drummond smiled at the young man. "I'd prefer to sit up front, if you don't mind."

The policeman looked baffled. "We go now, yes?" he asked, the door still held open.

So, thought Drummond, *you don't all speak English.* He smiled at the policeman again. "Okay. We go now," he said, and climbed into the cramped back seat of the BMW.

Cop cars the world over have an aroma all their own, and this one was no exception. The pong of urine and sweat, blood, vomit, and fear permeates the back of any police car. Drummond rolled the window down a few inches to let in some fresh air and settled back to endure it as best he could.

At police headquarters, he was escorted upstairs by his driver and ushered into a well-appointed office where three other men were waiting for him. Their conversation changed immediately from German to English when Drummond entered the room. One of the men, tall and on the thin side, with oversized square-framed glasses, immediately came over and offered to take Drummond's coat and hat, while another one, tending towards overweight, bald and wearing a bow tie, introduced himself to Drummond.

"Hi, I'm Joe Guzman, from the embassy." Drummond immediately picked up on the strong west Texas twang in Guzman's voice.

"That wouldn't happen to be the Embassy of the Lone Star State, would it?" he asked, as he shook Guzman's hand.

Guzman smiled at the joke and introduced Drummond to the two other men. "This is the Director of Criminal Investigations, Dr. Lauda."

The thin man with the glasses shook Drummond's hand.

"How do you do, *Kapitän*?" he said.

"And this," Guzman continued, "is State Attorney Milch." The state attorney bowed slightly.

"If you have no objections," Guzman went on, "we'll tape-record the proceedings and then prepare depositions in English and German for you to sign. Please sit down and make yourself comfortable, Captain." Guzman looked at his watch. "I don't think this will take more than about half an hour."

The deposition opened with the usual questions concerning Drummond's name and address, age, and occupation. The state attorney asked the questions in impeccable English, in a voice that reminded Drummond of James Mason's portrayal of Erwin Rommel in the film, *The Desert Fox*. The formalities over, Drummond was asked to tell what happened after he returned to his hotel from dinner.

Drummond carefully detailed his movements from the moment he and Eberle parted at the beer hall until he was attacked in his room. At that point, Dr. Lauda interrupted.

"*Kapitän* Drummond, is it possible that you may have met this young man as you walked back to your hotel and invited him into your room?" Lauda's implication was clear.

"No, I did not." Drummond's voice was firm but without any trace of emotion or annoyance.

Lauda bowed slightly in Drummond's direction. "Very well. Please proceed."

Drummond completed his story, although he left out any mention of seeing his attacker impaled on the fence and then pushing himself free and walking away. When he had finished, the state attorney asked if there was anything else he'd care to add to the transcription.

Drummond shook his head. "No, I've nothing to add."

They offered him a coffee then, while a secretary transcribed the tape and prepared the depositions. When he had signed everything necessary, Guzman walked him to the door.

"Sorry you had this trouble, Captain. I assure you, this isn't the way Vienna treats most Americans. I hope it hasn't put a damper on your vacation."

"No, it's a beautiful city, Mr. Guzman. Thanks very much for your help."

Outside in the corridor, Eberle was waiting for Drummond.

"How did it go?" Eberle asked as they walked toward the elevator.

Drummond shifted his leather coat onto his left arm and put on his hat. "Well, they took my statement, but I doubt they'll catch the guy."

"I'm sorry you have such a low opinion of our professional capabilities." Eberle grinned, his two stainless steel teeth glinting as they stepped into the elevator.

"It's not that I doubt it, Markus, it's that I know

it's *not* the crime of the century. Besides, there must be a couple of hundred skinhead punks running around here in Vienna—though the rose tattoo might be a lead."

The elevator stopped, and both men got out.

"Can I buy you lunch?" Drummond asked.

"God, I wish I could, John, but I'm afraid I'm stuck in court all day." Eberle looked genuinely disappointed at not being able to take up Drummond's offer of hospitality. "Maybe tomorrow."

Before Drummond could tell his friend that he wouldn't be here tomorrow, that he was heading for Munich, Eberle glanced at his watch and winced. "Jeez, gotta run, John. I'm late again. Catch you later!"

Outside it had stopped raining, and as the sun broke through the clouds, steam rose off the pavement. Drummond glanced at the sky, took off his hat, and caught a taxi back to his hotel. In his room, he changed his suit for cords and a pullover, threw a few essentials into his carry-on, and packed the rest into his larger canvas bag. When he appeared at the desk with them, the manager greeted him with an anxious bow.

"Good afternoon, *Kapitän* Drummond. I hope you are not leaving us?"

"I've decided to do a little sightseeing for the next few days, so I'd like to settle my account and, if possible, leave one of my bags here until I get back." Drummond reached into his pocket for his wallet and started to pull out a credit card.

"There is no charge for the room, *Kapitän*. After last night, it would be impossible to charge you for your stay." The manager grimaced at the necessity to even allude to the attack on Drummond the night before. "As for your bag, just leave it with the porter. It will be here when you return."

"Thank you. I appreciate the kindness."

The porter was placing Drummond's smaller bag in the trunk of his car when the Bentley silently drove up and crunched to a stop on the gravel drive. Despite his usual preference for German cars, Drummond found himself reluctantly admiring the graceful lines of the pre-war Bentley, the bright blue sky and fluffy white clouds reflected in miniature on the large headlamps and nickel-plated radiator.

The door of the pale blue and black car opened, and Anton von Liebenfalz slid from behind the wheel, immaculately clad in a gray three-piece suit with a heavy gold watch chain swagged between his vest pockets.

"Ah, *Kapitän* Drummond," he said. "Not leaving Vienna so soon, are you?"

"No, not at all. I'm just going out into the countryside for a day or two." Drummond tipped the porter, then turned back to von Liebenfalz. "What brings you to Palais Schwartzenberg?"

"Two things." Von Liebenfalz smiled and, with the thumb and index finger of his right hand, brushed up the ends of his moustache. "The first is this," he said, reaching into an inside pocket of his suit coat to produce a thick buff-colored envelope. "I was able to gather some further information on the Order of the Sword."

"Ah. Thank you very much," Drummond said.

"As to the other reason—" Von Liebenfalz leaned forward and lowered his voice as if he were about to betray a state secret. "I am having lunch with the Countess von Hohenrobertin." He winked at Drummond.

"Well," Drummond said, glancing at the envelope in his hand, "I can certainly recommend the dining room here at the hotel."

"Dining room?" The baron arched an eyebrow. "My dear *Kapitän,* ours is an *assignation,* not a business meeting. No, we shall drive to some discreet country inn, where our presence will not be noticed."

Drummond looked at the pale blue Bentley with the swooping black fenders. "Of course," he said. "Where you won't be noticed."

Apparently deaf to the droll understatement, von Liebenfalz pulled a large gold watch out of his vest pocket and snapped it open. "Well, I see it is late, *Kapitän,* so I really must be going. *Auf wiedersehen.*"

As von Liebenfalz turned and started up the granite steps leading to the hotel, Drummond called after him.

"Just one more thing, Baron—"

Von Liebenfalz stopped in mid-stride and turned to face him.

"Yes?" he said.

"About the research fee?" Drummond was careful not to associate von Liebenfalz with anything so common as money, especially in public.

"Ah. I have been instructed to inform you that in this instance, all services have been provided *gratis.*" With a click of his heels and a curt bow, von Liebenfalz turned and, before Drummond could reply, vanished into the hotel lobby.

Instructed? Drummond returned to his car, pondering just what von Liebenfalz could have meant by his last remark. *Instructed by whom?* he wondered.

Still trying to figure out von Liebenfalz, Drummond tossed the fat envelope on the seat beside him and started the Mercedes, buckling up before pulling out the gates of Schwartzenberg Palace. As he turned onto Prinz Eugen Strasse, a motorcycle, its rider clad in black leathers, pulled out from the opposite curb and followed at a discreet distance.

Vienna was as congested as Los Angeles, and it took Drummond several wrong turns before he finally found the road that pointed him out of the city and toward the ancient town of Salzburg. Within a few miles, the road became autobahn, and Drummond put his foot down.

Cruising the Mercedes at well over one hundred miles per hour, Drummond followed the signs for Salzburg, stopping in that town only long enough to refuel his car. Swinging northwest of Salzburg, he followed the signs on toward Munich. The road to Munich was significantly faster, and Drummond was able to blast along at speeds approaching one hundred fifty miles per hour, before he had to slow for the transition to the ring road that curved east around the city, heading back toward Riem, and Munich's international airport. A mile behind him on the autobahn, the rider in black leathers gave a slight squeeze to the brake lever and shifted down from sixth to fifth gear, following Drummond's Mercedes off the super highway and into the parking lot of the largest of the airport hotels.

As Drummond got out of the car and went in to register, the big Suzuki purred into the lot and quietly rolled past Drummond's parked car. The rider stopped opposite the glass doors of the airport hotel and watched as Drummond bent over registration documents and credit card slips and was handed a key by the receptionist. Satisfied, the rider gave the bike's throttle a deft twist and eased the machine forward, weaving through the parking lot to a huge gas station next to the hotel.

The rider dismounted stiffly after nearly five hours in the saddle, but moved with purpose toward a rank of telephones that lined one wall of the service plaza. Stepping into one of the phone booths, the rider pulled off the shiny black helmet and ran a black-gloved hand through sweat-matted, mousy-brown hair. From a jacket pocket came a plastic phone card, which the rider inserted into the appropriate slot in the telephone box. Black-gloved fingers pecked out a phone number, and after a few seconds someone answered.

"This is Magda Krebs," the woman in the motorcycle leathers said. "Tell the Master that Drummond has checked into a hotel at Munich airport."

Chapter 17

Father Freise was pushing a baggage trolley with a large suitcase on it as he came through customs and into the arrivals hall at Munich airport. He was wearing his clerical collar under a black trenchcoat, but even without it, Drummond would have had no trouble recognizing the priest he had last seen at the sanitarium in New Hampshire. Pushing his way through the crowded concourse, Drummond walked over to where Father Freise had stopped near a sign marked "Meeting Point" in half a dozen different languages.

"John!"

The priest spotted Drummond before Drummond could get to him, and hurried to embrace him like an old friend.

"John, dear boy! God, but it's good to see you!"

Taking his cue from Freise, Drummond played along, pumping the old man's hand and grinning self-consciously as Freise stood back to look at him, pretending long-time familiarity.

"It's good to see you, too, Father. How was your flight? Did you get any sleep?"

They kept up the pretense all the way to the car, Drummond pushing the trolley and Freise chatting animatedly of inconsequentials but watching around them all the while—looking for what, Drummond

271

had no idea. It would not have been evident to anyone but a professional who was looking for it, but Drummond had the definite impression that Freise had spent many years glancing over his shoulder.

They reached the car, where Drummond opened the trunk and stashed Freise's big suitcase inside with his own. Freise fell silent as they got into the car, not looking at Drummond until they had threaded their way past the parking kiosk and were easing onto the autobahn.

From her vantage point near the taxi stand, Magda Krebs watched the white Mercedes head up the access ramp and onto the Munich ring road before she gunned her motorcycle to life and followed.

In the car, Drummond decided it was time to drop the pretenses.

"I don't understand what all that was about, back in the terminal, Father, but I want to thank you for coming," Drummond began.

"I had my reasons, Captain," Freise replied. "However, for the next however long it takes, I'm officially off-duty, in a manner of speaking. So I'd appreciate it if you'd call me Frank."

To emphasize the point, Freise reached up to his collar and pulled out the white tab showing at the center, then opened the top button, transforming the clerical attire into an ordinary black shirt. "How's that?" he asked, turning to look at Drummond almost in challenge.

"Okay, Frank. You'd better call me John, then. Fair enough?"

"Fair enough," Freise agreed.

Drummond stole a sidelong glance at Freise as they headed up the on-ramp to the autobahn. Looking quickly in his rearview mirror, he thought he caught a glimpse of a motorcycle cop, and so refrained from pushing the car much over eighty.

"So, tell me about your vampires," Freise said.

Trying to remain professionally detached, Drummond briefly related the incident of the attack in his room, and how his assailant had impaled himself on an iron fence and then walked away. In the cold light of day, he found himself thinking that if someone had come to *him* with such a bizarre story, he would have dismissed the guy immediately as a nutter.

"Is that it?" Freise said, when Drummond had faltered to a pause in his narrative.

Drummond braced himself to go on, beginning to wonder if it had been such a good idea to call the priest. But there was no point in holding back now.

"No, there's more. There's a series of unsolved and seemingly unconnected murders involving blood banks, back in the States and here—except that I think they may *be* connected. And the apparent suicide of an old Jew named Stucke—except that I think he was murdered. And a guy who may be a former SS officer named Kluge—except that he *can't* be Kluge, because Kluge would be well into his seventies by now. I have a copy of his SS file in the glove box. Take a look, if you like." He swung the Mercedes around to overtake a slow-moving truck in the lane ahead.

Father Freise opened the glove box and pulled out the copy of the file from the Weisenthal Center. On top was the buff-colored envelope von Liebenfalz had given Drummond the previous afternoon. Ignoring the file, Freise held up the envelope.

"What's this?" His voice was hard-edged.

"Oh, *that*. It's a report on the Order of the

Sword, the group that belongs to that coat of arms you sketched for me back in New Hampshire." Drummond was distracted by something in the rearview mirror. "Why?"

"Because this seal on the back," he held the envelope up so Drummond could see the purple seal stamped across the envelope's opened flap, "is the seal of the Vatican library." Father Freise stared intently at Drummond for several seconds before he spoke again. "Are you working for the Church?"

"God, no," Drummond said. "I'm not even Catholic. I fell into this in Los Angeles about six months ago, and the first I knew of any church involvement was just now, when you told me about that seal. Other than their cover-up for you, of course. Why?"

Ignoring Drummond's question, Freise opened the flap of the envelope and took out a thick sheaf of papers. "Do you mind if I read these while you drive?"

"Not at all," said Drummond. "Go right ahead."

Egon lay on the floor of the van breathing shallowly. The two wounds in his chest had finally closed, and he was no longer wheezing air with each breath, but it hurt less if he didn't breathe too deeply. He was still very weak. Actually, he no longer felt very much pain—just total exhaustion.

Turning his head, he looked blearily at the girl in the torn fishnet stockings and Doc Martins. She had been nice to him, dragging him into the van when they were getting ready to go, instead of leaving him in the abandoned warehouse. He thought he had overheard her talking to someone else about him, something about it taking too long for him to recover, but he knew he was not going to die from his wounds. Kluge had seen to that. Egon was immortal. He was going to live forever.

He had not been so sure of that last night. After impaling himself on the railing outside of Drummond's hotel room, he had managed to free himself, with a strength he had not known he possessed; but the superhuman strength had faded rapidly as he sprinted for safety toward the Belvedere Park. He had lost a lot of blood, between the fence and the running. He managed to hide himself in some shrubbery before collapsing, and tried to pinch his wounds closed, the way he had seen Kluge do that first night; but it hadn't seemed to work as well for him as it had for the Master. He knew he mustn't stay there indefinitely, but he couldn't seem to summon up enough energy to do more than lie there on his back, listening to the wheezing in his lungs.

After an hour or so, he became aware that relief of a kind was near. A dog had wandered into the bushes, attracted by the sound and the smell of blood on Egon's clothes, and had come sniffing too close. Using all of his strength, Egon had grabbed the dog and squeezed it around the throat until it passed out. Biting through the dog's skin had been hard, especially as Egon was missing his front teeth, but eventually he managed to chew through to a vein. He had felt the dog die in his arms as he drank its blood, and its body had still been warm when he slid into exhausted sleep. He mildly regretted what he had done, because Egon liked dogs.

The morning rain had revived him. The dog's body now was cold and stiff, but Egon felt a little better. Crawling out from the bushes, he somehow managed to stagger back to his Volkswagen van. By driving slowly, he made it to the all the way to the warehouse before collapsing again behind the wheel. When next he came to, his head was in the lap of the girl in the torn fishnet stockings, and everyone was climbing into shiny white vans with the Euro Plasma logo on the side.

Egon let himself float and dream as the van rumbled along, not caring where it was going. When it finally stopped, the door on the side was rolled back and everyone hopped out, the girl and two of her friends dragging Egon to the door. There, two clean-cut young men wearing white lab coats lifted him out of the van and helped him walk over to a large stone barn about fifty feet away.

Egon could hardly believe his eyes. Maybe his loss of blood was making him hallucinate. The interior of the barn was like the audience chamber of a medieval castle, lit only by torches. High overhead, a hammer-beam ceiling soared up to the center of the roof, and the walls were hung from ceiling to floor with long, narrow banners of crimson, like tapestries, each bearing the white circle and black swastika symbol of the Third Reich.

Twelve stone seats were arranged along three of the walls, each of the seats flanked by torches in tall, wrought iron standards. The fourth wall was pierced by a large window done in stained glass, mostly in reds, with a granite throne set beneath it that could only belong to the Master. In the center of the room, a long granite altar carved with runic symbols and the curved swastikas called sun-wheels rose organically from the stone floor.

Taking it all in, Egon suddenly felt very lightheaded. He must have swayed a little on his feet, because the clean-cut young men brought him into the great hall and gently helped him lie down on the altar, as the others from the vans filed in and quietly jostled into places behind the twelve empty stone seats. From Egon's vantage point, if he lifted his head just slightly and forced his eyes to focus, he could make out the design in the window set above the Master's granite throne. Golden eagles holding wreathed swastikas filled each corner of the blood-red window, while its center displayed the white roundel dominated by the black swastika of the Third Reich. The dark and brooding splendor of the room overwhelmed Egon, filling him with joy that the Master had finally seen fit to allow him into the sanctum of the holy knights of his new order.

With tears of pride staining his cheeks, Egon laid his head down again. From somewhere high above him, the strains of *Tannhaüser* began to intertwine with a hush that descended as a door closed somewhere behind him, the music building powerfully in the flickering torchlight. As steel-shod footsteps echoed hollowly on the stone floor, Egon turned his head slightly to behold a sight even more awesome than anything he had seen thus far.

From out of the torchlit shadows before the closed door, a dark procession approached—a glimpse, at last, of the powerful knights of Kluge's new order—cloaked in black, the *Sigrunen* flashing on their collar tabs, each with a great two-handed sword carried at the salute, and crowned with the distinctive coal-scuttle helmets that had been modelled on the sallets of medieval knights. There were six of them, marching by twos, giving proud escort to a seventh knight with an eye patch who bore the sacred *Blutfahne,* the Blood Flag of the old Third Reich.

Egon could scarcely believe what he was seeing. So far as he knew, none of the rag-tag crew of punker youths he ran with had ever seen even one of the almost-mythic warriors whom Kluge had told them were the knights of his new order. Yet here were seven of them, and two more flanking the Master himself as *he* followed the sacred banner—the clean-cut young men who had helped Egon out of the van, white coats now exchanged for long black cloaks like the other knights wore, helmeted as well. They had actually touched Egon!

The procession passed to the left, behind Egon's head, the column then splitting before the dais to form a sword-arch for the *Blutfahne* as it was carried up the steps and reverently set in a standard close beside the Master's throne. Then the banner-bearer stood to attention on the other side of the throne, giving a stiff-armed salute as Kluge passed under the sword-arch and mounted the steps to his throne, looking like a god as he turned and seemed to set his gaze directly on Egon.

The moment was too intense. Egon had to close his eyes for a few seconds, too overcome to bear the awe of it. When he could look again, the knights with the swords had withdrawn to stand motionless before the six stone chairs nearest the dais, three to either side, black-gloved hands folded on the pommels of their great swords. Behind them, cowed before the potency of their very presence, the watching punkers had shrunk back almost to the banners on the walls. The two knights who had been Kluge's personal escort stood at ease at the foot of the dais, facing Egon and the altar. But it was Kluge himself who drew all eyes to look upon him, Kluge who was the center and focal point of all that was coming to pass.

He was wearing the formal black uniform of an SS *Sturmbannführer,* with the silver braid and the lightning flashes and the high, peaked cap with the

SS pattern eagle and swastika cap-badge. A blood-red arm band circled his arm above the left elbow, with the same black and white swastika and roundel that graced the banners and the window behind him. The torchlight glittered off the lightning runes and the silver braid and the mirror shine of his riding boots as Kluge set black-gloved hands on his belt and looked out upon them.

"Tonight we dedicate ourselves to the resurrection of our holy cause," the Master said. He hardly raised his voice, but every word carried in the vaulted stone hall. "We bind ourselves together with our oath of blood and honor, made more sacred by sharing the sacrament of one of our own knights."

Majestically, Kluge descended the dais steps to the altar, his escorts flanking him and diverting to head and foot, acolytes now, in the ritual about to unfold.

"Tonight one of us shares himself before joining Odin and the great heroes of Valhalla," Kluge went on. "We shall drink to his glory as he carries our aspirations unto Valhalla's halls."

As Kluge held out a black-gloved hand, the knight at the head of the altar handed across an SS officer's dagger, its broad, spear-shaped blade flashing in the torchlight. Egon, lying dreamily beneath it, only half-comprehended Kluge's words. As Kluge held up the dagger like a sword at salute, pointing it then toward the stained glass window, Egon could only conceive that he was somehow being honored by the Master.

"Your Honor is True. You are a knight."

Egon trembled at the words. As the Master's eyes locked on his, a shiver of anticipation drained away his will and left him limbless, in ecstatic echo of that first time the Master had bade him drink his blood. As the dagger descended flat-bladed to touch his right shoulder, lifted over his head to touch the left, Egon knew only that his Master was according him the very highest honor. The noble music of Wagner swelled, and Egon hardly felt the dagger's steel kiss as Kluge drew the edge sharply across the left jugular.

He did not see Kluge handing off the dagger, for tears of joy and pride were streaming down his cheeks. He was a knight! He was *Kluge's* knight! He felt the blissful light-headedness of knowing he would live forever as a willing servant of this darkling god who now was receiving the most beautiful chalice from one of the knights beside him.

Gem-studded and beguiling in the torchlight, it winked and dazzled before Egon's tear-blurred gaze, twice the size of a man's cupped hands, with handles on either side by which to lift it and wonderful designs carved deeply in the ruddy gold. Golden eagles adorned the sides of the chalice, their wings outspread to bracket the brim, and each held a wreathed swastika in its claws, sapphire-set with gems the size of a man's thumbnail. Egon got a very good look at it as Kluge brought it down past his left eye, tilting it a little to press its rim against Egon's neck.

"Your honor is true," Kluge repeated, the voice soothing as Kluge caught Egon's gaze again. "You are a knight of the new Reich. And a knight is ever willing to lay down his life for his lord."

Slowly it dawned on Egon what Kluge was saying, what the words meant, what the chalice was for. But by then it was too late to question, too late to object, too late to tell the Master that he did not want to die yet—that he wanted to live forever! He tried to move his chilling limbs, but the acolytes moved in to hold him at ankles and shoulders—not roughly, but not relenting, either.

Gradually any resistance at all became simply too much bother, and he let the lethargy wash over him in ever-increasing waves, gazing up into Kluge's eyes in slack-jawed surrender as his life flowed into the chalice Kluge held. He managed to turn his head a little as the pressure of the chalice against his neck suddenly ceased, and before Kluge lifted it away, Egon caught just a glimpse of what it now contained, filled to the brim with his blood. As the strains of Wagner swelled in glorious paeans of victory, heralding the entry of the gods into Valhalla, Egon could summon no anger or resentment or even sorrow—only joy and pride, as Kluge raised the chalice high above his head with both hands.

"This is the blood of the new Reich!" Kluge thundered, as his holy knights looked on, and his awed disciples surged closer behind them, drawn by the power. "Through the bond of our blood, we attain Valhalla! *Sieg Heil! Sieg Heil! Sieg Heil!*"

The knights made no outward response to the exhortation, but the punkers took up the chant with ecstatic fervor, thrusting their right hands upward in stiff-armed salute as the words pounded at the hammer-beam ceiling like a slow, steady pulse-beat. As they chanted, Kluge drank deeply from the chalice, served his two assistants and the banner-bearer, who came down from the dais to meet him, then moved majestically to either side of the hall to administer the gory communion to the knights, denying the cup to the less exalted of his vampire army.

The chanting of the punkers slowly died away as they realized they had not yet earned the right to partake of this most coveted sacrament, of the blood of one of their own, so that by the time Kluge returned to the foot of the altar, he did so in silence—for the music of Wagner had come to an end during the chanting.

In utter silence, Kluge turned toward the *Blutfahne* on the dais beside his throne, raising the chalice in ultimate salute as he murmured, *"Die Fahnen hoch. . . ."*

His words were the cue for new music—the throbbing power of "Das Horst Wessel Lied," the official song of the Nazi Party, sung by a massed choir of male voices, the powerful arrangement orchestrated by Carl Orff. *Die Fahnen hoch*—the flags are high, the ranks are tightly closed. . . .

It pulsed and pounded among the rafters of the high-ceilinged hall as Kluge brought the chalice to his lips once more; the punkers joined their rougher voices to the choir's, clenched fists hammering out the tempo, stamping their feet, all eyes fixed fervently on their *Führer*. In triumph, Kluge tipped back his head to drain the chalice to its dregs, raising it high once more, up-ended to show that it was empty, before setting it thus between the feet of the man who had filled it with his life's blood.

That done, Kluge stood to rigid attention and gave Egon a final stiff-armed Nazi salute. The action was mirrored in unison by all the black-clad knights—their first movement since taking up their impassive sentinel positions—and then, raggedly, by the punkers as well. Kluge's murmured, *"Sieg Heil!"* was not audible above the final strains of the Nazi hymn, but Egon no longer could have heard it anyway, as the final tears of pride rolled down his lifeless cheeks.

The sudden ending of the song left behind it an utter and profound silence, hardly broken as Kluge's knights formed up smartly before the dais and escorted him and the *Blutfahne* from the hall by a side exit. The nearly twenty punkers remained subdued when the doors had closed behind the dark procession, only slowly daring to make their way outside to gather by a small moving van and await final instructions. When Kluge finally reappeared, he was carrying a cloak like those his knights wore, and two of them were lugging a large box.

"Put it down here," Kluge said, indicating a place near one of the vans.

The knights obeyed, and one of them lifted the lid of the box to reveal a lethal assortment of pistols and submachine guns. Without changing expression, Kluge picked up one of the Schmeissers, pulled back the cocking lever, then raised the muzzle to fire a quick burst into the air. As intended, the sound got all of their attention.

"Toys," Kluge said with a cold smile, by way of explanation. "It's playtime, boys and girls— playtime."

Chapter 18

In Drummond's white Mercedes, Father Frank Freise paged quickly through the report supplied by Anton von Liebenfalz, spent rather more time on Kluge's SS file—stiffening as he looked at the ID photo—then glanced up sharply at the direction signs flashing by on the autobahn.

"Where are you headed?" Freise demanded.

"Back to Vienna. Why?"

"I think we'd better talk first," Freise said, closing the folder and staring straight ahead. "Pull over at the next service plaza." His tone of voice had the ring of a command, and Drummond shot the priest a cold glare in response. "Please," Freise added, in a gentler tone. "It's important."

Drummond said nothing, merely easing the Mercedes into the slow lane and down-shifting to check their speed as they pulled into a rest area parking lot. When he had set the parking brake and switched off the ignition, he turned a cool, measured gaze on the priest.

"All right, Father. Let's talk."

"It's Frank—please." The priest looked down at his hands, clenched tautly around the edges of the file in his lap, and forced himself to take a deep breath.

"I'm sorry, John. I didn't mean to sound imperious. But you've put it all together."

"I have?"

"Yes. You've provided *me* with a vital missing link, too. This man—" He hefted the SS file in his hand. "You aren't going to want to believe this, but this Wilhelm Kluge is the same man who led the raid on the castle in 1944, and slit one of the knight's throats, and drank his blood. He's your master vampire, John."

"You're right. I don't want to believe this."

"All right. Let's try another approach," Freise said, squaring his shoulders. "Did you read this report that von Liebenfalz gave you?"

"Yes."

"Did you know what you read?"

"By your tone of voice, apparently not," Drummond replied. "It's a history of the Order of the Sword. They were an order of crusader knights who fell out of grace with the Church in the thirteenth century. If I catch your drift, it sounds like you're trying to suggest that they're the knights in the castle, the same guys you met up with in the Ardennes in 1944. I'm not sure I can buy the idea of vampire knights, Frank."

"Do you buy the idea that Wilhelm Kluge is a vampire?" Freise replied, staring bleakly out the windshield ahead.

Drummond looked at him in consternation for several seconds, then gave a grudging nod.

"Yeah, I guess I do. I guess that's why I called and asked you to come."

"I see." Freise nodded slowly. "Well, I don't want to sound ungrateful, but now that I've come, suppose you tell me what you'd planned to do next."

The priest turned and looked him full in the face, and Drummond swallowed, quickly retreating from vampires to the more familiar territory of police work, where at least he knew where he stood.

"All right. I thought we should go back to Vienna. I did some checking on your story in America, before I came over here. You said that you spotted the first of your vampires at a local blood drive—and that it wasn't run by the Red Cross."

"That's right."

"Okay. So it had to be a private company. I did some digging and found out that about the time of the vampire killings in L.A., a blood products company called Euro Plasma Services went out of business. Could be just coincidence, right?"

"Right again."

"However," Drummond went on, "there have been companies with slight variations of that name in San Francisco, in Vancouver, British Columbia, and in Hamburg, Germany. I haven't been able to tie anything to San Francisco—yet—but in Vancouver and Hamburg, there's definite proof that *some-one* has been killing people and draining their blood. And then there was Stucke's murder, in Vienna, which also fits the pattern."

Freise nodded. "Tell me about Stucke."

Drummond wrapped his hands around the steering wheel and stared straight ahead. "I made a police contact right after I arrived in Vienna—a professional courtesy sort of thing—an inspector named Eberle. Nice guy, and seems to be a good cop. We hit if off. He invited me to go along on a call-out a couple of nights ago. It's something cops do when they visit other departments—to compare notes, see how other departments do things.

"Anyway, the call-out was about a DB—"

"A what?" Father Friese interrupted.

"A dead body. The police were treating it as a probable suicide. The old guy gets in the shower and cuts his throat with a straight razor—body isn't found for about a week, when the woman in the apartment below notices water coming through her ceiling and realizes the rent hasn't been paid." Drummond allowed himself a deep breath.

"It was the purest coincidence that I went along on this particular call, but guess what? The dead man has no blood in his body. None. And there's none sprayed all over the bathroom, such as you'd expect if he did himself there. And that's not all. Seems he'd been to the police three weeks earlier, swearing up and down that he'd seen a former SS officer in Vienna, name of Wilhelm Kluge."

Freise nodded wordlessly, listening avidly to Drummond's every word as he continued.

"The police did some checking; confirmed that there *had* been an SS officer named Kluge during the war, but that the guy Stucke'd seen was a successful Austrian businessman, name of Hartmann—who *couldn't* be Kluge, because he was forty or fifty years too young—but Stucke wouldn't accept that.

"So he went to the Simon Wisenthal Center—the place that tracks down Nazi war criminals. He got a copy of Kluge's SS file. That's it you've been reading. I liberated it from Stucke's apartment, when I went back the next morning after the police were through. I hadn't put anything together yet, but something just didn't feel right."

"Do you think it was Kluge who attacked you?" Freise asked.

Drummond shook his head. "No way. It wasn't the guy the police say is Hartmann, either. Some skinhead punker."

Drummond realized his clasp on the steering wheel had turned into a death-grip, and he consciously made himself relax, flexing and unflexing his fingers before he went on.

"I think that the man Stucke saw *is* Kluge, Frank. I think that Kluge found out he'd been spotted, so he killed Stucke—or had him killed. And once he thought I was on to him, he tried to have me killed as well."

Freise nodded slowly. "I hope you realize what you're implying. Do you have any idea how this Kluge covers his tracks in Vienna?"

Drummond reached into his jacket pocket and pulled out a folded piece of paper which he handed to Father Freise. "Before I left the hotel yesterday, I tore this out of the phone book. Look for yourself."

Halfway down the page, circled in red, was a Vienna telephone listing for Euro Plasma Technik.

"I don't suppose you had time to discover whether one of the directors is a man named Hartmann, did you?" Freise said mildly.

Drummond swallowed audibly and shook his head.

"No matter," Freise went on. "I agree with everything you've said. It all begins to fit together. Except for one thing. The man who attacked you may not have been Kluge, but he had to be a vampire, to haul himself off that fence the way you described. That confirms that there are more of them than just Kluge. I guess I knew that twenty years ago, when I staked those six in L.A. But we'd be fools to try tackling him alone. We need help, and I know from experience that the police aren't about to lend a hand." Father Freise refolded the page from the phone book and handed it back to Drummond.

"Yes, that's what we'll have to do," he said. "We'll go to Luxembourg."

"Luxembourg?" Drummond repeated, not wanting to believe what Freise was suggesting.

"That's right. We'll ask the Order of the Sword to help us."

"Jesus Christ, Frank, they're *vampires*, the same as Kluge, if what you say is true!" Drummond retorted. He was stunned by Father Freise's suggestion. "What makes you think they're going to help us?"

"It doesn't matter what I think, John. The Church sent me, and they think the Order of the Sword will help us."

"Oh, yeah? Well, what makes them so sure that the Order of the Sword won't kill us and then link up with Kluge?" Drummond was beginning to wonder if Freise wasn't crazy after all.

Father Freise picked up the report from the Vatican Archives and brandished it between them.

"According to this, they've been under the special protection of the Church for nearly seven hundred years. I think that if we talk to them, they'll listen. And if they listen, they'll help."

"Yeah, and if they don't listen, we're dead." Drummond let out a long breath. "Besides, I don't really think it's such a hot idea to go looking for a castle full of seven-hundred-year-old vampires, alone and unarmed."

Father Freise smiled at Drummond.

"Let's go back to the trunk, John. There's something there I want to show you."

"Yeah, I'll bet," Drummond muttered under his

breath, picturing a suitcase full of wooden stakes, or garlic, or God knew what all else.

But he got out of the car and unlocked the trunk for Freise, standing back then, while the old priest hefted the suitcase around and opened it. On top was the expected assortment of socks and underwear and neatly-folded priest-shirts, with the bright embroidery of some gold and white vestments showing beneath. Lifting those up, Freise rummaged under a neatly folded cassock and brought out a leather-bound box with a silver cross on the lid. He laid it on top of the spare tire, next to his suitcase.

"Go ahead," he said. "Open it up."

Drummond lifted the lid off the box. Inside was a compact 9mm Beretta pistol and a box of ammo. Freise look smugly at Drummond.

"How on earth . . ." Drummond's voice trailed off in disbelief.

"I'm a regular reader of *Guns & Ammo*," Father Freise explained. "Bit of a black powder enthusiast. Anyway, I read some time back that the LAPD had gone over from Smith and Wesson to the Beretta, and I thought it might come in handy."

"But, where did you get it?" Drummond asked.

"New Hampshire. Remember? 'Live Free or Die'?" Freise looked around furtively. "I guess I did take a bit of a chance, putting it in my luggage like that, but I figured—heck, what customs man is going to dig around in a priest's suitcase? And I was right. Those Germans just waved me right through." He snorted. "And they're supposed to be efficient."

Drummond popped the magazine out of the pistol and quickly thumbed in fourteen rounds of 9mm hollow-points, keeping the operation shielded behind the raised lid of the trunk. Slapping the magazine back into the pistol, he snapped the slide back, chambering the first round before he set the safety and tucked the pistol into the waistband of his trousers.

"Well, this helps," Drummond said, zipping up his leather jacket, "but I wish we had some backup, just in case."

"We do," said Father Freise, pointing toward the heavens.

Still dubious, Drummond closed the old priest's suitcase, slammed the trunk, and he and Freise got back into the car. There was a gas station across the parking lot from where they had stopped, and he moved the car over to the pumps.

"I don't suppose you speak any German?" he said, getting out to start filling the tank.

"Are you kidding? My folks came from Düsseldorf. Why?" Freise asked.

Drummond nodded toward the small shop next to the gas pumps. "Why don't you go in there and see if you can get us a map? I don't even know which direction Luxembourg is in, much less how far it is."

"Can do," said Father Freise, climbing out of the car and heading into the shop.

Inside, next to the candy bars and magazines, was a rack filled with maps and road atlases. Overwhelmed by the selection, Father Friese looked at several, trying to decide which was best.

"Enschuldigen Sie mir, Vater, kann ich helfen Sie?"

Freise turned around to discover that the pleasant voice belonged to a plain, squat woman with mousy-brown hair, wearing motorcycle leathers.

"Ja, danke, das ist sehr gütlich, Fräulein," Freise murmured gratefully. *"Welches karte . . ."*

"Oh," she said in excellent English. "You are American. Tell me, where do you go?"

"We're headed toward Luxembourg," Father Freise volunteered. "To the Ardennes."

The woman pulled an oversized road atlas down off the rack. "Here is the one for you," she said. "I use it myself. It is easy to read."

"Well, thank you," Freise said.

"Not at all. *Auf wiedersehen."*

The woman turned and headed for the door, pulling on her helmet as Drummond came in to pay for the petrol.

"Did you find it?" he asked Freise.

"Sure did. Got it right here," he said holding up the *Collins Road Atlas of Europe.*

Outside, Magda Krebs went to the nearest phone, inserted her phone card in the slot, and dialed a long series of numbers. Nearly a hundred miles away, a cellular telephone rang in a pale green Mercedes van with the rear window blanked out. The doors bore the logo of Euro Plasma Technik, Hamburg. The moving van following half a mile behind bore no markings. The passenger in the front seat of the lead van, now wearing a white Euro Plasma coverall over his SS uniform, leaned forward and picked it up.

"Yes?"

"They're headed for Luxembourg," Magda reported.

"I see," Kluge said. "And who are 'they'?"

"Drummond and an old American priest. Drummond met him at the airport this morning."

Kluge did not answer right away, and Magda

sensed that he was thinking, deciding what to do next.

"Very good, Magda. Stay with them—and call me, once they reach their destination."

"I will, Master. Thank you."

The line went dead, and Magda slowly replaced the receiver in the rack. For a moment she stood motionless, basking in the warmth of the Master's compliment. Then, withdrawing her phone card, she walked over to her motorcycle, kicked it into life, and roared off after Drummond's white Mercedes.

Back on the autobahn, Drummond dropped the stubby gear lever into fifth and settled back to cruise at a rock-steady one hundred miles per hour, following the signs toward Augsburg, Ulm, and Stuttgart. Freise started nodding off after only a few miles, his jet lag catching up with him, so Drummond explained how to make the seat crank back to a semi-reclining position. Soon the priest was dead to the world, leaving Drummond to brood by himself as the lines on the road flashed by and the Mercedes ate up the miles.

The skies opened up as they bypassed Augsburg, and a torrential downpour forced Drummond to slow down to a sluglike fifty. Finally, on the outskirts of Stuttgart, after nearly two hours of slogging along in the rain, Drummond decided to call a halt, if only for long enough to stretch and grab a fast lunch. When he had pulled in at a roadside service plaza and turned off the ignition—and paused to lock the Beretta into the glove-box, lest he cause a panic in the cafe—he shook Freise awake and they went inside, running to dodge the rain.

Meanwhile, Magda Krebs also wanted to get out

of the rain. Pulling her Suzuki under the shelter of an overpass, numb to the bone, she resigned herself to a miserable wait. She shivered in her damp leathers, imagining the hot lunch that Drummond and the priest must be enjoying, and she tried to put her own hunger out of mind, consoling herself with the memory of Kluge's praise.

Less than an hour behind, the Euro Plasma van and its lumbering rear escort rolled on through the worst of the storm without bothering to stop. Inside the vans, Kluge had provided small, half-liter bags of liquid refreshment for the storm troopers of his new order, and charged the two SS men driving the larger van to make sure that no one overindulged—only enough to keep each at the peak of efficiency. He had no such worries about those in the van with him, of course. They all were his knights, sitting quietly and conserving their energy—cool professionals, biding their time until ordered to proceed.

Kluge sat back in the passenger seat of the lead van and watched the woods roll by, supremely confident. He was gaining on Drummond and the priest, although neither of them realized it yet, or even that they were being pursued. And he now knew, beyond a shadow of a doubt, exactly where Drummond and the priest were headed in Luxembourg.

That also told him who the priest was. Kluge remembered him from the war, that long-ago night when Kluge first had tasted immortality. The priest had *seen*. He had been among the American prisoners working in the triage camp—young, hardly old enough to be a priest, Kluge remembered thinking at the time. The Knights of the Sword—or the Knights of the Blood, as Kluge preferred to think of them—the knights had captured the priest along with a handful of Kluge's men, and hauled them back to the castle where all of them now were headed. Kluge couldn't remember the priest's name, if he'd ever even heard it, but he called up the memory of the face, and pictured how it might have changed after nearly fifty years.

Kluge had not changed, of course. Kluge smiled as he imagined the priest's reaction, when they eventually met—very mortal priest, nearing the end of his days, and immortal Master of a coming new world order. It had to be the priest who somehow had put all the pieces together and set the American policeman onto Kluge—the priest or that nosy Jew! At least Kluge had drunk *that* vessel to the dregs. The vengeance had been sweet, even if it *had* been Jewish blood. . . .

But *why* was the priest taking Drummond to the castle? The question gnawed at Kluge.

The most dangerous possibility was that Drummond somehow had gotten information out of Stucke before Kluge was able to silence him, and knew that Hans Hartmann was Wilhelm Kluge, and a vampire, somehow putting the Stucke information together with whatever he must have learned from the priest, back in America. If the two had decided to hunt down vampires, maybe they were going to the castle to try to kill the knights who had made Kluge what he was—*if* they still lived there, of course.

If that *was* their purpose, then Kluge's arrival would be construed as reinforcements by the beleaguered warriors. Once Kluge had finished off Drummond and the priest, the knights would be happy to form an alliance with him. *Those* were the sorts of knights Kluge really wanted for his new order—

not miserable, mouth-breathing punks like the ones following him in the larger van.

But what if Drummond and the priest had decided that Kluge was the danger, not the knights, and were going to ask the knights' help in destroying Kluge? What if Drummond and the priest convinced the knights to join forces against Kluge and his followers?

Kluge lifted the car rug tucked between the front seats of the van and patted the breech of the 9mm Walther submachine gun hidden beneath it.

Well, in that case, he thought, *it will be a triumph of the will*. Then, chuckling to himself, he added, *Of will, and superior firepower. . . .*

Chapter 19

In the cafe, perhaps an hour ahead of Kluge, Freise pored over his road atlas as Drummond finished his second cup of coffee.

"About how far do you think we are from Luxembourg?" Drummond asked over the rim of his cup.

"Hard to say," Freise said, studying the map. "It's autobahn from here to a little past Karlsruhe—maybe forty or fifty miles—but then there's about a thirty-mile stretch of *route régionale* between there and the Euroroute around Saarbrücken.

"After that, I'd suggest that we skirt the French border instead of going into France, heading northwest out of Saarbrücken to pick up this Euroroute to cross into Luxembourg. That looks to be—oh, another fifty or sixty miles to the border, and then a bit beyond that, to where we're going. Ordinarily, I'd say three to four hours." Freise feigned a scowl. "But the way you drive, my guess is we'll be there in two. Even if this rain lets up, it'll be dark by then, in any case."

The unspoken menace of that last statement kept both men silent until they were back in the car and accelerating back onto the autobahn.

"What *about* it being dark by the time we get there, Frank?" Drummond said, deliberately keeping his eyes on the road. "You gave me a rosary that first time we met at the sanitarium. Is that kind of thing going to give me any protection? While you were asleep, I kept scaring myself with all the horror films I've ever seen about vampires. Somehow, I don't get the impression that the standard protections are going to do too much good."

Freise nodded slowly, exhaling with a sigh. "I wish I could reassure you, John. All I can tell you is what I know from my own experience. A stake through the heart will kill them. Cutting their heads off will kill them, too, if I'm remembering correctly from that battle in the castle, back in '44. None of the Germans actually *cut* their heads off, with a blade—but blowing someone's head off with a grenade, or shearing it off with a machine gun, accomplishes the same thing. Other than that, I saw some of those knights take some *terrible* wounds and just keep coming."

Drummond felt a chill creep up his spine, and he forced himself to keep his eyes focused on the road ahead.

"What about crosses, holy water, all that stuff?"

Sighing, Freise shook his head. "I honestly don't know. I can't imagine that they affect the knights, at any rate. They asked me to say Mass, for God's sake! There were crosses all over their chapel—they *wear* crosses on their surcoats!

"And if the Germans hadn't come bursting in when they did, I would have given them all communion. You explain *that* one for me! Unless they were trying to commit suicide, I have to conclude that a consecrated host doesn't harm them. At least not our vampire knights."

Drummond felt like he'd just been kicked in the stomach.

"Jesus, Frank!" he whispered. "You sure know how to reassure a guy. What about Kluge's bunch?"

"Well, they aren't going to bite you in the neck like Count Dracula, if that's what you're thinking," Freise replied. "I've never once seen that MO, as you police call it. The ones in Los Angeles drained blood from their victims in blood banks."

"Yeah, and the ones in Vienna use a straight razor," Drummond interjected with a grimace. "Are they evil, or are they deranged?"

"Well, I don't think the ones in the castle are either," Freise said after a thoughtful pause, "or the Church wouldn't have protected them all these years.

"Kluge, now—he's another case, entirely. I *watched* him coldly cut the throat of one of the injured knights and drink his blood. If the knights are vampires, that has to be how Kluge became one—unless he was one to start with." He shuddered and shook his head.

"I don't think I'm ready to think about that just yet. If someone can become a vampire simply by drinking another vampire's blood, and there's none of this un-dead nonsense, it begins to sound more like a disease than an evil curse. The whole notion of good and evil goes out the window. We'll just have to wait and see."

He fell silent again after that, and Drummond returned his full attention to the road, little more enlightened or reassured than he had been before their latest conversation. The rain continued for another half hour, Freise dozing while Drummond continued to hold their pace to a steady fifty, until suddenly the rain stopped and the late afternoon sun came out with a vengeance.

Accelerating back up to a hundred, Drummond

let Freise sleep until they had skirted Saarbrücken and the border with France and were approaching the crossing into Luxembourg. The forest of the Ardennes had closed in thick and black as they headed north. The border crossing looked more like a toll booth for the Golden Gate Bridge than a national frontier, and Drummond slowed to the mandatory ten miles per hour and nudged Freise awake as he approached the border checkpoint. He was prepared to produce his passport, but the German border guard in the kiosk hardly bothered to look at Drummond as he waved him through, and the booth on the Luxembourg side didn't even seem to be occupied.

"I guess this European Community stuff is working," Drummond remarked, as the frontier post disappeared from his rearview mirror. "That was about as complicated as crossing an American state line."

Freise chuckled. "Its a far cry from what it was the *last* time I was here," he said.

A few minutes later, Magda Krebs eased her Suzuki through the barriers with no more formality than Drummond had encountered, and within forty minutes, Kluge's two vans also had been waved through the checkpoint.

After another half hour, following Freise's directions, Drummond headed the white Mercedes north out of the city of Luxembourg. They were on a rural road now, and Drummond had to keep his speed to a modest thirty to forty miles per hour. After they had ridden in silence for about fifteen minutes, Drummond looked over at Freise, who was glancing out the window and consulting the map. Twilight was approaching, and Drummond was beginning to become concerned.

"Do you know where we are?" Drummond asked.

"Oh, certainly," the priest said distractedly, tipping the map slightly as he scanned it up and down. "I know exactly where we are."

"Let me rephrase that," Drummond replied. "Do you remember where we go from here?"

"That," said Freise, "is a more difficult question. Everything has changed since I was here in '44— not that that's particularly surprising."

"Well, then, what do you propose we do?" Drummond pulled the car into a lay-by that presented itself and took the car out of gear.

"Well, I was captured just south of Clervaux . . ." Freise said uncertainly. "Ah!" The priest jabbed his finger against the map. "There should be a turn to the left, sign-posted 'Marbourg'." He closed the atlas and tossed it on the back seat. "Just stay on this road and keep heading north. Once we get closer, I'll find it. Don't worry."

" 'Don't worry,' the man says," Drummond murmured, rolling his eyes heavenward as he put the car back into gear.

About forty miles north from where they had crossed into Luxembourg, a small sign pointed the way toward Marbourg and Clervaux.

"Turn there!" Freise said.

Slowing, Drummond made the left turn and carried on, heading them westward into the densely forested mountains of the Ardennes.

"Slow down," Freise said, as the road started to climb up toward the mountain village of Clervaux. "It was along in here that I was captured. *This* road hasn't changed that much since then."

Hoping to catch sight of some familiar landmark, Freise craned his neck out the window as they continued, occasionally shaking his head, until finally he said, "Stop the car."

Drummond pulled off onto the grassy verge and looked at Freise expectantly.

"Is this it?"

"I'll let you know in a minute. Stand by."

Hopping out, Freise backtracked for several yards, then disappeared into the undergrowth. He was gone for only a couple of minutes, but to Drummond it seemed like hours. The priest was grinning as he trotted back to the car.

"I found it—my old jeep." His smile went suddenly somber as the memory came flooding back. "That's been nearly fifty years ago," he said. "Back in '44, I was racing up this road when we hit a land mine. The jeep was blown off the road. My driver, Corporal Costanza, was killed." He blinked and looked away briefly. "The Germans picked me up about ten minutes later, and marched me off to the camp where I was taken prisoner by the knights."

"So, how far do you reckon we are from the castle?" Drummond asked.

"Well, we'll have to go on foot from here," the priest replied, recovering his composure. "I'd say half an hour or so, maybe a bit more. If we hustle, we should be there before it gets completely dark." Freise walked around to the back of the Mercedes. "Open the trunk, will you? I need my stuff."

Wondering what he was letting himself in for, Drummond opened the glove-box to pull the trunk-release and also retrieved the Beretta. He was wishing he had a holster, if they were going to be covering any kind of rough ground, but he decided to be grateful that he even *had* a gun as he got out of the car and went around to help Father Freise, grabbing his leather jacket from the back seat.

Fortunately, Freise didn't want his whole suitcase. By the time Drummond got around to the trunk, the priest had stuffed what he thought he needed into a lightweight nylon zipper bag that he'd apparently packed flat for just such a purpose. He had also buttoned his collar and put back the collar tab, returning to clerical uniform for the coming venture. A flashlight and a pair of binoculars were going in on top, and Drummond nodded approvingly as he reached into the leather-bound box to scoop the rest of the ammunition into his pocket. The zip bag wasn't very heavy, and Drummond took it from the priest and slung it over his shoulder before slamming the trunk lid to follow Freise into the woods.

Half a dozen yards off the road, they came to the twisted hulk of an old jeep, slowly rusting into the earth. Freise started to lead them past it, then paused, turning slightly to Drummond.

"If you don't mind, I like to say a little prayer for Tommy Costanza."

Drummond nodded, waiting silently while the priest knelt down next to the rusted remains of the jeep, one hand caressing a twisted fender. After a few minutes, he crossed himself and stood up, reaching blindly into a pocket for a handkerchief, with which he wiped his eyes and gave his nose a good blow.

"Thank you," he murmured, not looking at Drummond. "He was a good kid."

Without further comment, he headed on deeper into the woods, Drummond silently following.

Their passage had not gone unnoticed. Magda Krebs had watched the two men abandon their car and plunge into the woods, lugging a zipper bag. When they did not emerge after several minutes, she parked her motorcycle and cautiously approached the Mercedes on foot.

Far back in the woods, almost beyond the range even of *her* heightened senses, she could just hear the sound of their passage receding into the other sounds of the twilight—twigs snapping underfoot, the crackle of trodden leaves, a muffled cough. When she could hear them no longer, she returned to her machine and doubled back the way she had come, returning to the main road to intercept Kluge.

She had traveled south on the main road for only about ten miles when the vans carrying Kluge and the others passed her going the other way. They slowed as they saw her, and she slowed, too, making a U-turn in the middle of the two-lane road and then racing back to overhaul Kluge just before the junction with the Clervaux turn-off.

Pulling alongside the lead van, she signaled it to pull over. Slowing, the convoy pulled off to the side of the road, allowing several other vehicles to overtake them before they finally stopped in a bus turn-out.

Kluge watched through the windshield of his van as Magda switched off her motorcycle and, tugging off her helmet, ran back to where he and the others were parked. She arrived at Kluge's van breathless from the exertion of running in the heavy motorcycle leathers.

"Drummond and the priest," she gasped. "They've headed into the woods on foot." She slumped against the van, gulping air.

"Where?" Kluge demanded.

"Up—" Magda had to take several deep breaths

before she could continue. "Up the road, then turn left. Their car is parked where they entered the forest. You can't miss it. It's a white Mercedes."

Kluge reached under his seat and brought out a battered German Army map case. Snapping it open, he looked at the faded yellow Wehrmacht map and, with a gloved finger, traced an invisible path through the woods. Closing the map case, he looked back at Magda.

"Take us to where you left them."

Magda blinked uncomprehendingly, still numb from two days on her motorcycle.

"I told you wh—"

"Now!" shouted Kluge. "Now, you bitch, or I'll kill you!"

Magda reeled as though she'd been hit. Stunned, and on the verge of hysteria, she staggered back to her motorcycle, swinging a leg over the machine and dropping into the saddle. After a moment's hesitation, she pressed the starter button, pulling on her helmet as she looked back at Kluge in his van. Then she pulled out on to the highway, the others following along behind.

Drummond and Freise had hiked through the woods for nearly three miles before they came to the edge of the grassy meadow that surrounded the castle of the Order of the Sword on all sides. In the fading dusk, the castle loomed dark and eerily silent, with just a sheen of dying sunset washing the western aspect with rose-gold. A moat followed the circumference of the castle wall, its murky water darkly reflecting the darkening sky.

Keeping low, they had circled all around the edge of the meadow, looking for the entrance, but they had come to no road leading toward it. The en-

trance was in the south wall, and looked firmly
closed and barred but disused. The drawbridge was
down, but didn't look like it had moved for decades. As Drummond scanned it with the field
glasses, he wondered whether the place was deserted or if the vampires were simply asleep until
the darkness fell—though Freise had assured him
that these vampires did not shun the light. Twilight
had deepened into darkness as the two men huddled in the murky shadows of the woods, contem-
plating their next move.

"What do you think?" Freise whispered, as
Drummond lifted the binoculars to scan the front
of the castle again.

"I think we're crazy to even be *thinking* about
going in there at night," Drummond replied. "You're
sure this is the place? It looks as quiet as a—forget
I said that. I don't suppose you've got any garlic
tucked away in that bag of yours?"

"No, 'fraid not. Why do you ask?"

"Well," said Drummond, continuing to scan with
the binoculars, "in all the movies, they use garlic
to keep vampires at bay. Even your friend Lupe
had it all over her house. Since I'm going in there,
I thought some garlic might come in handy." He
looked over at Father Freise and grinned. "You've
assured me these vampires are good guys. Well, the
only one I've ever met was a real bad sonofabitch,
so I'd rather not take too many chances."

Freise gave him an odd look and shrugged. "If I
thought that garlic might help, I'd have brought
some," he said. "I know what all the legends say,
but I haven't a clue how it might work."

"What about Lupe Gonzales, then?" Drummond
asked, remembering the woman's tidy house, with
its festoons of garlic, and crucifixes on every wall.

Freise smiled wistfully. "Well, she *thought* it might give her some protection—and I don't suppose it did any harm. She's a good woman, John—very devout."

Yeah, and she let you put a stake through her husband's heart, Drummond thought to himself, though he didn't say it. He still wasn't sure whether he believed the priest's story or not; it all seemed so very farfetched. And yet—

"Guess I'll just have to put my faith in firepower, then, if you haven't got any garlic," Drummond finally said, lowering his binoculars and handing them off to Freise.

"Oh, I think we can do better than that," Freise replied. He was struggling out of his jacket, starting to rummage in the top of his bag. "God will be with us."

"Well, God might be, but you won't," Drummond said. "I'm going in alone."

"The hell you are. . . ."

Sighing, Drummond rocked back on his haunches, wondering if he was going to have to slug the priest to make him listen to reason.

"Frank, listen to me. You're in great shape, but you've *got* to be over seventy. If anything goes wrong—" Drummond bit off what he had been about to say and stood up, checking his watch.

"Look. You wait here, and I'll scout out the castle. We don't even know if we can get in, for God's sake. If we can't, it's over—at least for now. If I *can* get in, and there *is* somebody there—well, I can't tell you what to do, but if I'm not back in—say, ten minutes—then if I were you, I'd haul ass back to the car and head for the nearest Catholic church I could find, and then I'd call my boss in Rome." Drummond gave Freise the steadiest look he could manage. "Listen, it's more than I could do for *you*, if positions were reversed."

With obvious reluctance, Father Freise nodded.

"I suppose you'd better give me the car keys, then," he said.

"They're in the ignition," Drummond replied.

"Okay, dammit. Ten minutes. Just one thing, though." Freise reached across to hug Drummond, pressing his forehead against the younger man's shoulder for just a second.

"Go with God," he whispered.

Drummond let the old man hold him for a second or two more, then patted him awkwardly on the shoulder and pulled away, not looking back as he stood and moved off into the darkness, keeping low. He had shifted the Beretta into the pocket of his leather jacket as he crouched with Freise back in the forest, and now he shoved his right hand into the pocket to steady the weapon as he broke into a jog, his other hand going into the left-hand pocket to balance himself as he ran. Along with the extra ammo he had put there, the hand closed unexpectedly on the rosary Father Freise had given him what seemed like a lifetime ago. He pulled it out as he flattened himself against the side of the barbican arch that guarded the approach across the castle's drawbridge.

With the rosary beads in one hand and Beretta at the ready in the other, close beside his head, he thumbed off the safety and listened, straining for any hint of sound that might be reaction to his approach. Nothing moved. When he had counted to twenty by his racing pulse, he cast a quick look back the way he had come, then looped the rosary beads over his head and tucked the cross inside his jacket—it *might* help!—and began slowly sidling along the barbican wall toward the open arch.

Back at the edge of the meadow, Freise watched Drummond through the field glasses until he passed from the moonlight to the shadow of the barbican arch, then put the glasses aside and pulled a black cassock from his bag. His fingers trembled a little as he put it on and did up the buttons, and for courage he made himself recite the proper prayers as he started donning the other priestly garments that he hoped would reassure the men inside—for they had seemed to value the fact he was a priest, fifty years before.

"Place upon my head, O Lord, the helmet of salvation," he murmured, as he laid the white rectangle of the amice over his head like a hood, "that Thy servant may be free from evil." He pushed it back around his neck and tied the strings across his chest, then pulled an alb over his head.

"Endow me, O Lord, with the garment of innocence and the vesture of light, that I may worthily receive Thy gifts and worthily dispense them," he whispered.

Over the long white alb with its white cord cincture he donned a stole, the set prayers turning to wordless supplications for protection as he kissed the cross on the center and looped it over his head, crossing the ends on his chest and securing the ends under the cincture, the way priests had done since before the Order of the Sword was founded, more than seven hundred years ago.

What had happened to the order was clear, reading between the lines of the history of the order that Freise had seen that morning. The document had never mentioned the word *vampire,* but putting the account together with what Freise knew from his own experience, that had to be the nature of the offense which had put them beyond the pale for 700 years—though their undoubted piety and repentance during that time had mitigated against the Church actually setting out to destroy them.

Of course, the Church *could* be wrong; the knights *could* be evil, as Kluge and his minions undoubtedly were. But Freise didn't want to believe that; and was willing to wager his life—and indeed, his soul, if the old legends about vampires were true—on the supposition that the Knights of the Sword were *not* evil.

And if he was wrong? Well, he had God's armor to protect him. As he drew the white cope around his shoulders, snapping the clasp of the cross-adorned morse that was almost like a breastplate, he hoped it was more effective than garlic or sunlight or crosses. . . .

Thus adorned in the whole armor of God, he ducked his head to look at his watch, then squared his shoulders and turned to look out at the castle in the moonlight.

"Never *could* tell time by the moonlight," he grumbled to himself, by way of excusing what he was about to do—for he knew Drummond had not been gone for more than five minutes, at the most.

Then, pocketing the flashlight he had brought, he set out across the meadow after Drummond.

Back at the road, Kluge walked over to the white Mercedes and opened the door, leaning in to pull the keys from the ignition. He had shed his Euro Plasma coverall, and he slipped the keys to the Mercedes into one of the outside pockets of his black SS tunic as he walked back to where his followers were waiting obediently by the van, his knights and the rabble in two distinct groups. It was nearly dark, but he had no need of light, for he could see as well as other men saw on a rainy afternoon, and knew that they could, too.

He had allowed his "expendables" another round of "refreshment" before disembarking from the van, and they were restless, keen for the hunt. The eighteen leather-clad punkers were armed with a variety of weapons, mostly left over from the Second World War. The girl in the fishnet stockings and Doc Martins cradled a Schmeisser submachine gun under her arm, as did one or two others. A thin, ascetic-looking boy with closely cropped hair held a Mauser machine pistol and had a pair of Lugers stuffed into the waistband of his red plaid trousers. Magda and the rest were similarly armed, and all carried knives in imitation of Kluge, although none of them dared to carry the sacred black SS dagger like the one worn by their master and the knights.

Kluge studied their faces, looking for any sign of weakness before he spoke.

"When we go into the woods, spread out, but keep in sight of one another. If you stumble upon Drummond and the priest, *take them alive,* understand? I need to know how much they know about us before they die. If you disobey, it will not be nice."

Looking at their faces as he spoke, Kluge knew that the lesson they had learned as Jurg's executioners had not been forgotten. And the knights standing silently behind them, with folded hands resting on their sword hilts, would be certain that no one forgot in the heat of battle.

"When we get to the castle," he continued, "no one shoots unless I give the command. Got it?"

The punkers nodded in mute agreement.

"All right, then. Let's go."

Cocking his Walther submachine gun, Kluge led his followers into the woods.

Drummond crouched down on his haunches and kept as low as possible as he slowly worked his way toward the barbican arch. At the drawbridge he paused, testing it with only part of his weight, then slowly proceeded on tip-toe, careful not to make any sound.

Across the drawbridge, Drummond came to the gates themselves. Shoving against one and then the other, first tentatively and then with all his might, he failed to budge either of the massive, iron-studded doors. Looking around, he noticed another, much smaller door to the left of the gates, so he glided silently over to that.

Pistol at the ready, Drummond flattened himself against the wall next to the small door. Crouching down, he leaned slightly forward and used his free hand to shove experimentally against the bottom of the door. The door swung open easily and bumped against the inside wall. The hollow bang sounded like a thunder-clap to Drummond's taut senses.

Straining every muscle in his body, Drummond tried to hear hear any sound coming from beyond the open door, but nothing stirred the silence of the night. Still crouching, Drummond leaped into the doorway, assuming a combat stance, eyes and pistol sweeping the darkness ahead, ready to blast anything that moved.

Nothing.

Slowly Drummond stood, raising the muzzle of the pistol close beside his face again, and stepped through the open doorway. He found himself in a small room at the base of a narrow turnpike stair that led upward into even greater darkness.

Drummond's mouth was dry with fear as he slowly began to climb the winding stairs. The absolute blackness was pierced only by the occasional shaft of moonlight that edged in through the arrow slits in the curved wall. The steps were uneven, and he stumbled. Fear had become a tangible, coppery taste in Drummond's mouth by the time he reached the top of the stairs.

There was no landing at the top—just another small door set into the wall. Drummond turned the stirrup-shaped latch and gently pressed against the door. Silently, on well-greased hinge pegs, the door swung open. The high-ceilinged room beyond was filled with the machinery used to raise and lower the portcullis of the castle. Two large, cross-shaped arrow slits admitted a flood of moonlight to the room, casting an eerie checkerboard pattern on the floor as it passed, wraithlike, through the raised portcullis. Barely visible in the half-light was another small door on the opposite wall.

Carefully, his back to the wall, Drummond made his way past the first of the two huge windlasses used to raise the portcullis—and had just about reached the center of the room when he felt the floor vanish beneath him.

Throwing his arms out wide, Drummond let out a yelp as he tried to catch himself. His knee banged sharply against the stone edge of the murder hole set into the floor above the castle's gates, as he careened into an awkward half-sitting position and somehow managed not to fall through.

He was still gasping with panic by the time he became sure he was not going to fall any farther. After carefully feeling about him in the gloom, he managed to shift his footing and scramble precariously to a standing position again, feet straddling the opening. But as he blessed his good fortune at not having fallen victim to the hole, he realized that he no longer held his pistol.

Drummond felt around on the floor for what seemed like hours trying to find his gun, but with no success. Finally, fearing the worst, he peered down through the hole. There, twenty feet below, lying in a brightly illuminated patch of grass, Drummond could see the Beretta.

"I still wish I had some garlic," he muttered to himself, as he stood up and cautiously resumed his approach to the other door.

He took the stirrup-shaped latch handle and tried to turn it. Nothing happened. The door was locked. Drummond tried shoving against the door with all of his might, but it didn't budge.

Drummond took a deep breath and let it out slowly. It was a dead end. And even as he decided that all he could do was go back the way he had come, he heard the only other door slam shut behind him.

Panicking, Drummond turned and launched himself across the chamber, terror clawing at his belly, but he never made it to the door. From up in the rafters, three men in hooded white capes dropped down on Drummond, knocking him unconscious as they landed on him. Then two of the men dragged Drummond to his feet, while the third produced a large key and unlocked the door that led down into the courtyard of the castle of the Order of the Sword.

Chapter 20

Father Freise stood motionless before the castle gates and stared up at them for what seemed like a very long time before bending down to pick something up. Watching from the woods at the edge of the moon-drenched meadow, even with his heightened senses of sight, Kluge couldn't tell what the priest had recovered before he vanished into the shadows.

Curious, but only mildly so, Kluge turned and retreated into the darkness where his followers waited, ignoring the punkers to pass directly to where his knights stood silently awaiting the coming confrontation.

Of the nine knights, only one of them remained from the original dozen he had selected to form the nucleus of his Knighthood of Blood. Besides himself, Baumann alone wore the blood-red arm band of the old order—a visible link with the *Blutfahne*, the blood-soaked flag that Hitler and his comrades-in-arms had carried in the Munich Pustch in 1923. The knights were as yet untried in battle, *although after tonight,* Kluge thought, *no doubt they will have earned the right to wear the arm band that will bind them to the fallen heroes of the Reich.*

Beneath the polished steel helmets, eight handsome faces followed every move that Kluge made, their blue eyes shining eagerly with devotion to their master. Kluge allowed himself a rare smile. Racially pure, these young men had been selected from among the very best of the Aryan people. Hiding them, training them, and finally initiating them into the immortal chivalry of the Knights of Blood had been no easy task, but it was one to which Kluge had dedicated not only his life, but his very soul.

Pulling his cape close about his shoulders, Kluge walked over to Baumann, the only man on earth he possibly regarded as a friend.

"When I give the order to go in," he said very quietly, "I want you to remain behind, just in case."

"Jawohl, Herr Sturmbannführer," Baumann replied, clicking his heels as he brought his right hand up to the brim of his helmet in a sharp military salute. Kluge returned the salute, then turned to survey the rest of his cohort.

Most of the punkers were sprawled on the spongy ground, as lacking in discipline as they were in pride. The punkers and their nihilistic attitude revolted Kluge. As part of the black-uniformed SS of fifty years ago, he had helped try to destroy one civilization so that another, greater civilization could replace it—a civilization that would last a thousand years.

But these modern-day Germans—Kluge hated to even use the word "German" in connection with them—were bent on the total destruction of society, and themselves with it. Kluge had experienced the total destruction of *his* society, and had risen, phoenix-like, from the ashes to perpetuate it anew. Looking at the punkers, he knew that for them, there would be no return from *Gotterdämmerung*.

Deep in the woods, four hooded men with long-bows patiently watched as Kluge turned back toward the castle. With a hand signal, their leader sent one of the men moving silently away from his comrades, to disappear into the black shadows of the night.

Torches were blazing in the great hall as Armand du Gaz led in two men-at-arms dragging the unconscious Drummond between them. De Beq and four other knights sat at a table drawn up at the far end of the room, while half a dozen serjeants and men at arms sat attentively on benches pushed back against the unrelenting stone walls.

"And the other one?" de Beq asked, looking up from the parchments spread before him on the table.

"Still in the woods," du Gaz replied, signaling his men to lower Drummond onto the flagstone floor.

"Are they alone?"

"I think so," du Gaz answered, "but I left four men from this evening's patrol in the forest, just in case."

De Beq grunted his approval. There once was a time when he hadn't been sure that du Gaz would fulfill the duties and vows of a knight. As the years had passed, however, du Gaz had blossomed, and de Beq now was happy to accord him the full respect due a brother knight.

"Have him searched," de Beq commanded.

"I have already seen to it, Sire." Du Gaz stepped forward and placed Drummond's wallet and watch on the table. William of Etton, who was seated closest to du Gaz, slid the objects over to de Beq.

"Well, Henri," William said, "it looks as though Sir Armand has done a trusty job."

"So it would seem," said de Beq, sorting through

Drummond's possessions. "See if you can revive your captive, Armand. I've a great many questions."

At du Gaz' signal, one of his men-at-arms went over to the corner of the great hall and filled a gourd with water standing in a bucket. Returning to Drummond, he dashed it in his face. Then kneeling, he lightly slapped Drummond's cheeks.

Ignoring the efforts of du Gaz's men to bring Drummond around, de Beq stared fixedly at the silver badge that was attached to Drummond's police ID.

"William," he said. "Take a look at this."

William of Etton took the badge case from de Beq and studied it carefully for several minutes, finally bringing it up to his mouth and licking it.

"Well, it's not silver, so it can't be too valuable," he said. "Still, it *is* finely wrought. What do you make of it?"

"Look closely, William. The shape of the thing." De Beq's voice took on the tone of a teacher speaking to a not-too-bright pupil.

"I don't follow, Henri." William of Etton looked slightly confused and handed the badge back to de Beq.

"It's shaped like a shield, Will." De Beq's voice was almost hushed. "And look—this design on it— like some sort of temple." His finger traced the outline of Los Angeles City Hall. "And here— look—the coat of arms of some great prince."

William squinted at the seal of the city of Los Angeles.

"It's not very good heraldry," he said.

"The heraldry doesn't matter." De Beq's voice betrayed a hint of good-natured exasperation. "What does matter, Will, is who this man is, and whether or not he is a knight."

Drummond began to stir, and one of du Gaz' men helped him into a sitting position. Slowly Drummond's eyes came into focus, and the rushing sound in his ears subsided to something less than a dull roar. Looking about him, the first thing that Drummond saw was the golden swastika set into the hilt of du Gaz's sword.

He tried to stand up and make a dash for the door, but one of the men-at-arms—Cullen, a short, thick-set Irishman—put a heavy hand on Drummond's shoulder and shoved him back down onto the flagstones.

Distracted by the commotion, Henri de Beq got up from his chair and came around the table to question his prisoner.

Father Freise closed the postern door that opened onto the turnpike stairs and, pulling his flashlight out of his cassock pocket, turned it on. Playing the bright beam of light around the edge of the door, he spotted the smooth wooden handle of the bolt. He drew the heavy oak beam across, seating the end into a square recess cut deep into the opposite wall. Then, with the door firmly barred behind him, he lifted the skirts of his cassock and alb and slowly began climbing the uneven stone stairs leading to the gatehouse.

Drummond's implication that, at seventy-plus Freise was over the hill galled the priest, although by the time he gained the top of the turnpike stair, he did have to admit that perhaps he was slowing down just a tad. Still, turning the latch and pushing open the door into the gatehouse, he doubted that many men even half his age would have climbed these steps under any circumstances.

Shining his flashlight into the gatehouse, Father

Freise took in the mechanism that operated the portcullis, as well as noting the murder hole in the floor, directly above the massive oak gates. The heavy weight of Drummond's automatic bumped against Freise's thigh.

Well, he thought, *at least John got this far.*

He couldn't imagine Drummond giving up his gun without a struggle, though, so perhaps the knights weren't as friendly as he'd hoped they would be.

Spotting the door in the opposite wall, Freise went over, avoiding the murder hole, and tried the handle. The latch turned, and the door swung easy on its hinges. Careful not to lose his footing going down the steep flight of worn stone stairs, Freise steadied himself with one hand against the wall while the other held up his skirts. Stepping into the courtyard at the bottom of the stairs, he patted the automatic in his pocket and then walked briskly toward the great hall.

Inside, de Beq was trying to question Drummond while du Gaz and his men held him in his place. They were making little progress. De Beq paced across the flagstone floor like a caged tiger, trying desperately to comprehend what his prisoner was saying. Finally he turned toward the man being held in a sitting position on the floor and, tapping his own chest, said, "Henri de Beq."

He pointed at Drummond. *"Et vous?"*

"John . . . Drummond," came the measured reply.

De Beq held up the badge. *"Jean Drummont. Chevalier?"*

Drummond didn't understand de Beq's question. "John Drummond . . . policeman," he replied.

De Beq was getting a headache. He turned to

William of Etton. "What, in the name of sweet Jesu, is a *poleecemond*?"

Before William could offer an opinion, a strange voice spoke out in Latin.

"A policeman is a constable." Father Freise stepped out of the shadows.

The effect of Father Freise's entrance couldn't have been more dramatic if he'd had two heads. For an instant, no one moved; then total chaos ensued as du Gaz and another knight rushed forward to grab Father Freise, only to be frozen in their tracks by de Beq's booming voice.

"Halt! No one touches this man." He looked at Father Freise for several seconds—staring at his face, taking in the cope and other priestly accoutrements—before speaking to him in a coarse form of Latin.

"I remember you. You were here when you were young." De Beq's voice was slightly tinged with wonder.

"Yes," said Father Freise. "And now the Church has sent me to you."

De Beq found Father Freise's modern Latin difficult to understand. "Forgive me, but what other languages do you speak?"

Freise took the question in stride. "German," he said. "And English."

De Beq and William looked at each other. "Englesh," de Beq said. "Spake us that."

"Aye, Sire," said Freise, nodding in agreement.

"Who be this man?" asked de Beq, pointing at Drummond.

"He be Constable of the Shire," Father Freise replied, hoping that somehow the title he had just invented would equate with Drummond's job as a cop.

"Be he knightly?" asked William of Etton.

"Nay, of captain's rank," Father Freise said.

"Be this the mark of his order?" asked de Beq, holding up Drummond's badge.

Father Freise looked at the badge for several seconds before even attempting to translate Los Angeles Police Department into something approaching fourteenth-century English.

"Aye," Freise finally said, a smile playing on the corners of his mouth. "He be a captain of the castle of the Order of the Queen of the Angels."

De Beq translated the conversation into Norman-French for the benefit of the rest of the men, who now looked at Drummond with a sense of curiosity, rather than hostility.

"And why be you here?" asked de Beq.

That, thought Father Freise, *is going to take some real explaining.*

The hooded and armored warrior crouched low as he ran through the woods skirting the castle of the Order of the Sword. Once he had reached the far side of the castle, he trotted to the edge of the moat and, making sure that he was directly opposite a small, cross-shaped arrow slit set high in the wall, began to wade into the murky waters.

Instead of slowly sinking into the water, the warrior seemed to walk upon it, pausing in mid-moat to feel around beneath the surface with the end of his bow. Striking a stone pylon set to his right, the man stepped upon it and repeated the process, now casting to the left, left again, right, in an apparently random pattern until he had reached the castle walls and stood under the opening of a machicolation projecting from the wall some ten feet above his head.

Then, after slinging his bow across his back, he used shallow finger and toe-holds cut into the pointing between the wall's massive stones to slowly climb up the wall and vanish into the opening of the garde-robe. When he had heaved himself into the courtyard of the castle at last, he ran toward the great hall to warn de Beq and the rest of the Order of the Sword about the intruders in the woods.

"So the Holy Father in Rome has sent you to ask for our help?" de Beq said, shooting a sidelong glance at Father Freise.

"Yes, he has," Freise replied.

"How long has the Holy Father been in Rome?" de Beq asked. "The last I heard, he was a captive of the French king in Avignon."

Freise stared coolly back at de Beq. "The Pope has been in Rome for more than six hundred years. Who told you he was in France?"

"Some Templars that we sheltered many years ago," de Beq said. "They told us that the French king had suppressed their order and was holding the Holy Father against his will. Was that true?"

Before Father Freise could answer, one of the men-at-arms came running through the door of the great hall and came to a stop directly between the priest and de Beq.

"Sire," Pageau said in Norman-French, "there is a large body of men in the woods," he gestured toward Freise and Drummond, "near where we first sighted these two."

"How big a force?" asked de Beq.

"About thirty, perhaps a bit less. Eight or ten of them are in uniforms, like those of the last men to attack our castle."

"And the others?" De Beq stared first at the priest, then at Drummond.

"Peasants, I should think, by the way they behave and are dressed." Pageau, his report finished, stood waiting for de Beq to speak, but de Beq turned to Freise instead.

"This man has just told me that there are thirty soldiers in the woods, not a hundred paces from where you were waiting." De Beq's nostrils flared. "Are they with you, priest? Are they?"

"I give you God's word, they are not!" Freise crossed himself. "I fear that they are the ones I told you about."

"The Nazis?"

Father Freise nodded.

"Then in that case, none of them will leave here alive." De Beq looked back at Pageau. "Open the gates."

Then, turning to Father Freise, he said, "God's will be done."

The man-at-arms in the woods crouched down, reaching into a leather box on his belt. Pulling out a strip of oil-soaked rag, he wrapped it around the shaft of an arrow and knotted it in place. Then, taking up flint and steel, he struck several sparks onto the rag before it ignited. Blowing on it, he waited until it was burning nicely before he set the arrow to his bow and, drawing the nock to his cheek, sent the flaming arrow skyward.

Kluge and his force were halfway to the castle when the arrow arched over their heads and fell, like a shooting star, into the courtyard of the castle. De Beq, waiting for the signal, picked up the fiery brand and quenched it with a steaming hiss in a nearby barrel of rain water.

"They're coming," he said to the two men watching with him. Then, hand on the hilt of his sword, he turned and headed back into the great hall.

Cullen, one of the men-at-arms, still stood over Drummond, one mailed hand clasped to Drummond's shoulder and the point of his dagger pressed firmly to the soft flesh behind Drummond's ear. De Beq walked over to them and ordered Cullen to fall in with the others. Then, looking at Drummond, he extended his hand and pulled him to his feet.

"Come," he said, leading Drummond by the arm.

"Sire de Beq," Father Freise began as de Beq came abreast of him.

"Priest, stay!" de Beq barked, almost as if speaking to an over-affectionate dog.

Grabbing a torch off the wall, de Beq headed down a narrow stair, half-dragging Drummond along behind him. The smooth stone steps wound their way down into the cellars beneath the great hall. At one end of the cellar was a stout oak door, with a wrought-iron grill set over a small opening near its top. Taking a key from a nearby hook, de Beq opened the door and shoved Drummond in.

Dungeons, thought Drummond. *Vampires and dungeons.*

He stood facing the wall, waiting for de Beq to slam the door, lock it and, in all probability, throw away the key, but instead, de Beq came into the cell with him, crouching down to wrench at the lid of a large wooden box. Lifting it open, he held the torch close so that Drummond could see inside.

The box was filled with guns. Or rather what had *been* guns, when the knights had gathered them from the surrounding fields more than half a century ago, after the Battle of the Bulge. Drummond wasn't an expert on military hardware, but from the looks of the guns in the box, he guessed that they had been down here since the Second World War, at least.

"*Prennez*," said de Beq—then, sticking out his right hand, grasped Drummond around the right wrist. Drummond immediately gripped de Beq's right wrist in return, and for a moment neither man spoke. Then de Beq broke the silence with a single word.

"Honor."

Drummond nodded his head almost imperceptibly. "Honor."

Without further words or need for words, de Beq handed Drummond the torch and headed back up the courtyard. Looking into the box, Drummond rummaged among what was mostly rusty junk until he found a P-38 that looked as if it was in working condition. Releasing the magazine catch on the bottom of the grip, he counted the rounds.

Seven. Pulling the slide back just a tad, he could see another round in the chamber of the pistol. Eight rounds. Better than nothing, but a long way away from enough.

Enough, Drummond reflected for just a moment. *How many slugs is enough, when you're shooting vampires? And where do you shoot them?*

Drummond decided to go for head shots. *If it'll drop a speed freak on PCP, it ought to at least slow down a vampire,* he reasoned.

Farther down in the box of rusted weaponry, Drummond struck pay dirt. Rusted solidly to a Luger was the remains of a Schmeisser submachine gun, its magazine filled with nearly fifty rounds of ammo that would fit the P-38. Pulling a bayonet out of the box, Drummond managed to pry the aluminum magazine out of the gun, and using his thumb he dumped the live ammo into the palm of his hand, quickly transferring it to his jacket pocket. Sticking the bayonet under his belt crossways behind him, he headed back up the stairs to join the others in the great hall.

The flaming arrow looked like a shooting star as it streaked down into the courtyard of the castle, as Kluge and his followers ran across the meadow that separated the castle from the woods. At the edge of the moat, they slid to a halt, then carefully made their way across the drawbridge.

In the pale moonlight, Kluge saw the doorway through which Drummond and the priest had entered the castle. Pushing against the door with the sole of his riding boot, he found it locked solidly closed. For just a moment he hesitated, wondering how the priest had entered, when suddenly the gates swung open as Magda and the girl in the fishnet stockings pushed against them. With no more time to worry about Drummond and the priest, Kluge bolted through the gates with the rest of his horde.

Chapter 21

The door to the great hall was open, spilling a swath of reddish-orange torchlight across the uneven cobblestones of the courtyard. The punker shock troops of Kluge's first wave instinctively made for the light, weapons at the ready, their blood lust rising in their throats as a chorus of frenzied screams.

The first punker had reached the steps leading up to the great hall when from out of the darkness a crossbow bolt smashed through his skull and embedded itself in the heavy timbered door-frame. Brains and blood bursting out of his forehead and streaming down his face, the punker spun with the impact and fired wildly into the darkness.

"Fuckerrrrs!" he screamed.

His legs buckled beneath him, and still trying to crawl, he slowly fell forward.

The first burst of gunfire triggered an immediate reflex reaction in the rest of the punkers. Wound tight by their blood-high and the surging adrenalin, for a few seconds they fired wildly at anything they imagined to be in the dark shadows of the courtyard. All discipline momentarily vanished as they went on a full auto rampage, slugs smashing through window glazing and ricocheting off the stone walls of the buildings.

Suddenly, as quickly as it had begun, it stopped, and an awesome quiet descended over the castle. From inside the great hall, only the voice of Father Freise could be heard, chanting the psalms of Evensong.

"Rush 'em!" someone screamed, and the punkers broke toward the great hall, now firing random bursts to lay down covering fire as they ran.

Before they had gone twenty paces, a skirmish party of half a dozen men-at-arms, led by du Gaz and Etienne Lefroi, came bursting out of the great hall and collided with them, scattering the startled punkers like ten pins.

The suddenness and ferocity of the resistance were totally unexpected. Lulled by the glamor of their superiority of firepower, the punkers fell back before the steel-edged might of warriors in red surcoats, men who were not afraid to throw themselves against withering gunfire. Blades flashing pearlescent in the moonlight, the armored knights began hacking their way through the punkers, whose bravado changed to obscene terror as cold steel clove through vampire flesh to kill and maim.

Kluge and his knights had held back in the shadows, not moving toward the great hall until after du Gaz and his party sallied forth and engaged the punkers. But now, surging past that struggle and bounding up the steps, Kluge's black-caped knights burst into the hall to look for the rest of the castle's inhabitants, their great hand-and-a-half broadswords flashing in the torchlight.

Kluge, in the vanguard, cut down the serjeant nearest the door and slammed his shoulder into another red-clad knight, sending him crashing to the floor. Swinging his broadsword two-handed, he turned in time to deflect a blow from a short battle-axe aimed at his head. Recovering, he lunged forward, jabbing his attacker in the face.

The knight staggered back, recovered, and gripping his axe in both hands, came at Kluge again, only to be hamstrung by a Nazi who had taken him from behind. Collapsing, the knight pushed himself up into a kneeling position, only to have Kluge's blade cleave down, decapitating him.

Backed into a corner, one of the Nazis was holding two serjeants at bay, feinting first at one and then the other with his broadsword. Pushing past two more men who were locked in hand-to-hand combat, Kluge came up behind one of the serjeants and, swinging his sword as if it were an axe, split the man's head down to his chin.

The remaining serjeant turned to defend himself against the threat of Kluge's attack, giving his former opponent the opening he needed. Swinging his broadsword like a baseball bat, the Nazi's titanium-edged blade sliced through the serjeant's body armor and opened his abdomen. Slipping in his own entrails, the serjeant fell screaming to the floor.

Adding to the chaos of battle, de Beq and his reserves now entered the fray, sweeping across the courtyard to systematically take out the remainder of the punkers, some of whom were still trying to put up a fight. One of the punkers broke through to the hall, spraying a burst of machine-gun fire which did little damage but shifted some of the fighting to that part of the hall for long enough to overwhelm him.

Drummond, meanwhile, was doing his best to stay clear of the swordplay, rationing his meager supply of ammo and determined to make every shot count, concentrating most of his effort on protecting Father Freise and keeping himself alive. His face was a mask of grim determination as he stood shielding Father Freise, his P-38 held rigidly in front of him in a two-handed combat stance. One of the Nazis came for them, his sword held out to his side, taunting Drummond to fire.

Without changing his expression, Drummond fired two rapid shots, both of which slid neatly under the rim of the black coal-scuttle helmet. The Nazi, completely rigid, toppled forward, landing at Drummond's feet.

Turning to his right, Drummond pumped three quick shots into the chest of another of the Nazis. The impact of the bullets caused the man to stagger back, but he recovered almost immediately, continuing his advance on Drummond and Father Freise.

Aiming at the Nazi's face this time, Drummond squeezed the trigger again.

CLICK. Nothing happened. Drummond tried again, but after fifty years in the castle dungeon, the damp and corroded ammo refused to go off.

Reaching behind his back, Drummond grabbed his bayonet and, taking it by the point, threw it at the advancing Nazi.

Cartwheeling through the air, the bayonet struck him in the chest butt-first and clattered harmlessly to the floor.

The Nazi smiled unpleasantly, and blind panic seized Drummond for just an instant.

Then Father Freise shouted, "The sword, John! Grab the sword!"

Drummond threw himself onto the floor, grabbing the sword that lay next to the body of the Nazi he had just shot. Rolling clear of the black-clad corpse, he came up into a crouch, the sword held menacingly in front of him.

The Nazi was pressing one hand against the

wounds in his chest, trying to heal himself while he decided whether to finish off Drummond or Father Freise first. Abruptly, spinning towards Freise, he cocked his sword arm back and then snapped it forward, his sword arching overhead and flashing down toward Freise's shoulder.

Drummond's own reactions were faster, as he swung his sword in a desperate attempt to block the blade, but his aim was off. Instead of stopping the Nazi's sword, he felt his own blade slice through the wrist of his opponent's sword arm. The Nazi screamed, and his sword, still clutched in a black-gloved hand, spun through the air, narrowly missing Father Freise. In a frenzy, Drummond began to beat at the Nazi with his sword until the man collapsed, a large pool of blood spreading from the end of his right arm.

Behind Drummond, one of Kluge's black knights was locked in a hand-to-hand struggle with one of de Beq's men-at-arms, the Nazi repeatedly driving his knee into the warrior's crotch with little or no effect. Finally, the two combatants tripped and crashed to the ground, where the Nazi was able to get on top of his opponent and gouge his thumbs deep into his eye sockets. Howling in pain, the blinded man-at-arms furiously rammed his hands deep into the pit of the Nazi's stomach and then, wrenching upwards, grabbed the bottom of his rib cage and split his chest open.

The Nazi screamed and staggered back against the wall, his heart and lungs hanging out of his body. Slumping into a seated position, his heart thumped feebly to a halt and the lungs slowly deflated. A wheezing scream caught in the Nazi's throat as he died.

Still clutching his sword, Kluge staggered out of

the great hall, hacking and slashing at the mailed men in red surcoats, who had made short work of his punker vanguard and now were slowly gaining the edge on his black knights as well. Even on the run, unable to take a close count, Kluge could see that four or five of his SS men were down, some of them to rise no more. It was not supposed to go this way!

A serjeant lunged at Kluge with a spear. Sidestepping the attack, Kluge swung his sword at the man's midriff and felt the blade embed itself in the man's spine. Unable to free his weapon from the body of the badly wounded serjeant, Kluge let it go, and was turning to bolt for the safety of the gatehouse and the forest beyond when he saw Drummond and Father Freise coming cautiously out of the hall, Drummond with one of Kluge's swords in his hand.

Bending down, Kluge seized the spear the serjeant had dropped and, drawing back his arm, launched it at Drummond with all his strength. The six-foot oak shaft flew just shy of its mark, its iron head grazing Drummond's head with great force and opening a nasty wound in his scalp, but not killing him.

Shock waves of pain exploded in Drummond's brain as the impact of the spear jarred him into Father Freise's arms. The sword fell from his hand. A great rushing sound filled Drummond's ears, and his vision narrowed, until he felt that he was at the bottom of a well looking up at the priest's face. Then even that faint vision was extinguished, and everything went black.

Kluge paused just a moment to savor the satisfaction as Freise anxiously lowered Drummond to the ground, blood streaming from the wounded man's head. And as the old priest looked up, searching for the one responsible, Kluge grinned and ran for the open gates and the safety of the forest. He did not see how Father Freise stood and, drawing Drummond's Beretta pistol out of the pocket of his cassock, took careful aim and fired a single shot at Kluge's retreating form.

The bullet hit Kluge just above the knee. Its impact spun him, flailing, to the ground. Stunned, he tried to stand, only to have his leg collapse under him. It took him several seconds to comprehend that he had been shot, and that the wound was bad.

In the half a century that Kluge had been nearly immortal, he had not experienced pain, real pain, like he now felt coursing up his leg. Unable to stand, he began to crawl out through the gates—until suddenly he felt a woman's hands grabbing him and lifting him up.

Magda Krebs had hidden in a doorway by the gates once the shooting started, watching with horror as the red-surcoated knights made short work of Kluge's first wave and then started cutting a swath through the black knights. She had been about to run for it when she heard the shot and saw Kluge stagger and collapse, shot through the leg. For a moment, shock had paralyzed her, that her beloved master should be felled by the priest's bullet. But then, ardor overcoming her fear, Magda ran out and helped Kluge to his feet.

Gasping, Kluge pressed his hands against his wound, hardly even aware of who she was, much less of the devotion that had fired her to action.

Blood, he thought, *I've got to have blood—blood to heal, blood to stop the bleeding!* And the blood of another vampire was best.

Panting with the exertion, Magda threw Kluge's

right arm over her shoulder and struggled to her feet, starting to drag him through the gates.

"Hang on, Master! Hang on!" she cried. "Just through the gates. I'll get you help!"

But as he leaned on her, pain pounding in his leg and strength waning by the second, Kluge realized that help was already at hand. Reaching down with his left hand, he closed his palm around the hilt of the SS dagger and quickly brought it up to plunge into the side of Magda Krebs' neck.

Her startled squeak was drowned in the gurgling of her own blood gushing in a frothy torrent into her throat. Kluge twisted the knife and pulled it out, sinking down, dragging Magda down to him, sealing her wound with his mouth and drinking in the hot vampiric blood that would immediately jolt his body into an even higher healing mode than normally possessed by the near-immortal. Unlike most of his other victims, Magda didn't even struggle after that first, startled reflex from the pain, but instead seemed to press herself closer to Kluge's body, unable even to whimper, as if in this one final act, her passion for Kluge was at last returned.

He kept drinking even when she moved no more, taking the blood as fast as he could, feeling its power surge through his limbs. Letting her fall, he pressed his hands on the wound above his knee and felt the bullet hole close, and the electrifying jolt of pure bliss as strength returned to his limbs. Still a little shaky on his feet, he stood, keeping to the shadows as he hobbled away from the turmoil in the courtyard and passed through the gates, headed toward the drawbridge, only to have a hurtling figure suddenly burst from the shadows and nearly bowl him over—the girl in the fishnet stockings and

Doc Martins, making a break for the safety of the woods.

"Master!" she gasped, only then realizing who he was.

Viciously, Kluge threw her off and lashed out at her with his good leg, sending her sprawling to the ground. Enraged, he kicked out at her again, this time catching her under the jaw with the toe of his boot. Turning then, he started to head for the open field, only to have the girl grab his foot, nearly wrenching him to the ground.

The conflict in the castle courtyard began to subside and de Beq, seeing Kluge trying to escape, bellowed for the men in the gate house to drop the portcullis. High above Kluge in the gate house, two armored men seized heavy mallets and began hammering at the safety block that held the portcullis in place, pounding on it with all their might.

The hollow rumble of the falling portcullis gave just enough warning for Kluge to react. Though hampered by the girl hanging onto his leg, he used his newly recovered strength to launch a powerful leap that barely threw him clear. He was still in midair when the falling portcullis crashed to the ground, its sharpened spikes spearing the body of the girl in the fishnet stockings and pinning her to the earth like an insect mounted on a specimen card. The hands gripping Kluge's boot relaxed, and with a jerk he was free of the mangled vampire. His wounds now nearly healed, he sprinted for the safety of the dark woods.

Baumann had remained motionless against the tree trunk since Kluge led the raiding party into the castle. Taking short, shallow breaths, he had watched undetected as the three men-at-arms moved to the edge of the woods not fifteen feet from where he stood. They were standing there now.

From the sounds drifting over from the castle, it was obvious that things weren't going as planned. The shooting had been too concentrated, too intense, to have been effective against the armored knights. Baumann's own experiences of half a century ago told him that.

There was movement near the gate. Baumann strained his one good eye to make out what was happening, but couldn't quite see who or what was coming out of the castle. The portcullis dropped, and then a black-caped figure broke into the moonlight and ran towards the woods. At once Baumann recognized his commanding officer. Kluge was limping, retreating toward the safety of the forest.

The men-at-arms had seen the figure leave the castle, too, and the tallest of the three had unslung his bow and was nocking an arrow to the string when Baumann, gliding up from behind, rammed his bayonet up under the archer's chin and drove it into his brain.

Turning, he drew his sword, smashing the pommel into the forehead of the man on his right and then spinning around to slash his blade deep into the shoulder of the other man before his sword was halfway out of its scabbard. The man on the ground tried to get up, but Baumann stepped astride him and used both hands to drive his sword down hard through his opponent's chest. Standing on the dead man, he grunted as he pulled his sword out of the corpse, and turned to finish the man with the wounded shoulder.

He was gone. Baumann cast a quick glance around and, satisfied that the wounded man had made a run for it and was not preparing to attack again, turned and headed out across the field to help Kluge. All gunfire had ceased by now, and even the clash of arms no longer resounded from within the castle walls. It was time to make good their escape.

An hour later, Kluge and Baumann emerged from the woods not far from the vans and headed unhurriedly toward Drummond's parked Mercedes. Kluge was unbuttoning his tunic as he walked, and when he reached the back of the car, he pulled out the keys and unlocked the trunk. Shedding his tunic, he tossed it into Father Freise's nearly empty suitcase and gestured for Baumann to do the same.

Then, while Baumann manhandled Magda Krebs' motorcycle into the larger of the two vans, Kluge climbed into the back of the lead van and opened one of the lockers to remove a small bag containing a change of clothes. Pulling off his breeches and boots in the cramped confines of the van, he changed, then went back out and placed the rest of his uniform in Father Freise's suitcase. In a few minutes Baumann returned, also changed to other clothes, and placed his own breeches and boots in the suitcase, which he then took back to the van with the motorcycle.

Climbing behind the wheel of the lead van, Kluge revved the engine a few times, put the car in gear, and after signaling Baumann to follow, made a U-turn, heading back toward Germany. Under the full moon, Drummond's white Mercedes-Benz parked in the shadow of the dark forest took on a lonely, ghostlike appearance as the glowing red taillights of the vans receded into the shadows of darkness.

Later that night, Father Freise and de Beq moved together through the great hall, where de Beq's wounded had been brought and laid out on the floor. Nearly all of the men had suffered cuts of varying degrees of seriousness, and some had taken appalling wounds. A few, like William of Etton, had been shot, some repeatedly. As the less seriously injured moved among their comrades to treat them, Father Freise was amazed at how stoically the men endured their wounds, with only the most grievously injured making any sound.

With de Beq he moved among the wounded men, offering what consolation he could to those who seemed the most helpless. He knelt with de Beq next to one of the men-at-arms who had a blood-soaked bandage wrapped over the empty sockets of his eyes. In obvious pain, the man grabbed de Beq's arm and said something to him in Norman-French. De Beq, unable to speak for a moment, merely nodded. The blind man repeated what he'd said, and de Beq emotionally replied, *"Oui, mon confrère."*

"What does he want?" Father Freise asked.

"The misericord," de Beq said flatly.

"I don't understand."

"He wants the *coup de grace*. He wants me to kill him, and share his blood with the other less seriously wounded." De Beq's voice was drained of all emotion.

"But his wounds—he'll recover . . ."

"As a blind man," de Beq interrupted Father Freise. "He would rather be dead."

De Beq called out, and one of the knights brought over a large pewter tankard. Helping the blinded man into a sitting position, de Beq took his knife and, before Freise could do or say anything to stop it, drew the blade swiftly across the man's wrist. Blood welled up strongly, and de Beq quickly caught it in the tankard. As the vessel filled, it was replaced by another, and then another, as the blind man slowly faded into death.

Father Freise, for his part, could only kneel by the dying warrior and, in Latin, offer him the Last Rites of the Church, which the man gratefully accepted. Toward the end, de Beq brought the cross hilt of his sword to the dying man's lips, remembering another man and another gentle death in a far away desert oasis where it all had begun. The man-at-arms relaxed into de Beq's arms then, with a last strained breath whispering, "Gramercy," before he finally died.

And de Beq, bowing his head over his departed brother, whispered the words he had spoken that other time, and many times, in the more than seven hundred years of his long life.

"Not to us, Lord, not unto us, but unto Thee be the Glory. . . ."

He spoke them in Latin, but Freise understood and crossed himself as he whispered, "Amen."

Gently laying his companion down, de Beq took one of the tankards and moved with it to the side of one of the knights who had been shot in the thigh by one of the punkers. Placing it to the knight's lips, de Beq held the cup while the wounded man drank deeply of its crimson draught, softly murmuring, *"Ceci, c'est le cadeau de notre confrère."*

The knight lay back with a sigh, closing his eyes. As Freise watched, within mere seconds, the ugly black hole began to pucker around the edges and slowly seal itself closed, the skin glowing an angry red where, but minutes before, had been an open wound. Friese was astonished.

"How—how can this be?" he stammered.

"I don't know," de Beq replied. "It is one of God's mysteries—part of His punishment of us, for having profaned the sacraments and having defiled the Lord's cup."

"But, how can you say you are punished by the Lord," Father Freise asked, "when He heals you in this way, and grants you the age of Methuselah?"

"Because we can only survive by drinking the blood of beasts—or of men, which we *will* not do, save when the gift is freely offered, and no other help will avail," said de Beq. "And we are punished because we are cut off from men and cannot do God's intended work, staying as we must, here in our castle."

De Beq and Father Freise moved on to another wounded man, suffering from a stab wound to the lung. The man's own blood frothed at his lips, but after de Beq had given him to drink, again speaking of the gift of their *confrère*, Freise noticed that at once the labored breathing grew easier, and a touch of color returned to the man's cheeks. Within a minute or two, the man slipped into healing sleep.

"But you *must* leave this place," Friese argued, as they moved on to another wounded man. "You have to help us track down the man who attacked the castle tonight."

"Why?" asked de Beq. "I doubt he'll be back soon."

It amazed Father Freise that the kind of mind that could conceive of a Gothic cathedral could at once be so naive.

"Because he is *evil,* what he *represents* is evil, and he must be *stopped*." Freise stood up. "You are a knight, de Beq, sworn to protect the Church and those who are weak, and yet you would fail to fight this evil. It is beyond comprehension."

De Beq said nothing, but followed Father Freise over to the corner of the room where Drummond lay propped up against the wall, dried blood matted to his face and shirt and a bloody bandage wound around his head.

"How'm I doing, Frank?" Drummond asked, his thick tongue slurring his speech.

"Well, to be honest, you could be better." Freise bent down and looked into Drummond's eyes, comparing the size of the pupils and relieved that both of them reacted equally. "You've got a nasty cut along the side of your head, but I don't think you've got a concussion."

Drummond closed his eyes, sighing deeply.

"That's good. Did we get 'em, Frank? All of 'em?"

" 'Fraid not. Kluge got away, and I'm not sure if there were more where he came from." Freise checked Drummond's bandage, and decided that a change could wait until daylight, when he could see. "We did get some prisoners, though. Maybe one of them will talk."

"Just make sure you read 'em their rights first." Drummond tried to laugh, but the pain made it come out more like a moan. "Jesus, I feel like shit. How long was I out?"

"About an hour and a half, I'd guess," Freise replied.

"An hour and a half? Then we've gotta get after them!" Drummond tried to get to his feet, but the pain made him black out.

Freise eased Drummond down flat on the floor, rearranging the rolled-up cloak that was supposed to be cushioning his head, then turned to de Beq, who had watched and listened in silence.

"You'll need an interpreter with the prisoners," he said. "Where are they?"

Outside, five badly wounded punkers were propped up against the wall of the great hall, hands tied behind their backs, guarded by two men with crossbows. Over by the gates, three of Kluge's SS men were crouching on their knees, their elbows tied behind their backs and their hands tied together in front of them—all except for one knight, whose stump of a right arm prevented tying his remaining hand to anything other than his belt.

De Beq and the priest walked over to the punkers.

"You can speak their language?" de Beq asked.

"I speak German, if that's what you mean," Freise replied.

"Ask these peasants where the Nazi is." De Beq looked at Freise. "Tell them that if they cooperate, they will die quickly. Otherwise I will tie them all together and set fire to them."

Freise's face went ashen. "I can't tell them that. . . ."

"Why not?" de Beq asked. "It is all perfectly true."

Freise turned slowly to the punkers and began to translate de Beq's ultimatum.

"Fuck you," one of them said, spitting at Freise.

Without changing expression, de Beq stepped over to the boy who had spit on Freise and grabbed a handful of the punker's stringy hair, at the same time whipping out his dagger and placing its tip against the punk's Adam's apple. Even as the teenager's eyes were widening in disbelief, and Freise gasped, de Beq's hand rammed the dagger through the punk's throat and held him pinned to the wall behind him.

The heels of the Doc Martins drummed up and down as the punker writhed and gurgled in the agony of death for nearly a minute—to the horrified dismay of his fellow prisoners. When he was still at last, de Beq released the filthy, matted hair and pulled his dagger out of the teenager's throat, letting the body slump forward. Walking across the courtyard then, he stopped in front of the SS men who had been made prisoners.

"Father Freise," he called over his shoulder, "I need you over here."

Friese walked over to where the three men knelt, belligerently glaring up at their captor. They had been stripped of their helmets and cloaks, and the sight of their SS uniforms gave Freise a brief flashback to the war and a scene in an SS triage camp.

"Tell these three the same thing you told them," de Beq said, gesturing toward the punkers with his thumb.

Without inflection, Freise relayed de Beq's earlier ultimatum to the three men in black, who stared back at him in stony silence. He was about to turn back to de Beq, when one of them spoke.

"Tell him we are knights," the man said in German, "and we demand to be treated as such."

"And tell him," said the one with one hand, "that he dishonors himself by asking us to betray our master."

"Yes," added the first knight, "tell him that we welcome death as much as we loathe dishonor."

De Beq smiled slightly when Freise turned back to him after speaking with the SS men.

"So, did they tell you where their leader is?" de Beq asked.

"No," said Freise. "They wanted me to tell you

that they are knights and demand to be treated as such."

The color drained out of de Beq's face. "Are you sure that's what they said?"

"Yes," said Father Freise. "That, and that you dishonor yourself by asking them to betray their master."

De Beq's jaw tightened behind his beard. "The first one," he said quietly. "He spoke twice. What else did he say?"

Father Freise tried to avoid de Beq's steely gaze, but couldn't. Finally, after an anguished silence, he answered.

"He said that they welcomed death as much as they loathed dishonor." Freise felt like a judge passing sentence of death.

De Beq let out a long breath.

"Then in that case, holy Father, tell them they shall die—like knights."

Just before dawn, the three remaining SS men were brought to the center of the castle courtyard, hands still bound, and made to kneel at three-yard intervals. Opposite them, the punkers were drawn up in a straggling line against the wall of the great hall. Standing to the right of each of Kluge's SS men and slightly behind them was a knight with a large two-handed sword: Hano von Linka, William of Etton, and Etienne Lefroi.

De Beq raised his hand, and the knights began to slowly circle the big swords over their heads, increasing the speed with each pass of the blade. The eastern sky was brightening with the faint colors of the coming day, and as the first golden rays of the sun broke through the clouds, de Beq dropped his arm. In a single flashing instant, all three of Kluge's knights were dispatched to Valhalla. Behind him, de Beq could hear one of the punkers puke.

Turning to Armand du Gaz, de Beq jerked his thumb in the direction of the punks.

"Cut their throats," he said.

Du Gaz made quick work of the four remaining vampires. When it was done, he leaned down and wiped his blade on the shirt of the last to die and then, being careful not to step in the spreading pool of blood that was slowly sinking in between the cobblestones, he followed de Beq back to the temporary hospital in the great hall. Despite their need, they would have nothing to do with *this* blood.

Inside, de Beq paused to speak with one of the serjeants, both of them glancing toward the corner of the room where Father Freise was bending over a now conscious and vocal Drummond.

"Ow! That really hurts," said Drummond, as Father Freise tried to remove the bandage that was stuck to his matted hair.

"Well, it's off, so let's have a better look at that cut, now that we've got some daylight." Father Freise carefully probed the edge of the gash that ran along the side of Drummond's scalp. "I'm afraid this is going to leave quite a scar, my friend."

"I'll just comb my hair over it," Drummond quipped.

De Beq squatted next to Father Freise and set down a small leather bag. Opening it up, he scooped out a liberal amount of something that resembled gray lard.

"Here," he said, plopping the dollup in Freise's hand. "Put this on the wound. It will stop it scarring or going rank."

Freise looked at the glop in his hand, then over at Drummond.

"Sure, go ahead, Frank. Don't want to offend the man," Drummond said.

"Okay, but if your hair falls out, don't blame me," Freise replied, carefully spreading the greasy concoction along the side of Drummond's head before tying on a clean bandage.

De Beq watched closely, inspecting Freise's handiwork with an experienced eye. As the bandage was tied off, he spoke to the priest.

"I have taken counsel with my knights," he began, "and we would esteem it a great honor if you would say a Mass for us before you leave." The speech had taken a great deal of effort on de Beq's part, and Father Freise knew how much this simple service would mean to them.

"Well," Father Freise said slowly, "I could offer up a Mass of Dedication." He looked straight at de Beq.

De Beq knew at once what the priest was driving at.

"Father," he began, "I cannot lead my men out of this castle to fight your Nazis. The world is much too changed a place. Even the best knights need leadership, and there are none among us who know your world." He lowered his eyes. "Most of us have forgotten our world." He paused for a moment, his voice trailing off, and whispered, "We are lost."

"I could lead you," said Drummond, propping himself up on one elbow.

"How could you?" asked de Beq. "You are not one of us. You are not even a knight."

"If I *were* a knight, would you follow me?" Drummond asked.

"If you were a knight," de Beq retorted, "would

you join with us, and live as we live, and keep to our holy vows?"

"If I could, yes," said Drummond. "As far as any man can."

De Beq turned to Father Freise. "You said a Mass of Dedication, yes?"

Freise looked at Drummond, who drew a deep breath.

"We need them Frank. We've gotta have the backup." Drummond pushed himself up into a seated position and felt himself going light-headed. "I don't know what it's going to take, but we've got to stop Kluge, no matter what the cost."

De Beq looked at Father Freise beseechingly.

"Well, Father?"

Chapter 22

Dozens of candles flickered in the chapel that evening, casting ghost-like shadows over the helmets of departed knights that hung from pegs set high in the walls. Beneath each helmet was a sheathed sword, the name of a knight carefully illuminated on the scabbard. The heady perfume of incense filled the air, and in the stillness the sound of a silver bell added to the rapture that filled the hearts of those present. One by one, the men of the Order of the Sword came forward, and each received the cup from Father Freise's trembling hands.

The last to approach the altar rail was a postulant dressed in the purest white. Like the others he knelt at the altar step, his hands pressed together in an attitude of prayer, but unlike the others, the priest did not approach. Instead, a lean, grizzled man with a short-clipped salt-and-pepper beard came forward, clad in burnished chain mail and wearing a surcoat of deepest red.

Kneeling in front of him, the knight placed his hands around those of the postulant. Together the two men exchanged the simple vows of an ancient order of chivalry. The knight stood, and taking his sword from the altar held it in front of him, pommel topmost, forming the sign of the cross. Kissing the sword where the simple guard crossed the blade, he turned it so that it pointed skyward and then solemnly brought it down flat-bladed on the postulant's shoulder.

"Soit Chevalier," he said as the steel touched the right shoulder. Then lifting the sword over the head of the postulant, he touched him lightly on the left shoulder. *"Au Nom de Dieu."*

Two more knights stepped forward and placed a surcoat over the head of the kneeling man—bright red, emblazoned with a pale blue, gold-limned cross set with four golden sun-wheels. The knight by the altar bent down, and taking the newly made knight by the hands, lifted him up.

"Avaunce, Chevalier," he said, and led him by the hands to the topmost altar step, where both of them knelt, the older knight behind and a little to one side. The chalice lay on the altar, set before a bank of flickering candles, and Father Freise lifted it with reverence, bringing it over to the kneeling new knight.

"The blood of Christ, my son," he said, as he offered Drummond the cup—a simple thing of horn, bound with brass. . . .

Placing his hands around those of the priest, eyes locked with his, John Drummond drank deeply of the communion of the Order of the Sword.

COMING NOVEMBER 2007

AT SWORD'S POINT

Created by Katherine Kurtz,
Written by Scott MacMillan

A group of Knights Templar and a cadre of Nazis
have been affected with the same affliction—
vampirism—and have fought one another since the
closing days of World War II. Now, LAPD detective
John Drummond knows about their secret war and
will stop at nothing to end it...

THE ULTIMATE IN
SCIENCE FICTION AND FANTASY!

From magical tales of distant worlds to stories of
technological advances beyond the grasp of man, Penguin has
everything you need to stretch your imagination to its limits.

penguin.com

ACE
Get the latest information on favorites like
William Gibson, T.A. Barron, Brian Jacques,
Ursula K. LeGuin, Sharon Shinn, and Charlaine Harris,
as well as updates on the best new authors.

ROC
Escape with Harry Turtledove, Anne Bishop,
S.M. Stirling, Simon R. Green, Chris Bunch, Jim Butcher,
E.E. Knight, and many others—plus news on the
latest and hottest in science fiction and fantasy.

DAW
Mercedes Lackey, Kristen Britain, Tanya Huff,
Tad Williams, C.J. Cherryh, and many more—
DAW has something to satisfy the cravings of any
science fiction and fantasy lover.
Also visit dawbooks.com.

*Get the best of science fiction and fantasy
at your fingertips!*